I0641579

Raw Law: The Complete Cases of MacBride & Kennedy, Volume 1

Frederick Nebel

RAW LAW: THE COMPLETE CASES OF

MACBRIDE & KENNEDY

VOLUME 1, FROM THE PAGES OF BLACK MASK

FREDERICK NEBEL

Illustrations by
ARTHUR RODMAN BOWKER

Introduction by
EVAN LEWIS

Series Editor
KEITH ALAN DEUTSCH

Another Volume in the BLACK MASK LIBRARY

Boston • Philadelphia • New York
2013

© 2013 Altus Press • First Edition—2013

DESIGNED AND PUBLISHED BY
Matthew Moring

BLACK MASK SERIES EDITOR
Keith Alan Deutsch

PUBLISHING HISTORY
"Introduction" appears here for the first time. Copyright © 2013 David Lewis. All
Rights Reserved.
Owing to limitations of space, permissions to reprint previously published material
appear on pages 365-366.

Published by arrangement with Black Mask Press/Keith Alan Deutsch
(keithdeutsch@mac.com).

THANKS TO
Ed Hulse, Evan Lewis, Ken McDaniel, Rob Preston & Ray Riethmeier.

Visit altuspress.com for more books like this.
Printed in the United States of America.

Another volume in the BLACK MASK LIBRARY.

Table of

CONTENTS

Introduction

EVAN LEWIS

Preface: For much of the personal information contained herein, I am indebted to the author's wife, Mrs. Dorothy Nebel. In letters and telephone conversations in the early 1980s, she was extremely gracious in answering my often-nosy questions. Dorothy was an avid reader of her husband's work, and one of her favorite characters was Captain Steve MacBride. She passed away in 1996.

THIS has been a long time coming.

Nebel fans like me have been waiting not just years—but *decades*—for this series to be reprinted.

In the heyday of *Black Mask*, two series stood head and shoulders above the rest: Dashiell Hammett's adventures of the Continental Op, and Frederick Nebel's saga of Richmond City. Both authors excelled in their mastery of the hard-boiled style, the depth and humor of their characters, the richness of their settings and the varied scope of their stories. But while Hammett is now a household name, Nebel has been largely relegated to the shadows.

The reason is simple. While Hammett and many of his contemporaries went on to write mystery novels, Nebel stuck to novelettes. As the pulps gave way to paperbacks in the 1950s, the novel became the dominant fictional form, rendering the novelette almost defunct. *Black Mask* writers like Erle Stanley Gardner, George Harmon Coxe, W.T. Ballard—and a guy named Raymond Chandler—remained in the public consciousness thanks to their books, while Nebel was remembered only by pulp collectors.

Nebel was a skilled craftsman who put his own stamp on the hard-boiled school of writing. His prose, packed with crackling dialogue and keen characterization, is as fresh today as it was in the 1930s. Altus

Press has brought the bulk of his detective writing back into print. Now, at long last, they introduce new legions of readers to his most important body of work—the adventures of Captain Steve MacBride and his pal, reporter Kennedy of the *Free Press*.

WHEN this series debuted in the September 1928 *Black Mask*, it was called "The Crimes of Richmond City." The title was appropriate. This is the story of MacBride and Kennedy, it's also the story of a city. The series lasted nine years, and from first to last, Richmond City was seen as a living, breathing and growing metropolis—almost a character in itself.

Nebel's secret was simple. In writing about Richmond City, he was writing about his home town. The borough of Staten Island, where he was born, was then known as Richmond. It comprised most of Richmond County, with Richmond Valley at one end, Richmond Terrace at the other, Richmond Creek in the middle, and joined by Richmond Avenue and Richmond Road. He took the harbor and residential areas of Staten Island and combined them with elements of the Bronx and Manhattan to create his own scaled-down version of New York. Richmond City seemed very real—because to Nebel, it was.

Nebel's father Louis was Swedish (there's a Nebel River in Sweden) and his mother Mathilda was German-American. When their son Louis Frederick came into the world on November 4, 1903, they were 21 and 18, respectively. The marriage quickly went sour, and two years later Mathilda sued for divorce, receiving full custody. Young Louis, who much preferred the name Fred, grew up in Staten Island without a father until he was ten, when his mother married a restaurateur. When he was twelve, they gave him a half-brother. It was also at age twelve that he recalled meeting, for the only time, his real father. In his years away from the family, the elder Nebel had become a captain on the Staten Island Ferry and a decorated hero of the harbor.

At fifteen, while still in school, Fred worked as a car checker on the wharf front. He would later tell reporters he had spent exactly one day in high school, but this was not the case. Much as he disliked school, he stuck it out until he was seventeen, though he did leave before graduating. Fred's formal education was cut short when his mother's uncle, who had a huge homestead near Alberta, Canada, invited him to help out on the farm. Fred's stepfather offered to stake him to college, but he was already educating himself on the side and had begun selling stories to magazines. (Sadly, where these early stories appeared—and under what name—is not known, but Nebel later told his wife his mother saved them.) In Canada Fred soaked up plenty of North Woods atmosphere, which would later serve him well in the pulps.

By 1925 he was back in New York, now writing full time. His earliest located stories appeared that year, three in *North-West Stories* and one in *Action Stories*.

1926 was an even better year, with thirteen appearances in *North-West*, four in *Action* and three in *Lariat*. His first series character, introduced in *North-West*, was a detective of sorts—Corporal Chet Tyson of the RCMP. For *Lariat* he created a gunslinger called The Driftin' Kid. And, most importantly, he broke into *Black Mask*.

That first *Black Mask* sale, "The Breaks of the Game," appeared in March 1926 under the pen name Lewis Nebel. The editor at that time was Phil Cody, and the magazine's star attractions were Carroll John Daly, Erle Stanley Gardner and Dashiell Hammett. Nebel's story ran only six pages, but was enough to demonstrate his aptitude for the new hardboiled style and set him apart from the others.

The story's protagonist, small-time heist artist "Shrimp" Darcy, nearly avoids a murder rap by altering his appearance, but gives himself away with an unconscious shoulder twitch. Had Daly written the story, he would have played up the action at the expense of all else. Gardner would have gone for speed, sacrificing detail. Hammett would have focused on the irony of Shrimp's capture. Nebel handled all these elements well, but his sharp characterization stole the show.

Nebel's third-person narration, even in this early effort, is more than tough and tight. It's also rich, a quality sometimes missing from the work of the others. Almost every word works toward developing Shrimp Darcy's character, and he emerges as a real crook interacting with real people.

Later that year, when Joseph T. Shaw took the reins of *Black Mask*, he began reading back issues in search of stories he liked. Impressed with "The Breaks of the Game," he asked Nebel for more. Shaw's first issue, in November 1926, featured the Nebel story "Grain to Grain," about two police detectives—an ex-gangster and an ex-prizefighter—working the New York waterfront.

In December, Nebel joined a Scandinavian tramp streamer for a three-and-a-half month trip to the Caribbean. He was strictly a passenger on the voyage, but it gave him time to soak up plenty of sea lore and formulate new characters.

In 1927 Nebel made his first "slick" sale, to *Elks Magazine*, and began his first *Black Mask* series. Again drawing on his waterfront experience, he created an adventurer named Buck Jason. Unlike Nebel, who was no more than 5'9", Jason is a whale of a man with eyes that glint like chips of blue steel. Jason appeared in March and April, returning for the last time in August. Meanwhile, *Air Stories* introduced wisecracking freelance pilots Bill Gales and Mike McGill. The series was an instant hit. With two leads, Nebel was able to inject more witty dialogue and deepen the characters by exploring their friendship. This was a technique he would use to even greater effect in the MacBride and Kennedy series.

Black Mask quickly became one of his major markets, and the fact that it paid two cents a word—twice the usual rate—probably had a lot to do with it. When Buck Jason didn't catch on, Nebel experimented with a variety of cops, crooks and detectives, honing his hardboiled style.

Shaw had quickly learned that series characters sold magazines, and to be successful he had to maintain a balance of character types. The lone-wolf private eye spot belonged to Daly's Race Williams. The number one agency man was Hammett's Continental Op. Gardner's Ed Jenkins was the lead crook. With these roles filled by the magazine's most popular writers, the area of greatest opportunity was in the police story.

Cops were nothing new in *Black Mask*. The first major police series, from author Francis James, began in October 1922, featuring a Harvard-trained criminologist-turned-cop by the name of Prentice. By the time Shaw took over, Prentice was gone and the magazine's leading cop was a New York police detective called "Mac," the creation of Tom Curry. "Mac" appeared off and on for several years without achieving star status.

Nebel's police series was something new.

"THE CRIMES OF RICHMOND CITY," a sequence of five connected stories, introduced readers to a setting so well realized they could have drawn a map. The city has at least thirteen precincts, a large rail yard and a busy harbor. There are shoe and garment factories, woolen mills, a novelty jewelry business, a dowel factory, a racetrack and sports auditoriums. The many distinct neighborhoods include the theater district, the swank West End, Little Italy, dark and dangerous Jockey Street, and Craig Square, home to many of the speakeasies. Nebel added to the reality with details of the city's history, even telling us who certain streets are named after.

Fred and Dorothy in New Hampshire, 1941

Early in the series, we learn that Richmond City is only a few miles from the Atlantic and on a navigable river. Readers must have suspected it was based on Richmond, Virginia, because Nebel eventually went out of his way the squelch the idea. When MacBride takes his wife on vacation, touring the "Southern States" in his new flivver, we're told he drove through a red light in Richmond, Virginia.

It seems that almost no one in a position of power in Richmond City is above corruption. Judges, party chiefs, commissioners, aldermen, magistrates, comptrollers, State's Attorneys, and even mayors are susceptible to graft. But standing above it all is the city's toughest police captain, Stephen J. MacBride.

We meet MacBride in the first scene of the series, and while he's "tough as a hard-boiled egg," he's no stereotype. We see him not merely as a cop, but as a husband, father, friend and lifelong citizen of the town. Just as Richmond City seems a real place, Steve MacBride emerges as a real man.

The next character we meet is reporter Kennedy of the *Free Press*. He's laconic and world-weary, but a keen observer of the Richmond City scene. When Kennedy leaves the office, MacBride says, "Sharp, that bird. Pulls ideas out of the air, and every idea hits you like a sock on the jaw."

Like Richmond City, MacBride and Kennedy carry the stamp of authenticity. In developing the characters, Nebel did his homework, spending time with two friends—one a New York newspaperman and the other a police captain—and deluging them with hundreds of questions.

Though Nebel eventually came to think of this as the MacBride-Kennedy series, it's clear that for the first few years this was MacBride's show and Kennedy was merely the most important member of the supporting cast. It wasn't until "Wise Guy" (June 1930), that Nebel began toying with other points of view, and not until "Backwash" (May 1932), halfway into the series, that Kennedy got a scene of his own.

IN this opening volume, comprised of stories published between September 1928 and February 1930, we see Richmond City at its most violent. As the series begins, crooked politicians and racketeers have such a stranglehold on the city that MacBride is powerless to act. It's only when his best detective quits the Force to fight fire with fire that the grip is broken, and MacBride can start cleaning up. He does this with a vengeance. We see pitched battles in the streets, usually with MacBride himself leading the charge, and the death toll is high on both sides. The worst offenders are weeded out, but the corruption runs deep, keeping MacBride on the defensive. Things are so bad that the precinct house seems the last bastion of law and order.

When we first meet MacBride, he's running the city's toughest precinct, where crookdom's elite brush up against the high hats and the evening gowns of the city's great white way. At forty, he's the youngest captain on the Force, and already known as "a holy terror against the criminal element."

Kennedy sums him up nicely: "The skipper is a big bull-headed mutt. He's got a one-track mind and he thinks that shield he wears is another kind of bible. It never occurs to him to walk around a tree, he's got to batter his head against it. To him the law, my friend, is the law: good, bad or indifferent, it's the law. He carries it out as strictly on himself as on any heel he picks up."

A minor female character puts it more succinctly: "This gent looks as if he never goes in reverse."

But strict as MacBride is, he knows that sometimes the law goes too far and sometimes not far enough. When an acquaintance asks,

"How's every little thing?" he replies, "I let the little things slide and get headaches over the big ones."

Realizing that certain types of victimless crimes must be tolerated, MacBride turns a blind eye to speakeasies, bootleggers, and reasonably honest gambling houses. This rational approach to crimefighting also finds its way into Headquarters. His desk sergeant drinks home-brew on duty and must be warned to wipe the suds off his chin. MacBride himself keeps a bottle of liquor in his desk (often as not confiscated in a raid), and drinks five percent beer with his lunch. And though it gripes him, he puts up with detectives playing poker and craps in the office and a vice squad sergeant who runs a horseracing book. The one crime MacBride will not tolerate under any circumstances is murder.

MacBride is also savvy enough to know when extra-legal methods are justified. When a crook tells him, "You're overstepping the law—" MacBride snaps, "I sure am, Morio—I sure am. What this town needs." When suspects refuse to talk, he doesn't hesitate to send them to the sweat room, or as he once calls it, "to play kick-the-wicket." And he's not above promising a heroin addict a fix in return for ratting out her supplier.

"I'm no master mind," MacBride says. "I don't go in for solving riddles. I'm just a cop who tries to beat crime to the tape." And he usually wins the race. When a hood tells him to come back with a warrant, he comes back with a Thompson machine-gun instead. "If it's a fight," he tells his men, "use everything you've got—guns, rocks, clubs, feet and your brains." Often as not he's at the thick of the battle, inspiring them with his vigor and spirit. When he gets mad, his safety valve pops and steam roars. As one of his detectives describes it, "MacBride's boiling so hard that if you put a hat on his head it'd bubble off."

What sets MacBride apart from other *Black Mask* heroes is his dedication to family. His lives with his wife and daughter in a vine-clad bungalow on an elm-shaded street in clean but modest Grove Manor. He owns a shabby Ford, though he usually rides a streetcar to work, and owes three thousand on the house. When the series begins his wife is thirty-eight, still retaining much of her youthful charm. She's proud of him and cuts his pictures from the newspapers, displaying them on their wall. When it rains, she makes him wear galoshes to work.

Suspecting he'll die young in the line of duty, he carries twenty thousand in life insurance, double indemnity. Consideration for his family's welfare is the one thing that can make him back off. As a crusader against crime and corruption he is fearless, but an implied threat to his family—such as losing his job—makes him gnash his teeth in frustration.

MacBride grew up in Richmond City, and his hardass tendencies surfaced early. When he was kid, he busted his next door neighbor's nose for cheating at marbles. At twenty-two, when he joined the Force as a beat cop, he admits he was "a hellion." By the time he made detective first grade he was still inclined to "hit first and ask questions afterwards," but command has mellowed him. A little. As a captain, he usually asks questions *before* he starts hitting—or, more often, has his subordinates do the hitting for him.

Kennedy lives alone in one nondescript boarding house, and while we occasionally meet old friends, they shed little light on his history. "My old man was Irish," he once says, "and mother was a McNulty." He's seen corruption before, in San Francisco, Chicago and New Orleans, but whether close up or from afar is not clear. He was once a fairly good amateur boxer, but now gets by solely on his brains and his nerve.

Kennedy says he's "hard-boiled as hell," and his actions bear this out. Eyeing the bodies of a mobster and a crooked judge, his reaction is "Oh, boy! Where, oh, where is a telephone? What a scoop!" And though he's frequently beaten up, he takes it in stride.

He's at his best when he's dishing out samples of his cockeyed philosophy. "Work is the curse of the drinking classes," he proclaims, and "Blessed is the earth, for it shall inherit the meek." When he says, "Cast your bread upon the waters and it will come back all wet," the ever-pragmatic MacBride responds, "I can't stand water. That's why I never go to sea. I always get seasick."

Lackadaisical as he appears, Kennedy never lets down on the job. "I have big ears and I have a habit of putting them to door panels." In one instance, too drunk to walk, he crawls to a house to get a story.

NEBEL contrasts the two characters in nearly every way possible.

MacBride is tall, angular and square-shouldered, "built of whipcord, hard bone, tough hide." Kennedy is small and slim, with round shoulders and a hollow chest. He looks like "a scarecrow or the shadow of an emaciated tree," and is so skinny he can take cover behind a lamppost.

MacBride has thick, black, wiry hair, a ruddy-brown face and eyes that could "lacerate a man to the core." Kennedy has unruly blond hair, a sallow complexion, and "the whimsical eyes of the wicked and the wise."

MacBride's clothes are neat, clean and sharply pressed, and his shoes reflect light. Kennedy's attire is always "haphazard and ill-assembled." His suits are wrinkled and his topcoats threadbare. His hats are faded, misshapen, and sometime on backwards.

MacBride drums his heels and slams into a room like "a blast of wind." Kennedy drifts, slopes, slouches or sways.

MacBride's words are barked, clipped, bit off or ripped out. Kennedy chuckles, sighs or grins, then speak with dry humor.

Kennedy addresses MacBride as "old tomato," "old horse," and "Skipperino." MacBride responds with such endearments as "fat-head," "pot-head" and "bozo."

While nothing seems to faze Kennedy, he causes MacBride plenty of grief. "You're like a burr in a man's sock," he tells Kennedy. "You start dropping ideas around and me, like a fool, I go picking 'em up and losing sleep over 'em." "You're a cynical, cold-blooded, snooping, wisecracking example of modern newspaperdom. But, Kennedy, you've got brains—and you're on the square." From MacBride, there can be no higher compliment.

Different as these two are, there's no doubt their friendship runs deep. When Kennedy is missing and feared dead, MacBride goes looking, coming back with "his face drawn, dark circles under his eyes." Seeing Kennedy standing in the station house, "wild joy" leaps to his face. As for Kennedy, while he does not always approve of MacBride's hardheaded attitude, he genuinely likes him, admitting, "He's probably the best friend I've got."

Though Nebel was only 23 when he began the Richmond City series, the stories—and the setting—carry the weight of an author with far more life experience.

His flare for understatement produced lines Hammett would have admired:

> Guns empty, the men clashed, hand to hand, clubbing rifles. Nightsticks became popular. (from "The Law Laughs Last")
> Sergeant Flannery blundered in, full of news. (from "Graft")
> She cursed and added something relative to his maternity. He trotted her down the stairs. (from "Graft")

"Listen, lady, pipe down, will you? Give your ears a chance." (from "Lay Down the Law")

"Fingerprints don't walk into a place without fingers." (from "Too Young to Die")

"If you know where your alley is—stay up it." (from "Die-Hard")

Nebel's quick wit provides MacBride with a great sense of humor. In "Tough Treatment," when he advises a hardboiled dame he's running her into the station, we get the following exchange.

Dame: "You're sure a pain in the neck, MacBride."
MacBride: "Try liniment, sister."
Dame: "Get wise that I'm only taking an overnight bag."
MacBride: "You get wise and take a trunk."

This one comes from "Shake-Down":

Acquaintance: "How's the gumshoe trade?"
MacBride: "Slow. Not a thing stirring. We're having day-beds put in Headquarters."

And this from "Beat the Rap":

MacBride: "Mr. Bergman, have you ever seen the inside of a Police Headquarters?"
Bergman: "No."
MacBride: "It's kind of worth seeing. Put your hat on."

Kennedy gets in plenty of great lines, too, as in "It's a Gag":

Kennedy's editor: "The repercussions of this are going to be far-reaching, or I'm a horse's neck."
Kennedy: "Horse's neck? My, you're a champion of understatement."

IN 1928, around the same time the first Richmond City stories were appearing in *Black Mask*, Nebel had his first brush with the silver screen. His *Action Stories* tale "The Isle of Lost Men" was made into two short silent films, one bearing the story title and the other called "Ships in the Night." Each featured entirely different casts and characters.

Late that year, Nebel traveled to France, where he planned to share a villa with other writers and artists. This plan went by the wayside when fellow *Mask* writer Nels Leroy Jorgensen offered to introduce him to some nice American girls. "I can meet them at home," Nebel replied, "How about some French ones?" But he went, and one of the girls was Dorothy Blank, daughter of a St. Louis department store manager. Nebel was entranced enough to invite her to lunch the following day. And that was that. Dorothy was visiting France with her mother, so Nebel abandoned his villa plans and found a small apartment near their Paris hotel. In the spring, the three traveled to London, where he rented a furnished flat. Fred and Dorothy spent much of the next three weeks touring the English countryside.

When Dorothy and her mother sailed for home, Nebel stayed on for another two months. It's odd to think of him pounding out hardboiled tales of Richmond City from a London flat, but that's how it was. He also kept up a stream of stories to other markets. In 1929 alone his work appeared in *Action Stories*, *Air Stories*, *Argosy*, *Five Novels Monthly*, *Flying Stories*, *North-West Stories*, *Real Detective Tales*, *Sea Stories*, *Wings* and *Young's Magazine*, along with two slicks, *Columbia* and *Elks Magazine*.

Nebel returned to New York in early summer. His chief companions there were Dashiell Hammett and Raoul Whitfield, with whom he did a lot of carousing in bars. One night he and Hammett carried an open umbrella—despite the lack of rain—just to see if anyone would notice. No one did. Naturally they had plenty to drink, and Nebel slept it off on Hammett's couch. In the morning, Hammett presented him with an inscribed copy of *The Maltese Falcon*, a book Nebel kept for the rest of his days. When Nebel left for St. Louis to prepare for his wedding, Hammett wrote him a few lines of sympathy almost every day.

Nebel admired *The Maltese Falcon* and reviewed it in *The St. Louis Post-Dispatch*: "It seems a pity that this should be called a detective story.... Truly, it is a story about a detective, but it is so much about a detective that he becomes a character, and the sheer force of Hammett's hard, brittle writing lifts the book out of the general run of crime spasms and places it aloof and alone as a brave chronicle of a hard-boiled man, unscrupulous, conscienceless, unique."

To Fred Nebel, in memory of the night of the cloud-burst when we were companions under the umbrella — Dashiell Hammett

February 16 - 1930

While in St. Louis, Nebel kept busy turning out stories for *Black Mask* and his adventure markets, and also made his first appearance in *Detective Fiction Weekly*.

LATE in its second year, the Richmond City series entered a new phase. In the next Altus Press volume, featuring stories published between April 1930 and February 1933, we'll see MacBride on the lookout for new rackets and new forms of corruption, hell-bent to nip them in the bud. Though he takes heat from other cops—and the commissioner himself—for overstepping his bounds, MacBride is on a crusade. And when his efforts finally earn him a spot at Headquarters, he must face the reality that some of his fellow officers are on the take.

Fred and Dorothy were married in St. Louis on May 12, 1930. St. Louis made its presence known in Nebel's writing almost immediately. He took a break from MacBride and Kennedy to create detective "Donny" Donahue, an operative of the Interstate Detective Agency, on assignment in St. Louis. Donahue made his debut in the November 1930 *Black Mask*, appearing four straight issues before MacBride and Kennedy returned, after a seven month hiatus, in March 1931. With the Continental Op all but retired from service, Donahue was now the magazine's number one agency dick.

The Nebels made frequent trips back to New York. On the first after their marriage, Nels Jorgensen brought flowers, while Hammett brought a funeral wreath. Mrs. Nebel thought her husband looked "comically short" next to Hammett. (Joe Shaw once listed him among his authors who were over six feet tall, but this was meant as a joke.) One night as Fred and Dorothy were having dinner at a speakeasy, Hammett appeared in a doorway on the far side of the dance-floor. Next to him stood a tray of silverware. While the Nebels watched wide-eyed, Hammett scooped up handful after handful of forks, flinging them across the floor, until he was forcibly removed. Hammett had recently returned from Hollywood, and despite being dead broke took a room at the Waldorf, throwing parties and running up a bill. Eventually Nebel and other friends had to chip in and bail him out.

Nebel provided *Black Mask* with a dozen stories in 1931—a personal record. That total included four MacBride and Kennedy novelettes, four Donahues and four non-series tales. Two of the stand-alones, published in the same issues as Richmond City stories, appeared under the pen name Grimes Hill ("I was born at the foot of Grimes

Hill," he explained). In addition to a full slate of adventure stories, he made two more appearances in *Detective Fiction Weekly*, and began two new mystery series.

For *Detective Action Stories* he created Inspector Peter Larsen—a character much like Steve MacBride. Larsen battles crime with his likeable but less bright subordinate, Sergeant Brinkhaus, in the fictional city of Portsend, a doppelgänger of Richmond City.

In *Dime Detective* Nebel introduced Cardigan, an agency operative in the mold of Donahue. When the series begins, Cardigan is heading up the St. Louis branch of the Cosmos Detective Agency. Like Donahue, he works best alone, but sometimes teams up with a smart-mouthed female operative named Pat Seaward. Unlike Donahue, who normally works well with the police, Cardigan has more of an adversarial relationship. It would have been interesting to see him butt heads with the equally tough Steve MacBride.

In 1932 Nebel got a taste of better money, selling a story to the *Saturday Evening Post* for $1,700. This was big stuff, seeing that his *Black Mask* and *Dime* stories brought in between $200 and $270 each. Deciding it was time to write a novel, Nebel abandoned his adventure markets in July and cut back his detective writing to two or three novelettes a month. He completed the novel, *Sleepers East*, in October.

Nebel's inspiration for *Sleepers East* was Vicki Baum's novel *Grand Hotel*, released as a hit film in 1932, in which a large and varied cast of characters are thrown together in a limited space (in Nebel's case an eastbound train) to affect each others' lives.

Sleepers East is not a mystery novel, but the crime element is prominent because five of the twelve main characters are on their way to an upcoming murder trial. Among them are a lawyer defending a notorious mobster, a dirty private dick and an inept railroad detective. But there's no whodunit here, no crime committed on the train, and very little violence. Most of the conflict revolves around personal aspirations, political problems and romantic entanglements.

With a dozen point-of-view characters, it's hard to pick a protagonist, but the guy who starts and finishes the novel is a henpecked husband trying to leave his boring life behind. He fails, but feels richer for this brief taste of freedom. Other characters go through changes of their own. Some lose love and find it elsewhere. One gets her first taste of happiness and pays for it with her life. One is forced to see the ugly truth about himself, while another faces the ugly truth about someone else.

MacBride and Kennedy took a back seat to Donahue in 1932, with only two stories to his four. The Larsen-Brinkhaus series jumped from *Detective Action* to *Detective Fiction Weekly*, where Brinkhaus stepped out of Larsen's shadow to take the lead in three stories. And Cardigan, now working out of New York City, topped them all with nine stories in *Dime Detective*.

By 1933, the Nebels had settled in Laguna, California, and for a little more than a year he kept a journal.

On an average day he'd rise early, fix his own breakfast and take a walk into town, which he called "the village," visiting the post office to pick up mail. He'd begin writing around 10:30, break for lunch, and sometimes read or take a short nap. He'd then work a couple more hours before dinner. When up against a deadline he'd stay at his desk longer and sometimes return late in the evening. His output fluctuated between 1,000 and 5,000 words a day.

Nebel could usually turn out a novelette in three to five days. The only *Black Mask* story mentioned by name in the journal, the Donahue novelette "Save Your Tears," is a good example. Work got underway slowly on January 21. On the 22nd he worked in spurts, and felt the story moved along pretty well. That evening he had a guest and "drank more than I should have," for which he blamed a mediocre 1,000 words on the 23rd. He progressed fairly well on the 24th, and turned out 3,000 words ("a good day") on the 25th. On the 26th he worked until 5:30, finishing, editing, and mailing the novelette, which he deemed, a "fair yarn—considerably more than adequate." He received a $230 check for the story on February 6, which Shaw praised very highly.

On January 31 his agent advised him that Little, Brown and Company had bought *Sleepers East*. He received an advance of $250 and royalties on a sliding scale, retaining all motion picture and dramatic rights. The novel was immediately sent to Twentieth Century Fox for consideration. Their lack of response nettled Nebel until April, when Paramount expressed interest and Fox finally got off the dime, buying the film rights for $5,000.

THE Richmond City stories published between March 1933 and February 1935, to be collected in the third Altus Press volume, take on a more personal note. Rather than combating large scale corruption, MacBride and Kennedy apply their talents to murder cases, often involving old friends. This group also includes "Bad News" (March 1934), in which MacBride is away on vacation and Kennedy takes the lead for the first time. This story, as you might expect, is the most comedic of the entire saga.

With the series in its fifth year, Steve MacBride begins to feel his age. He gets more and more frustrated with the job, particularly when men he considers friends don't support his actions. "It just breaks my heart with gratitude," he says. "Some fine day I'm going to start out and systematically change the shapes of a lot of schnozzles in this man's town." And, "The longer I work at this job, the more I think I should have taken up farming." He's tired of the long, irregular hours, and sick of "the blood and intrigue" that goes with police work.

While MacBride ages, Kennedy seems to grow younger. His drinking reaches the point that he is always either drunk or slightly drunk. His actions become more erratic, and he's played for slapstick, tumbling out of taxi-cabs and getting caught in revolving doors. More and more, Kennedy is seen as an almost-magical sprite who flits in and out of danger but is never seriously hurt.

Nebel had always been a voracious reader, and his journal reveals a wide range of interests. Among the many books and articles he noted reading in 1933 were *A High Wind in Jamaica* (which impressed him greatly), *The Craft of Writing* by Percy Lubbock, a *Fortune* article about the rolling of Cuban cigars, Sinclair Lewis' *Ann Vickers*, Zola's *Nana*, Tolstoy's *Anna Karenina* and *The Death of Iván Ilyitch*, a *Fortune* article about the history of the banana monopoly in the Caribbean, Fowler's *Modern English Usage*, *Cities of Sin* (a record of prostitution in the Orient which he called "a fair piece of erotica, of no importance whatever"), H.E. Wortham's *Chinese Gordon*, an unnamed book by Gertrude Stein ("most times she irritates me, at other times I find myself intensely interested"), W.R. Burnett's *Dark Hazard*, and Somerset Maugham's *Moon & Sixpence* (Nebel had a collection of Maugham's first editions).

While living in California, Nebel bought a Smith & Wesson .38 and sometimes went shooting with friends, many of whom were other writers. Though he refers to most by only first names or initials, one he identifies is pulp writer (and future screenwriter) Eric Taylor. During this period Nebel also paid a visit to Erle Stanley Gardner, encouraging him to quit his law practice and write full time.

In his own writing, Nebel was firing on all cylinders, working on a novel, slick stories and detective tales at the same time. While the slicks paid more, he was not yet ready to abandon the pulps. Shaw and *Dime Detective* editor Harry Steeger had become close personal friends, and he felt a certain loyalty. Equally important, those sales were a sure thing, proving a steady income while he sought a solid footing in the higher paying markets.

To free more time for the new novel (one he would eventually set aside), Nebel began churning out the pulp stories faster than ever, and the rush jobs did not go unnoticed. In March, Shaw asked him to revise the beginning of his latest novelette. This was the first time in two years Shaw had asked him for a revision, and he complied, but it cost him two and half work days. When Shaw requested another revision in April, Nebel refused, noting, "I honestly did not agree with his point of view, and told him so." Meanwhile, because *Dime* had just begun a twice-monthly schedule, Steeger wanted two stories a month instead of one—more than Nebel could provide. Later that month Doubleday's Crime Club requested a full-length mystery novel. This idea apparently fell by the wayside, because it was not mentioned again.

In June 1933 Nebel received a check for $2,500, the first installment toward the movie rights for *Sleepers East*. This was the largest check he had yet received for his work, and he was pleased. "I really feel that I am getting somewhere," he wrote. "Joe gave me a big spread on the current issue of his magazine, and continues to be one of my great enthusiasts. His enthusiasm and encouragement have meant much to me ever since we came to know each other as author and editor."

The Nebels had developed the habit of spending the latter half of each year on the East Coast, and did so again in 1933. In New York, Nebel had dinner and cruised the bars with Nels Jorgensen, then headed for Scarsdale, where he and Shaw played golf, both pretty badly. He attended a cocktail party at Raoul Whitfield's place, which he termed "a menage in the upper east Eighties," and saw Hammett, who told him *Cosmopolitan* and *Collier's* had turned down an abridgement of his new novel, and "admitted his shorts in *Collier's* were lousy." (The novel Hammett referred to was *The Thin Man*, which was finally accepted by *Redbook* and published in hardcover the following January. After reading it, Nebel wrote, "I can't see it at all, though the critics are whooping it up.")

Sleepers East was published in June and was a big success. By June 16, when he paid a visit to Little, Brown the book was already in its third printing, and he was unable to get any more firsts. The book received a good review from *Time*, calling it better than *Grand Hotel*, and it was number two on the bestseller list, behind *Anthony Adverse*. Critics praised the crisp dialogue and fast-moving story.

Nebel felt that his photograph accompanying the review in the *Saturday Evening Post* made him look "dark and forbidding." He did look stern and serious in that often-used picture, but he actually had a great sense of humor. As a storyteller, he was in great demand at parties, and was a talented mimic. Attending a Laguna New Years Eve party as Groucho Marx, he was nearly thrown out for his antics with the ladies. And he once dressed as Adolf Hitler, goosestepping and sieg heiling for a camera.

While in New York, having abandoned the novel he'd been working on since February, he started a new one, which would eventually become *But Not the End*. He planned to spend the next month or six weeks on the novel, "unless it knots up and an idea for a short appeals to me."

In June he received a letter from "a new writer named George H. Coxe, Jr.," asking if he might pay a visit and get his copy of *Sleepers East* autographed. This was the beginning of a lifelong friendship. That fall, he spent the night with Coxe and his wife on Cape Cod, where Coxe was eager to talk shop. Nebel encouraged him to submit his work to Shaw, resulting in the addition of Flashgun Casey to the cast of *Black Mask*.

In November WABC bought the rights to broadcast one of the MacBride and Kennedy stories, "Lay Down the Law." When the show was broadcast in December, Nebel wrote, "Joe is a little disgruntled… they did not give credit to his magazine."

Nebel worked on his new novel almost exclusively between July and October, averaging a thousand words a day. His working title "Beginning Again" would go through several name changes, including "Crash and Resound" and "Bridges to Burn" before finally becoming *But Not the End*. Little, Brown accepted the novel in November, though two of their five readers were "luke-warm."

Nebel was at the top of his form while writing *But Not the End*, and it's loaded with fine prose. But because it's set during the Great Depression, most of its characters are depressed, making it a largely downbeat read.

The primary point-of-view character, an investment broker, faces financial ruin and watches helplessly as his partner and several clients commit suicide. His nymphomaniac wife is having her sixth not-so-clandestine affair, and his daughter is about to marry a daredevil flyer. A once-rich immigrant is forced to accept a menial job and is ashamed to return home in disgrace. A champion prizefighter loses his title, his career and half his vision. Those who deserve a second chance at happiness are rewarded in the end, while those who don't are lost beyond redemption.

But Not the End paid one unexpected bonus. In the thirteen issues of *Dime Detective* published between October 1933 and March 1934, Nebel had only three stories. Harry Steeger wanted Cardigan back so badly that he bumped Nebel's rate to four cents a word, bringing complaints from other writers. Shaw would no doubt have offered Nebel a higher rate too, but his publishers were trying to economize.

With Cardigan bringing in twice as much as Donahue, it would have been bad business to keep Donahue working. Only one more story appeared, and that a year and half later. Still, out of loyalty to Shaw, Nebel continued to bang out four or five Richmond City novelettes a year.

Nebel must have been feeling flush, because in December he bought a new Pierce-Arrow, "relinquishing the old roadster." He loved big cars, and this one filled the bill. He and Shaw taxied to the dealership to pick up the car, then headed to Joe's place for a round of martinis.

That same month, a check from Fox bounced, and Nebel discovered that a Little, Brown payment was overdue. For these and other irregularities he blamed his agents, and vowed to seek new representation. He soon put his work in the hands of Carl Brandt, for whom he had the greatest respect. He would stay with the Brandt agency for the rest of his career.

Nebel was in New York before and after the 18th Amendment repealed Prohibition and saw apprehension among speakeasy owners. "I daresay," he wrote, "that we shall look back upon speakies with tender, sentimental regrets." Folks in Richmond City were not so sentimental, but MacBride noted that even after repeal, bootleggers were far outselling the legal suppliers.

Fred and Dorothy spent Christmas with her family in St. Louis. On New Year's Day of 1934 he reported, "I of course celebrated in the usual manner and added nothing especially new to the occasion. I got quite tight and enjoyed myself...."

On January 27 he wrote, "The James Warner Bellahs stopped by. He had been fencing and there was a small cut on his cheek. We convened in my bar and I think limericks were popular." And, "Joe argued me into doing a story for him and I did one and he said it was the best story I had ever given him. I thought it was fair." Meanwhile, a friend reported seeing Fox's first version of *Sleepers East* (which would not be officially released until April) and deemed it terrible. "It's no more like your book than I'm like chalk," the guy said.

Nebel's journal entries were becoming steadily less frequent, and the last were made in February. Galleys of *But Not the End* had been sent to movie studios, and Nebel had high hopes. He wrote, "I heard that Fox paid Lewis $25,000 for the picture rights to *Work of Art*; that Metro paid Hammett $22,500 for *The Thin Man*." Whether the rights to *But Not the End* ever sold to a studio is unknown, but no film was produced.

In his last journal entry, Nebel says his agent suggested doing a 17,000 word story for *American Magazine* for $2,000, and he agreed to think it over. The fact that he would not immediately accept such an offer is a fair indicator that his spirits were flying high.

LITTLE, Brown published *But Not the End* in March, and reviews were good. Sales, however, were down, probably due to the Depression theme.

But Not the End established Nebel as a novelist, and he found a warm reception in the slicks, especially *Collier's*. At the same time, the book's poor sales had shown him there was more sure money in magazine stories. "I have no ideas for a new novel and don't propose to look for any for several months," he wrote. "I shall concentrate on short stories." Now officially between novels, he bore down on his novelettes. But his focus was more and more on the higher-paying markets. He made only four *Black Mask* appearances in 1934, versus nine in *Dime Detective*.

Sleepers East, released by Fox in April, starred Wynne Gibson—who made an undistinguished career of playing hardboiled blondes—as the woman pressured to clear a gunman of a murder frame. Preston Foster was Jason Everett, the henpecked man running away from his dull life. Also in the cast (though uncredited) was J. Carrol Naish as the unscrupulous private detective.

After several years of coast-hopping, the Nebels found and renovated a huge 200-year-old farmhouse on four acres of land in Ridgefield, Connecticut. This was just where they wanted to be, fifty miles from New York, and they would live there for the next twenty-five years.

After the move to Connecticut, Nebel and George Harmon Coxe got together several weekends a year, and Nebel helped convince him to write his first novel. Some of those weekends included writer and former journalist Thomas Walsh, who also became a close friend.

Nebel had not given up on his aspirations as a novelist. By 1935, the extra money from *Dime* and *Collier's* had given him enough cushion to support another lengthy project, and he tried again to repeat the success of *Sleepers East.*

Fifty Roads to Town, published 1936, came closer but still fell short. Once again, reviews were good but sales were not. Like *Sleepers East,* the novel features a large cast of characters, and like *But Not the End* it has no crime content.

Two of the major players are Edwin Henry, a henpecked salesman of fire protection equipment and assorted sundries, and Peter Nostrand, a man on the run from an aggrieved husband. Nostrand's hideout is a secluded cabin in the Maine woods, and Henry blunders in, hoping to make a sale. When a storm hits, the two are snowbound together. Most of the action takes place either in the cabin or in an ancient hotel called the Outpost House, where we find the rest of the characters. These include the county attorney heading the search for Henry, the wronged and sexually repressed husband, a fun-loving but tenth-rate torch singer, and Henry's harpy of a wife.

When Henry's disappearance goes public, reporters descend upon the Outpost House and the search turns into a circus. The governor gets involved, a famous aviator flies circles over the landscape, and a champion sled-dog driver arrives with his team, merely to get drunk.

Compared to Nebel's first two novels, *Fifty Roads* is a fun read, laced with humor and satire, and it's obvious Nebel had fun writing it.

IN the fourth and final volume of the Richmond City stories, featuring stories published between May 1935 and August 1936, we'll see secondary characters assume larger roles, and the introduction of two new regulars. By this time Nebel had come to think of himself as a novelist and wanted to delve deeper into his characters. This results in longer scenes, and sometimes longer stories.

MacBride's two best detectives, Ike Cohen and "Mory" Moriarity, were introduced early in the series, but in the final years their personalities grew stronger, providing more comic relief. They're often found sneaking drinks in the station or matching quarters in the back of the police car, and both spend a lot of time in speakeasies. The medical examiner calls them MacBride's cowboys. Kennedy calls them his stooges. MacBride calls them apes or tramps, but trusts them implicitly. "I've got two palookas working for me," he sums them up, "who think of me first and then the department."

The new regulars also add to the comedy. Kennedy's wacky bartender pal, Paderoofski, is always ready to lend Kennedy an ear, and sometimes other essentials like money or a gun. And MacBride's driver, Gahagan, is an all-around dimwit who pays not the slightest notice to safety or traffic laws, but has an uncanny ability to get places in a hurry.

At this point in the series, the humor is welcome, because MacBride's moods have grown increasingly dark. He reaches the lowpoint of his career in "Fan Dance" (January 1936), when he finds himself suspended. "I ought to have been kicked in the head," he says, "the first day I ever put on a uniform." Kennedy's scenes are darker, too. Both the author and his characters seem to realize Kennedy's drinking is out of control, posing a threat to his health and life.

As the Richmond City series was nearing its end, Steve MacBride was popping up in other media. 1936 saw him featured in a CBS Radio program called "Meet McBride" (apparently a one-shot deal) and his first movie, Warner Brothers' "Smart Blonde." The film, based on the *Black Mask* story "No Hard Feelings," gave "McBride" a backseat to a Hollywood-created femme fatale, torch singer Torchy Blane. But it was successful enough to spark eight sequels, most featuring Glenda Farrell as Torchy and Barton McLane as McBride. Jane Wyman and Allen Jenkins took the roles in one film, Lola Lane and Paul Kelly in another. Nebel received "based upon" screen credit for the sequels, but none utilized his stories.

Nebel's chief project in 1936 was a novel-length work called "Nothing to Lose." This one had more of his pulp-style crackle and speed, and point of view stayed with one character, an adventurer not unlike Nebel's pulp heroes. No records survive to show whether it was offered to Little, Brown or other publishers, but it did find a home, in abridged form, in the January 1937 *Cosmopolitan*.

Nebel devoted himself more and more to the slicks, and found success in new markets like *Liberty*, *Maclean's* and *Redbook*. When Joe Shaw was replaced in late 1936, Nebel took the opportunity to drop out of *Black Mask*, closing the saga of Richmond City after nine years and thirty-seven stories. In mid-1937, after a total of forty-four Cardigan adventures, he left *Dime Detective* as well.

In April 1937 Dorothy Nebel gave birth to their first and only child. The boy, Christopher, had trouble with his lungs and nervous system, but there was nothing wrong with his mind. He quickly learned to read, and particularly enjoyed his father's copies of *Fortune* and *The Encyclopedia Britannica*. At ten, teachers judged him to be reading at the level of a sixteen year old.

In June 1936 Fox released their version of *Fifty Roads to Town*, transformed into a romantic comedy. Don Ameche starred as Nebel's character Peter Nostrand, but rather than an adulterer hiding from a murderous husband, he's a good guy trying to avoid testifying in a friend's divorce. Ann Sothern, playing a character not in the book, is his romantic interest. Nebel thought the movie was fairly well done, though it had little to do to with his novel.

Two more Nebel-based films were released in 1941. The second adaptation of *Sleepers East*, now called *Sleepers West*, came out in March, an entry in the Michael Shayne franchise. Lloyd Nolan starred as Shayne—a character who had no parallel in the book, and instead of running from Chicago to New York, the train went from Chicago to Denver. Nebel found it amusing that they made his book into a 'B' picture both times.

In April, Fox released "A Shot in the Dark," a second version of the MacBride and Kennedy story "No Hard Feelings." This one starred William Lundigan as reporter "Pete" Kennedy, with Nan Wynn as torch singer Dixie Wynne and Ricardo Cortez (the screen's first Sam Spade) as nightclub owner Phil Richards. Fourth billing went to Regis Toomey (in the MacBride role) as Detective Lt. Bill Ryder.

On this and other occasions, the studios tried to lure Nebel to Hollywood, but he resisted all offers. He had seen too many friends come back broke.

Nebel's best magazine markets at this time were *Collier's*, *Liberty*, *Good Housekeeping* and *Cosmopolitan*. Some stories were marginally mysteries, and a few featured cops or detectives, but most plots revolved around romance rather than crime.

During the war, he was in charge of the Ridgefield rationing board. "He was a tough baby," his wife said, "running it no doubt like Steve MacBride would have—fairly but equitably." When a New York steamship magnate wanted his Ridgefield home heated to protect his antique paneling, she recalled this exchange:

> Nebel: "I understand that paneling of yours dates back to the 1600s."
> Magnate: "That's right."
> Nebel: "Well, they didn't have central heating back then. You'd better not heat that house or you might ruin it."

NEBEL did not like looking back at his pulp work. In 1945, he found the *Black Mask* material too dated and rejected Joe Shaw's suggestion to submit a paperback collection to Avon. "I've looked over some of those novelettes," he wrote his agent. "They were published over a dozen years ago and I think we ought to forget about them." He also refused, much to Shaw's chagrin, to be included in *The Hard-Boiled Omnibus*, published in 1946. He did, however, suggest that a 50,000 word story from *McCall's* might interest one of the paperback outfits. He was right, and "Weekend to Kill," appeared in a Century Mystery digest that same year, combined with Hugh Pentacost's "Secret Corridors." Nebel received a $500 advance and a royalty agreement.

"Weekend to Kill" does qualify as a mystery, because one of the main characters is an ex-cop working to solve a murder. But it's really more a play of manners and romantic foibles, using the murder as mainly an excuse to create conflict among the characters. There are faint echoes of the Richmond City series. The narrator is a reporter, his pal an ex-cop, and there's talk about a crusading editor striving to expose a corrupt political regime. But the characters are creampuffs compared to Kennedy and MacBride, and the corrupt politicians remain offstage.

In 1948 Nebel had his best-ever payday. He received $15,000 for the movie rights to "The Bribe," a story from *Cosmopolitan*. MGM released the film in 1949, featuring Robert Taylor, Ava Gardner, Vincent Price and Charles Laughton. Nebel's neighbors were surprised he didn't travel the fifty miles to the New York premiere, but he resolved to wait until it came to their local theater. His mother *did* attend the premiere, and phoned to say she enjoyed it, especially the deep-sea fishing scene. Nebel's response was "*What* deep-sea fishing scene?"

When the reprint question arose again in 1949, Nebel had changed his tune. His high blood pressure had made it difficult to produce more than a few stories a year, and revenue was welcome from any source. Robert Mills, managing editor of *Ellery Queen's Mystery Magazine*, requested a collection of Donahue stories for consideration as a Mercury Mystery digest, and possible inclusion in *EQMM*. Nebel was enthusiastic, selecting six Donahue stories for his agent to submit.

At the same time, he put together a possible collection of MacBride and Kennedy stories, including the first, "Raw Law." He marked up tear sheets from the magazine to make minor revisions. One change would have increased Richmond City's population from "almost a hundred-thousand" to "almost 500 hundred-thousand." What had seemed a good-sized city in 1928 was much smaller by 1949 standards.

After several months, the Donahue stories were returned. Frederic Dannay had found them a bit too dated for either *EQMM* or the digest line. The collection went next to Avon, where it sold. The publisher initially planned to call the book *The Black Mask Murders*, but Popular Publications objected. Avon settled on *Six Deadly Dames*, a title Nebel didn't like, for which he received a $500 advance. The book appeared as a wonderfully lurid paperback in 1950.

With *Six Deadly Dames* a reality, Nebel was faced with a decision. He could submit another Donahue collection or switch to Richmond City. "I think we'd better offer the MacBride-Kennedy series next," he told his agent, "and hold back on a second Donahue group. Reason: I've got more MacBride-Kennedy, enough for four books. If Avon doesn't want 'em, then we can go elsewhere and throw the second Donahue at Avon." But by the time the stories were submitted, Avon had decided to cut back on story collections, following the trend toward hardboiled novels. They also declined to reprint *Sleepers East* and *Fifty Roads to Town*, which were by no means hardboiled. Popular Library and Mercury Mysteries also passed on both books. Around the same time, Gold Medal wrote requesting an original mystery novel, but Nebel's health would no longer permit such a sustained effort.

Over the next few years Nebel's income was augmented by occasional sales of movie and television rights. In 1956, after *EQMM* and *The Saint* reprinted some of his old stories, he wrote several new ones for *EQMM*. His agent helped squeeze every dime of income out of each story. For "Try It My Way," from the June 1956 *EQMM*, he got $300 from the magazine, $200 for an Ellery Queen anthology, $1,000 for television rights from CBS, $100 from Japanese TV, and $75 for Danish newspaper rights. The Japanese sale gave him a laugh. He told his wife he'd give "anything" to see their version on TV.

In November 1958 the Nebels were forced to sell the house in Connecticut. The place had thirty-three storm windows, and every one of them had to go up and down each year. When Fred's blood pressure would no longer permit this they returned to California, where they still had friends. Their son Christopher, then in his twenties, lived in San Pedro, where he worked at the local branch of the L.A. Library.

Nebel sold his last stories to *EQMM* in 1961 and 1962, the magazine that said "Including Black Mask Magazine" on its masthead. Though he continued working, his health grew steadily worse, and he found stories difficult to complete.

The possibility of a MacBride-Kennedy collection surfaced again in 1966. Sherbourne Press had recently published Ron Goulart's *The Hardboiled Dicks* and Frank Gruber's *Brass Knuckles*, reviving interest in detective pulps. Nebel's agents approached Avon about the possibility of reprinting *Six Deadly Dames*, and proposed a Richmond City collection. Nebel selected six stories for the book, to be called *Too Young to Die*. Along with the title story, they were "Be Your Age," "He Was a Swell Guy," "It's a Gag," "Crack Down," and "Deep Red." Avon considered the idea until September, when they passed on both projects. The MacBride-Kennedy collection was then submitted to Sherbourne Press, but for some reason never materialized.

Nebel never stopped writing. At the time of his death, from a cerebral hemorrhage on May 3, 1967, he had an outline for a new novel, and his typewriter held the first page of a new mystery.

Though Nebel had a long and varied career, his greatest legacy was the saga of Richmond City. To you who are about to enter the city limits and fight crime with MacBride and Kennedy, I offer a word of advice:

Hold onto your seat. It's going to be a wild ride.

Raw Law

A city of graft and crime; a man's buddy, a victim; then the deadly game of vengeance—and justice.

Chapter I

CAPTAIN STEVE MacBRIDE was a tall square-shouldered man of forty more or less hard-bitten years. He had a long, rough-chiseled face, steady eyes, a beak of a nose, and a wide, firm mouth that years of fighting his own and others' wills had hardened. His face shone ruddily, cleanly, as if it were used to frequent and vigorous contact with soap and water. For eighteen years he had been connected, in one capacity or another, with Richmond City's police department, and Richmond City today is a somewhat hectic community of almost a hundred-thousand population.

MacBride sat in his office at Police Headquarters. He sat at his shining oak desk, in a swivel chair, smoking a blackened briar pipe, with the latest copy of the Richmond City *Free Press* spread before him. In one corner a steam radiator clanked and hissed intermittently. There were a half dozen chairs lined against the wall behind him. The floor was of cement, the ceiling was high and, like the walls, a light, impersonal tan. About the room there was something hollow and clean and efficient. About the borders of the two windows at MacBride's left there were irregular frames of snow left by a recent blizzard. But the room was warm and, except for the clanking of the radiator, quite silent.

Reading on, MacBride sometimes moved in his chair or took his pipe from his mouth to purse his lips, it seemed a little grimly and ironically. Once he muttered something behind clenched teeth, way down in the cavern of his throat. Presently he let the paper drop and sat back, drawing silently on his pipe and letting his eyes wander back and forth over the collection of photographs tacked on the bulletin board on the wall before him—photographs of men wanted for robbery, murder, and homicide. One of the telephones on his desk rang. He took off the receiver, listened, said, "Send him in." Then he leaned back again and swung his chair to face the door.

It opened presently, and a man neatly dressed in a blue overcoat and a gray fedora strolled in. A cigarette was drooping from one corner of his mouth. He had a young-old face, a vague smile, and the whimsical eyes of the wicked and wise.

"Hello, Cap." He kicked the door shut with his heel and leaned against it indolently, as if he were a little weary—not in his bones, but with life.

"Hello, Kennedy," nodded MacBride. "Sit down."

"Thanks."

Kennedy dropped into a chair, unbuttoned his overcoat, but did not remove it.

MacBride creaked in his chair, looked at the newspaper on his desk and said, with a brittle chuckle, "Thanks for the editorial."

"Don't thank me, Mac."

"Your sheet's trying to ride us, eh?"

"Our business is to ride everybody we can."

"M-m-m. I know."

Kennedy knocked the ash from his cigarette. "Of course, it's tough on you." He smiled, shrugged. "I know your hands are tied."

"Eh?" MacBride's eyes steadied.

"You heard me, Mac. This little boy knows a lot. Y' know, you don't run the Department."

MacBride's lips tightened over his pipe.

"You," went on Kennedy, "would like to put the clamps on this dirty greaseball, Cavallo. Now wouldn't you?"

MacBride's eyes narrowed, and he took his pipe from his mouth. "Would I?" His hand knotted over the hot bowl of the pipe.

"Sure you would. But—" Kennedy shrugged—"you can't."

"Listen, Kennedy. What did you come here for, to razz me?"

"I don't know why I came here. It was cold out, and I know you keep it warm here. And—well, I just thought I'd drop in for a chat."

"You thought you'd get some inside dope. Go ahead, come out with it. Well, Kennedy, I've got nothing to say. News is as tight here as a drumhead. What a bunch of wisecracking eggs you've got down in your dump. Gink Cavallo'll laugh himself into a bellyache when he reads it. The lousy bum!"

"Something's got to break, Mac. When a bootlegging greaseball

starts to run a town, starts to run the Department, something's got to break."

"He's not running *me!*" barked MacBride.

"The hell he isn't! Don't tell me. I'm no greenhorn, Mac. Maybe not you personally. But your hands are tied. He's running somebody else, and somebody else is running somebody else, and the last somebody else is running you."

"You're talking through your hat, Kennedy."

"Oh, am I? No, I can't lay my hands on it all, but I can use my head. I know a few things. I know that Gink Cavallo is one of the wisest wops that ever packed a rod. He's a brother-in-law to Tony Diorio, and Diorio is president of the Hard Club, and the Hard Club swings two thousand sure votes and a thousand possible votes. And, you know, Mac, that these wops stick together. Most of the bohunks in the mills are wops, and they've sworn by the Hard Club, and—get this, Mac—it was the Hard Club that put Pozzo in for alderman and Mulroy for state's attorney. And it's the state's attorney's office that's running the Department—the rottenest administration in the history of Richmond City. It's just putting two and two together.

"You can't move, Mac. You've got your orders—hands off. What can you do? You're a captain. You've been with the Department for eighteen years. You've got a wife and a kid, and if you were kicked out of the Department you'd be on the rocks. I know you hate Cavallo like poison, and I know you're just aching to take a crack at him. It sure is a tough break for you, Mac."

MacBride had not batted an eyelash, had not shone by the slightest nicker of eyes or expression, how he took Kennedy's speech. He drew on his pipe meditatively, looking down along his beak of a nose. It was in the heart of MacBride that seas of anger were crashing and tumbling. Because Kennedy was right; he had hit the nail on the head with every charge. But MacBride was not the man to whimper or to go back on the Department. Loyalty had been ground into him long years ago—loyalty to his badge.

His voice was casual, "Finished, Kennedy? Then run along. I'm busy."

"I know, Mac. Kind of touched you on the quick, eh? It's all right, old-timer. Your jaw's sealed, too. You'd be one hell of a tool to tell Steve Kennedy how right he is. Well." Kennedy got up and lit a fresh butt. "It's all right by me, Cap. But when the big noise breaks, don't forget yours truly. It can't go on, Mac. Somebody'll slip. Some guy'll yap for more than his share. I've seen these rotten conditions before—'Frisco, Chicago, New Orleans. I'm hard-boiled as hell, Mac, and there's no one pulling any wool over my eyes. I'm just standing by and laughing up my sleeve." He took a pull on his cigarette. "There's one wild Mick in your outfit who's very liable to spill the beans, get himself shoved out to the sticks and maybe poked in the ribs with a bullet, besides."

"You mean—?"

"Sure. Jack Cardigan. S' long; Mac."

"Good-bye, Kennedy."

When the door closed, MacBride let go of himself. He heaved to his feet, spread-legged, his fists clenched, his eyes narrowed and burning intensely.

"God, Kennedy, if you only *knew* how right you are!" he muttered. "If I was only single—if I hadn't Anna and Judith. I'm tied all around, dammit! Home—and *here!*" He sank back into his chair, his head drooping, age creeping upon him visibly.

Chapter II

HE was sitting there, in precisely the same position, fifteen minutes later. And fifteen minutes later the door swung open swiftly, silently, and Jack Cardigan came in. A tall, lean, dark-eyed man, this Cardigan, rounding thirty years. Men said he was reckless, case-hardened, and a flash with the gun. He was.

"You look down at the mouth, Steve," he said, offhand.

"I am, Jack. Kennedy—"

"Oh, that guy!"

"Kennedy dropped in to pay me a call, Sharp, that bird. Pulls ideas out of the air, and every idea hits you like a sock on the jaw."

"Been razzing you?"

"Has he! Jack, he's got the whole thing worked out to a T. He'd just need my O.K. to spill the whole beans to the public, and likely Police Headquarters'd be mobbed. He's right. He's got the right slant on the whole dirty business. Jack, if I was ten years younger, I'd tell the Big Boss to go to hell and take my chances. That lousy wop is sitting on top of the world, and his gang's got Richmond City tied by the heels."

Cardigan sat down on the edge of a chair. There was something on his mind. You could see that much. He tapped with his fingers on the desk, his lips were a little set, the muscle lumps at either side of his jaw quivered, his dark eyes were close-lidded, active, flashing back and forth across MacBride's face.

"Brace up, Steve," he clipped. "I've got some news that might knock you for a row of pins."

"Eh?" MacBride straightened in his chair.

Cardigan's lips curled. "I came up alone. The sergeant said Kennedy'd gone up to see you. Didn't notice if he'd left. So I came up beforehand—to see."

"Kennedy left fifteen minutes ago. What's up?"

"Enough!" Cardigan took a vicious crack at the desk with his doubled fist. "The dirty pups got Hanley!"

"What!" MacBride's chair creaked violently. He leaned forward, laid his hand on Cardigan's knee, his breath sucked in and held.

"Two shots—through the lung and the heart! Somebody's going to pay for this, Steve! Joe Hanley was my partner—my sister's husband! There's nobody'll stop me—nobody! I'll—"

"Just a minute, Jack," cut in MacBride gently "How'd it happen?"

Cardigan got a grip on his temper, bit his lip. "I was out at Joe's place for dinner tonight, on Webster Road. Marion was a little upset. Kid had a bad cold, and she had a streak of worrying on, just like her. I mind five years ago, how she used to say she'd never marry a cop. She used to worry about me all the time. Not that a cop wasn't good enough—hell, no. But she used to say if she married a cop she'd be laying awake all night worrying. So, like a woman, she married Joe, and Joe's been a buddy of mine since we were kids. Well, you know that. Then she had two to worry over—Joe and me.

"And she was worrying tonight. Joe laughed. So did I. She got me alone in the hall and told me to watch out for Joe. She'd always been doing this. I kidded her. She said she meant it, and that she felt something was going to happen. I remember how she hung on to him when we breezed. God!"

"Steady, Jack!"

"I know. Well, Joe and I hoofed it to the park, to get a bus into the city. There was none in sight, so we began hiking down Webster Road till one 'd come. Pretty lonesome there. A car came weaving down behind us, and we heard a girl scream. We turned around and held up our hands for it to stop. The driver swerved to one side, intending to duck us. He slid into a ditch, roared his motor trying to get out. The girl was yelling hysterically. We saw her pitch out of the car. Then it heaved out of the ditch and was getting under way when Joe hopped it, pulling his rod. Two shots slammed out, and Joe keeled. I had my hands full with the girl. The car skidded and crashed into the bushes.

"I had my rod out then and ran up. Two guys in the back had jumped out and ducked into the bushes. I nailed the chauffeur. He wasn't heeled, but he was trying to get away, too. He started giving me a line and I socked him on the head so he'd stay put till I looked after Joe. Well, there wasn't much to look after. Joe was dead. The girl—she was only a flapper—was bawling and shaking in the knees. She'd been pretty well mauled. A machine came along and I stopped it."

"Wait, you say you got the chauffeur?"

"Sure. He says his name's Clark, and he's downstairs barking for a lawyer."

"Who's the girl?"

"Pearl Carr's her name. Just a wise little flapper who thought she was smart by taking a ride. She was waiting for a bus—she told me this—when this big touring car stopped and one of the guys offered her a lift. Sure, she got in, the little fool, and these guys started playing around."

"Know the guys?"

Cardigan growled. "Two of Cavallo's guns or I don't know anything. Her description of one tallies with Bert Geer, that walking fashion-plate. You remember two years ago they nabbed Geer on suspicion for that girl out in St. Louis they found strangled near Grand Gardens. But he got out of it. The other guy sounds like that rat "Monkey" Burns. I took the number of the touring car. I looked up the records downstairs and found the plates had been stolen from a sedan two weeks ago. If they're Geer and Burns, it means that Cavallo's in the pot, too, because they're the wop's right-hand guns. If we make them take the rap, they'll draw in Cavallo, and just as sure as you're born Diorio and Pozzo and our estimable State's Attorney Mulroy'll get in the tangle, and there'll be hell to pay all around. But I'm going through with this, Steve, and the state's attorney's office be damned! Joe was my buddy, closer to me than a brother—my sister's husband! God—can you picture Marion!"

MacBride was tight-lipped, a little pale, terribly grim. The ultimate had come. Would they tie the Department's hands now?

"Did you let Clark get a lawyer?" he asked.

"No—cripes, no!"

"Then get him up here. Where's the girl?"

"Downstairs, still bawling. I sent a cop out to get her a dress or something. I phoned her old man and he's driving in to get her."

"All right. Leave her there. But get Clark."

Cardigan went out and MacBride settled back, heaved a vast sigh, crammed fresh tobacco into his pipe. When, a few moments later, the door opened, he was puffing serenely, though deep in his heart there was a great numbness.

Clark came in, aided by a shove in the rear from Cardigan. The detective closed the door, grabbed Clark by the shoulder and slammed him not too gently into a chair.

"Say, go easy there, guy!" whined Clark, a charred clinker of a runt with a face of seeming innocence, like a mongrel dog.

"Close your jaw!" snapped Cardigan.

Clark spread his hands toward MacBride. "Tell this guy to leave me alone, Captain. He's been treatin' me hard. First off he beans me with his gat and since then he's been chuckin' me around like I was a rag. I got my rights. I'm a citizen. You can't go cloutin' citizens. I got my—"

"Soft pedal," said MacBride heavily. "So your name's Clark, eh? How'd you come to be driving that car?"

"I was drivin' it, that's all. I'm all right. I don't know nothin'. I was just drivin' it. You can't make a slop-rag outta me."

"Shut up," cut in MacBride.

"All right, I'll shut up. That's what I'm gonna do. You gotta let me get a lawyer. I got rights. Them's a citizen's rights."

"Listen to the bum!" chuckled Cardigan.

"There, see!" chirped Clark. "He's still insultin' me. He's just a big wise guy, he is. I got my rights. I'll see you get yours, fella. I was drivin' a car. All right, I was drivin' it. I know you guys. I ain't gotta talk."

"You're going to talk, Clark," said MacBride ominously. "And none of this cheap chatter, either. Talk that counts—see?"

"I ain't. No, I ain't. I want a lawyer. Gimme that phone."

He scrambled out of the chair, clawed for the telephone. Cardigan grabbed him by the nape of the neck, hurled him back so hard that Clark hit the chair aslant and, knocking it over, sprawled with it to the floor. He crouched, cringing, blubbering.

"You leave me alone, you! What the hell you think you're doin'? You leave me—"

"Get up—get up," gritted Cardigan. "That's only a smell compared with what's coming if you don't come clean. Get up, you dirty little rat!" He reached down, caught Clark, heaved him up and banged him down into another chair.

Clark's teeth chattered. His hands fidgeted, one with the other. His mouth worked, gasping for breath. His eyes almost popped from his head.

"Now," came MacBride's low voice, "who were the two guys that got away?"

"You can't make me talk now. You can't!" Clark gripped the sides of his chair, the stringy cords on his neck bulged. "I ain't talkin'—not me. I want a lawyer—that's what. Them's my rights, gettin' a lawyer. There!" He stuck out his chin defiantly.

MacBride turned in his chair and looked at Cardigan. Cardigan nodded, his fingers opening and closing.

"Take him into the sweat room, Jack," said MacBride. "Sweat him."

Clark stiffened in his chair, and sucked in his nether lip with a sharp intake of breath. He writhed.

"You can't do that, you can't!" he screamed. "I got my rights. You can't beat up a citizen."

"Citizen are you?" chuckled Cardigan. "You're a bum, Clark. You were driving a car with somebody else's plates. You tried to get away with the other two birds but you weren't fast enough. My buddy was killed, see? Now you'll talk. I'll sweat it out of you, Clark, so help me!"

"You won't! I ain't gonna talk. Gawd almighty, I want a lawyer! You can't stop me from gettin' one!"

"You're stopped, Clark," bit off Cardigan. "Get up and come on along with me."

Cardigan reached for him. Clark squirmed in his chair, lashed out with his feet. One foot caught Cardigan in the stomach and he doubled momentarily, grimacing but silent. MacBride was out of his seat in a flash, and Clark was jerked to his feet so fast that he lost his breath. He was wild-eyed, straining at the arms that held him, his lips quivering, groans and grunts issuing from his throat.

"You ain't gonna beat me—you ain't! You'll see! I won't talk! I got my rights. I—I—"

"I'll take him, Steve," said Cardigan.

MacBride stepped back and Clark struggled frantically in Cardigan's grasp as the latter worked him toward the door.

The telephone bell jangled.

"Wait," said MacBride.

Cardigan paused at the door.

MacBride picked up the phone, muttered something, listened. Then, "What's that?" His hands knotted around the instrument, his eyes narrowed, his mouth hardened. "Are you sure of that?" He groaned deep in his throat, rocked on his feet. Then, bitterly, "All right!"

He slammed the receiver into the hook and banged the instrument down upon the desk violently. He turned to face Cardigan.

"It's no use, Jack. A runner for that lousy firm of Cohen, Fraser and Cohen, is downstairs, which means this bum slides out of our hands."

Cardigan's face darkened. "How'd they know we had this bird so soon?"

"That's their business. They work on a big retainer from the head of the gang Clark belongs to."

There was a knock at the door, and a sergeant and a patrolman came in. The sergeant showed MacBride a writ, and the patrolman marched Clark out of the office. Then the sergeant left, and MacBride and Cardigan were alone.

"Wires being pulled again," muttered Cardigan. "This guy will never come to trial."

"Of course not," nodded MacBride grimly.

"What a fine state of affairs! We nab a guy, and have every chance to make him come across, and then he's taken out of our hands. What's the use of a Police Department, anyhow?"

"Clark is one of Cavallo's boys. No doubt about it. And we can't do a thing—just sit and curse the whole thing. It's tough to be on the Force eighteen years—and have to stand for it."

"I know, Steve, you can't move. Your wife and kid to think of. But there's one way to get back at these wops, and the only way. They killed Joe, and they've got to pay for it! I'm going to make 'em pay—pound for pound! By God, I am, and the Department and the State's Attorney and everybody else be damned!"

"Jack, you can't—alone. You're a dick and—"

"I'm no longer a dick. I'm single and free and my resignation goes in now! I'm going to fight Cavallo, Steve, at his own game!"

"What do you mean?"

"Just what I said. I'm resigning from the Department. I'm going on my own and wipe out Cavallo and every one of his dirty gunmen! Richmond City is going to see one of the biggest gang wars in its history! When they killed Joe Hanley, they killed the wrong man, for my part! I'm going to fall on 'em like a ton of brick!"

"Jack, you can't do it!"

"Watch me!" chuckled Cardigan, his eyes glittering.

Chapter III

MEN said Jack Cardigan was reckless and case-hardened—men meaning cops and reporters and Richmond City's generous sprinkling of gunmen. Something might be added; he was ruthless. As a detective, he'd been hated and feared by more crooks than perhaps any other man in the Department—inspectors, captain, lieutenants and all the rest included. Because he was hard—tough—rough on rats; rats being one of his favorite nicknames applied to a species of human being that shoots in the dark and aims for the back.

For three years Joe Hanley had been his partner, in the Department. In life, they'd been partners for years—and the bond of friendship had been welded firmly and topped off with the marriage of Cardigan's sister Marion to Joe. It was a far, long cry from that happy, flowered day to the day when Marion and Cardigan rode home from the cemetery, after the burial of Joe. Cardigan held his sister in his arms on the slow journey. There was nothing he could say to comfort her. Pity, condolence, make empty, meaningless words on such a tragic day. So he held her in his arms and let her sob.

His own face was a mask, grim and carven, the eyes dark and close-lidded. Home, he put her into the hands of their mother. No one spoke. Glances, gestures, conveyed far more. For a long while he sat alone, motionless and thoughtful. The funeral was over, but the dread pall of it still lingered. Even the house seemed to take on a personality of mourning—quiet and hollow and reverent.

A week later Cardigan sat in a speakeasy on the outer circle of Richmond City's theatrical district. He was sipping a dry Martini when Kennedy of the *Free Press* drifted in and joined him.

"What's the idea of shaking your job, Cardigan?"

"What's that to you?"

"Or were you *told* to resign?"

"Maybe."

Kennedy chuckled. "Sounds more like it. What you get for bringing in Clark. Lord, that was a joke! His lawyer was a sharp egg. Clark played the dope all through. Bet his lawyer spent nights drilling him how to act. Clark was just a hired chauffeur. How did he know the plates were stolen? He was hired a week before the mess out on Webster Road to drive a car. They gave him a car to drive. The whole thing was a joke, and the presenting attorney gave the defense every possible opening. What are you doing now?"

"Nothing. Taking life easy."

"Don't make me laugh!"

"Well, have it your way."

"Listen, Cardigan," said Kennedy. "You know a lot. The *Free Press* would sell its shirt to get some straight dope from you. That's no boloney. I mean it. I've got the whole thing figured out, but what we need is a story where we can omit the 'alleged' crap. Man, you can clean up!"

"Yeah?" Cardigan laughed softly. "Be yourself, Kennedy. Run along. You're wasting time on me."

"I don't know about that."

"Then learn."

Kennedy had a highball and went on his way. Alone, Cardigan took another drink, and looked at his watch. It was half-past eight at night. He looked across at the telephone on the wall. He drained his glass and lit a cigarette.

The telephone rang. He got up and beat the owner to it. "This is for me," he said, and took off the receiver. "You, Pete?... O.K. Be right over."

He hung up, paid for his drinks and shrugged into his dark overcoat. Outside, it was damp and cold, and automobiles hissed by over slushy pavements.

Cardigan did not walk toward the bright glow that marked the beginning of the theatrical district. He bored deeper into the heart of Jockey Street. Where it was dirtiest and darkest, he swung in toward a short flight of broken stone steps, reached a large, ancient door, groped for a bell-button and pressed it. It was opened a moment later by a huge, beetle-browed negro.

"Pete Fink," said Cardigan. "He expects me."

"Who yuh are?" asked the negro.

"None of your damned business."

"I'll get Fink," said the negro and slammed the door in Cardigan's face.

"Takes no chances," muttered Cardigan. "Well, that's good."

Fink opened the door this time, while the negro hovered behind him, his face like shining ebony under the single gas-jet.

"Take a good look, big boy," Cardigan said, as he passed in.

And the negro said, "Got yuh, boss."

Fink led the way up a flight of crooked stairs that creaked under their footfalls. They reached the upper landing. Cardigan placed six doors in a row. One of these Fink opened, and they entered a large, square room, furnished cheaply with odd bits of furniture, no two pieces the same in make or design.

Cardigan stood with his hands in his coat pockets, idly running his eyes about the room.

Fink was leaning against the door he had closed. He was a big, rangy man, with one of his shoulders higher than the other. His nose was a twisted knot; a tawny mustache sagged over his mouth. He had a jaw like a snowplow, and eyes like ice—cold and steady and enigmatic. His hands were big and red and bony. He wore brown corduroy trousers, a blue flannel shirt, a wide belt with an enormous brass buckle. He looked like a tough egg. He wasn't a soft one.

Cardigan sighed and poured himself a drink. He downed it neat, rasped his throat, and looked at the empty glass.

"Good stuff, Pete."

"Cavallo sells the same."

They faced each other. Their eyes met and held and bored one into the other. At last Fink grinned and rocked away from the door, sat down at the table and lit a cigarette. Cardigan sat down opposite him, opened his overcoat and helped himself to one of Fink's cigarettes.

"Well, Pete?…"

Fink leaned forward, elbows resting on the table, his butt jutting from one corner of his mouth and an eye squinted against the smoke that curled upward.

"Six," he said. "I got six."

"Who are they?"

"Chip Slade, Gats Gilman, Luke Kern, Bennie Levy, Chuck Ward and Bat Johnson. All good guns."

"Yeah, I know. How do they feel about it?"

"Cripes, they're ripe!"

"They want to know who's behind you?"

"I said a big guy—somebody big, who's in the know."

Cardigan chuckled. "Remember, Pete, it stays that way. I'm—it sounds like a joke—the mystery man in this. The master mind!" He chuckled again, amusedly, then grew serious. "To come out in the open would be to shoot the whole works. I'm too well known as a gumshoe. But I'll manage this, Pete, and supply the first funds. I've got a measley two thousand saved up, but it's a starter. And I'm out to flop on the bums that got Hanley, my buddy. If everybody holds up his end, you'll all make money and Cavallo and his crowd will get washed out."

"You say the word, Jack. I'm takin' orders from you. The rest take orders from me and no questions asked."

"Good. I'll give you five hundred bucks to buy a second-hand car. Get a big touring. To hell with the looks of it; buy it for the motor— for speed. Buy half-a-dozen high-powered rifles and plenty of am- munition. Pick up some grenades if you can. How about a storehouse?"

"Got one picked—an old farmhouse out on Farmingville Turnpike."

"Sounds good. Rent it for a month."

"It's way out in the sticks," added Fink. "Off the main pike, way in on a lane, and no other house inside of a quarter mile. I can get it for fifty bucks a month."

"Get it. We've got to watch out for tapped wires, though. Here, I'm staying at the Adler House. You know that number. If things get hot and you've got to talk a lot, just call me up and say, 'I've got something to tell you.' I'll hang up and run down to the drug-store on the corner. There's a booth there and I'll get you the number. We'll choose booths all over the city where we can make calls, and we'll get the numbers."

"O.K."

"How about the dinge downstairs?"

"He owns the dump. Sees a lot and says nothin'."

Cardigan ground out his cigarette. "Then it's all set. Get me straight, Fink. Leave the cops alone. Tell your boys that. We're after Cavallo and his rats—not the cops. If the cops show up, run. I've got a grudge against that wop and the crowd he runs with. I'm playing my grudge to a showdown. If I make some jack out of it, all right. But I'm after rats first—not jack. You and your guns can clean up sweet in this racket, if you use your head and move how I tell you."

"I got you, Jack," nodded Fink.

"All right. Let me know when you're all set and I'll map out our first move. Get the rifles, ammunition, grenades. Get a fast car and see that the tires are good." He drew a wad of bills from his pocket. "There's a thousand as a starter."

Fink shoved the money into his pocket and poured another brace of drinks.

"You got guts, Jack," he said, "to chuck the Department—for this."

"Guts, my eye!" clipped Cardigan. "I've got a grudge, Pete, a whale of a grudge—against the dirty, rotten bums that killed the best friend I ever had." He raised his glass. "Down the hatch."

On that they drank.

Chapter IV

TWO days later Cardigan was sitting in his room at the Adler House, when the telephone rang. It was the desk, and he said, "Send him up." Then he settled back again in his over-stuffed easy-chair. It was ten in the morning and he was still in pajamas and bathrobe. On a settee beside him was a detailed map of Richmond City and its suburbs. Here and there he had marked Xs, or made penciled notations.

There was a knock on the door and he called, "Come in, Steve."

MacBride came in, closed the door and stood there stroking his chin and regarding Cardigan seriously.

"Sit down," said Cardigan. "Take the load off your feet, Steve. You'll find cigars in the box on the table. How's tricks?"

MacBride took a cigar and eased himself down on a divan. "My day off and I thought I'd drop in and see you."

"Is that all you came for, Steve?"

MacBride lit up and took a couple of puffs before replying. "Not exactly, Jack."

"Spill it."

"Oh, it's not much. Only I was worrying. You still thinking of butting in on Cavallo's racket?"

"What a question! Why'd you suppose I left the Department?"

"M-m-m," droned MacBride. "I wish you hadn't, Jack. You were the best man I had, and, Jack, old boy, you can't buck that crowd. It's madness. You'll get in trouble, and if you make a bad step, you'll get the Department on your neck. You haven't got politics behind you. You'd be out of luck. That's straight. How do you think I'd feel if it came to the point where you faced me as prisoner?"

"I've been thinking about that, Steve," admitted Cardigan. "It's the one thing I'd hate."

"No more than I would." MacBride licked a loose wrapper back into place on his cigar. "Kennedy's been in to see me again. That guy's so nosey and so clever it hurts. Look out for him. *He's* got an idea you're up to something."

"I know. That bird's so sharp he's going to cut himself some day."

"Made any moves yet—I mean, you?"

"Some—getting things ready."

"What's up your sleeve anyway?"

"Steve—" Cardigan paused to flex his lips. "Steve, we've been mighty good friends. We are yet. But I can't tell you. I'm playing a game that can't have any air-holes. You understand?"

MacBride nodded. "I guess so. But I'm worrying, Jack. I've got a hunch you're going to get in wrong and somebody's going to nail you."

"Don't worry. Forget it. If I pull a bone I'll take the consequence. But I'm not counting on pulling a bone. This town is going to shake.

Somebody's going to get hurt, and, Steve, before long some pretty high departmental offices are liable to be vacated so damned fast—"

"I'd go easy, Jack."

"I am—feeling my way."

MacBride shrugged and got up. They shook, and the captain went out, a little mournfully and reluctantly.

Ten minutes later the phone rang and Fink asked, "How soon can you come out?"

"Five minutes."

"I'll pick you up at Main and Anderson in the car."

Cardigan hung up and snapped into his clothes. Five minutes later he shot down in the elevator, strode through the lobby and out onto Main Street. Two blocks south was Anderson. He saw the big touring car idling along—the one that Fink had bought for five-fifty; five years old, but it could do seventy-five an hour. The curtains were on, all of them.

The door opened and he hopped in, settled down beside Fink. They pounded down Main Street, swung into a side street to avoid a traffic stop, and cut north until they struck Farmingville Turnpike.

Then Cardigan said, "Well?"

"I got the rifles and ammunition and some grenades," said Fink. "I want to show you the farmhouse. The boys are ripe to go, soon as you say the word."

It took them half an hour to reach the ramshackle farmhouse. It was quite some distance from the hub of the city. It stood well off the main highway, hidden behind an arm of woods and reached by a narrow lane where the snow still lay. Fink pulled up into the yard and they got out. He had keys and opened the kitchen door. They entered and Cardigan looked it over. Two big rooms and a kitchen downstairs. Three bedrooms upstairs. Dust, the dust of long neglect, covered the floor. The windows were small and set with many little squares of glass. The place was old, years old. The walls were lined with brick, a relic of days when houses were built to last for more than one generation.

"Just the thing," nodded Cardigan. "Maybe we'll use it tonight."

"Huh?"

"Tonight. Cavallo keeps a lot of his booze on North Street. Know the old milk stables?"

"Yeah."

"That's the place. There are three in a row, all joined together. The one in the middle is our meat. It has sliding doors, and there's always a reserve truck inside."

"How do you know all this, Jack?"

"What do you suppose the Department does, sleep all the time?"

"Oh... I gotcha. Yeah, sure."

"Get your map out."

Fink dived into his pocket, came out with a folder that opened to large dimensions. Cardigan also had his out.

"I've figured out the route you're to take," he said. "Mark these down now, so there'll be no slip up. The truck is a type governed to do thirty-five per and no more. Four speeds ahead. All right." And he proceeded to give Fink precise directions to follow, street by street to Black Hill Road which leads into Farmingville Turnpike. "Got the route all marked?" he asked, as he finished.

"Yeah, all marked."

"Who'll drive the truck?"

"Bat Johnson and—"

"No—Bat's enough. The rest of you drift along ahead in the touring car and lead the way. One man on a truck'll cause no suspicion. More might. And get this. Maple Road runs parallel with North Street—behind the stables. You park on Maple Road and watch across the lots till you see three blinks from a flashlight. That will mean to come on and take things over. When Bat takes the truck out you boys beat it back across the lots, into the car and fall in ahead of the truck on Avenue C."

"Who's goin' to blink the lights?"

"I am."

"Huh?" Fink seemed incredulous.

"That's what I said. I'm going ahead to see if the road's clear. I'll take care of the watchman. If there's more there—the gang, I mean—we'll give up for the night. And mind this, if you don't see any flashes by ten o'clock, breeze. Be on Maple Road at exactly nine-fifty, no sooner or later. If everything turns out all right, if you get the booze out to the farmhouse and away safe, call me up and just say, 'Jake'; that's all. And about the truck. Drive it back and abandon it on Black Hill Road."

"But, hell, Jack, why can't me and the boys bust in the stables and crash the place proper?"

"You would say that, Pete. That's just the way to ball up the whole works. We're not out to butcher our way if we can help it. That's the trouble with you guys. You don't use your head. That's the main reason why Cavallo and his rats are going to blow up. They're too damned free with their gats."

"Um—I guess you're right there, Jack."

"All right, then. Come on, let's breeze. Drive me to the bus line and drop me off."

An hour later Cardigan was eating lunch at his favorite haunt in Jockey Street, with a bottle of Sauterne on the side. It was one of fifteen restaurants circulated throughout the city and owned by a syndicate of brokers that paid a fat sum monthly to the authorities for the privilege. Four were in the financial district, six in the theatrical district, the rest scattered. More would open for business in time. You didn't need a card. The places were wide, wide open. Where the syndicate got the liquor, was nobody's business.

The Jockey Street place was managed by an ex-saloon keeper named Maloney. Cardigan had been a frequent visitor there since his resignation from the Force, and they got on well. This day he called Maloney over and asked him to sit down.

He asked, "Between you and me, what does your outfit pay for good Scotch?"

"That's our business, buddy, if you know what I mean."

"I know what you mean. Come on, I'm *talking* business."

"You in the game?"

"I know somebody who is."

Maloney thought hard. "Sixty-five bucks a case."

Cardigan nodded. "You can get it for fifty-five. Work the deal with your boss and you'll get a rake-off of five bucks on the case."

"Your friend must be hard up."

"He's just starting in business."

"Oh. We'll have to sample it first."

"Sure. But are you on?"

"It sounds good. How—how many cases?"

"Maybe two hundred."

"Cripes!"

"Think it over. Speak to your boss. I'll see you again in a day or so."

He left ten minutes later, pretty certain that he had paved the way nicely. To kill the afternoon, he dropped in at a vaudeville theatre, and ate dinner at the hotel. Later he sat in his room smoking a cigar and going over his plan step by step, searching for a loophole. He couldn't see any. Tonight would start the ball rolling. His vengeance would be under way. They'd murdered Joe Hanley. Now they'd pay—pound for pound. It was law of his own making, a hard, raw law—fighting rats on their own ground with their own tactics. Yet he had one advantage; a reasoning, calculating mind, thanks to his service in the Department; strategy first, guns—if it should come to that means—later.

He had a hard crew under him. Pete Fink, a product of the bootleg age—one time in the prize ring, once a sailor. Cardigan knew that he was a tough customer, and he also knew that he could rely on him. The other guns; he relied on Fink to take care of them. He'd arrested Bat Johnson only a year ago for petty larceny. Chip Slade had once felt the rap of his blackjack.

"Hell," he mused, "if they only knew who was behind Fink!"

Chapter V

EIGHT-THIRTY came around. Cardigan put on his overcoat and shoved an automatic into his pocket. He took his time. He wandered leisurely out of the hotel, walked a couple of blocks down Main Street and boarded a bus bound for the suburbs. Half an hour later he got off, lit a cigarette and strolled north. He was a little ahead of time, so he went on at ease.

He reached Maple Road, and continued south. Houses were scattered, and fields intervened. Then, squatting dimly in the murk beyond a field of tall grass, the old milk stables. Cardigan paused behind an ancient oak tree and looked at the illuminated dial of his watch. It was nine-thirty-five. His hand slid into his pocket and gripped the butt of his automatic.

He slipped away from the tree, hunched over and weaved his way through tall weeds. His feet slushed through snow. At intervals he paused briefly, to listen. Then he went on, bit by bit, until he reached the old picket fence behind the stables. In this he found a gap and muscled through, and squatted still for a long moment. From his coat he drew a dark handkerchief and fastened it about his face, just below his eyes. His hat brim he pulled lower.

There was a faint yellow glow shining from a window, and toward this Cardigan crept. A shade had been drawn down to within an inch or two of the bottom of the window. Smoke was drifting from a tin stove chimney. In a moment Cardigan was crouched by the window.

He saw two men sitting in chairs by a little stove. On the stove a kettle was spouting steam. A lantern stood on an empty box nearby. One of the men was asleep. The other was half-heartedly reading a newspaper; Cardigan recognized him, a huge brute of a man called "Dutch" Weber, with a record. The other he placed as Jakie Hart, sometimes called the Creole Kid, a one-time New Orleans wharf rat. A dirty pair, he mused.

Minutes were flying, and so much depended on chance. Cardigan bent down and felt around on the snow. He found a two-foot length of board, and hefted it in his left hand. His right hand still gripped the automatic. Again looking in, he raised the board, set his jaw and crashed the window. The shade snapped up. The man with the paper spun in his chair, clawed at his gun.

But Cardigan had him covered, his head and shoulders thrust through the window.

"Drop that gat, Dutch!" he barked. "You too, Jakie—drop it! Fast, you guys, or you'll get lead in your pants!"

The Creole Kid blinked bleary eyes. Dutch Weber cursed under his breath, his huge face flushing, murder in his gimlet eyes, his big hands writhing. But he dropped his gun, and the Creole Kid imitated him a moment later.

"Stand up—both of you," went on Cardigan. "Face the wall! Move out of turn and God help you!"

"You lousy bum!" snarled Weber.

"Can that crap, buddy! About face!" bit off Cardigan.

Sullenly they faced the wall, hands raised.

A moment later Cardigan was in the room. He yanked down the shade, picked up the men's discarded guns, thrust them into his pockets. And from his pockets he drew two pairs of manacles.

"Back up six paces, Dutch! Stay where you are, Jakie! Never mind looking, Dutch—just back up. Now put your hands behind your back. Don't get funny, either." In a flash he had the manacles on Weber. "Get over against the wall again. Move!" He jabbed the muzzle of his gun in Weber's back. "Now you, Jakie—back up!"

In a moment he had the other pair of bracelets on the Creole Kid, and forced him back against the wall. Then he took a small bottle of chloroform from his pocket and saturated a handkerchief.

"Back up again, Jakie! As you are, Dutch!"

He clamped his arm around the Creole Kid's neck, forced the handkerchief against his nostrils and into his mouth, held it there, while he still warned Weber to stay where he was. Presently the Creole Kid went limp, relaxed, and Cardigan let him fall to the floor, unconscious.

Then he soaked another handkerchief, approached Weber and planted his gun in the big man's ribs.

"Not a stir, big boy!"

His left hand shot out, smacked the saturated handkerchief against Weber's mouth. The big man struggled, but Cardigan reminded him of the gun.

"Damn your soul!" snarled Weber in muffled tones.

"Shut your trap!"

In a short time Weber joined the Creole Kid on the floor, muttering vaguely, his hands twitching slower and slower. Cardigan pocketed his gun, produced a coil of thin, strong wire and bound their ankles. Then he ripped away strips of their shirts and bound the handkerchiefs securely on their mouths. From Weber's pockets he took a ring of keys.

With his flashlight he started a quick, systematic search of the stables. The large, covered truck was in the main stable. Its tank registered seven gallons of gasoline. Under tarpaulins he saw case upon case of liquor—between two and three hundred. He also saw ten barrels of wine. These he tipped over and sprung the spigots, and the wine gurgled and flowed on the dirt floor.

Chuckling, he hurried into the back room, blew out the lantern and pulled up the shade on the window. He raised his flashlight and blinked it three times. Then he opened the back door, sped into the main stable and unlocked the big sliding doors, but did not open them.

He turned, jumped to a ladder and climbed up to a small loft, drew the ladder up after him. Then he lay flat on his stomach in the pitch gloom, waited and listened. After a few moments he heard a door creak, and then footsteps—saw the reflection of a flashlight in the back room.

"Huh," muttered a voice, "the Chief sure paved the way. Lookit the way them two babies is tied up!"

"Shut up, Bat. Come on, gang." That was Fink.

The beam of light jumped into the stable. Figures loomed in. The flash settled on the draining barrels. Someone chuckled.

"What he can't take he busts," said a voice. "This Chief knows his termaters, what I mean!"

The beam of light swept around the stable and found the stacked cases of liquor.

"*Ba-by!*" exclaimed someone, softly.

"Cut the gab!" hissed Fink. "Step to it! There's the truck! Come on, guys!"

Cardigan watched them spread out. They hauled off the tarpaulins. Two men jumped into the truck. The others leaped to the cases of liquor. They worked swiftly and for the most part silently, passing the cases to the pair in the truck, who stacked them rapidly.

One muttered. "Y' know, first off I thought this Chief was just a guy wit' brains an' no guts. I mean, like he wanted us to do his dirty work—"

"Pipe down, Gats!" snapped Fink. "Y' see he's got guts, don't you now?"

"Sure. I'm all for him."

"You better be," muttered Fink. "Any one o' you guys that thinks he ain't's got a lot to learn."

"Where's he now?"

"None o' your business!" said Fink. "Prob'ly ridin' home in a bus or somethin'. Nemmine the talk. Step on it."

Cardigan smiled in the darkness. Yes, he could trust Fink; no doubt of it, now. Not even Fink knew he was up there in the loft, a silent watcher.

The minutes dragged by. Case after case went into the truck. The pile on the floor grew smaller and smaller. The men worked rapidly, and now silently. Cardigan looked at his watch. Half-past ten. He was stiff from holding his tense position.

"Cripes, what a load!" a voice said hoarsely.

"How many more?"

"Ten."

"That," said Fink, "'ll make two-hundred-and-forty-two."

"*Ba-by!*"

Cardigan saw the last case go in. Then Fink and two others spread tarpaulins over the rear and lashed them to the sides.

"All right, Bat," he said.

Bat Johnson climbed up into the seat, juggled the transmission lever. Another man grabbed the crank, heaved on it. The motor spat, barked, and then pounded regularly. Two men jumped to the doors, slid them back. They looked out, came back in and one said, "Clear! Let her go!"

Bat shoved into gear and the big truck rumbled out. The doors were pulled shut. The men bunched together and at a word from Fink slipped out through the back door.

Three minutes later Cardigan dropped from the loft. He strode into the back room, snapped on his flash, played its beam on the Creole Kid and Dutch Weber, still unconscious. Then he dropped their keys and guns beside them, snapped off his flash and made for the door.

With a brittle little chuckle he went out, crossed the fields and struck Maple Road. He sought the bus line by a different route than the one by which he had reached the stables. At a quarter to twelve he entered his room, took off his coat and dropped into an easy-chair. He lit a cigar and relaxed, a little weary after the strenuous night.

But deep within him there was a great calm. He thought of Joe, and of his widowed sister. He thought, too, of other cops who had met death in strange back-alleys at the hands of rats who always shot from the rear. What protection was a shield nowadays? Protection! He grimaced. More a target! But mainly it was Joe he thought of— mild-mannered, easygoing Joe. Joe with two bullets in him, out on Webster Road....

At half-past one the telephone rang. He picked it up.

" 'Jake'," said Fink.

" 'Jake'," said Cardigan, and hung up.

Chapter VI

IT did not get into the papers. Things like this don't. But the underworld rumbled ominously, and the echoes seeped into the Department, but got no further. The law-abiding element of Richmond City went about its daily tasks and pleasures as usual, all ignorant of the fact that in the world of shadows, wolves were growling and baring hungry fangs.

The very next afternoon MacBride dropped in to see Cardigan.

"Well, Jack," he said.

And Cardigan said, "Well?"

"M-m-m, you did it."

"You mean Cavallo?"

MacBride nodded.

Cardigan chuckled.

"We got a whiff of it this morning," went on MacBride. "Cavallo must have gone to his brother-in-law Diorio and I guess Diorio went to his friend Alderman Pozzo and then Pozzo had a chat with State's Attorney Mulroy. Jack, for God's sake, watch your step!"

"I am. Why, do they suspect?"

"No, but—" MacBride clenched his fists and gritted his teeth. "I shouldn't be telling you this Jack. But—we're—old friends, and I'd like to see that dago wiped out. And I guess—if I was younger and single—and a buddy of mine—like Joe was to you—was bumped off, I'd do the same. Maybe I wouldn't. Maybe I wouldn't have the guts. But, Jack, I've got to tell you, for old times' sake. McGinley and Kline, of the State's Attorney's office, have been detailed to get the guys who flopped on Cavallo's parade!"

"Oh, yes?"

"Yes. For my sake, Jack, shake this racket. You can't beat it. You see what you've got against you?"

Cardigan nodded. "I know, Steve. But I've started, and I'm not going to let the thing just hang in the air. The more I think of Cavallo and Bert Geer and Monkey Burns and all that crowd, the more I want to blow up their racket. Imagine Pozzo for Alderman—a guy that can hardly speak English and calls himself a one hundred per-cent American! Cavallo's bulwark! Mulroy having to take these wops' part because they put him in office, and getting a rake-off from their proceeds."

"I know, Jack, I know. But—"

"No, sir, Steve. I'm playing this to a showdown, and somebody's going to get hurt in the wind-up."

"It might be you, Jack."

"Here's hoping it won't."

"No one gets anywhere today trying to be a martyr."

Cardigan laughed shortly. "Martyr! You think *I'm* taking the godly role of a martyr? Hell, no! I'm just an ordinary guy who's sore as a boil. I'm a guy whose buddy got a dirty break, and I'm starting to go after these lads the only way they can be reached."

MacBride shrugged and remained silent. Then he got up, shook Cardigan's hand and went out.

A little later the phone rang and Fink said, "I got somethin' to tell you."

"All right," replied Cardigan briskly.

A few minutes later he walked into a drug-store on the corner, stepped into the booth and closed the door. A minute, and the bell rang.

"O.K., Pete," he said.

Fink explained, "Meet me in the dump on Jockey Street in half an hour. I've got a sample, and it's sure powerful stuff. I'll be waitin' outside the door there. Everything is jake, and the boys are feelin' good but wonderin' about their divvy."

"Be over," said Cardigan.

When, later, he strolled down Jockey Street, he saw Fink cross the street, pause on the steps of their rendezvous, look his way, and then pass inside. Cardigan swung up the steps and the door opened. He went in and Fink led the way up to the latter's room. The big man drew a pint flask from his pocket.

"They're all in pints," he explained. "Try it."

Cardigan took a pull on the bottle and let the liquor burn in. "Good," he nodded. "The best I've tasted."

Fink grinned. "If that stuff ain't come across the pond I don't know Scotch. It's the first time I ain't drunk dish water in a long time. D' you figger Cavallo's sore?"

"Sore!" echoed Cardigan, and laughed on it.

"Yeah," droned Fink, "I guess he's lookin' to kill. Um. Now the stuff's out there in the farmhouse, what?"

"I'll know by tonight. Keep your shirt on."

"I ain't worryin'. The gang. They're achin' to see some jack and have a good time."

"You tell 'em to watch their step, Pete. It's hard lines for any guy pulls a bone. We're not through yet. It would be just like Chip Slade, for instance, to doll up in new duds, pick up a broad, get tight to the eyes and blabber. We've got to watch out for that, Pete."

"Yeah, I know, Jack. I been keepin' my eye on Chip."

"I'll see you here tonight, Pete."

Cardigan went out with the pint flask on his hip and dropped in to see Maloney in the speakeasy. He talked business to him, and let him take a drink from the bottle.

"Boy!" whistled Maloney. "That's *Scotch*, what I mean!"

"What's the news?"

"The boss says all right, if he likes the stuff. Fifty-five a case."

"I can get two-hundred-and-forty cases. He can have the lot or none, and he's got to act fast. This is no young stuff—"

"Hell, I know! Ain't I just tasted it? And me—I get my share, when?"

"When your boss pays, you get twelve-hundred bucks, and then forget about everything. There are no names necessary."

"Of course not," nodded Maloney. "How do you get the money?"

"Your boss'll send it to John D. Brown, at a post office box. You'll get the box number later. Send it in a plain package, with no return address. Thirteen thousand and two hundred dollars in one hundred dollar bills."

"Insure it?"

"Lord, no! Just first class—that's the safest way to send stuff through the mails. It beats registered mail four ways from the jack. I never lost a first class letter, but I've lost 'em registered and I've lost insured packages. A man will pick up the letter at the post office." He thought for a moment. "Get the dope from your boss, and let's know where the booze goes."

"I ought to get my share first," demurred Maloney.

"I know. You think I'll skip. You'll get yours through the mail, too. That's the proposition. It's up to you."

"I'll take the chance." Maloney got up. "Come in at six."

Cardigan nodded and left. He took a box at a suburban post office under the name of John D. Brown. When he met Maloney at six that night the ex-saloon keeper was flushed with elation. Everything was settled, and the liquor was to be delivered as soon as possible.

"That means tonight," put in Cardigan.

"The boss stores it at the Tumbledown Inn. Say the word and

there'll be somebody there tonight to meet the truck."

"It'll be delivered sometime after midnight."

With that Cardigan went out and met Fink in the latter's hideout. He explained what had transpired, and Fink rubbed his hands in joyful anticipation.

"I know where I can get a truck, Jack. Leave it to me."

"I am," said Cardigan.

He explained in detail how the liquor should be transported, how Bat Johnson should drive the truck alone and the others ride in the touring car ahead. The Tumbledown Inn was on Farmingville Turnpike, four miles beyond the farmhouse where the liquor was stored at present.

"It's a cinch," said Fink.

"When it's all over, ring me up and say the O.K. word."

They parted, and Cardigan headed for the Adler House. He had proved a successful general on his first try. He believed he could repeat a second time, and then some more. He turned in at eight and set his alarm to wake him at one. He figured that he should get a report from Fink at about two.

When he got up at one a.m., he dressed, in the event of an emergency. He drank some hot black coffee from a thermos and ate some sandwiches which he had brought up before. Then he lounged on a divan with a cigar and watched the clock. The hands moved around the hour and passed two. They passed two-thirty and wheeled on toward three. At three, Cardigan sat up.

He looked grave, a bit tight-lipped. He stared at the telephone. It was black and silent. The hotel was silent as a tomb. Up from the street floated the sound of a lone trolley car rattling across a switch. He sat down, clasping his hands around one knee, tapping an impatient foot. Half-past three.

"Something's gone wrong," he muttered. He cracked fist into palm, cursed under his breath, bitterly.

Dawn came, and then the sun. And still no word from Pete Fink.

Cardigan put on his overcoat and went out. He bought a paper, thinking he might find some clue there, but he reasoned that if anything had happened in the early hours, the morning papers wouldn't have it yet. The next edition might. He ate breakfast in a dairy restaurant. Then, reasoning that he ought to be at his room in case Fink might call, he hurried back.

At nine Fink called. He said two words, "My room."

"Right," said Cardigan.

Chapter VII

TWENTY minutes later he was striding down Jockey Street. The negro let him in and he climbed the rickety staircase. He knocked at Fink's door. There was a slow movement.

Then, "You, Jack?"

"Yes, Pete."

The door opened. Cardigan went in.

Fink was dropping back into a chair.

"Lock it," he muttered.

His face was haggard. His left arm was in a sling, and blotches of dry blood showed on the bandage.

"I thought so," said Cardigan.

"Yeah," nodded Fink, and forced a wan grin. "They got Bat."

Cardigan sat down. "Go on."

"They got Bat. It was all a accident. We delivered the booze and was on the way back. We took Prairie Boulevard. Bat wanted to bring back the truck. The tourin' car got a flat and we stopped to make a change. Bat went ahead slow all by his merry lonesome. We got the spare on, all right, and whooped it up to catch him. You know where Prairie Boulevard goes through them deep woods. It's pretty lonely there.

"Well, our headlights pick up Bat and he's stalled. But we see another car stopped in front of him, facing him. It looks phony, and we take it easy. We see some guys standin' around on the road, but they duck for the car. We stop our car and wait. We think maybe they're dicks, see. Then their car starts and roars towards us. It looks like they're goin' to crash us, but they cut around and slam by, scrapin' our mudguard. A lot of guns bust loose and I'm socked in the arm. Chip gets his cheek opened. Nobody else is hurt. Gats turns around and empties his rod at the back of it. I don't know who he hit, but the car kept goin'.

"I get out, holdin' my arm and Bennie tears off some of his shirt and sops up the blood. Chip is holdin' his cheek and cursin' a blue streak. Gats runs up to the truck and we go after him. Bat is layin' on the road, pretty still. Him and Gats was buddies, you know. You should hear Gats curse!

"Bat is dyin'. They'd busted his knob with a blackjack. He says he was ridin' along when this car stopped him. See, just by accident. Monkey Burns and Bert Geer and two others. They smell there was booze in the truck, and ask him what's he been doin'. He tells them where they can go. They wanter know who he's been runnin' booze for. He ain't talkin'. They sock him, but he don't chirp. That's Bat all over. More you sock him the worse stubborn he gets. Gawd, they batted hell outta him! Ugh! Then they see us. Bat croaks after he spiels us his story. Poor Bat. He was a good shuffer."

Cardigan stared at the floor for a long minute, his hands clenched.

Fink was saying, "I took the plates off the truck and disfiggered the engine number and the serial number with a couple o' shots. Then we drove to the farmhouse. The boys are there now. I got here alone, quick as I could. I could ha' sent one o' the boys to call you up, but I didn't want any o' 'em to know where you was."

"You're aces up in a pinch, Pete," said Cardigan, and he meant it.

"I did the best I could."

"I'll say you did. Did Monkey and his gang see you boys?"

"No. And Bat didn't tell 'em. But they know, like everybody else, that Bat was buddies with Gats, and they'll be huntin' Gats. And Gats has gone wild. He wants to go out gunnin' for them guys. He swears he'll do it. And Gats is the best damn gunman I know about."

"You've got to keep him under cover."

"Yeah. I got to get back to the farmhouse. Bandage this arm tight so I can put it in a sleeve. I can't go walkin' around too much with a sling. It'll hurt without it, but what the hell."

"Good man, Pete. Get out there, see how things are. I'll hang around the corner drug-store between two and three. Call me there from a booth and give me a line."

When he had bandaged Fink's arm, he patted the big man on the back and left him. Below, in the street, he ran into Kennedy, of the *Free Press,* leaning indolently against a lamp-post. He brought up short, his breath almost taken away.

"Hello, Cardigan," said the reporter in his tired way. "What's the attraction?"

"You trying to crack wise, Kennedy?"

"Who, me? No-o, not me, Cardigan. See this yet?" He handed Cardigan the latest edition of the *Free Press.*

Rival Bootleg Gangs Clash

That was the headline. Something about an abandoned truck, empty, with license plates gone and engine number disfigured. Blood on the road. Empty cartridges. Nearby trees showing bullet marks. A farmer beyond the woods had heard the shooting about half-past one a.m. No cops on the job. The farmer himself had come out to investigate and reported the abandoned truck. It looked like the beginning of a gang feud.

Cardigan looked up. "Well that's news, Kennedy."

"Is it?" Kennedy had a tantalizing way of smiling.

"I'm in a hurry," said Cardigan, and started off.

Kennedy fell into step beside him. "I'm not green, Cardigan. You ought to know that by this time. And I know that one of the gangs was Cavallo's. Now the other gang.... Cardigan, be a sport."

"What do you mean?"

"Tell me about it."

"You're all wet, Kennedy."

"Oh, no I'm not. Listen, Cardigan. You're not pulling the wool over this baby's eyes. The Department knows who the guy was that was bumped off and then carried away by his buddies. They got the dope from Cavallo's friends—maybe Diorio to Pozzo to Mulroy. Then they tell the Department to get busy—just like that, and they're spreading for somebody. The riot squad's on pins and needles, waiting for another break. Now, it would take guts to head a gang to buck that outfit—you tell me, Cardigan."

Cardigan laughed. "Kennedy, you're funny. So long." He crossed the street and left Kennedy in perplexed indecision.

But he realized that Kennedy was one man he'd have to look out for. That newshound, in other words, knew his onions. He was nobody's fool.

After luncheon Cardigan went out to the suburban post office, opened his box and took out a solitary package. He thrust it into his pocket and returned to his hotel. There he opened it, and found thirteen thousand, two hundred dollars. Twelve hundred he put in a plain envelope and addressed it to Maloney. In each of five plain envelopes he placed a thousand dollars, for Pete Fink's boys. For Pete he placed aside two thousand. He lost no time in mailing Maloney's letter.

Later, he was at the booth in the corner drug-store to get Fink's prearranged call. Fink mentioned his room, but Cardigan objected, remembering Kennedy, and told Fink to pick him up at a street corner well out of the city. Then he hung up and took a bus out, got off at the street he had named, and waited for Fink. He did not have to wait long. The touring car came up, and Fink was driving with his one good arm. Cardigan got in and they rolled off.

"Gats," said Fink. "He slipped out on the boys. He's out gunnin' for the guys who got Bat Johnson."

"What!"

"Yup."

Cardigan saw his nicely made plans toppling to ruin. This was one of those things the best of tacticians cannot foresee. An accident. A bad break. Gats' gone gun-mad because his buddy 'd been killed by the wops.

"We've got to get him," he said.

"Yeah, but where?"

Cardigan cursed the luck. Then he said, "Well, I've got the money. It's all here. A thousand each for the boys. Two thousand for you. Twelve hundred went to the go-between for the booze." He passed over the envelopes. "That'll make the boy's feel better." After a moment he said, "The riot squad's ready for action."

"It won't take long, if we don't get Gats. He'll start the fireworks sure as hell."

"Drop me off when the next bus comes along. Look for Gats. Go to all the places you think he'd be. Ring me at the hotel and say 'Jake' if you get him. Then stay out at the farm—all of you—until this blows over."

A few minutes later he got out of the car, boarded a bus and went back to his hotel. He was very much on edge, and he mused that no matter how perfectly you lay a plan, something is liable to happen that will bring down the whole framework.

At four o'clock the telephone rang, and Fink said, "Jake."

"Jake," said Cardigan.

A great burden was automatically lifted from his mind. He even whistled as he got into his bath. He hummed while he shaved. Then he dressed, spent half an hour with a cigar and the evening paper, and at five-thirty put on his overcoat and went out. As he swung out of the hotel, he heard the scream of a siren. He looked up the street.

Three police cars were roaring down Main Street. Traffic scattered. People gathered on the curb. The three cars shot by the hotel doing fifty miles an hour. They were packed with policemen, and automatic rifles were clamped on the sides. The sirens snarled madly.

Cardigan's breath stuck in his throat. A chill danced up and down his spine. Then his jaw set and he crossed to a taxi-cab.

"Hit Farmingville Turnpike," he clipped, and jumped in.

He started to close the door, but something held it. He turned around. Kennedy was climbing in after him.

"Mind if I go?"

Cardigan sank into his seat, his fists clenched. But he managed to grin. "Sure. The old gumshoe instinct in me always follows a riot call. I'm anxious to see what this is all about."

"Yeah?" smiled Kennedy.

"Yeah. I'm in the dark, just like you."

Kennedy frowned after the manner of a man who wonders if after all he isn't wrong in what he'd been supposing.

Chapter VIII

CARDIGAN had a hard time masking his inner emotions. He said to the chauffeur, "Follow those police cars. It's all right. We're reporters."

Kennedy lit a cigarette. "You've got me guessing, Cardigan."

"Me? Same here, Kennedy. You've got me guessing, too."

"Have a butt."

"Thanks." It was casual, everything he said, but inside of him there was turmoil. What was going on? What had happened to Fink and the boys? He'd formed a strange liking for Pete Fink. In his own way Pete had proved his fidelity, his worth.

The sirens went on screaming. People were still looking out of windows when the taxi shot past in the wake of the police cars. Pedestrians had gathered on street corners and were speculating. Some were talking to traffic cops, asking questions. The cops only grinned and shrugged and waved them away. Other cars were joining in the impromptu parade, breaking all speed laws. The people had been reading of a fresh outbreak in gangdom, of a bitter gang feud. They were obsessed now, rushing to get a bird's-eye view, for human nature is fundamentally melodramatic and its curiosity very close to the morbid.

It was already dark, in the early winter gloom. The taxi struck Farmingville Turnpike, fell into the stream of vehicles that pounded along. Horns tooted, and big, high-powered cars shot by so fast that the taxi seemed to be standing still. Mob curiosity was at it's peak. Anything draws it—a fire, an accident, a soap-box orator, a brawl between school-boys, a man painting a flagpole.

Then suddenly the cars began parking. In the gleam of the headlights two policemen with drawn nightsticks were shouting hoarsely, waving the people away.

"I guess we get out here," said Kennedy.

"Looks that way."

"Come on."

Cardigan paid the fare and they walked ahead. Kennedy showed his card and Cardigan went through with him. They strode briskly along the edge of the woods.

"Hear it?" asked Kennedy.

Cardigan heard it—the rattle of gunfire. Yes, the farmhouse. Alternate waves of heat and cold passed over him. The shadows in the woods were pitch black. Soon they could see the flash of guns, hear the brittle hammering of a machine-gun, firing in spasmodic bursts.

A figure in plainclothes loomed before them.

"Hello, Mac," said Kennedy.

"Who's your friend?" muttered the captain.

"Cardigan."

"Oh-o!"

Kennedy pushed on. Cardigan stopped and MacBride came closer.

"Well, Jack, you see?"

Cardigan bit his lip. "What are you doing, blowing the place up?"

"Yes. Captain McGurk in charge."

"How'd it start?"

"Headquarters got a phone call about a lot of shooting going on out here."

Cardigan growled. "Can't you get 'em to offer a truce? God, Steve, it's pure slaughter!"

He was thinking of Pete Fink and the other boys, trapped in the house.

"There's no use. We came up in the bushes and let go with a machine-gun as a warning. A lot of rifle fire was our answer. This looks like the end."

"Cripes, Steve, stop it—stop it!" He lunged ahead.

MacBride grabbed him, held him in a grip of steel.

"Easy, Jack. You can't do a thing. Don't be a fool. You took the chance and this is the result."

"Let me go, Steve—let go!"

"No, dammit—no! By God, if you make a move I'll crack you over the head!"

"You will, will you?"

"So help me!"

Cardigan swore and heaved in MacBride's grasp. They struggled, weaving about, silent and grim. They crashed deeper into the bushes. Then MacBride struck, and Cardigan groaned and slumped down.

MacBride knelt beside him, white-faced and panting. "Jack, old boy, you hurt much? I didn't mean to hit so hard…Jack, but you can't do a thing. It's the breaks of the racket. God!…" He was rubbing Cardigan's hand.

The battle was still on. Daggers of flame slashed through the dark. Lead drummed against the walls of the house, shattered the windows, pumped into the rooms. Spurts of flame darted from the house. A policeman crumpled. Another heaved up, clutching at his chest, and screamed.

"Oh, God!" groaned MacBride.

Captain McGurk, in charge, swore bitterly. He looked around. "That's three they got. We'll have to give 'em the works. Charlie, you got the grenades?"

"Yes, Cap'n."

"Go to it."

A machine-gun, silent for a moment, cut loose with a stuttering fusillade that raked every window in sight. Intermittent flashes came from the windows. Lead slugs rattled through the branches and thickets. The breeze of evening carried acrid powder smoke. The men in the bushes moved about warily.

Cardigan lay in a daze, conscious of the shots and the din, but in a vague, dreamy way. He wanted to yell out, and he imagined he was yelling, at the top of his lungs, but actually his lips moved only in a soundless whisper. His head throbbed with pain. MacBride had clipped him not too gently. And the captain was now bent over him, with one arm beneath him, rocking him.

The man called Charlie had worked his way closer, crawling on hands and knees, from tree to tree. Finally he stood up, and his arm swung. A small object wheeled through the dark, smacked on the roof of the house. There was a terrific explosion, and a sheet of ghastly flame billowed outward. Stones and bits of timber sang through space, clattered in the woods. The roof caved in, parts of the walls toppled in a smother of smoke and dust.

Out of the chaos groped a man, with hands upraised. He stumbled, sprawled and hit the earth like a log. He never moved once after that. Another crawled out of the ruins, turned over on his back and lay as still as the first. The policemen advanced out of the woods. Nothing stopped them now. They closed in around the house, entered here and there through torn gaps.

MacBride hauled Cardigan to his feet, put on his hat. "You've got to get out of this, Jack," he muttered.

Cardigan was able to stumble.

"It's all over," said MacBride.

He half-dragged him back through the woods to the road, walked him along it.

"Brace up!" he ground out. "I'll put you in a taxi. Look natural. Keep your hat down, your collar up. Get back to your hotel. Stay there, for God's sake. It's all over, you hear? There is no use making a fool of yourself."

They found a taxi, and Cardigan got in. MacBride gripped his hand.

"Good luck, Jack!"

"Thanks, Steve."

Cardigan rode to his hotel in a sunken mood. He got out, paid his fare, and sagged up to his room. He locked the door and slumped into a chair. He groped for a cigarette and lit it, and stared gloomily into space. He muttered something old—something about plans of mice and men....

"Hell!" he mumbled, and sank lower.

Ten minutes later the telephone rang. He looked at it darkly. He didn't know whether he should answer it. But he got up, laid his hand on it, then took off the receiver.

"Hello," he muttered.

"Jack—my room," said Fink, and that was all.

Cardigan snapped out of his mood, sucked in a hot breath. He slammed down the receiver and dived for his overcoat.

Chapter IX

HE climbed the rickety stairs in the ancient house in Jockey Street. He did not know what to expect. He paused a whole minute before the door until he knocked. Then he rapped. There was the sound of quick steps. Then the door swung open and Fink loomed there, grinning. He pulled Cardigan in, closed the door and locked it.

"Park your hips, Jack," he rumbled. "Have a drink."

Cardigan crossed the room, dropped to a chair and slopped liquor into a glass. He held it up. "I need this." He downed it neat. "Well?"

Fink rubbed his big hand along his thigh vigorously. "Well, Cavallo and his gang oughta be done for. Cripes, it was a great break for us! Well, I picked up Gats all right, and we drove back to the farmhouse. Then I figgered maybe one o' Cavallo's guns was trailin' us. I seen a closed coupé follerin' all the way out, but I didn't let on. I swung in by the farm and I saw this coupé slow down and then shoot ahead.

"I put Gats in with the boys, and then I went out and hid in the bushes by the road. An hour later I see a big tourin' car stop down the road and a guy get out. It was Monkey Burns. I run back to the house and plan a trap. I pull down the shades and leave a light lit. Then me and the boys skin out and hide in the bushes with our rifles.

"Little later the bums sneak up. Monkey and Cavallo and Bert Geer and six others. They creep up on the house, and Monkey tries a door. It's open. He turns to his guns and whispers and they all bunch. Then they crash the door and go in shootin'. Before they know what's what, Gats busts loose with his gun and gets the last mutt goin' in. They see they're trapped and they slam the door.

"We surround the place. Then I explain things to the boys. Then I drive off in the car, get to a booth and call Police Headquarters and tell 'em a gunfight's goin' on out there. Then I drive back and park up the road a bit. The boys was takin' pot-shots at the winders now and then. I tell 'em what I done and then run back to the road. When I see a mob o' cars whoopin' down, I whistle and the boys beat it through the woods. We sit in the car until we hear guns goin'. Then we know the cops is at it, and Cavallo and his bums still thinkin' it's us. Then we drive off, and the boys scatter in the city. Just like that."

Cardigan regarded Fink for a long moment. Then he wagged his head. "Pete, you've got a sight more brains than I ever gave you credit for. Every man in that house was killed."

"Humph. What ammunition we saved. So the cops got 'em after all. Well, who has more right than the cops?"

Cardigan went back to his hotel with a light heart. He turned in, slept well, and got the whole thing in the morning extras. At ten MacBride came in to see him. The captain looked full of news.

"Well, you know it all by this time, eh, Jack?" he asked.

"Yes."

"No, you don't." MacBride sat down and took off his hat. "There's a big shake-up. Cavallo and all his rats were wiped out last night. But Cavallo's brother-in-law, Diorio, president of the Hard Club, goes wild this morning. He got in an argument with Pozzo, his friend, the alderman, and blamed him for it all. Claimed Cavallo was framed because he knew too much—framed by Pozzo and Mulroy. It wound up by Pozzo getting shot. Pozzo passed the buck and drew in State's Attorney Mulroy. Kennedy, that wiseacre reporter, crashed in on the row and got the whole story. What dirt they raked up! It's something nobody can hush. Diorio was pinched and he sprung the whole rotten story of graft and quashed criminal cases. Pozzo threatened to have him sent up for twenty years, but Pozzo can't do a thing. He's in the net. So is Mulroy. The governor's wires have been buzzing, and in a short time we're going to see a new state's attorney and a new alderman. It's the biggest shake-up in the history of the city. And you, Jack, in your own little way, caused it, thank God!"

Cardigan smiled. "Not me, Steve—exactly."

"Who, then?"

Cardigan shrugged. "Well, let it drop. A lucky break—and a certain friend of mine." He grew grave. "Now I'm satisfied. Joe Hanley, my buddy, is vindicated. I swore he would be. I was counting on some good breaks. For a while it looked like I was wrong. But the good ones came in the end."

MacBride nodded. "It's funny, there wasn't a trace of the gang that was riding Cavallo and his guns—not a trace."

Cardigan grinned. "I hoped there wouldn't be."

"M-m-m," mused MacBride. "Well, what are you going to do now?"

"That's a question," replied Cardigan. "I was thinking of starting a detective agency. I know the ropes, and I'm through with the Department, and I know where I can get a good right-hand man."

"Who's that?"

Cardigan chuckled. "You may meet him some day, Steve."

He was thinking of Pete Fink.

Dog Eat Dog

A city where crime and politics are organized as one business; an honest, hard-fighting Police Captain who is bucking the crowd of graft-takers and their gunmen when his own daughter is caught in the slimy mesh.

Chapter I

WHEN Captain MacBride was suddenly transferred from the Second Precinct to the Fifth, an undercurrent of whispered speculations trickled through the Department, buzzed in newspaper circles, and traveled along the underworld grapevine.

It was a significant move, for MacBride, besides being the youngest captain in the Department—he was barely forty—was known throughout Richmond City as a holy terror against the criminal element. He was a lank, rangy man, with a square jaw and windy blue eyes. He was brusque, talked straight from the shoulder, and was hard-boiled as a five-minute egg. Now the Second Precinct is in the very heart of Richmond City's night life, hence an important and busy station. The Fifth is out on the frontier, in a suburb called Grove Manor, and carries the somewhat humorous sobriquet of the Old Man's Home. Plenty of reasons, then, why MacBride's transfer should have been made matter for conjecture.

MacBride said nothing. He merely tightened his hard jaw a little harder, packed up and moved. To his successor, Captain O'Leary, he made one rather ironic remark: "Well, I'll be nearer home, anyhow." He had a bungalow, a wife and an eighteen-year-old daughter in an elm-shaded street in Grove Manor.

He landed in the Fifth in the latter part of August. It was a quiet, peaceful station, with a desk sergeant who played solitaire to pass the time away and a lieutenant who used his office and the Department's time to tinker around a radio set which he had made and which still called for lots of improvement. MacBride's predecessor, retired, had spent most of his time working out crossword puzzles. All the patrolmen, and three of the four detectives, were local men, and well on in years. The fourth detective had just been shifted from harness to plainclothes. Ted Kerr was his name; twenty-eight, sandy-haired, and

a dynamo of energy and good-humor. He was ambitious, too, and cursed the luck that had placed him in the Fifth.

"Gee, Cap, it sure is a shock to see you out here," he said.

MacBride could remember when Kerr wore short pants. He grinned in his hard, tight way. "Forget it, Ted. Now that I'm here, though, I'm going to clean out a lot of the cobwebs. They say time hangs heavy on a man here. Too bad I haven't got a hobby."

"Why did they shift you, Cap?"

"Why?" MacBride creaked his swivel chair and bent over some reports on the desk, tacitly dismissing the subject.

A month dragged by, and the hard captain found ennui enveloping him. He was lounging in his tipped back chair one night, with his heels hooked on the desk, reading the newspaper account of a brutal nightclub murder in his old district, when an old acquaintance dropped in—Kennedy, of the city *Free Press*.

"Oh, you," grumbled MacBride.

Kennedy helped himself to a seat. "Yeah, me. Gone to seed yet, Mac?"

"Won't be long now."

"What a tough break you got," chuckled Kennedy.

"Go ahead, rub it in. Pull a horse laugh, go on."

"I'll bet Duke Manola's laughing up his sleeve."

"That pup!"

Kennedy shrugged. "Serves you right for taking the law in your own hands. You birds can shake down a common sneak thief or a wandering wop that goes off on a gun spree coked to the eyebrows. But, Mac, you can't beat organized crime. You can't beat it when it's financed by silent partners—and those silent partners"—he arched a knowing eyebrow—"on the inside, too."

"Man, oh, man, I'm going to get that grease-ball yet!" MacBride's lip curled and his windy eyes glittered.

"Still got him on the brain, eh?" Kennedy lit a cigarette and spun the match out through the open window. "He's fire to fool with, Mac. He'll burn you surer than hell. Anyhow, you're out here in the sticks keeping the frogs and the crickets company, and you're not worrying Duke much. He's planted you where you'll do no harm. Oh, I know, Mac. There's a lot I know that the paper can't afford to print. When you raided the Nick Nack Club you stepped on Duke's toes. Not only his—but his silent partner's."

"Easy, Kennedy!"

"Easy, hell! This is just a heart-to-heart talk, Mac. Forget your loyalty to the badge when I'm around. You've kept a stiff upper lip, and you'll continue to. But just keep in the mind that here's one bird who knows his tricks. I know—see?—I know that Judge Haggerty is the Duke's silent partner in those three nightclubs he runs. Haggerty's aiming for Supreme Court Justice, and he needs lots of jack for his campaign. And he's not going to let a tough nut of a police captain get in his way."

MacBride bit the reporter with a keen, hard eye. After a long moment he swung his feet down from the desk and pulled open a drawer.

"Have a drink, Kennedy."

He drew out a bottle and a glass and set them down. Kennedy poured himself a stiff three fingers and downed it neat, rasped his throat.

"Good stuff, Mac," he said.

"Have another."

"Thanks."

Kennedy measured off another three fingers and swallowed the contents at a gulp, stared meditatively at the empty glass, then set it down quietly.

"Now, Mac," he said, looking up obliquely, while the ghost of a smile played around his lips. "I'll tell you what I came here for."

"Came to razz me, I thought."

"No. That's just my roundabout way of getting at things. One reason why I got kicked off the city desk."

MacBride felt that something important was in the wind. Sometimes he liked Kennedy; other times, he felt like wringing the newshound's neck. Clever, this Kennedy, sharp as a steel trap.

"Well," he said, leaning back, "shoot."

"Just this, Mac. Maybe you're going to run up against Duke again."

"Go ahead."

Kennedy's smile was thin, almost mocking. "Duke's bought that old brewery out off Farmingville Turnpike."

MacBride's chair creaked once, and then remained silent. His stare bored into the lazy, whimsical eyes of the reporter. A sardonic twist pulled down one corner of his mouth.

"What's that wop up to?" he growled, deep in his throat.

"I've got a hunch, Mac. He's getting crowded in the city. He's going to make beer there—the real stuff, I mean. And gin. And—" he leaned forward—"he's going to rub it in—on you."

"He is, eh?" MacBride's voice hardened. "He'll take one step too many. He's getting cocky now. I never saw a wop yet who didn't overstep himself. Riding on my tail, eh? Well, we'll see, Kennedy. Let him move out of turn and I'll jump him. That wop can't kick me in the slats and get away with it. The booze I don't give a damn about. I wouldn't have cared how many speakeasies he ran in the city. But when he ran stud games in the back rooms and reached out for soused suckers I got sore. That's why I broke the Nick Nack Club. It was three in the morning, and among the bums in the back room were two guns from Chicago."

Kennedy chuckled. "That was when Captain Stephen MacBride pulled one of the biggest bones in his career. What a beautiful swan song that was! Hot diggity!"

MacBride rose to his lean, rangy height and cracked fist into palm.

"Boy, but I'm aching to meet that dago! I hope to hell he does make a bum move!"

"He put you out in the sticks; out," added Kennedy whimsically, "in the Old Man's Home. And you're sore, Mac. I can foresee some hot stuff on the frontier, and Grove Manor on the map."

MacBride swung to face him, his feet spread wide. "Just that, Kennedy—just that. They shoved me out here to cool off and grow stale. But I'm not the guy to grow stale. Duke's cracking wise. Maybe he thinks that the transfer has shut me up. Maybe he thinks he can ride me and get away with it. Let him—that's all—just let him!"

There was a knock at the door, and then Sergeant Haley looked in, his beefy face flushed with excitement.

"Carlson's on the wire, Cap'n. There's been a smash-up out on Old Stone Road. Carlson was riding along in the patrol flivver when he saw a big touring car tangled up against a tree half in the bushes. There's a dead man in the car but Carlson can't get him out 'count of the wreckage."

MacBride snorted. "Is Carlson so hard up for company that he has to call up about a wreck?"

"No, but he says he thinks there's something fluky about it. He says there's a woman's footprints near the car, but he didn't see no woman."

"Maybe she walked home," put in Kennedy. "Lot of that going on these days."

"I'll speak to him," clipped MacBride, and sat down at his desk.

Sergeant Haley went out and switched over the call and it took MacBride only a minute to get the details. Then he hung up and, pouring himself a drink, corked the bottle and dropped it back into the drawer.

"The ride will do me good," he remarked as he slapped on his cap.

"Me, too," added Kennedy.

MacBride looked at him. "You're out of your territory, aren't you?"

"What the hell!"

On the way out MacBride told the sergeant, "When Kelly and Kerr drift in—God knows where they are now—tell 'em to hang around. Call up the nearest garage and tell 'em to send a wreckage crew out to Old Stone Road, about a mile north of Pine Tree Park. Buzz the morgue and tell 'em to send the bus to the same place. Tell 'em tonight, not sometime next week. When Lieutenant Miller gets fed up on monkeying with his radio, ask him to kindly take care of things till I get back. When you work out your present game of solitaire, I'd appreciate your getting those delinquent reports as near up to date as you're able. I won't be long."

Outside, he stopped on the curb to light a fresh cigar. Then he followed Kennedy into the police car, and said, "Shoot, Donnegan," to the man at the wheel.

Chapter II

OUT of the hub of town, the car struck Old Stone Road and followed it past neat, new bungalows and later, past fields and intermittent groves of piney woods. Once through Pine Tree Park, the road became darker, lined by heavier woods, with not even an occasional house to relieve the gloom.

Donnegan, at the wheel, pointed to a pair of headlights far up the road, and when they drew nearer, MacBride saw a small two-seater flivver parked on the side and a policeman in uniform spreading his arms to stop them. Kennedy hopped out and MacBride followed him.

"There it is," said Carlson, and pointed to a tangled heap of wreckage against a tree alongside the highway. MacBride strode over, and Carlson followed, snapped on a flashlight and played its white beam over the ruined car.

"Three thousand bucks shot to hell," observed Kennedy. "And still insurance companies make money." He sniffed. "Who's the stiff?"

"Don't know," muttered MacBride and made a gesture which indicated that the man was so deeply buried beneath the wreck that they could not get him. He turned to Carlson. "You said something about footprints."

"Yeah, Cap. See?" He swung his flash down to the soft earth around the car. "Sure, a woman's."

MacBride nodded, then said, "But she never got out of this car after it struck."

The wreck offered mute evidence to that statement. Its radiator was caved in half the length of the long, streamlined hood, and the cowl and part of the hood were crushed up through the windshield frame. Beneath this, and wedged in by the left side of the car, lay the man who had been at the wheel, face downward, the steering-wheel broken and twisted around his chest.

"I been wonderin' where the woman could have went," ventured Carlson.

"Whoever she was, she must have walked away," said MacBride. "Her footprints wouldn't show on the macadam." He added, after a moment, "At any rate, I'll bet my hat she wasn't in the car when it socked that tree."

Donnegan called out, "Guess this is the wrecker."

It was. The wrecking outfit from the garage rolled up, and two men in overalls got out.

"Hello, boys," greeted MacBride. "Before you haul this piece of junk away, there's a dead man inside. See if you can chop away some of the wreck."

The two men pulled axes from their car and set to work and hacked away at the snarled mass of metal. MacBride stood at one side, sucking on his cigar, offering no suggestion to men who knew their business and were doing the best they could. Presently he saw them lay down their axes, and he stepped over to help.

Bit by bit they hauled out the broken, bloodstained body, and laid it down on the ground. MacBride bent down on one knee and taking Carlson's flashlight, snapped on the switch. He grimaced, but gritted his teeth. A swarthy young face, the face of a boy in his early twenties.

"Hot diggity!" exclaimed Kennedy.

MacBride looked up. "What's eating you?"

"Don't you know him?" cried Kennedy, his usually tired eyes alight with interest.

"Frankly, I don't."

Kennedy slapped his knee. "Duke Manola's kid brother!"

"Hell!" grunted MacBride, and took a swift look at the discolored face.

"He was always a sheik with the ladies."

"I've heard of him," nodded MacBride. "Now what the cripes kind of a stunt did he try to pull?"

"Simple," shrugged Kennedy. "Got fresh with some broad probably."

"But how did the broad shake the wreck? I still say she wasn't in the car when it hit. Man alive, there'd been no chance of her walking after that!"

"The crack reporter of the *Free Press* agrees with the astute captain's common sense remark. But wait till Duke gets wind of it. You know these wops. Tweak the nose of a forty-eighth cousin and the whole shooting-match sharpens up their stilettos. Boy, don't I know!"

"Well, if he started playing around it's his tough luck. The trouble with a lot of these sheiks is that they're so used to the yes-girls that when they meet another kind they get sore—and nasty."

Kennedy rasped his throat. "Picture a decent gal trotting out with a marcelled sheik like Joe Manola! Don't tell me!"

MacBride shrugged as he stood up. He took his flashlight and mounted the wreck, shooting the beam down through the twisted metal. A moment later he stood up and held a short, stubby automatic in his hand.

"One shot fired," he said. "Not long ago, either." He had rubbed his finger across the muzzle, and looked at the black streak it left.

A siren screamed through the night, and two headlights came racing down the road. It was the morgue bus, and it pulled up behind the patrol flivver.

"What kind of a gun?" asked Kennedy.

"Thirty-two," shot back MacBride, and with a sudden movement crossed to the body and knelt down.

Kennedy trailed after him and bent over his shoulder. Then Mac-Bride stood up, wiping his hands, a glitter in his eyes.

"He was shot, Kennedy. Shot through the right side."

"And then he hit the tree!"

"Exactly."

Kennedy whistled. "When the Duke hears this!"

MacBride turned to one of the men from the morgue bus. "You can take him. But there's a slug somewhere inside. I want it after the autopsy."

A few minutes later the bus shot off with its dead cargo, and MacBride turned to watch the wrecking-car tugging at the smashed machine. Its derrick hoisted up the front end, and thus the rear wheels were in a condition to move.

"Keep it in the garage," said MacBride, "and I'll take care of your bill."

When the wreck had gone, with the rear red light winking in the distance, Kennedy made for the police car. "Well, let's be going, Mac. This'll be in the early editions."

MacBride started to follow, but turned and retraced his steps to where the wreck had lain. His flash played on the gashed tree and down on to the gouged ground. His eyes narrowed and he bent over, picked up something that shimmered in the white light.

In the palm of his hand lay an emerald pendant, attached to a thin gold chain that had been broken. His lips parted in a sharp intake of breath, and his hand knotted over the pendant.

"Oh, shake it up, Mac," called Kennedy.

MacBride turned and strode to the police car with hesitant steps. He climbed in and closed the door softly behind him. His hand, still holding the emerald pendant, slid into his pocket and remained there.

"Shoot, Donnegan," he clipped.

Chapter III

O N the way back through town, MacBride had the car stop in front of a cigar store.

"Want to get some cigars," he told Kennedy, and strode into the store.

He bought half-a-dozen cigars, spent no more than a minute in a telephone booth, and then returned to the waiting car.

"Have one," he offered Kennedy.

"You were always a good-natured Scotchman," grinned Kennedy.

A couple of minutes later they walked into the station, and Kennedy made for the telephone, and shot the news into his office. Then he said, "Duty calls, Mac. Something tells me I'll be seeing you often."

"Don't make it too often," growled MacBride.

Kennedy waved and strolled out to catch a trolley back to the city.

MacBride tipped back his cap, revealing strands of damp hair plastered to his forehead by perspiration. His chiseled face looked a bit drawn.

He addressed Sergeant Haley huskily—"Call up the Nick Nack Club. Leave word to be delivered to Duke Manola that his brother was found dead at ten-thirty tonight—"

"Dead!" exclaimed Haley, who hadn't recorded a killing in his precinct in ten years.

"Don't butt in," recommended MacBride, lazily, as though deep within him he was very, very weary. "Do that. Found dead in a wrecked car on Old Stone Road, near Pine Tree Park. Tell 'em the body's at the morgue and may be reclaimed after the autopsy. No hint as to who shot him. No"—his teeth ground into his lower lip—"no clues. Make out your regular report and file it. Joseph Manola. We'll get his age and other incidentals later."

"Looks like murder, Cap'n!"

"Ye-es, it looks like murder," droned MacBride, sagging toward his office.

Ted Kerr came in briskly from another room, stopped short in the path of the captain.

"In here," said MacBride, and led the way into his office.

He sank into his chair, slammed his cap down on the desk and took a stiff drink.

"Hear you went out to investigate a wreck," ventured Kerr.

"Ye-es. And ran into a murder." MacBride's hand was in his pocket fingering the emerald pendant.

"Well!"

"Don't get worked up," dragged out MacBride.

"You look all in," said Kerr, seriously.

"Never mind me. What's on your mind?"

"Well, nothing much. Kelly and I were out to the Blue River Inn. You know there's been some complaints about raw parties being pulled off there. Pretty quiet tonight. Couple of drunken dames and a few soused college boys. And then—well...." He hesitated, and looked away, his lips compressed.

"Well, what?"

"Oh, nothing much. Just...." He paused again.

"Come on, Ted. Let's have it."

"Well, I just got a bit of a shock, that's all." His clean-cut face bore a vaguely hurt expression. "Well, Judith was there—"

MacBride snapped forward, his eyes keened. "Yes!"

"Why, what's the matter, Cap?"

"Keep talking. Judith was there. Who with?"

"Oh, hell, I shouldn't have said anything about it. But I've sort of liked Judith—"

"Don't say like when you mean love. And?"

"Well, she was there, that's all. Was another girl with her. Never saw the other girl. Kind of—well, brassy type. Chic looking and all that but— brassy. And two fellows. The one with Judith was young and dark—looked like an Italian sheik. The other fellow was older— so was the girl. I didn't let on I saw them. They had a couple of drinks, then breezed in a big, classy touring car. Don't bawl Judith out, Cap. I shouldn't have told you, but—well, it just came out. Judith's a good girl. I guess I've got a nerve to think I ever had a chance—me just a dick. Promise me you won't say anything to her about it."

MacBride drew in a deep breath and held it trapped in his lungs for a long moment. Then he let it out, slowly, noiselessly, and followed it with a sigh.

"Ah-r—it's a rough, tough world, Ted, old timer."

Kerr attempted to change the subject. "But what about this murder, Cap?"

"It's going to start something—something big—big! Well, I've got my wish—but not in the way I'd expected." He was thinking of his wish that Duke Manola would face him again for a showdown.

"What wish, Cap?" asked Ted Kerr.

"No matter. Joe Manola was the bird got killed. He's Duke Manola's brother, and the Duke can call two dozen gunmen any time he wants to."

The telephone on the desk jangled. MacBride leaned forward, picking up the receiver and said, "Captain MacBride—"

"Yes, MacBride," came a voice with a hint of a nasal snarl. "This is your old playmate, Manola."

"The elder," supplemented MacBride.

"Be funny," snapped Duke Manola. "I just heard my kid brother was bumped off out in the sticks. What's the lay?"

"No lay yet, Duke. When I get the lay I'll send you an engraved copy of the report, autographed."

"Crack wise, big boy, crack wise."

"And—"

"You better snap on it, MacBride. I'm just telling you, get the pup or pups that winged the kid before I do. And don't get tough, either. Kind of a sock on your jaw, eh? You having to work for the guy gave you a buggy ride out to God's country!"

"Lay off that, Duke. And don't *you* get tough. You keep your hands out of this. And take a tip: Try to play around in this neck of the woods and I'll flop on you like a ton of brick. I'll handle this case, and I don't want any dirty greaseball getting in my light."

"I may drop in for tea soon, big boy."

"If I never saw you, Duke, that'd be years too soon. There's no Welcome sign hanging out here, and there's no good-luck horseshoe parked over the door. In short, I'm not entertaining."

"Whistle that, guy, and go to hell!" With that a sharp click indicated that Duke Manola had hung up.

MacBride slammed down the receiver, and Kerr offered, with a half-grin, "You men don't seem to get along so well."

"We get along worse every day," replied MacBride.

Kerr lit a cigarette. "Any clues on that murder, Cap?"

MacBride's hand was in his pocket, and it clenched the emerald pendant in sweaty fingers.

"No, Ted," he muttered.

Chapter IV

MRS. MacBRIDE was a woman of thirty-eight who still retained much of her youthful charm. The onyx sheen of her hair was not threaded by the slightest wisp of gray. Ordinarily, at breakfast time, she was a bright-eyed, animated woman, with a song on her lips and pleasant banter for her husband; and occasionally, as she passed back and forth from the kitchen, a kiss for the captain's cheek. Secretly, MacBride cherished this show of affection.

But something in his attitude that morning—or it may have been something in the heart of his wife—tended to eliminate this little by-play. There was a song on her lips, but it was in an unnatural, off-tone key.

When they sat down at the table facing each other, MacBride, without looking up from his morning paper, said, "Judith up yet?"

"Yes. She'll be right in, Steve." She went about sprinkling sugar on the grapefruit. "Grove Manor must have gasped this morning when they read the papers about—about—"

"Yes," nodded MacBride. "Haven't had a murder here in ten years."

"You'll be careful, Steve."

He glanced up. "Careful, Ann?"

"Well—you never can tell. I'm always worried."

"Oh, nonsense, Ann. You shouldn't worry—"

There was a step on the stair, and Judith came in, quietly. Ordinarily she entered at a skip, vivacious, animated. Her hair was jet black, and bobbed short, in the extremely modern manner. Likewise was her mode of dress extremely modern.

"Morning, dad. Morning, ma." Cheerful the tone, but with a faintly hollow ring.

As she crossed to the table she limped a trifle, but it escaped MacBride's eyes. His gaze was riveted on the newspaper.

"Morning, Judith," he said.

When she was seated, he folded his paper and laid it aside.

It seemed that Mrs. MacBride was holding her breath.

Hard on the outside, hard with men who were hard, he had always found it difficult to be hard at home. He wanted to eliminate a lot of preliminary talk. Somehow, he did not want to see a woman of his own crumpling bit by bit under a lightning parry and thrust of words.

He drew his hand from his pocket and laid the emerald pendant on the table.

"Yours, Judith?"

But the girl had already blanched. Mrs. MacBride sat stiff and straight, her hands clenched in her lap, the color draining from her tightly compressed lips.

"It was found," went on MacBride slowly, clumsily gentle, "beside a wrecked car on Old Stone Road last night."

"Oh!" breathed Judith, and looked to left and right, as if seeking an avenue of escape.

"Come, now, little girl," pursued MacBride. "Tell me about it. What happened?"

Judith jerked up from her chair, started for the stairs leading to her room.

"Judith!"

She dragged to a stop and turned.

"Please, Steve!" choked Mrs. MacBride. She got up and put an arm around her daughter.

"Ann, please stay out of this," recommended MacBride; and to the girl, "Judith, tell me about it. I know you were out in the company of the man who was murdered last night! I'll have to have an explanation!"

"I—I can't tell!" came her muffled, panicky voice.

"But you must!" he insisted sternly.

"No—no! I can't! I won't! Oh, please!…"

He crossed the room and laid his hand on her shoulder. "Do you realize the significance of this? I don't say you killed Manola. But you were out with him, and you know what happened on that road. Judith! Out with one of the worst rakes in the city—the brother of Duke Manola, the gang leader and—my enemy! My God, girl, what have you been thinking of? Isn't Ted Kerr good enough for you? Or does a classy car and a marcelled wop win you?"

She was crying now, but through it all she kept reiterating—"I won't tell! I won't tell!"

"Judith, so help me, you will!"

"No—no! I won't! You can beat me! You—can—beat—me! I won't tell! Oh-o-o-o!…"

"Steve," implored Mrs. MacBride, "don't—please!"

"Ann, be still! Do you think I enjoy this? How do you think I felt last night when I picked that pendant up by the wreck? God, it's a wonder the hawkeyed Kennedy didn't see me! Judith, listen to reason. You've got to tell me!"

She spun back, her hands clenched, a storm of terror in her moist eyes—tense, quivering, like a cornered animal, and defiant.

"No—no—never! You can't make me. Dear God, you can't!"

She pivoted and clawed her way up the stairs, fled into her room and locked the door.

Halfway up the staircase, MacBride stopped, turned and came down slowly, his face a frozen mask.

"To think, to think!" he groaned.

His wife touched him with her hands, and he took them in his own and looked down into her swimming eyes.

"Ann, I wish you could make me happy, but just now—you can't. I'm as miserable, as sunk, as you are."

Years seemed to creep upon him visibly. He picked up the pendant and dropped it into his pocket.

Chapter V

AT five that evening MacBride was sitting at his desk in the precinct, when Ted Kerr breezed in, closed the door quietly and stood, wiping perspiration from his forehead.

"Well?" asked MacBride.

"I was out there. Kline, the bird that runs the Blue River Inn, acted dumb. He didn't remember the party of four. Had never seen them before. In short, didn't know them."

"Think he's on the level?"

"No." Kerr dropped to a chair. "I could see he was walking on soft ground, watching his step. It's my bet that he knows the two fellows." He paused. "How—how's Judith?"

"Still love her?"

"Well, God, Cap, she's in trouble—"

"Sh! Soft pedal, Ted!"

Kerr spoke in a husky whisper. "I don't believe she's done bad. She wouldn't. Just lost her head. Damn these oily birds with their flashy cars!"

"Listen. If you saw the guy who was with Manola again, would you recognize him?"

"Sure."

"Then take a trolley to Headquarters and look over the Rogues' Gallery. Call me up if you have any luck."

Kerr took his departure, and a little later Kelly entered and said, "Yup, Cap, there's men out in that brewery where you sent me. I heard some hammerin' goin' on like, and the windows on the third floor— that's the top, you know—them windows was open, they was. Then I seen two cars parked inside the fence, under the sheds where the beer used to be loaded on trucks. Classy cars—one a big sedan, all black—number A2260. The other was a sport roadster, C4002. Nobody was around them."

On his desk pad MacBride marked down the type and number of the two cars. He dismissed Kelly and then called up the automobile license bureau. The sport roadster, he found, belonged to a man named John A. Winslow. The sedan was owned by Judge Michael Haggerty.

MacBride sat back with a bitter chuckle. "That sounds like 'Diamond Jack' Winslow, the race-track kid. H'm. And Mike Haggerty. Cheek and jowl with Duke Manola."

He lit a cigar and looked up to find Detective-Sergeant O'Dowd, from Headquarters.

"Hello, O'Dowd."

"Hello, Mac. I just dropped in with a little order from the big cheese. Know that brewery out off Farmingville Turnpike?"

MacBride nodded.

O'Dowd said, "Well, don't let it worry you, Mac. They're making some good beer there, and orders are to leave 'em be."

"I've been waiting for those orders," said MacBride. "So long as they bust the Volstead Act and don't make any noise, it's O.K. by me. Anything else, though—"

"Let your conscience be your guide, Mac," grinned O'Dowd, and left.

The machinery of the underworld and politics, mused MacBride, was getting under way. Kerr called up a little later, and he had information.

"I'm sure it's the same guy, Cap," he said. "Chuck Devore. The records show he was arrested two years ago in connection with the shooting of a taxi driver named Max Levy. But he wasn't indicted."

"We're hot, Ted," shot back MacBride. "Devore is a gangster, and a pretty tough egg. He used to run with Duke Manola. In that killing two years ago we had the hunch that Manola tried to frame Devore to take the rap. Then they broke and Devore drifted. If he's back in town, there's a pot of trouble brewing."

"You mean a gang war?"

"Right. Dog eat dog stuff, and hell's going to pop or I miss my guess. All right, Ted. Hop a trolley home."

MacBride slammed down the receiver and sat back rubbing his hands. Devore back in town! But what had he been doing in the company of Duke Manola's brother? And who was the woman in the case—besides Judith? A chill shot through MacBride. His own daughter mixed up in an underworld feud!

He snapped up to his feet, changed from his uniform coat and cap into a plain blue jacket and a gray fedora. He strode out of his office, told Donnegan to get the car out, and left brief instructions with Sergeant Haley.

Outside, he climbed into the car and said, "Know the Blue River Inn?"

Donnegan said, "Yes."

"That's where we're going. Don't run right up to it. Park back a distance, out of sight."

The car shot off through town, hit Old Stone Road and followed it into Farmingville Turnpike. Half an hour later Donnegan pulled up on the side of the road, in the shadow of a deep woods. Up ahead they could see *Blue River Inn*, picked out in electric light bulbs.

"You wait here, Donnegan," said MacBride. "I won't be long."

The inn was large and rambling, two storied, with many windows. MacBride entered the large, carpeted room that served as a lobby, and the headwaiter, with a menu in his hand, bowed.

"I'm not eating," clipped MacBride. "Who runs this dump?"

"Sir?"

"Cut out the flowers, buddy. I'm from the precinct." He flashed his badge. "Snap on it!"

A short, rotund man in dinner clothes came strolling in from the main corridor, and the headwaiter, a little troubled, beckoned to him.

"You the owner?" asked MacBride. "What's your name?"

"Hinkle, owner and manager. What can I do for you?"

"I'm MacBride, from the precinct. There were two couples in here last night— *You!*" he suddenly shot at the headwaiter. "Stay here! Now," he went on, "who were the two men?"

"Of course," said Hinkle, "there are so many people come here, we cannot recall them. So many are transients."

"Look here," pursued MacBride. "One of those men was Joe Manola, who was later killed in a wreck last night. Now who was the other guy—the guy with him?"

Hinkle moistened his lips and his eyes shifted nervously. "I'm sorry. I don't know. Nor does my headwaiter."

The girl at the desk trilled, "Mr. Hinkle, telephone."

Hinkle went over to the desk, and MacBride followed, stood beside him. Hinkle picked up the telephone, and said, "Yes, Hinkle talking." And then his face blanched, and his lips began to writhe.

MacBride's gun came out of his pocket, jammed against Hinkle's adipose paunch. He tore the receiver from Hinkle's hand and clasped it to his own ear, heard—

"…and get that, Hinkle. Act dumb, all the time, see. And if it gets too hot, call me on the wire. Got that number? Main 1808?"

MacBride's lips moved silently, forming the words, "Say yes, Hinkle."

"Yes, yes," said Hinkle, his face pasty white.

"O.K. then," was the reply, and the man at the other end hung up.

MacBride hung up, set down the telephone, a thin, hard smile on his face.

"Who was that, Hinkle?"

Hinkle wilted, blubbered, kept shaking his head.

"Chuck Devore, eh?" grinned MacBride, without humor.

"Oh, G-God!" choked Hinkle, gasping for air and reeling backward.

MacBride picked up the telephone and called the precinct. To Sergeant Haley he said, "Send a man out around to the telephone exchange. Tell the operators there to allow no calls incoming or outgoing from"—he looked down at the number on the phone— "Farmingville 664. Also, no calls to be connected, outgoing or incoming, to Main 1808. Until further notice from the station. Also, get me the address of Main 1808, quick, and ring me at Farmingville 664 before the order to shut off. Snap on it, sergeant!"

He hung up, stepped to the door and blew his whistle. When Donnegan came in on the run, MacBride said, "No hurry. Just stay here and keep your eyes on these two men till you get word from the precinct. Don't let them get out of sight. Go in the dining-room and tell all the guests to clear out."

There were only a dozen-odd persons in the dining-room, and they made an angry and protesting exodus. When they had gone, MacBride said to Donnegan. "Let no more in. See that no more cars leave."

The telephone rang, and he picked it up, listened. "All right, sergeant," he said. "I'll have to pass there on the way through. Tell Kelly and Kerr to be ready and I'll pick them up."

He turned from the telephone, looked at the group of waiters and at Hinkle and his steward. Then he looked at Donnegan. "Keep them salted, Donnegan, right in this room. You, Hinkle, have your sign shut off and all the lights in the house except in this room. You're temporarily closed for business."

"It's an outrage!" choked Hinkle.

"See if I care," chuckled MacBride; and to Donnegan, "I'll take the car."

Chapter VI

KELLY and Kerr were waiting outside of the precinct when MacBride drew up.

"Hop in, boys. We're going for maybe a little target practice."

Kelly shifted his chew and climbed in, and Kerr, eagerness sparking in his eyes, followed. MacBride stepped on the gas and they shot off.

"What's the lay, Cap?" asked Kelly.

"We're going to look up Chuck Devore, at a dump in lower Jockey Street. There may be a fight. You boys well heeled?"

They were. And as they drove on, MacBride explained about his pilgrimage to the Blue River Inn.

They made good time into the city. Traffic on Main Street, the artery of theatres and cabarets, held them up.

Presently MacBride turned into Jockey Street and followed it west. Near Main Street, small restaurants, Chinese or Italian, displayed their signs. Further along, it changed to blank-faced brick houses, old and peeling, with here and there a single globe of light marking out a speakeasy. The municipal lighting system was poor, and the way was dark.

MacBride pulled up in the middle of a block and said, "It's on the next block, but we'll leave the car here. Come on."

They got out and continued down Jockey Street with MacBride taking long strides in the lead. There was a noticeable jut to his teakhard jaw and a windy look in his blue eyes. He was not the man to grow stale from sitting on his spine in a precinct office. The game on the outside still lured him—the somewhat dangerous game of poking into back alleys and underworld hideouts.

He slowed down, but did not stop. "This is the house, boys. Number 40. Don't stop. All dark except the third floor. Shades drawn there, but you can see the light through the cracks. I know this neighborhood. They have a lookout in the hall, and a man needs a password to get in. A red light dump without the red lights. We'll see if there's a way to it from the next street."

At the next block they turned south, and then east into the next street. Between the houses here they could see the backs of the houses on Jockey Street.

"There it is," pointed out MacBride. "That three-story place, taller than the others." He stopped. "Here's an alley. Come on."

They swung into a dark, narrow passageway that led between two wooden houses and on into a small yard criss-crossed with clotheslines. Separating this yard from that of the one belonging to the house in Jockey Street was a high board fence. Behind this, the three paused and looked up. All floors were dark except the third and top-most.

MacBride gripped the top of the fence, heaved up and over, landed in soft earth. Kerr and Kelly followed and they stood hunched closely, whispering. MacBride pointed to the fire-escape.

"Up we go. You boys trail me. Easy!" he warned.

He led the way up the ladders, his gun drawn. Nearing the top story, he went more cautiously, more quietly, and turned once to recommend silence with a finger tapping his lips. At the third floor he stopped, hunched over. The window was open, a half-drawn shade crackling in the draft.

Slowly MacBride raised his head and peered in over the sill. Four men were sitting around a table in shirt-sleeves, their collars open. A bottle and glasses were on the table, and MacBride caught whiffs of cigarette smoke. He saw Chuck Devore in profile. Devore was a tall, smooth-shaven man of thirty, with curly brown hair and a cleft chin. His eyes were deep-set and peculiarly luminous. In repose, his face was not bad to look at—except for the strange, impenetrable eyes. MacBride had never seen the others, but all of them bore the stamp of hard, dangerous living. The most outstanding, besides Devore, was a huge bull of a man with flaming red hair and a heavy jaw.

"It will be a cinch," Devore was saying. "We can bust in about three a.m. and stick up the works, and you can take it from me, there'll be no small change. Not with Diamond Jack Winslow in on the show and a lot of big political guns. And they can't yap. That's where we've got them. They're playing a crooked game, and if the public got wind of it, Perrone would have about as much chance of getting in the aldermanic show as I would. And Haggerty'd land on his can, too."

"And won't Duke Manola get sore!" chuckled the red-head.

"Yes, the lousy bum!" snapped Devore. "Cripes, his kid brother spilled a lot of beans. Wild sheik, that bird was."

"Yeah—*was*," nodded the red-head.

"I feel a draft," said Devore, and got up, coming toward the window.

He walked into the muzzle of MacBride's thirty-eight.

"Nice, now, Chuck!" bit off MacBride. "Up high."

He stepped in through the window, and Kerr was halfway through behind him, his gun covering the startled group at the table.

Then came Kelly, slit-eyed, dangerous.

"What's the meaning of this, Mac?" snarled Devore.

"Be your age, Chuck," said MacBride.

No one saw a hand sliding in through a door that led to another room. This hand, slim and white, felt for the lightswitch, found it, and pressed the button.

The room was thrown into sudden darkness. Chairs scraped. A door banged.

A dagger of flame slashed through the gloom, and a man screamed, his body hit the floor with a thud.

MacBride found Devore on his hands, and the gangster was trying to twist the captain's gun arm behind his back.

"No, you don't, Devore!"

MacBride heaved with him, spun through the darkness, crashed into other struggling figures. He slammed Devore against the wall, and Devore tried to use his knee for a dirty blow. MacBride blocked with his hip and banged Devore's head to the wall, again and again. Then Devore twisted and dragged out of the jam, but MacBride heaved against him and they crashed to the floor.

Struggling feet stumbled over their twisting bodies, and curses ripped through the darkness. Another shot banged out, went wild and shattered a light bulb in the chandelier. The table toppled, and somebody crashed over a chair.

Then the door leading to the hall was flung open and dim figures hurtled through it on the way out, their feet pounding on the floor. Devore planted his knee brutally in MacBride's stomach and the captain buckled, gasping for breath. Then Devore tore free, reeled about the room and dived for the open door.

But MacBride caught his breath, heaved up and lunged after him. Doors opened and banged, but nobody came out to get in the way. Somewhere far below MacBride heard a sharp exchange of shots. He catapulted after Devore who was racing down the staircase. Near the bottom, he leaped through space and landing on Devore's neck, crashed him to the floor.

Devore groaned and relaxed. MacBride straddled him, drew out manacles and settled Devore's status for the time being. He stood up, wiping blood from his face, shoving wet strands of hair back from his forehead. He heard footsteps rushing up from below and swung around with his gun leveled.

It was Ted Kerr, his clothes in tatters and a couple of blue welts on his face.

"They got away, Cap," he explained. "Through the back. Went through a door, slammed it and locked it. Kelly and I tried to bust it, but no can do. I came up to see if you were all right. One was wounded. Here's Kelly."

Kelly puffed up, his collar gone but his tie still draped around his neck.

"Take this guy," MacBride said, jerking a thumb toward Devore. "I'll be right down."

He went upstairs two steps at a time and entered the gang's quarters. He lit a match, found the light switch and snapped it. The room was in ruin, and the shade still clicked in the draft. He crossed to another door, stood to one side, then turned the knob and kicked the door open. A light was burning inside, and a breeze blowing through an open window.

Entering, MacBride set it down as a room used by a woman. There was a littered dressing table, and a bureau with several drawers half out and signs indicatory of somebody having made a quick getaway. A cursory examination revealed no tell-tale clues. MacBride turned out the lights, left the rooms, and descended the staircase.

Devore was standing up now, between Kerr and Kelly, and venom was burning in his strange, enigmatic eyes.

MacBride said, "Now for a little buggy ride, Devore."

"You're going to regret this, MacBride," the man snarled. "By cripes, you are!"

"Cut out the threats, you bum!"

"Cut out hell! Before you know what's what I'm going to have you tied by the heels."

"Should I sock him, Cap?" inquired Kelly.

"No. He'll get a lot of that later, where it's more convenient." MacBride's hand clenched, and his lips flattened back against his teeth.

Devore smiled, mockingly. "We'll see, MacBride—*we'll see!*"

Chapter VII

IT was about half-past ten when the police car rolled into Grove Manor. Ted Kerr was at the wheel. Devore sat in the rear, between MacBride and Kelly.

"Looks like a crowd in front of the station," sang out Kerr.

"Swing into the next block," said MacBride. "Probably some photographers and—no doubt—that very good friend of mine, Kennedy, with his nose for news, and his wisecracks."

The car turned into a dark street several blocks this side of the police station and halted.

"What should I do, Cap?" asked Kerr.

MacBride was thinking. "Let's see. H'm. Drive around the back way, Ted. Park a block away from the station. I'll run this bird in the back way, right into my office. You and Kelly drive up a little later. And don't spill any beans—keep your traps shut. Then you come in my office, Ted, and we'll see."

Kerr drove off slowly, cut around the back of the town and came up a dark, poorly paved street that ran back of the station. When he pulled up, MacBride hauled Devore out and marched him off. They took a path that led through a vacant lot and on up to the back of the station.

Here MacBride, using a key, opened a door and shoved Devore in, then followed and, locking the door, guided the gangster along a dark hallway that ended against another door. MacBride unlocked this and stepped into his office, relocked it quickly and crossing to the door that led into the central room, shoved shut the bolt. Then he turned with a sigh of relief, took off his cap and sailed it across his desk.

"Take the load off your feet, Devore," he droned, and pulling open a drawer in his desk, hauled out a bottle and downed a stiff bracer. He turned to Devore. "Dry?"

"I don't drink slops, thanks."

"You can go to hell," chuckled MacBride, slamming shut the drawer.

"Listen," jerked out Devore. "Let me use that phone. I gotta talk to my lawyer."

"Try setting that to music, guy. You're calling no lawyer. You're seeing no one. And the newspapers aren't going to know I've got you. I'm top-dog, you dirty slob, and you're going to come across!"

"About what?"

"Ask me another," scoffed MacBride. "About the killing of Joe Manola. Now don't try to hand me a song and dance, Devore. I was listening outside the window on the fire-escape. I heard you and your guns talking."

"How did you get the lay on me, MacBride?"

"Don't worry about that, Devore. The thing is, I've got you, and you're going to come across."

Devore leaned forward, his teeth bared, but not in a smile. "How about your kid daughter, big boy?"

"Yes, you pup, how about her?" exploded MacBride, a bad light in his eyes.

"Sound nice, won't it? Daughter of Captain MacBride linked up with gangsters. Think it over, MacBride."

"I'm thinking it over, Devore. It's a blow—a sock flush on the button, but I'll weather it. She'll have to talk, sooner or later, even though she is my daughter. But she's been framed somehow. And what I want to know is, who's the woman who was in the quartette last night at the Blue River?"

"Ah, wouldn't you like to know!" Devore snarled; and then snapped, "Try and find out, you big bum!"

There was a knock on the door. MacBride walked over and asked, "Who is it?"

"Ted."

He opened the door and Ted Kerr slipped in. MacBride snapped shut the bolt. Kerr scowled at Devore.

"Right at home, eh, Devore? You won't be," he threatened.

MacBride said, "Keep your eye on him, Ted. I'm going out and give the gang the air."

There was a sizable crowd waiting for news. Four reporters, three photographers. And Kennedy, with his whimsical smile.

"Ah, captain," he chortled, "and now you broadcast."

MacBride bored him with a keen stare. "You're wasting your time, Kennedy. On your way—all of you boys. No news tonight."

"But who's the bird you've got?" demanded a reporter from the city news association.

"You heard me," shot back MacBride. "No news. There's a trolley goes through here in five minutes. Take a tip. Hop it."

"Aw, for cripe's sakes," protested Kennedy. "Be a sport, Cap. Think of all the good breaks I've put in your way."

"Think of all the good drinks I've handed out," replied MacBride. "No use, Kennedy. Beat it, all of you. You're cluttering up the station."

The outer door opened and a man strolled in nonchalantly smoking a cork-tipped cigarette. He was of medium height, slight in build, dressed in the acme of fashion. He wore a gray suit that could not have been made for less than a hundred dollars, a cream-colored silk shirt, a blue tie, and a rakish Panama hat. He carried a Malacca stick, and now he leaned on it, his hand aglitter with diamonds, a lazy, indolent look in his slitted brown eyes.

"Hello, MacBride," he droned through lips that scarcely moved.

"Aren't you late for tea, Duke?" asked the captain.

"Kind of. But I heard you've been shooting the town up. Where's the catch?"

"Rehearsing. No public showing just yet, Duke."

"Forget it. I got a right to a private interview."

MacBride shook his head. "That's a lot of noise. You've got no rights at all so far as I'm concerned. The door's behind you, Duke. The air'll do you good."

Duke Manola snarled, "Can that tripe, Mac. I didn't come out here to chin with you. I came out to see who you picked up. Cut the comedy!"

"Soft pedal, Duke. You're in bad company right now."

"Why, damn your soul, MacBride!—"

"Shut up!" barked the hard captain. "You might be a big guy in other circles, but just now, as far as I'm concerned, you're only a little dago shooting off a lot of hot air." He stepped to the outer door and yanked it open. "Now get the hell out!"

Manola's lips moved in a silent oath, and his eyes flamed behind lids that were almost closed. Then he shrugged. "All right, MacBride. Have your way. I see you're not tamed yet."

"Not by a damned sight, Duke!"

"Maybe—I'll try a little more—taming." With that he sauntered out, a leer on his dark, smooth face.

A moment later the newspapermen followed.

From then on until midnight MacBride sat in his office, behind locked doors, and raked Devore with a merciless third degree. But Devore only taunted him. He made no confession. He gave no details. He weathered the gale with the hardness of his kind, and at midnight MacBride, worn and haggard, torn inwardly by emotions that he never revealed, called it a day.

"All right, Devore. That'll do for tonight. More later, buddy."

He called in a policeman and directed him to put Devore in a cell.

"Listen here, MacBride," the gangster protested on the way out of the office. "I want a lawyer. I want him mighty quick."

"Dry up. You're not getting out on bail while I'm alive."

Still protesting, Devore was dragged away to a cell.

Weary, sunk at heart, MacBride slumped back in his chair, his chin dropping to his chest, his tousled hair straggling down over his red-rimmed eyes. He was up against it. He dared not look ahead. There was no telling what the morrow would bring. But one thing was certain. His daughter would be drawn into the net, linked with a gangster's crime, her name and likeness published throughout the country. Judith MacBride, daughter of Captain MacBride, feared by the criminal element of Richmond City. A stickler for the law. A hard man against crooks. Possessed of an enviable record.

He shuddered; the whole, big-boned frame of him shuddered.

And then the telephone rang, and he picked up the receiver.

"Is this you, Steve?" came his wife's anxious voice.

"Yes, Ann."

"Steve! I don't know where Judith is. She went to a movie tonight—to—forget for a little while. She'd promised to go with Elsie, from the other end of town. You know the show's out at eleven. And she hasn't come home yet. I called up Elsie and she said they parted in front of the theatre at eleven and Judith started walking home.

"And Steve, listen. At about ten some woman called up and asked for Judith. I said she wasn't in, that she'd gone to the movies. Then she hung up. What do you suppose could have happened?"

Under the desk, MacBride's clenched fist pounded against his knee.

"I don't know, Ann. But don't worry. I'll be home right away. Don't worry, dear. I'll—be—home."

The color had drained from his face by the time he slipped the receiver back on to the hook. He sat back, his arms outstretched, the hands knotted on the edge of the desk, the eyes wide and staring into space. And then the eyes narrowed and the lips curled.

He heaved up, banged on his cap and strode out of the station. When he reached home his wife was sobbing, and she came to his arms. Hard hit as he was, he, nevertheless, put his arms around her and patted her gently.

"Buck up, Ann. That's a brave girl. Maybe it's nothing after all. Maybe—"

The ringing of the telephone bell interrupted him. Slowly, he approached the instrument, unhooked the receiver.

"Who is this?" grated a voice.

"MacBride."

"Get wise to yourself, MacBride. You see that Devore gets free by tomorrow midnight, or your daughter gets a dirty deal. This is straight. The gang's got her at a hideout you'll never find. I'm calling from a booth in the railroad station. By tomorrow midnight, MacBride, or your daughter gets the works! Good-bye!"

A click sounded in MacBride's ear. He turned away from the telephone, met his wife's wide-eyed stare.

"Steve! Steve!" she cried.

"Judith's been kidnaped by Devore's gang. Devore's the man I've got in jail. His freedom is their price—for Judith."

"Oh—dear—God!"

Ann MacBride closed her eyes and swayed. The hard captain caught her, held her gently, carried her to a sofa and laid her down, kneeling beside her.

For the first time in his life MacBride prayed—for his daughter.

Chapter VIII

NEXT day he sat in his office, with the doors bolted, and Ted Kerr facing him.

"Ted, I'm cornered," he muttered. "I've got to pay through the nose."

"The skunks!" exclaimed Kerr. "God, can't we comb the city? Can't we run the pups down?"

"It would take two or three days. They demand Devore by midnight. I've got to swallow my pride and let him go."

"But, Cap, you can't let him just walk out."

"I know I can't. There must be another way. He must escape."

Kerr bit his lip, perplexed. "Escape? Can you imagine the razzing you'll get?"

MacBride nodded. "Yes, more than you can. I've been called a tough nut, Ted. Well, I won't deny it. And my pride's been one of the biggest things in me. Swallowing it will damn near choke me. But my daughter—my flesh and blood—is the price, and, by God, I can't stand the blow!"

"But can't it be fixed so the blame'll fall on me? Hell, Cap, you've got so much more at stake."

"No. I'm the guy pays through the nose. Devore must escape."

"What about those birds at the Blue River?"

"They're not in the know. I hauled Donnegan off last night. Devore was just their bootlegger. Hinkle came across. He said Devore warned him to close his trap and keep it closed, or wind up wrestling with a bullet. No, there's no alternative. Sometime tonight I've got to pull a bone-head move and let Devore blow. Afterwards, Ted, I'll clean him out. But Judith comes first."

"Suppose they double-cross you?"

"I'll take care of that before Devore goes."

The day dragged by, and at nine that night MacBride had Devore brought in from the cell. He dismissed the officer with a nod. Devore sat down—he was without manacles—and helped himself to a cigarette from a pack on the desk. He needed a shave, and he looked down at the mouth—and nasty.

"What a crust you've got, MacBride! Dammit, I want a lawyer. I want to see something besides polished buttons. I gotta right to that, MacBride."

MacBride rocked gently in his swivel chair. "Pipe down. And listen. You're going to slide out of here tonight."

Devore looked up, suspecting a trick. "What d' you mean?"

"The rats you run with kidnaped my daughter last night. Their price is—your freedom. They've got me buffaloed, and I know they'd slit her open if I didn't come across."

"Told you I'd get you tied by the heels."

"Shut up. It's a bum break, and I'm not yapping. You slide out tonight."

Devore looked around. "Which way?"

"Not yet, buddy. You're going to call up your gang and tell 'em to let my daughter go."

"Do you see any green on me, Cap?" snarled Devore.

"You can take my word or leave it. I've never framed a guy yet, Devore. You ought to know that. Here's my proposition. You call up your gang and tell 'em it's all fixed. They let my kid go. You breeze. I'll give you twelve hours' grace. But after that I'm going after you. I'll know what number you call up, so don't hang around there after you're out. You're getting a lease on life, a twelve hours' lease. Grab it before I change my mind."

Devore leaned forward, his luminous eyes roving over the captain's face.

"Call Northside 412," he breathed.

MacBride reached for the telephone and put through the call.

When he heard the operator ringing, he passed the phone over to Devore and watched him intently.

"Hell—hello," snapped Devore. "This you, Jake?... Yeah, this is Chuck. It's all fixed. Let the dame go—right away. Put her in a taxi and send her home. Then clear out and I'll meet you at Charlie's.... Of course, I mean it. For God's sake, don't act dumb!... Yeah, right away. S' long."

He hung up, his eyes narrowed. "Now, MacBride!"

MacBride pulled open a drawer and laid an automatic on the desk. "The gun you shot Joe Manola with. It's empty. You grab it and cover me and beat it out the back way, through the lots, and run for three blocks. There's a main drag there, and a bus goes through to the city in five minutes."

Devore grabbed the gun, his eyes brilliant in their deep sockets, his lips drawn tight.

"Paying through the nose, eh, MacBride?"

"Shut up. When I meet you again, Devore, I won't be taking any prisoners. The morgue bus will gather up the remains. Breeze!"

Devore snapped to his feet, leered, and sped out through the rear door. MacBride sat still, his face granite hard, his fingers opening and closing, his teeth grinding together. For two minutes he sat there. Then he jumped up, ran to the door leading into the rear hall and banged it shut.

He spun around and dived for the door leading into the central room. Sergeant Haley was playing solitaire. Kerr was sitting at a table playing checkers with Kennedy, of the *Free Press*.

"Snap on it!" barked MacBride. "Devore's escaped! He pulled a fast one. Grabbed a gun lying on the desk. Come on!"

Kerr kicked back his chair. Two patrolmen came running from another room, drew their nightsticks.

MacBride led the way out, and on the street said, "We'll split." He directed the patrolmen to head for the trolley line. To Kerr he said, "We'll watch the bus line."

A moment later he and Kerr were running for the bus line, and when they reached the highway, MacBride pointed to a red light just disappearing around a bend.

"That's the bus," he said. "And Devore."

"So you did it, Cap."

"Hell, yes!"

Chapter IX

A N hour later, MacBride and Kerr stopped in at the captain's house. Judith was weeping in her mother's arms and her mother was shedding tears of happiness.

"Judith just came in," she said.

MacBride took his daughter and stood her up, placing his hands on her shoulders. "Poor kid—poor kid. Now tell me, Judith, tell me—all you know."

Ted Kerr stood a little back, ill at ease.

"Oh, daddy, I've been a fool—a little fool. When I was walking home from the movies last night that girl drove up in a car, called to me—and then two men jumped for me, gagged me, and they drove off."

"What girl?"

"Arline Kane. I met her a month ago at a hairdressing parlor in the city. She said she was an actress, and marveled at my hair. She said I ought to go on the stage. She took me to lunch, and then promised to introduce me to some theatrical men. She was going with a man named Devore. I met him several times, and then the other night we went to the Blue River and there was another fellow— for me. Mr. Manola. I—I didn't like him. He—he drank too much.

"When we drove away from the Blue River, he wanted to park on a dark road. But I didn't want him to. He was pretty drunk, and he wanted to make love to me. I fought him off, and then he turned to the others and said, 'I thought you said I'd find a good time.' And Mr. Devore said, 'Don't crab, Joe. Drive on.' And Mr. Manola said, 'Nothing doing. I've got a mind to make you all walk. Go on, get out, all of you.' Well, he meant it, and he was pretty angry, too. And Mr. Devore got angry. They began swearing. Then Mr. Manola said, 'You *will* get out, all of you!' And he drew his gun. But Mr. Devore, who was sitting in the back, jumped on him, and the gun went off, but it was twisted around so that the bullet struck Mr. Manola.

"He screamed, and then he shouted, 'I'll wreck all of you!' He seemed crazy, and threw into gear, and the car started. Then Mr. Devore yelled, 'Jump! We'll have to jump!' And we all did. And the car gathered speed, and Mr. Manola must have fainted, because it swerved to right and left and then hit a tree.

"We fled through the woods, after I'd gone to the wreck to see if he was alive. But he wasn't. Then Mr. Devore told me to say nothing about what had happened. He threatened that if I did he'd wipe out my whole family. That's why I wouldn't tell you, dad. I've been terrible—a fool—a fool!"

"Yes, you have," agreed MacBride. "But did Devore and Manola talk about—well, business?"

Judith thought; then, "No. But I remember, at the Blue River, when Arline and I had come back to the table from the ladies' room, Mr. Devore was saying to Mr. Manola, 'And they think hooch is being made there! A good blind!' And then he laughed."

MacBride stepped back, stroking his jaw. Judith threw Kerr an embarrassed look, but he came to her and took her hand. "It's all right, Judith. I'm awfully glad you're safe."

"I've been awful, Ted. And yet you're so kind." Feeling his arm about her, she laid her head on his shoulder. "I'll never—never do it again, Ted—never."

MacBride clipped suddenly, "Ted, I've got a hunch. That brewery. I wonder if something besides beer and hooch is being made there."

Kerr looked up from Judith. "What do you mean?"

"I don't know. But I'm going to find out. Come on."

Leaving Judith, Kerr flicked her cheek with his lips, and she pressed his hand.

But MacBride was calling him, and he hurried out at the captain's heels. They strode back to the station, and MacBride hauled out Donnegan and the police car.

"Drive to that old brewery," he clipped. He sat back beside Kerr and lit a fresh cigar. Kerr said, "I thought the orders were to lay off that place?"

"I said I'd lay off if they were busting the Volstead Act. But I've got a hunch something else is going on there."

"What, Cap?"

"That's what I'm going to find out. Shoot, Donnegan!"

Donnegan nodded, and as the car moved away from the curb, there were running feet on the sidewalk, and a moment later Kennedy was riding on the running-board.

"Mind if I tag along, Mac?" he grinned.

"You're like a burr in a man's sock, Kennedy. But get in beside Donnegan."

"What's the lay, Mac?"

"Stick around and see if you can find out. Here's a cigar. See if that'll keep your jaw shut."

"Thanks, Mac. Only I'm sore as hell that you didn't tell me beforehand it was Devore you had. Cripes, won't they hand you the razzberry! I shot the story right in. I said you were sitting with Devore alone in your office, with the automatic lying on the desk. You were trying to make him swear it was his gun, and in the heat of the argument Devore grabbed it and covered you. I had to make up a lot of fiction, but that was because you didn't explain. I ended up by saying that you were sure you'd recapture him, and all that sort of boloney."

"That's as good as anything," muttered MacBride. "Now jam that cheroot in your mouth and sign off."

Twenty minutes later they were driving along Farmingville Turnpike. The night was dark, and within the past ten minutes a chill Autumn drizzle had started, the kind of drizzle that is half rain and half mist—penetrating and clammy. The rubber tires hissed sibilantly on the wet macadam, and the beams of the headlights were reflected back from the gray vapor.

Presently Donnegan slowed down and swung in close to the side of the road, extinguished the lights.

"Can't you drive into the bushes?" asked MacBride. "We ought to get the car off the road and out of sight."

Donnegan tried this and succeeded. Then they all got out and stood in a group.

MacBride said, "We'll walk up. There's a lane a hundred yards on, leading into the brewery, which is a quarter of a mile off the Turnpike. You," he said to Kennedy, "better stay out of this."

"Try and do it, Mac. I didn't come out here to pick wildflowers."

MacBride growled, turned and plowed through the bushes. The others followed, and in short time they reached the lane. It led through vacant fields, fenced in, where in the old days horses belonging to the brewing company had grazed.

"Here comes a machine!" warned Kerr, and they dived into the tall grass by the fence.

Two beams of light danced through the gloom. The machine was bound in from the Turnpike, and presently it purred by—a big, opulent limousine. When its tail-light had disappeared behind a bend, MacBride stood up, motioned to the others, and proceeded. The visor on his cap was beaded with the drizzle.

Gradually the buildings loomed against the blue-black sky—the big main plant, surrounded by stables and storehouses. Not a light could be seen. They reached the first outbuilding, and from where he stood MacBride could see a half-dozen automobiles parked near the main building, by the loading platform. Here and there he saw a faint red glow near the machines.

"Chauffeurs, smoking," he decided, and his gaze wandered up the dark face of the big three-storied building, which an ancient brewing company had evacuated three years ago.

"Something phony going on there, or I don't know my tricks," remarked Kennedy.

"Guess this is the time you do," replied MacBride. "Let's work around to the rear."

They retraced their steps a short distance and then began creeping around the outside of the building, weaving through tall grass and dried-out weeds. Ten minutes later they were at the off-side of the main building, deep in shadows. MacBride found a window with broken panes, nodded to the others, and crawled through. He dropped a few feet into a chill, damp cellar, black as pitch; stood waiting while Kerr, Kennedy and then Donnegan, followed.

"Your flash, Donnegan," he whispered, and felt the cylinder pressed into his hand.

He snapped on the light. The beam leaped through the clammy gloom, shone on stacks of dusty kegs, long out of use, and on stacks of bottles musty with cobwebs. The odor of must and mold seeped into the men's nostrils.

MacBride led the way, winding in and out between the rows of barrels. Further on he came to a small, heavy door which, swinging open under his hand, led into another section of the cellar. Here were more barrels, but they were standing upright, and the smell of new wine was prevalent. Barrels of it. Kennedy licked his lips, then pointed ahead.

The beam of light swung back and forth across stacked cases of liquor. The men crept closer.

"Hot diggity!" whispered Kennedy. "Look at the Dewar's, and the Sandy MacDonald. And—say!... Three Star Hennessy!"

"Pipe down!" snapped MacBride under his breath.

"Maybe you got a bum steer after all, Mac. If it's only liquor, and you dragged me all the way out here—"

"Nobody dragged you out here, Kennedy! Quit yapping!"

"I know, but—"

Bang! Bang!

Kerr tensed and his breath shot out with—"What's that?"

Bang! Bang!

MacBride had his gun out, his lips pursed, his eyes looking up toward the unseen regions above.

"One thing," he muttered. "It's not just target practice. Come on!"

Chapter X

FOUR shots, muffled by floors and walls but, nevertheless, somewhere in that building.

MacBride, with his flash sweeping around furiously, finally located a staircase that led up to the ground floor. At his heels came Kerr, trailed closely by Donnegan and Kennedy. MacBride paused to get his bearings.

Another shot rang out, echoes trailing, commingled with the sounds of banging doors and the shouts of men.

"This way!" clipped MacBride, espying another stairway.

He ascended two steps at a time, reached the next landing. He looked up into the gloom above just in time to see a slash of gunfire rip through the darkness. In the sudden flare he saw a man with hands upthrown. Then there was a thumping sound, as the man fell.

MacBride's flash was out. His lips were set. He whispered to his men, "Watch it, boys! This place is a death trap! Stick close!"

A sudden exchange of shots burst out on the floor above, and the rebound of bullets could be heard intermingled with screaming oaths and pounding feet. Then, nearby, MacBride heard a body hurtling down the stairs. He jumped in that direction, caught a man in the act of scrambling to his feet. Heaving up, the man struck out and the barrel of a revolver whanged by MacBride's cheek and stopped against his shoulder.

MacBride struck back with his own thirty-eight and landed it on the stranger's skull. Then Donnegan was there to help him, gripping the man's arms from behind. They dragged him down the hall, felt their way into a room, and then MacBride snapped on his flash and looked at their catch.

It was the bull-necked red-head whom he had seen in Devore's hideout in Jockey Street. The man was streaked with blood.

"What the hell are you doing here?" MacBride wanted to know.

"Playin' Santy Claus—"

"Cut out the wisecracks! What's going on upstairs?"

"Go up an' find out. Go on. Slugs are sailin' around up there like flies in the summer time."

"I'll tend to you later," bit off MacBride; and to Donnegan, "Get out your bracelets and clamp him to the water pipe on the wall."

This done, MacBride again led the way back up the hall. As they reached the foot of the staircase leading to the floor, they partly heard, vaguely saw, a knot of men milling down the steps.

MacBride squared off and pressed on his flash.

"Good cripes almighty!" exploded one of the men.

"As you are!" barked MacBride.

The man in the lead was carrying a canvas bag. The man was Chuck Devore, and behind him were six others. One of these snapped up his gun and fired. The shot smashed MacBride's flashlight, tore through his left hand that held it. He cursed and reeled sidewise, and Kerr's gun boomed close by his ear, and the slug ripped through the gang on the stair.

"Back up!" one of them called to his companions.

MacBride thrust his wounded hand into his pocket and fired at them.

"Come on!" he snapped, and leaped up the staircase.

Kerr passed him on the way up, and let fly with three fast shots. A gangster crumpled near the top, spun around and came crashing down. He reeled off MacBride and pitched over the railing. At the top, a gun spat and a bullet grazed Kerr's cheek, leaving a hot sting. Then they were on the top floor.

In a close exchange of shots Kennedy gasped and clutched at his left arm, and Donnegan stopped short, his legs sagging. His gun dropped from his hand and he crumpled. MacBride stumbled over him and sprayed the gloom with three shots. A man screamed and another flung out a bitter stream of oaths that died in a groan. Mac-Bride plugged ahead, reeling over prone bodies, himself dazed with the pain of his wounded arm.

He saw a square of the night sky framed in a window, saw it blocked suddenly by a figure that stepped out to a fire-escape. The figure twisted and a slash of gunfire stabbed the darkness. MacBride's cap was carried from his head. His own gun belched and the man in the window doubled over and fell back into the hall.

Then he brought up short, looked out and saw, vaguely, a couple of automobiles tearing away into the night. He spun around, expecting another enemy, but a dread pall had descended after that last shot. Kerr limped up to him, panting. Kennedy was swearing softly. Mac-Bride snapped on his own flash and saw them, bloody and torn; Kerr with a gash on his cheek, Kennedy slowly sopping a wound in his arm. The beam picked out dead bodies on the floor. He swayed back and bent over Donnegan, then stood up, wagging his head.

"I'll never say, 'Shoot, Donnegan,' again," he muttered.

His light swung around and settled on the man he had shot by the window. It was Devore, still gripping the canvas bag. MacBride bent down and opened the bag, and saw a mass of bills—fives, tens, twenties. He gave the bag to Kerr, and moved on toward a door. He threw his light in here and saw a large, square room whose expensive furnishings were in ruin. He espied a light switch and pressed the button, and a big chandelier sprang to life.

"Hot diggity!" exclaimed Kennedy.

Dead men were here, too. But what had caused Kennedy's exclamation was the gambling layout. There was a roulette wheel. There was a faro table. There were a half dozen card tables, two of them overturned. There were cards and chips spread over the floor. The windows were covered by heavy curtains, and ventilators were in the ceiling.

"My hunch was right," nodded MacBride, bitterly.

"And look who's here!" cried Kennedy. "Duke Manola—dead as a doornail. And—oh, boy!—the late Judge Mike Haggerty—*late* is right. Where," he yelled, looking around, "oh, where is a telephone? What a scoop!"

There was a shot below, and MacBride whirled. He dived out into the hall, with Kerr at his heels, and went down the stairway on the fly. His flash leaped forth and spotted two figures running for the lower staircase.

"Stop!" he shouted.

His answer was a shot that went wild. But MacBride fired as he ran, and saw one of the figures topple. He kept going, furiously, and collided with the other.

"All right, Cap. You've got me."

His flash shone on the face of a woman.

The man lying dead on the floor was the red-head.

Chapter XI

"**W**ELL," said MacBride, "who are you?"

"Arline Kane, and what about it?"

"No lip, sister. What are you doing here?"

She laughed—a hard little laugh. "Came in to look around. I heard the fireworks from the road. I found Red tied to a pipe and I shot away the nice little bracelet."

"You come upstairs," directed MacBride, and shoved her toward the staircase.

Once in the hidden gambling den, Arline stood with her hands on her hips and looked around with lazy eyes.

"Hell," she said, "what a fine mess. Real wild West stuff. Jesse James and his boy scouts were pikers alongside these playboys. Well, there's Duke, the bum. Good thing."

"What do you mean?" asked MacBride.

She sat down and lit a cigarette. "Don't know, eh? Well, Duke used to be my boy friend, until he got hot over a little flapper not dry behind the ears yet. Gave me my walking papers. That was after he tried to frame Chuck Devore, and Chuck breezed for a while. But when Chuck came back, I looked him up and we consolidated our grudge against the wop.

"We got one good break. Duke and his kid brother were on the outs. The kid wanted more money, but Duke was nobody's fool. He told Joe where he got off. I understand they actually came to blows. Well, it was about that time I met Joe, and like a kid he handed me his sob story about Duke landing on him.

"I got him tight one night and he sprung his tongue for a fare-ye-well. Told me about Duke buying this brewery to make and store booze. But some politicians, and Diamond Jack Winslow—laying there, with the busted neck— were behind him. Diamond Jack installed the games here and Haggerty was to get a thirty percent split from Jack on the house winnings. Duke had some money in it, but he was mainly for the booze end. Haggerty promised protection, and Duke, in payment, promised three thousand votes for Haggerty's party.

"Well, Duke's kid brother was hard up for money, and Duke would never let him run with the gang. So Chuck and I got the kid one night and put it up to him: He could clean up by raiding this dump, by tipping us off when the games were running high. Then the other night, he got drunk and sore and—"

"Pulled a bone," put in MacBride, "on Old Stone Road. I know all about that. And then tonight Devore and his rats thought they'd pull a fast one—do what we'd least expect after their first fumble—jump this joint and clean out before we'd caught our breath. Well, they would have fooled me, sister. I *didn't* expect them. I came here on a hunch to look around, and found fireworks. And you—you're the last one."

"Out of luck again," she nodded.

"You could make some money," put in Kennedy, "writing a series of articles for the *Evening News* on 'How I Went Wrong.'"

"You would say that, ink ringers," she gave him, derisively. "But I'll do no writing. And because I'm the last straggler, I'll take no rap." She bit off the end of her cigarette and flung the other part away with a defiant gesture. "A pill was in the tip. Always carried one for just a tough break like this." Her eyes were glazed. "Not lilies, boys… something red… roses."

A DAY later MacBride sat at his desk in the station, his cap tipped back, one eye squinted against the smoke from his cigar while he read the *Free Press'* account of last night's holocaust. Sometimes he wagged his head, amazed at remarks which he was alleged to have made.

The city was shocked to the core. Election possibilities had turned more than one somersault during the past twelve hours. Big officials were making charges and counter charges. And MacBride, with his hunch, was mainly responsible for it.

He looked up to see Kennedy standing in the doorway. He put down the paper and leaned back. Kennedy's arm, like his own, was in a sling.

"Greetings, Mac. No end of greetings." He wandered in and slid down on a chair. "How do you like the write-up I gave you?"

"You're a great liar, Kennedy."

"Well, hell, I had to make up a lot of goofy stuff, sure. What's the biggest lie, Mac?"

"Where the account says, 'Captain MacBride, having received a tip from an unidentified person, probably a stoolie, that a certain gang was planning to raid the near-beer plant on Farmingville Turnpike last night, immediately drove out to forestall any such attempt.'" He jabbed the paper with a rigid forefinger. "That's the part, Kennedy."

Kennedy shrugged. "Yeah, you're right. When I got back to the office and wrote the thing up, I wondered how you *had* got the tip. Well, I was in a hurry, so I wrote in that—just that. It sounded all right, fitted all right—and look here, Mac. It just about cinches any chance of the big guns bawling you out. You were tipped off by a stoolie—a phone call—no name. You shot out there and the raid was under way. What developed later was not your fault. It's air tight!"

MacBride creaked his chair forward, sighed, and drew a bottle and glasses from his desk. He set them down.

"Have a drink, Kennedy."

Kennedy edged nearer the desk and, arching a weary eyebrow, poured himself a stiff three fingers. MacBride poured himself a drink, and leaned back with it.

"Kennedy," he said, "there have been times when I ached to wring your neck. You're a cynical, cold-blooded, snooping, wisecracking example of modern newspaperdom. But, Kennedy, you've got brains— and you're on the square. Here's to you."

Kennedy grinned in his world-weary way. "Boloney, Mac. No matter how you slice it, it's still boloney," he said.

The Law Laughs Last

Captain MacBride and organized crime have a showdown.

Chapter I

A **TOUGH** precinct was the Second of Richmond City, lying in the backyard of the theatrical district and on the frontier of the railroad yards.

A hard-boiled precinct, touching the fringe of crookdom's elite on the north—the con men, the nightclub barons; and on the south, the dim-lit, crooked alleys traversed by the bum, the lush-worker and poolroom gangster. On the north were the playhouses, the white way, high-toned apartments, opulent hotels, high hats, evening gowns. On the south, tenements, warehouses, cobblestones, squalor, and the railroad yards. The toughest precinct in all Richmond City.

Captain MacBride, back again in the Second, ran it with two fists, a dry sense of humor and a generous quantity of brass-bound nerve. He was a lean, windy-eyed man of forty. He had a wife and an eighteen-year-old daughter in a vine-clad bungalow out in suburban Grove Manor, and having acquired early in life a suspicion that he was going to die young and violently in line of duty, he had forthwith taken out a lot of life insurance. He was not a pessimist, but a hard-headed materialist, and he rated crooks and gunmen with a certain species of rodent that travels by dark and frequents cellars, sewers and garbage dumps.

He was sitting in his office at the station house a mild spring night, going over a sheaf of police bulletins, when Kennedy, of the *Free Press,* strolled in.

"Spring has come, Mac," Kennedy yawned.

"Why don't you set it to poetry?"

"I got over that years ago." He drifted over to the desk, helped himself to a cigar from an open box, sniffed it critically. "Dry," he muttered.

"I like 'em dry."

"I always keep mine moist."

MacBride chuckled. "That's rich! First time I see you smoking a cigar of your own I'll buy you a box of Monterey's. Well, what's on your mind?"

Kennedy looked toward the open window through which came the blare and beat of a jazz band muffled by distance.

"That," he said.

MacBride nodded. "I thought so. I'll bet if something doesn't bust loose over there you'll get down-hearted."

Kennedy shrugged, sank wearily to a chair and lit up. "And I'll bet you're happy as hell they're staging that political block-party. You look it, Mac."

"Don't I!" muttered MacBride, a curl to his lip. "Yes, Kennedy, I'm happy as a school kid when vacation time comes. Of all the dumb stunts I can think of, this block-party takes the cake. If this night passes without somebody getting bumped off, I'll get pie-eyed drunk and take a calling-down from my wife. A political campaign in Richmond City makes a Central American rebellion look comical."

"And how!" grinned Kennedy. "But I only hope Krug and Bedell get kicked out of office so hard they'll never get over it. As State's Attorney, Krug's made a fortune, and Alderman Johnny Bedell's his right-hand man. I'm all for Anderson for State's Attorney and Connaught for alderman of this district. They're square. But I wouldn't be willing to bet on the outcome. The Mayor and his crowd are behind Krug.

"And here's the nigger in the woodpile. Connaught and Anderson are square men. They deserve to get in office. But there's a gang in this city that's taken it into their own hands to make things hot as hell for Krug and Bedell, and by doing this they're going to cramp the Anderson-Connaught square style. Connaught and Anderson don't want their support, but they've got to take it—through the nose, too."

"Say who you mean, Kennedy," broke in MacBride. "Come on and tell me you mean Duveen and his guns."

"Sure—Duveen. Duveen hasn't got a good break since Krug's been State's Attorney. But who has? Simple. Bonelio, the S.A.'s friend. And Bonelio is sure tooting his horn for the Krug-Bedell ticket. If Anderson gets in for State's Attorney he'll put a wet blanket on Bonelio's racket; and if Anderson sweeps Connaught in with him, it'll mean

that Bonelio's warehouses this side of the railroad yards will be swept clean.

"And that's what Duveen wants, because he wants to run the bootleg racket in Richmond City, and so long as Bonelio has the present State's Attorney and the alderman for this district on his side, Duveen's blocked. What a hell of a riot this election is going to be!"

MacBride grunted, opened a drawer and pulled out a bottle of Three Star Hennessy.

"Have a drink, Kennedy," he said. "There are times when I'd like to kick you in the slats, but I admire your brains and the way you get the lowdown on things."

Through the window came another burst of dance music. On Jackson Street couples were dancing, political banners were flying, ropes of colored lights were glowing. And policemen were on the walkout, idly swinging nightsticks, watching, waiting, prepared for the worst and hoping for the best.

MacBride lit a cigar and looked up to find Detective Moriarity standing in the doorway.

" 'Lo, Cap. 'Lo, Kennedy." Moriarity was a slim, compactly built young man, short on speech, quick in action—one-time runner-up for the welterweight title.

"How do things look?" asked MacBride.

"Depends," said Moriarity. "Committeeman Shanz is a little tight. Bedell ain't there yet. Shanz expects him, though. Says Bedell's s'posed to speak at eleven."

"See any bums?"

"No. But pipe this. I just been tipped off that a crowd of Anderson-Connaught sympathizers from the Fourth Ward are making a tour of the town. About ten machines. Band and flags and all that crap. I figure this way. Ten to one all o' them have got some booze along, to make 'em feel better. They're mostly storekeepers and automobile dealers, but if they get tight they'll get gay. Like as not they'll wind up at the block-party and some wiseguy will haul off and talk outta turn."

MacBride doubled his fist and took a crack at the desk. "Just about that, Jake! All right. Get back on the job. Cohen with you?"

"Yeah, Ike's over there. Patrolmen Gunther and Holstein at one end the street. McClusky and Swanson the other. Things are running smooth so far. Don't see any o' Duveen's guns, or Bonelio's."

"That," said MacBride, "is what itches me. Bonelio ought to be there. He's Shanz's friend."

"He's not there. None of his guns, either. Tell you who is there, though, Cap."

"Who?"

"Bonelio's skirt. That little wren he yanked from the burlesque circuit and shoved in his ritzy nightclub on Paradise Street. Trixie Meloy. Ask me and I'll crack she still oughter be back in burlesque, and third rate at that."

"Who's she with?"

"Alone. High-hatting everybody. But she sticks close to Shanz."

"I got it!" clipped MacBride. "She's waiting for somebody, for Bonelio. Watch her, Jake. It's ten-thirty now. Bonelio should have been on hand long ago. He shows up at all of the district's balls and dances. Until he comes anything can happen. Tell the cops to keep their eyes open. Tell Cohen to tend to business and quit trying to date up the gals. I know Ike. On the way out tell the sergeant to see the reserves are ready for a break. First time you pipe a Duveen gun on the scene, run him off. If he cracks wise, bring him over here.

"Remember, Jake, this precinct is just about as safe as a volcano. We've heard rumblings for the past month, and God knows when the top'll blow off. It's a tough situation. I'm all for the Anderson-Connaught ticket, as you know, but no rat like Duveen is going to get away with anything. He doesn't give a damn for the Anderson-Connaught combine. He's sore at the present State's Attorney and the grease-ball Bonelio. Both of them ought to be in the pen, and before this election is over I've got a hunch one of them will be—if he doesn't get bumped off during the rush. On your way, Jake, and good luck."

Moriarity went out.

Kennedy said, "I'm going over and look around, too, Mac."

"You smell headlines for tomorrow's *Press,* don't you?"

"Yeah—the city of dreadful night. Hell, man, we ain't had a good hot story since that Dutch butcher tapped his frau on the knob with a meat ax. Years ago, Mac, old bean!"

"Two weeks ago last night," mused MacBride. "Ah-r-r, when will this crime wave stop? Wives killing husbands; husbands killing wives! College kids going in for suicide and double death pacts! Men braining little kids! Men willing to kill to get power!"

"That," said Kennedy, pausing in the doorway, "is what keeps the circulation of the daily tabloids on top. See you later."

Alone, MacBride stared into space for a long moment, his eyes glazed with thought. Then he sighed bitterly, flung off the mood with a savage little gesture, and continued looking over the collection of police bulletins.

Fifteen minutes dragged by. The dusty-faced clock on the wall ticked them off with hollow monotony.

Then the telephone rang.

MacBride picked up the receiver, said, "Hel-lo."

"MacBride?"

"Yup."

"Bedell's slated to get the works tonight."

The instrument clicked.

"Hello—hello!" barked MacBride.

There was no use. The man behind the mysterious voice had hung up. MacBride rang the operator, gave his name.

"Trace that call," He snapped. "Fast!"

Chapter II

HE pressed one of a series of buttons on his desk. The door opened. Lieutenant Donnelly tramped in wiping the cobwebs of a recent nap from his eyes.

"On your toes, lieutenant!" cracked MacBride. "Just got a blind call that Bedell's going to get bumped off. You'll take charge here tonight while I'm on the outside."

The telephone rang. MacBride reached for it, said, "Yes?" A moment later he hung up, snorted with disappointment. "Call was from a booth in the railroad terminal."

"Who d'you suppose it was, captain?" ventured Donnelly.

"How the hell do I know?" MacBride was on his feet, buttoning his coat. He reached for his visored cap, but changed his mind and slapped on a flap-brimmed fedora.

"I'll be over on Jackson Street," he told Donnelly crisply. "Bedell's supposed to pull a campaign speech at eleven. I'll put the clamps on that. Bedell's no friend of mine, but I'm damned if any bum is going to kill him in my precinct. If Headquarters wants me, give 'em the dope and tell 'em where I am."

He strode into the central room and shot brief orders to the desk sergeant. Then he drafted four policemen from the reserve room. They came out buttoning their coats, nightsticks drawn. The lieutenant, the sergeant, the four policemen—all were affected by the vigor, the spirit with which MacBride dived into the middle of things. No captain liked more to get out in the raw and the rough of crime than MacBride. The crack of his voice, the snap of his movement, made him a man whom others were eager to follow. Hard he was, but with the hardness of a man supremely capable of command. He had turned down a Headquarters job on the grounds that it was too soft—that he would stagnate and grow old before his time, grow whiskers and a large waistband.

He led the way out of the station house. His step was firm and resolute, and he carried himself with a definite air of determination. One block west, and two south, and they were at Jackson Street.

The band was playing a fox trot. The block was roped off at either end, and a hundred couples were dancing on the street pavement. On the sidewalks and the short stone flights before the tenement were a hundred-odd onlookers. Strung from pole to pole were rows of colored electric lights. Banners were waving; posters showing likenesses of Alderman Bedell and State's Attorney Krug emblazoned the houses and the poles. A temporary bandstand had been erected in the middle of the block, and from this, too, the candidates for re-election were expected to speak.

MacBride looked the place over critically. Detective Ike Cohen left a couple of girls to join the captain.

"Something up, Cap?"

"Maybe. See any old familiar faces around?"

"None that'd interest you. Here comes Moriarity."

At sight of the captain Moriarity frowned quizzically. "Huh?" he asked.

MacBride explained about the telephone call. Gunther and Holstein, the patrolmen stationed at that end of the block, mingled with the four reserves, all wondering what was in the wind.

"Where's Committeeman Shanz?" MacBride asked.

"I'll get him," said Moriarity, and faded into the crowd.

He reappeared in company with Shanz, district committeeman and chairman of the night's carnival. Shanz was a German-Jew, though he had more of the beer-garden look about him. A short, rotund man, beefy-cheeked and spectacled, with a jovial grin that was only skin deep.

"Well, well, captain," he boomed, waddling forward with his hand extended, "this is a pleasure."

MacBride shook and said, "Not so much, Shanz. You've got to bust up this picnic."

Shanz's grin faded. "How's this?"

"The ball is over," explained MacBride. "There's trouble brewing and it's liable to boil over any minute."

"But I got to make a speech," argued Shanz. "And Alderman Bedell is due here now." He looked at his watch. "He's going to make a speech, too."

"I don't give a damn! You're not going to broadcast and neither is Bedell. I tell you, Shanz, this block-party scheme is the bunk. It's the best way I know of to start a riot."

"Do you say that, heh, because you favor the opposition? Ha, I know where your sympathy lays, captain!"

"Don't be a fool! I just got a tip that Bedell's set to get bumped off, and it's not going to happen in my precinct."

Shanz leaned back and threw out his chest. "What is the police for? What are you for?"

"I've got a hunch I'm supposed to side-track crime. I'm no master mind, Shanz. I don't go in for solving riddles. I'm just a cop who tries to beat crime to the tape. Now don't stick out your belly and hand me an argument. I'm not in the mood."

Shanz was troubled. "I can't stop it. If I do that and Bedell can't make his speech he'll land on me. Wait till he comes. Talk to him. But I ain't going to call it off. We staged this so Bedell could make a speech."

MacBride, impatient, cracked fist into palm. "Cripes, I want to clear this crowd out before Bedell gets here! I told you he's not going to make a speech. I won't let him."

The dance number stopped. But from the distance came the sound of another band, with brass and drums in the majority. It drew nearer with the minutes, and then a string of cars appeared, flaunting banners that exalted the virtues of the Anderson-Connaught combine. Colored torches smoked from every machine, and the roving campaigners cheered their candidates lustily.

"What in hell is this?" roared Shanz, reddening.

"Competition," said MacBride.

The automobiles stopped, and the brass band attained new heights of noise commingled with the singing voices of the men. The carnival orchestra, not to be outdone, burst into action, hammering out a military march. The result was boisterous, maddening, and everybody began yelling.

The first symptoms of mob hysteria were apparent.

MacBride snapped quick orders to the policemen. "Chase this crowd! The dance is over!"

He pivoted sharply, set his jaw and plowed through the crowd on a beeline for the leaders of the parade.

"You move on!" he barked. "Come on, no stalling. Get out of here, and I mean now!"

"Aw, go fly a kite," came a bibulous retort. "Everybody havin' helluva good time. Who's all right? Hiram Anderson, the next State's At-torney's all right! Y-e-e-e-e!"

Others took up the cry. Somebody flung a bottle and it crashed against a house front, the glass spattering.

"Dammit," yelled MacBride, "you're starting a riot! Get a move on!"

One of the cars started moving. Others honked their horns. Many of the occupants had piled out and several of them, far gone with walloping liquor, hilarious as sailors on a spree, were trying to tear down the banners of the Krug-Bedell faction. The supporters of Alderman Bedell objected strenuously, and fists began flying about promiscuously. It was, now, anybody's and everybody's carnival. Admission fees were waived. The two bands continued to add to the din and clamor. The tempo of their combined efforts went far toward heightening the strain of hysteria that had taken hold of the mob. The streets were jammed with motor cars, and the horns honked and bleated.

Women screeched, and men began striking out without apparent provocation. The crowd surged this way and that, but never got anywhere. Nightsticks rapped more frequently on stubborn heads. Somebody heaved a brick that crashed through an automobile windshield and knocked the man at the wheel unconscious. The machine swerved, bounded and banged head-on into a doorway.

"Good God Almighty!" groaned MacBride.

He plunged through the mob, fought, pounded, hammered his way to the big touring car that carried the musicians. He leaped to the running-board, wrenched a trombone from the player's hand.

"Stop it!" he yelled. "I'll cave in the next mouth that pulls another toot!"

He silenced them.

He turned and weaved toward the bandstand, and on the way ran into Alderman Bedell.

"Who started this, MacBride? What is it? What's going on?"

"What the hell does it look like, a May party?"

"Don't get sore—don't get sore!"

"Listen to me, Bedell!" MacBride gripped his arm hard. "You're no friend of mine, but I'm giving you a tip. Get out of here! Jump in your car, go home and lock all the doors. Some pup is out to get you!"

"He is, eh?" snarled Bedell, a big whale of a man with gimlet eyes. "Let him!"

"Don't be a blockhead all your life! I tell you, man, you're in danger!" A whiff of Bedell's breath told him the man had been drinking. Drink always made Bedell cocky, and he spoke best from a platform when he was moderately soaked.

"I'm going to d'liver a speech here tonight, MacBride—"

MacBride snorted with disgust and went on his way. He reached the bandstand and ripped the baton from the leader's hand. He kicked over the drum and shot out short, sizzling commands. He left a silenced bandstand.

The policemen had managed to club into submission the instigators of the riot. Swollen heads, black eyes and bruised jaws were in abundance. The best argument in a riot is a deftly wielded nightstick. A clout on the head is something a temporarily crazed man will understand.

The hysteria was dwindling. A dozen of the rioters were hastily escorted away from the scene by four policemen and taken to the station house. The crowd quieted, took a long breath generally, and waited.

MacBride climbed back upon the bandstand, rumbled the drum in plea for silence, and then raised his voice.

"Please, now, everybody go home!" he demanded. "The party is over. It's too bad, but nothing can be done." He waved his arms. "Clear out, everybody—now!"

A figure bulked at his elbow. It was that of Alderman Bedell, and before MacBride could get a word in edgewise, Bedell roared, "La-dies and gentlemen, it grieves me to see this sociable gathering break up because of the undignified actions of the hirelings—yes, hirelings, I say—of the party which is trying to drive me out of office. As alderman of this district, I want to say—I... ugh!"

He clapped a hand to his chest, swayed, then crumpled heavily at MacBride's feet.

"Heart attack," cried someone in the crowd.

MacBride knelt down, turned the alderman over, felt his chest, ran his hand inside the shirt. It came out stained with blood. Bedell twitched, stiffened, and was dead.

Kennedy said over MacBride's shoulder, "Headlines, Mac, in the first edition. Hot diggity damn!"

Chapter III

AN hour later MacBride stood spread-legged in his office at the station house. His coat was unbuttoned, his hair was tousled, and his lean cheeks looked a little drawn.

Among the others present were Committeeman Shanz, Trixie Meloy, Moriarity and Cohen, and the inevitable Kennedy. No one had been apprehended. No shot had been heard. Obviously a silencer had been used on the gun that sent Bedell to his death. Bedell's body was at the morgue being probed by the deputy medical examiner.

"Now look here, Miss Meloy," MacBride said. "You say you were standing on Jackson Street near Holly. You saw a man wearing a light gray suit and a gray cap drift down Holly, get into a car and drive off when Bedell was shot. Why didn't you yell out?"

"Does a lady go shoutin' out like that?" she retorted, tossing her peroxide bob. "Besides I didn't know what it was all about. I didn't know he was shot. I thought he fainted or something. I didn't connect the two up until I heard you yell he was killed. Then I thought of the other man."

"In that case, how does it happen you remember what he wore?"

"Well, I got an eye for nice clothes. He was dressed swell, that's why. A woman notices clothes more than a man does."

"Remember the car?"

"Not so good. It wasn't so near. It looked like a roadster."

"How about the man—besides his clothes?"

"I didn't see his face—only his back as he was walkin' away."

"I see. You're a friend of Tony Bonelio's, aren't you?"

"Yes. Antonio's a good friend of mine."

"My mistake. Antonio." He smiled drily. "How come Antonio wasn't at the dance with you?"

"He was at his nightclub. I never seen a block party, so I come down to look it over. Mr. Shanz here invited me. He's a friend of Antonio's."

"Yes, that's right," put in Shanz.

"And listen," said Trixie, looking at her strap-watch. "I got to dance at the Palmetto Club tonight."

"All right, Miss Meloy. You run along. Keep in mind, though, that I may want to ask you more questions."

Shanz stood up. "I'll take Miss Meloy to the club in my car," he said.

"Suit yourself," shrugged MacBride. "Maybe this'll be a lesson to you about block parties."

"It cooks the Anderson-Connaught goose, too, captain," replied Shanz. "Connaught's a guy preaches a lot and then goes and hires gunmen."

"Careful how you talk," warned MacBride. "If it was a gunman of Connaught's I'll nail him. But I've got a hunch it wasn't."

"Then who was it?"

"If I could answer that right now, d'you think I'd be losing a night's sleep?"

"See you get him, anyhow. There's lots o' captains want this job here."

"That's my worry, Shanz, not yours."

"Well, I'm just telling you, see you get him."

"See you mind your own business, too."

Shanz and Trixie Meloy went out.

MacBride opened his desk and passed around the Hennessy. He downed a stiff bracer himself and lit a fresh cigar.

"Cripes," he chuckled grimly, "this'll mean one awful jolt to Connaught. It'll be hard to believe that the guy got Bedell wasn't on Connaught's payroll."

"If," said Moriarity, "we only knew who the guy was sent in that tip you got."

"That's the hitch, Jake," nodded MacBride. "The guy who called up is the key to who killed Bedell."

There was a knock on the door, and Officer Holstein looked in.

"Say, Cap, there's a Polack out here wants to see you. He lives on Jackson Street."

At a nod from MacBride, an old man came in, fumbling with his hat.

"Hello," said the captain. "What's your name?"

"Ma name Tikorsky. I got somet'in' to tell. See, I live number t'ree-twent'-one Jackson, up de top floor. I look out de window, watch de show, see. When de big feller drop down, I hear"—he looked up at the ceiling—"I hear noise on de roof, like a man run, see."

MacBride jerked up. "You heard a man run across the roof?"

Tikorsky nodded.

"Is there a fire-escape back of where you live?"

"Yeah, sure."

MacBride reached for the phone, called the morgue. In a moment he was speaking with the deputy medical examiner. When he hung up he pursed his lips, and his eyes glittered.

"All right, Mr. Tikorsky," he said. "You can go home. Thanks for telling me. I'll see you again."

The Pole shuffled out.

MacBride looked at Kennedy. "Out, Kennedy. Go home and hit the hay."

"Ah, Mac, give a guy a break," said Kennedy. "What's in the wind?"

"A bad smell. Come on, breeze, now. When there's any news getting out, I'll let you know."

Kennedy got up, shrugged, and sauntered out.

Moriarity and Cohen regarded the captain expectantly.

MacBride said, "I just got the doctor's report. The bullet was a thirty-eight. It hit Bedell in the chest, knocked off part of his heart and lodged in his spine. But get this. The angle of the bullet was on a slant. It went in and *down*."

"Then," said Cohen, "it couldn't have been fired from the corner where the broad saw this guy she was beefin' about."

"No," clipped MacBride. "The Polack was right. He heard a guy on the roof. That guy who was on the roof bumped off Bedell."

"What about this guy in the gray suit?"

"I'm wondering. But we know he couldn't have done it. A bullet from him would have gone up and hit Bedell on the left somewhere." He tapped his foot on the floor. "Well, the show is on, boys. Bonelio, the late alderman's buddy, has a whale of an excuse to oil his guns and start a war of his own. And Krug, the State's Attorney, will give him protection. Bonelio will suspect the same guy we do."

"Duveen," said Moriarity.

"Exactly. I know just what the greaseball will do."

"Let him," suggested Cohen, with a yawn. "Let the two gangs fight it out, exterminate each other. Who the hell cares?"

MacBride banged the desk. "You would say that, Ike. But I'm responsible for this precinct. I've got one murder hanging over my head as it is. Personally, I wouldn't care if these two gangs did mop each other up. But in a gang war a lot of neutrals always get hurt." He put on his hat. "Let's look over the Polack's roof."

The three of them went around to 321 Jackson Street, located the rooms where the old Pole lived, and then ascended to the roof. Moriarity had a flashlight. They discovered nothing to which they might attach some relative importance. They took the fire-escape down to a paved alley that paralleled the back of the row of houses and led to Holly Street.

"See here, boys," MacBride said. "Wander around and get the lowdown on Duveen's gang. If you see Duveen, cross-examine him. Better yet, tell him I want to see him."

The two detectives moved off. MacBride headed back for the station-house and requisitioned the precinct flivver. A man named Garret was his chauffeur. After brief instructions on MacBride's part, they drove off.

Twenty minutes later they stopped on Paradise Street, uptown. It was a thoroughfare of old brownstone houses that, following the slow encroachment of the white lights, had been turned into tearooms, night-clubs and small apartments, patronized mostly by people of the theatre.

Garret remained with the flivver. MacBride entered the Palmetto Club, to which an interior decorator had tried his best to give a tropical air. The manager did not know him, and said so.

"That's all right," said MacBride. "I don't want to see you, anyhow. Where's Bonelio?"

A moment later he met Bonelio in a private room handsomely furnished. Bonelio was a chunky Italian of medium height, dressed in the mode. He had smooth white skin, dark circles under his eyes, and an indolent gaze.

"Sit down, MacBride. Rye or Scotch?" he asked.

MacBride noticed a bottle of Golden Wedding. "Rye," he said.

"Ditto." Bonelio poured the drinks, said, "Well, poor Bedell."

"What I came here about."

They looked at each other as they downed their tots.

"About what?" Bonelio dropped on to a divan and lit a cigarette.

"Just this," said MacBride. "I'm banking on the hunch that you suspect who's behind the killing. I'm asking, and at the same time telling you, to keep out of it. We've never been friends, Bonelio, and don't get it into your nut that I'm making any overtures. But I don't want any rough work done in my precinct. I'll handle it according to the law. You just stand aside and keep your hands off. You get me?"

"Sure. But let me tell you, MacBride, that the first pup gets in my way or monkeys around my playground, I'll start trouble and I don't give a damn whose precinct it's in. I'm sitting on top of the world in Richmond City and no guy's going to horn in."

"I'm telling you, Bonelio, walk lightly in my precinct. I'm giving you fair warning. I'm putting on the lid and I'm locking up any guy that so much as disturbs the peace. That goes for you and your gang as well as anybody else. You can sell all the booze you want. Much as I dislike you, I've never bothered your rum warehouses down by the railroad yards—"

"You were told not to. The big guys are my friends."

"Don't take advantage of it. I could be nasty if I wanted to. And I will, if you butt in in my precinct."

"Here's hoping you get Duveen for the murder of Bedell."

"Make sure *you* don't try to!"

MacBride banged out, hopped into the flivver and Garret drove him back to the station-house.

Moriarity and Cohen were playing penny-ante, half-heartedly.

"What news?" asked MacBride.

"None," said Cohen. "Duveen hasn't been seen for the past week."

"Hasn't, eh? All right, we want him, then. Sergeant," he called to the man at the desk, "ring Headquarters. General alarm. Chuck Duveen wanted. Ask Headquarters to spread the news and start the net working. I want Duveen before"—his lips flattened—"before somebody else gets him."

Chapter IV

NEXT day the papers carried big headlines. The sheets that were in sympathy with the current administration bellowed loudly and asked the public to consider the drastic measures used by the opposition to gain its own end. The others, among them the *Free Press,* employed a calmer, more detached tone, and pleaded with justice to get at the root of all evil. Both Anderson and Connaught, aspirants for the offices of State's Attorney and alderman of the Sixth Election District respectively, deplored the tragedy and promised all manner of aid in running down the person or persons who had murdered their opponent, the late Alderman Bedell. State's Attorney Krug promised quick action in the event the criminal was apprehended. Charges and counter charges ran rampant.

MacBride, having gone home at three in the morning, did not get back on the job until noon. He felt rested and his clean-dipped face glowed ruddily from recent contact with lather and razor. He had read the papers on the way in from Grove Manor with the attitude of a man who knows the inner workings of politics and newspaperdom. In short, a slight morsel of what he read was worthwhile, and the rest was bunk—salve for an outraged public.

The one item that drew his attention was anent the fact that Adolph

Shanz was to run for alderman in place of the late Alderman Bedell. This made him chuckle bitterly. As committeeman Shanz had been, ever since he was elected, clay in the hands of Krug and Bedell. If elected for alderman, he would be one of Krug's most pliable tools.

The police net was spread for Duveen. The city was combed up, down and across. But the man was not caught. The only information available, gleaned as it was from old familiar hangouts of the gang boss, showed that Duveen had not been seen for a week. A day passed, and then two and three, with the man still at large.

Wherefore, on the fourth day, Captain MacBride was convened for a solid hour with the Commissioner of Police, a man who ran the Department and gave quarter nowhere. The meeting took place in the morning, and before noon MacBride was back in the station-house. There he held a brief consultation with his assistants.

In conclusion, he said to the sergeant at the desk, "When Kennedy, or any other of his breed drifts in, tell him I have a statement for the press."

Alone in his office, he drank his first bracer and started his first cigar of the day. He chafed his hands vigorously, paced the floor with a little more than his customary energy, trailing banners of excellent cigar smoke behind him. A beam of sunlight streamed through the open window. On the telephone wires that passed behind the old station-house, birds were swaying and chirping. MacBride's eyes were keen and narrow with thought.

An hour later, when he was writing at his desk, a knock sounded on the door.

"Come in," he yelled.

Kennedy came in. "What the hell's this I hear about—"

"Sit down. Glad to see something can work you up and make you look as if you weren't dying on your feet."

"Come on, spill it, Mac!"

"My wife's birthday."

"Cripes—"

"Should see the new spring outfit I bought her. Kennedy, she gets younger every day. Well"—he cleared his throat with a serio-comic air—"look who her husband is."

"For the love o' God, what's the matter, are you batty?"

MacBride grinned—one of his rare, broad grins that few people knew, outside of his wife and daughter.

"All right, Kennedy," he said. "I said I'd give you a break when I started broadcasting. I'm broadcasting. Tune in. Early this morning Detective Moriarity picked up a man for violating the state law regarding the possession of concealed weapons. This man was carrying an automatic pistol.

"He was cross-examined by Captain Stephen J. MacBride—don't omit the J. Intense questioning brought out certain interesting facts, in the light of which Captain MacBride hopes to apprehend—and don't insert 'it is alleged'—Captain MacBride hopes to apprehend the man who killed the late Alderman Bedell within the next twenty-four hours.

"For certain reasons known to the Department alone, the informant's name will not be divulged for the present. Suffice it to say that during the course of the cross-examination it was learned that this man was the one who phoned anonymously to Captain MacBride about one hour before Alderman Bedell was murdered, warning him that the murder was prearranged."

He rubbed his hands together. "How does that sound? Pretty good for a plain, ordinary cop, eh? And I never took a correspondence course, either."

"But who's this guy you picked up?" demanded Kennedy.

"You heard me, didn't you? He's under lock and key right here in the precinct. Put that in, too, Kennedy. He's locked up at the precinct. But who he is—that's my business for the time being. Headquarters is standing by me to the bitter end on that. Now pipe down and consider yourself lucky I've given you this much. Here, sink a drink under your belt and see that story gets good space."

Still curious, Kennedy, nevertheless, went out. Within the hour other reporters got the story. It would be on the streets at four that afternoon.

Moriarity dropped in, when MacBride was alone, and asked, "Think it will work, Cap?"

"Man, oh, man, I'm banking everything on it right now. It's a bluff—sure, a hell of a big bluff. And if it doesn't trap somebody or give me a decent lead I'll take the razz. Just now the underworld is stagnant, Jake. This will be the stone that stirs the water. We're supposed to have somebody here who knows who killed Bedell. Whoever killed him, will make a move. What that move will be, I don't know, but I'm ready to meet it."

Moriarity was frankly dubious. "Dunno, Cap. Maybe I'm short on imagination. You're taking a long chance giving out the news we got a mysterious somebody picked up and locked in."

"I'm willing to take it, Jake. It's a bluff—the biggest bluff I ever pulled in my life. Just play with me, Jake. Appear mysterious. All you've got to keep saying is that you picked a guy up—but no more. I've got all the keys to that cell and nobody, I don't care who he is, is going to see that it's empty."

"Gawd," muttered Moriarity, "I hope you don't get showed up."

"That's all right, Jake. Cut out worrying. Just play your part, and if the breaks go against us, I'll take the razz personally."

Moriarity wandered out, far from overjoyed.

At four the news spread. Quick work, mused many—an important prisoner in the hands of the police already, with the account of the murder still vivid in the city's mind. And the mysterious tone of it; that was intriguing, MacBride holding the man's name a secret.

MacBride read three different sheets.

The *Free Press* mentioned his name more than the others. That was Kennedy's work. Good sort, Kennedy, even though he did get on a man's nerves at times. Kennedy's column was well-written, concise, cool, almost laconic.

At four-thirty a big limousine pulled up before the station-house. State's Attorney Krug, a large, faultlessly groomed man, innately arrogant, strode into MacBride's office swinging his stick savagely.

"Look here, Captain," he rapped out, "what is the meaning of this? I refer to the late editions, and to this fellow Moriarity picked up."

"What does what mean?" MacBride wanted to know, unperturbed.

Krug struck the floor with his stick. "Why, as State's Attorney of this county, I think it is no more than pertinent that I should be informed of such important news before it comes out in the newspapers."

"Dark secret, Mr. Krug," said MacBride. "The Department's prisoner. When we get through with him, we'll turn him over to the State Attorney's office."

"But I should like to have a preliminary talk with the fellow, so that I may go about preparing briefs. I tell you, Captain, action is what is necessary."

"I agree with you. But as it is, Mr. Krug, the prisoner is still in the Department's hands."

"Nonsense! We can have just an informal little chat. I want to see the fellow. What is he called, by the way?"

MacBride shook his head. "The whole thing is a dark secret. When I spring it, everybody'll know."

"But dammit, man, I am State's Attorney! I demand to interview the prisoner!"

"I ought to add," put in MacBride, "that I have the backing of the Department. There's the phone if you care to call the Commissioner."

State's Attorney Krug departed in high heat, bewailing the fact that the Department was trying to double-cross the very efficient State's Attorney's office.

"You know why he's in such a hurry, Jake?" MacBride asked Moriarity.

"Sure. Stage a fast trial, get a quick conviction. It'd help him for re-election."

MacBride chuckled grimly. Moriarity drifted out, leaving the captain alone.

It was about half an hour later that the door swung open, and a tall, broad-shouldered man entered casually. He kicked the door shut with his heel, stood with his hands thrust into his coat pockets, a cigarette drooping from one corner of his mouth. His face was deeply bronzed, his eyes pale and hard as agate.

"My error," he said, "if I didn't knock. Thought I'd drop in and see why you've been looking for me."

"Sit down, Duveen."

"I'll stand."

MacBride leaned back in his chair. "Are you heeled?"

"No. Want to look?"

"I'll take your word. But you've got one hell of a lot of nerve to come in here."

"Open to the public, ain't it?" Duveen gushed smoke through his nostrils. "I want to know what's all this crap about you looking for me."

"Where have you been for the last ten days?"

"I don't see where that's any of your business. I was touring. I took a ride to Montreal. Get up on your dates, skipper. I've been gone two weeks. Scouting around for good liquor. Got two truckloads coming down for the election—and afterwards."

"Counting on Anderson and Connaught getting in?"

"Yup."

"Won't do you any good. Connaught's going to clean up this district, and you'll never be able to buy off Anderson."

"All I want is the bum Krug out. Well, you were looking for me. Here I am."

"About that Bedell killing."

"What about it?"

"You'll need a strong alibi to prove where you were on that night, Duveen."

"Talking of—arrest?"

"About that."

Duveen laughed. "Not a chance, MacBride. Krug would frame me so tight I'd never have a chance. Guess again."

"Nevertheless…" MacBride's hand moved toward the row of buttons on the desk.

Duveen snapped, *"Kid!"*

"Up high, Cap!" hissed a voice at the window.

MacBride swivelled. A rat-faced runt was leaning in through the open window, an automatic trained on the captain.

Duveen ran to the window, stepped out. There was an economy of words. With a leer, the rat-faced man disappeared.

MacBride yanked his gun, blew a whistle.

The reserves, Moriarity and Cohen came on the run. They swept out, guns drawn.

But the city swallowed Duveen and his gunman.

MacBride took the blow silently, choking down his chagrin.

"Did he wear a gray suit?" asked Moriarity.

"Yes," muttered MacBride. "Block all city exits, place men in the railroad station. Tell Headquarters to inform all outlying precincts and booths, motorcycle and patrol flivvers, Duveen's in town. What I can't understand is, why the hell he came strolling in here?"

"Crust, Cap. Duveen's got more gall, more nerve, than any bum I know of. Probably came looking for information."

"Yes, and I pulled a bone," confessed MacBride. "I should have played him a while, drawn him out. But seeing him here, I wanted to get the clamps on him right away. He had no gun—he's wise. But he had a gunman planted outside the window. If I can get him, get this Trixie Meloy gal to identify him as the man walked down Holly Street toward the roadster, we can crash his alibi. We know he couldn't have fired the shot, but it's likely one of his rats was planted on the roof, and Duveen was on hand to see things went off as per schedule."

An hour later the telephone rang.

"MacBride?"

The captain thought fast. "No. You want him?"

"Yes."

"Wait a minute."

MacBride dived into the central room, barked, "Sergeant, call the telephone exchange—quick—see where this guy's calling from."

The sergeant whipped into action, had the report in less than a minute. "Booth number three at the railroad waiting room."

"Good. Call the Information Desk at the railroad. Cohen's there. Tell him to nab the guy comes out of booth three. Fast!"

The sergeant put the call through, snapped a brief order to Detective Cohen.

MacBride was on the way back into his office. He stood before the desk, looked at his watch. He would give Cohen two minutes. The two minutes ticked off. He picked up the instrument, drawled "MacBride speaking."

"Just a tip, MacBride. Your station-house is going to be blown up. If you're clever, you'll get the guys. Sometime tonight."

That was all.

MacBride hung up, sat back, his fists clenched, his eyes glued on the instrument.

Chapter V

WHO was the man behind the voice? Who was he double-crossing, and why?

MacBride went into the central room, called out four reserves. "Look here, boys," he said. "I've got a tip somebody's going to try to blow up this place. One of you at each end of the block, the other two in the back. Let no machines come through the street. No people, either. Make 'em detour. Anybody around the back, pick him up. Anybody tries to hand you an argument, get rough. All right, go to it."

He went back into his office, clasped his hands behind his back and paced the floor.

Twenty minutes later the door opened. Cohen came in with a man. The man was a little disarranged. His natty clothes were dusty and his modish neckwear was askew. His derby had a dent in it, and wrath smoldered in his black eyes. Slim and lithe he was, olive skinned, with long, trick sideburns that put him in the category familiarly known as "Sheik."

Cohen's explanation was simple. "He tried to argue. Cap."

MacBride rubbed his hands together briskly. The mysterious informant was in his hands. His enormous bluff, recently put into print, that he had a valuable suspect in connection with the murder of Bedell, had worked out admirably.

"What's your name?" he asked.

"I'm not telling," snapped the high-strung stranger, struggling for dignity.

"I want to thank you for those tips," went on MacBride, "but I want to know more. Now cut out the nonsense."

"I'm not telling," reiterated the stranger. "It was a dirty trick, getting me this way. If those guys knew I'd been tipping you off, my life wouldn't be worth a cent."

"You tell me your name," proceeded MacBride, "and I'll promise to keep your name mum until the whole show is over."

"That's out. I don't want your promise. I didn't do anything. I'm not a gangster. I was just trying to help you out and keep my name out of it at the same time. It wouldn't do you any good to hold me. I've got no record. I didn't do anything."

MacBride told him to sit down, then said, "I'm sorry we had to grab you, buddy, but I've got a lot to answer for, and I've no intentions of getting tough with you. Just come across."

The man was losing his dignity rapidly. His black eyes darted about feverishly, his fingers writhed, his breath came in short little gasps. Fear was flickering across his face, not fear of MacBride, but of something or someone else. Mixed with the fear, was a hint of anguish.

"Please," he pleaded, "let me go. My God, if I'd thought it would come to this, that I'd be picked up, have my name spread around, I'd never have tipped you off. Give me a chance, Captain. Let me go. I told you this place is going to be blown up tonight."

"Who's going to blow it up?"

"Don't make me tell that! God, don't. I guess I've been a fool, but

I— I— Oh, hell!" He choked on a hoarse sob. "I told you what's going to happen. Lay for them. Get them when they try to blow you up. You'll learn everything then."

"Why have you been tipping me off?"

"I—for many reasons. A grudge, but behind the grudge—something else. It's been driving me crazy. Haven't been able to sleep. I was going to kill—but—I didn't." He raised his hands and shook them. "I'm lost, Captain, if you keep me, if you let loose who tipped you off. Dear God, give me a break—won't you?"

He leaned forward, extending his hands, pleading with his dark eyes, his face lined with agony.

MacBride bit him with an unwavering stare. What tragedy was in this fellow's life? He was sincere, that was certain. Something terrible was gnawing at his soul, making of him a shivering, palsied wreck, pleading eloquently for mercy.

"I don't want anybody to know I've been in this," he hurried on. "It's not only my life's at stake, it's something else—something bigger and deeper. Don't make me explain. I can't. Isn't it enough I warned you about this—this bombing?"

MacBride looked down at the desk, tapped his fingers meditatively. Then he looked up. "I'll give you a break," he said. "I'm going to lock you up for the night. If I get the men I want, you slide out quietly, and my mysterious informant remains a mystery. That's a promise. If Cohen here can find a Bible, I'll swear on it."

"Not a Bible in the whole dump," said Cohen.

The stranger was on his feet. "You promise, Captain? You will promise me that?"

"I've promised," nodded MacBride.

"Thanks. God, thanks! I've heard you were a hard-boiled egg. I—I didn't expect—"

"Pipe down. Ike," he said to Cohen, "lock him up and keep your jaw tight about what's just happened."

Cohen took the man out, and MacBride leaned back to sigh and light a fresh cigar, musing, "Maybe I ought to get kicked in the pants for making that promise. But I think the guy's hard-hit."

Half an hour later he was visited by State's Attorney Krug. Krug was pompous. "What are the latest developments, Captain?"

"Got some dope this joint is going to be blown up. You better get on your way."

Krug's eyes dilated. "Blown up!"

"Right."

"Then why don't you clear out?"

"See me clearing out for a lot of bums like that!"

"But this fellow you've got—this mystery man. Hadn't you better get him out of here? Don't you realize that it is possible they intend blowing up the place so that that man will be exterminated? Dead, he can give no evidence. I say, Captain, you ought to turn him over to me. Consider that I am eager to start a trial. We can use him, put the blame on him temporarily, at least make some headway. Come, now."

MacBride shook his head. "Nothing doing, Mr. Krug."

"This," stormed Krug, indignantly, "is monstrous!"

"If I were you, I'd get out of the neighborhood. Hell knows when these birds will show up. You don't want to follow in Bedell's footsteps, do you?"

"Damn my stars, you are impossible!" With that Krug banged out.

The echoes of his departure had barely died when Kennedy wandered in.

"How about some more news, Mac?"

"Thanks for mentioning my name so much in your write-up," replied MacBride. "When there's more news, you'll get it."

"Meaning there's none now."

"How clever you are!"

"Applesauce!"

"On your way, Kennedy."

"I'm comfortable."

"You won't be if you hang around here much longer. Now cut out the boloney, old timer. I'm busy, there's no news, and you're in my way."

Kennedy regarded him whimsically. "When you talk that way, Mac, I know there's something in the wind. All right, I'll toddle along." He coughed behind his hand. "By the way, I intended buying some smokes on the way over, but—"

MacBride hauled out his cigar box, and Kennedy, helping himself to a cigar, sniffed it as he sauntered to the door.

"I wish you'd keep 'em a little moist, Mac," he ventured.

He was gone before MacBride could throw him a verbal hot-shot.

The captain put on his visored cap, strode into the central room, looked around and then went out into the street. At the corner he paused for a brief chat with the policemen stationed there.

"Eventhing okey, boys?"

"So far, Cap."

"Keep a sharp lookout. If it comes, it will come suddenly."

The men nodded, fingering their nightsticks gingerly. A street light shone on their brass buttons, on their polished shields. Beneath their visors, their faces were tense and alert.

MacBride made a tour of the block, and then through the alley in the rear. Everything was calm, every man was in readiness. They spoke in voices a trifle bated. They exuded an air of tense expectancy, peering keenly into the shadows, moving on restless feet.

As MacBride swung back into the central room he almost banged into the desk sergeant.

"Just about to call you, Cap," the sergeant puffed. "Holstein and Gunther just picked up a touring car with three guys, and a machine-gun and half-a-dozen grenades."

"Where?" MacBride shot back.

"Down near the railroad yards. They were coming north and stopped to fix a flat. Holstein and Gunther are bringing 'em in."

"Good!" exploded MacBride, and punched a hole in the atmosphere. "By George, that's good."

Moriarity and Cohen were grinning. "Looks like them guys got one bum break," chuckled Moriarity.

"Sure does, boys!"

MacBride strode up and down the room grinning from ear to ear. He kept banging fist into palm boisterously. He was elated.

A little later there was a big touring car outside, and a deal of swearing and rough-housing. MacBride went out, and found Holstein and Gunther manhandling three roughnecks. Kennedy was there, having popped up from nowhere.

"Knew something was in the wind, Mac," he chortled.

"You'll get plenty of headlines now, Kennedy," flung back the captain.

Patrolman Gunther said, "Nasty mutts, these guys, Cap. One of 'em tried to pull his rod and I opened his cheek."

"G' on, yuh big louse!" snarled that guy.

"I'll shove your teeth down your throat!" growled Gunther, raising his stick.

"All inside," clipped MacBride.

The roughs were bustled into the central room. A reserve carried in the grenades and the machine-gun. There was a noticeable lack of politeness on the part of the three gangsters. Also, there was noticeable lack of gentleness on the part of the policemen. One of the gunmen, a big, surly towhead, was loudest of all, despite the gash on his cheek. He started to make a pass at Gunther, but MacBride caught him by the shoulder, spun him around and slammed him down upon a chair.

"That'll be all from you, Hess," he ripped out warmly. "I guess we're near the bottom of things now."

"Who is he?" asked Kennedy.

" 'Slugger' Hess, Duveen's strong-arm man."

"Hot diggity damn!"

"Now where's Duveen?" MacBride flung at Hess. "I want that guy. Every damn gangster in this burg is going to get treated rough. Now you come clean or you get the beating of your life!"

"And I'd like to do it, Cap," put in Gunther.

"Yah, yuh big hunk of tripe!" snarled Hess.

"Can that!" barked MacBride. "Where's Duveen?"

Hess was not soft-boiled. Despite the roomful of policemen, he stuck out his jaw. "Go find him, Captain. You can't bulldoze me, neither you nor that pup Gunther!"

"Where's Duveen?" MacBride had a dangerous look in his eyes, and his doubled fists were swinging at his sides.

"You heard me the first time."

Gunther flexed his hands. "Should I sweat him, Cap?"

"Sweat the three of them," said MacBride. "In my office. Ike, Jake, you'll help," he added to Moriarity and Cohen.

Eager hands took hold of the three gangsters and propelled them toward MacBride's office.

But before they reached the door there was a terrific explosion, and the walls billowed and crashed.

Chapter VI

STONE, splinters, plaster, beams thundered down. Yells and screams commingled with the tumult of toppling walls and ceilings. Lights were snuffed out. The roof, or what remained of it, boomed down. There were cries for help, groans, oaths. Tongues of flame leaped about, crackling.

MacBride found himself beneath a beam, an upturned table, and an assortment of other debris. Near him somebody was swearing violently.

"That you, Jake?"

"Yeah, Cap... if I can get this damn hunk of ceiling off my chest...."

MacBride squirmed, twisted, heaved. He jack-knifed his legs and knocked aside the table. He brushed powdered plaster from his eyes, spat it from his mouth. The beam was harder. It was wedged down at both ends by other weighty debris, and MacBride could not shove it off.

But he twisted his body from side to side, backed up bit by bit, finally won free and stood up. His face was bloody, the sleeve of his right arm was torn from shoulder to elbow. He did not know it. He stumbled toward the pinioned Moriarity, freed him from the weighty debris pressing upon him and helped him to the sidewalk.

Going back in, he ran into Cohen. Ike was carrying a semi-conscious desk sergeant.

A crowd had already gathered. People came on the run from all directions. Somebody had pulled the fire-alarm down the block. The flames were growing. From a crackling sound they had been whipped into a dull roar.

Two battered but otherwise able policemen came out and MacBride sent them to chase away the crowd. Blocks away fire-engines were clanging, sirens were screaming. The policemen fought with the crowd, drove it back down the street. MacBride and Cohen were busy carrying out those they were able to pry from beneath the debris.

The first fire-engine came booming around the corner, snorted to a stop, bell clanging. Helmeted fire-fighters with drawn axes ran for the building. A couple of flashlights blinked. The big searchlight on the fire-engine swung around and played its beams on the demolished station-house. The firemen stormed into the mass of wreckage, hacked their way through to the pinioned men.

MacBride plowed back into the cell where the mysterious stranger had been placed a few hours before. He had trouble finding him. The man was deep beneath the wreckage. MacBride ran out, got an ax and came back to chop his way through. He carried out a limp dead weight.

Other engines came roaring upon the scene. There was a din of ringing bells, hooting motors, loud commands. Hose was being strung out. Streams of water began shooting upon the building, roaring and hissing. A grocery store down the street was used to shelter the injured men, all of whom had been taken from the building. An ambulance was on the way.

MacBride and Cohen were bending over the stranger. He was a mass of bruises, scarce able to breathe, let alone talk.

"Guess… I'm… dying," he whispered, his eyes closed, his body twitching with pain.

"The hell you are!" said MacBride. "We'll have an ambulance here in a minute."

"Don't… tell." He struggled for breath, then choked. "Two ten… Jockey Street…. Get 'em!" Then he fainted.

One of the gangsters was dead. The two others had escaped in the wild mêlée.

Kennedy was alive, though pretty much the worse for wear. He was hatless, covered with soot and grime, one eye closed, a welt on his forehead. He limped, too, but he was not daunted.

"What next, Mac?"

MacBride turned. "God, Kennedy, you look rotten!"

"Feel rotten. I'd like to find the guy put his heel on my eye. I'm out of smokes. Who's got a butt?"

Moriarity had one.

The battalion chief for the fire department came up. "Hello, Mac. Bomb, eh? Yeah, I know. I've just been around. It was pitched through a window in the back." He looked up. "Good-bye, station-house, Mac!"

Even as he said this the front swayed, caved in with a smother of smoke, cinders and flame. Firemen rushed to escape the deluge. The hose lines pounded the place with water.

Detective Cohen appeared, with a bad wrist—his left hand.

"Where you been, Ike?" asked MacBride.

"Looking around. Guy in a cigar store around the corner said he was looking out the window a few minutes before the fireworks. Saw a big blue sedan roll by slow. He noticed because it's a one-way alley and classy machines don't often go through it. Runs back of the station-house, you know—Delaney Street."

"See here, boys." MacBride's voice was tense. "You all well heeled? Good. We're going to take a ride up to 210 Jockey Street, and I smell trouble. There's something here I don't understand. We were caught napping. I'll say I was—I'm the dumb-bell. There I thought I had the case all ready to bake, and we were blown up."

He found Lieutenant Connolly and gave him brief orders. He gathered together six reserves and Moriarity and Cohen. They used the big touring car in which Hess and the other two gangsters had been brought to the precinct. Gunther drove, and as he was about to slide into gear, Kennedy came up on the run.

"Room there for me, Mac?"

MacBride groaned. Getting rid of Kennedy was like getting rid of a leech. But taking a look at Kennedy, seeing him all banged up but still ready to carry on, the captain experienced a change of heart.

"Hop in," he clipped.

The big machine lurched ahead. Once in high gear the eight cylinders purred smoothly.

Two left turns and a right, and they were on a wide street that led north. In the distance the reflection of the white light district glowed in the sky. Ten men were in the car. There was no room for comfort.

The white light district grew nearer.

MacBride and his men ignored traffic lights. They struck Jockey Street. Jockey Street is like a cave. At one end it is lit by the glare of the theatrical district. As one penetrates it, it becomes darker, narrower, and the street lamps are pallid. Two and three-story houses rear into the gloom, lights showing here and there, but not in abundance. Most of the doors are blank-faced, foreboding. It is a thickly populated section, but pedestrians are rare. More than one man has been killed in lower Jockey Street. Patrolmen always travel it in pairs.

The machine stopped.

"Two ten's on the next block," said MacBride. "We'll leave the car here. Gunther, you and Barnes go over one block south and come up in the rear. Hang around there in case anybody tries to get out. The rest of us will try the front."

They all alighted. Gunther and Barnes, their sticks drawn, their pistols loose in their holsters, started off purposefully. MacBride, though he saw no one, had a vague feeling that eyes were watching him from darkened windows. People might have been curious in Jockey Street, like all humanity, but they differed materially in that they rarely came into the open to vent their curiosity.

As the men walked down the street, their footsteps re-echoed hollowly; a nightstick clicked against another. MacBride led the way, a jut to his jaw, his fingers curled up in his palms. Home, in peaceful Grove Manor, his wife was probably mending socks. Maybe his daughter was playing the piano; something about Spring from Mendelssohn or one of those Indian love lyrics. Well, he carried lots of insurance.

How about the men with him? Most of them married, too, with little kids. Moriarity, Cohen, Feltmann, Terchinsky, O'Toole, Pagliano. Gunther and Barnes in the back. Two hundred a month for the privilege of being a target for gunmen. They made far less—and paid double the life insurance premium—than many a man whose most important worry was a cold in the head or the temperature of his morning bath.

"This is it," said MacBride.

Kennedy said, "Dump."

"You stay out of it, Kennedy."

"If you've got a penknife I'll sit out here and play mumble-peg on the pavement."

In front of the house, which was a two-story affair built of red brick, was a depression reached by four stone steps that led down to the basement windows. At a word from MacBride, the men hid in this depression. A single step led to the front and main entrance, where there was a vestibule with glass in the upper half.

Alone, MacBride approached this, tried the door, and finding it locked, pressed a bell-button. Somewhere distant he heard the bell ring. He took off his cap of rank and held it under his left arm, partly to hide his identity. His teeth were set, his lips compressed. He rang again.

Presently he heard a latch click. It was on the inner door. There was a long moment before a face moved dimly in the gloom behind the vestibule window. MacBride made a motion to open the door.

The face floated nearer, receded, remained motionless, then came nearer again. Then it disappeared abruptly. The inner door banged. He heard running feet.

"We crash it, boys!" he barked in a low voice.

His revolver came out. One blow shattered the glass in the vestibule. He reached in, snapped back the latch. His men swarmed about him. He leaped into the vestibule, tried the next door. It was locked, built entirely of wood.

"All together, boys," he clipped.

En masse, they surged against the door. Again they surged. Wood creaked, groaned, then splintered. The door banged up under the impetus, and the law swept in. MacBride had a flashlight. It clicked into life, its beam leaped through the gloom. He turned.

"Holstein and Feltmann! Guard the front!"

"Yup, Cap!"

His flashlight swung up and down, back and forth, showed a stairway against one wall, leading to regions above. In the lower hall, he saw two closed doors.

"Bust these!"

He was the first to leap. The first door opened easily. The room was bare, unfurnished. He dived out and tried the next. It was unlocked. Empty. But it was meagerly furnished; a cot, a table, a rocking-chair, a gas stove.

"Lookout's room," he speculated. "Guy who came to the door."

Sentences, words, were clipped.

The flashlight's beam picked out the foot of the stairway.

"Up, boys!"

MacBride was off on the run. He led the way up the stairs.

Came two gun reports, muffled.

"Gunther and Barnes," he said. "These guys are trying for a break."

They were in the hall above. The first door they tried was locked. MacBride hurled his weight against it.

Bang!

A shot splintered the panel, passed the captain's cheek. He sprang back.

Moriarity, leaning against the bannister, shot from the hip. He plastered four shots around the doorknob. Pagliano put three more there. Then they waited, silent, all guns drawn. They listened. Men were moving inside the room. There was an undertone of voices.

MacBride turned to Cohen, "Ike, go downstairs and get the chair in that room."

Cohen departed, returned carrying a heavy kitchen chair. MacBride took the chair, hefted it, then swung it over his head and dived with it toward the door. The chair splintered; so did the door. A couple of shots banged from the inside. MacBride felt a sting on his cheek. Blood trickled down his jaw.

Two policemen stood side by side and pumped bullets into the room. There was a hoarse scream, the rush of bodies, the pound of feet. Glass shattered.

Firing, MacBride and Moriarity hurtled into the room. Moriarity saw a dim figure going out through the window. He fired. The figure buckled and was gone.

"They've made the roof!" clipped MacBride.

He jumped to the window, out upon the fire-escape, up to the roof. He could see vague blurs skimming over the roof of the adjoining house. For a block these roofs were linked together, trimmed with chimneys, ventilating shafts, radio aerials.

Cohen went past MacBride in leaps and bounds, stopped suddenly, crouched and fired two shots. One knocked a man over. The other whanged through a skylight. Moriarity cut loose, missed fire.

Then the gunmen, near the end of the row of roofs, stopped and hid behind chimneys and the projections that separated one roof from another. They sprinkled the night generously with gunfire. Officer Terchinsky went down with a groan, came up again.

The policemen advanced warily, darting from chimney to chimney, crouching behind a skylight, wriggling forward. MacBride was mopping the wound on his cheek with a handkerchief. His gun was in the other hand. Moriarity was with him. A slug chipped off the corner of the chimney behind which they crouched.

Moriarity fired.

"Got that bum!" he muttered.

Both sides suddenly opened a furious exchange of shots. Lead ricocheted off the roof, twanged through aerial wires, shattered the glass in skylights. Shouts rose, sharp commands and questions. The policemen rose as one and galloped forward, firing as they ran.

The gunmen loomed up in the darkness—four, five, six of them. Guns bellowed and belched flame at close quarters. Terchinsky, already wounded, went down again, this time to stay. Guns empty, the men clashed, hand to hand, clubbing rifles. Nightsticks became popular.

Below, crowds were gathering, machines coming from other districts. Police whistles were blowing.

Gunther and Barnes came up from the rear, joined the fight. From then on it was short-lived. Every one of the six gunmen, rough customers to the last man, were beaten down, and most of them were unconscious.

The policemen were not unscathed, either. Terchinsky, of course, was dead. Cohen was on the point of collapse. MacBride was a bit dazed. They handcuffed the gangsters. MacBride looked them over, one by one, with his flashlight, and then went off to examine the ones who had been shot down. Moriarity was with him.

"Recognize anybody, Cap?"

"One or two, but can't place 'em. I'd hoped to find Duveen."

"Didn't you pot a guy going through the window? Maybe he fell down the fire-escape."

"That's right, Jake. Let's look."

MacBride gave brief orders to his men, told them to carry the prisoners down to the ground floor. Then he went off with Moriarity, descended the fire-escape, followed it down to the bottom.

Lying on the ground, face down, was a man dressed in a tuxedo. MacBride turned him over.

"Alive," he muttered, "but unconscious."

"Who is he?" asked Moriarity.

MacBride snapped on his flash, leaned over, his eyes dilating.

"Bonelio!" he muttered.

Kennedy was coming down the fire-escape.

Chapter VII

A DAY later MacBride stood in a large room in Police Headquarters. He was a little pale. His cheek was covered with cotton and adhesive tape. Moriarity was there, strips of tape over his right eye. And Cohen's left arm was in a sling.

Against one wall was a bench. On this bench sat Trixie Meloy, Adolph Shanz, and Beroni, manager of the Palmetto Club. All three were manacled, one to the other. Shanz was despair personified. Beroni was haggard. Trixie wore a look of contempt for everybody in the room.

Kennedy came in, sat down at a desk and played with a pencil.

MacBride said, "I have a letter here that I'm going to read. It will interest you, Miss Meloy."

He spread a sheet before him, said, "It was dictated to a stenographer at the hospital by a man named Louis Martinez."

Trixie bit her lip.

MacBride read, " 'To Captain Stephen MacBride: The man you want is Tony Bonelio. I worked in his club. I was Miss Meloy's dancing partner. We'd danced before, all over the country. I loved her. I thought she loved me. Maybe she did until Bonelio won her with money. It drove me crazy. I wanted to kill him. But I didn't. But I learned a lot. He killed Bedell. I heard the plans being made. Bedell was getting hard to handle. State's Attorney Krug and Shanz and Bonelio got together. Shanz was to get Bedell on the speaker's platform, so Bonelio could shoot him from the roof. Shanz and Krug staged the block-party just for that. When Bonelio read that you had a man prisoner who was in the know, I heard him phone Krug. Krug promised to go down and get the man from you. Whoever he was, they were going to pay him a lot of money to take the rap. But when you wouldn't give him up, Bonelio told Krug there was only one way—blow the station up.

" 'I tipped you about all this because I wanted to see Bonelio get his. I wanted to win back Trixie's love. But I knew if she knew I'd done all that, she'd never look at me again. I was crazy about her. I was, but that's over. I was lying here, dying, and I called her up to come over. She told me to go to hell and croak. I've been a fool. I see what she is now. But go easy with her, Captain, anyhow. The only thing she did was to go to the block-party and say she saw a man in a gray suit walking away. She didn't see anybody. It was just a stall. That's all she did, except what she did to me. I don't know, maybe I still love her.' "

MacBride concluded, and you could have heard a pin drop. Then he said, "That was Martinez' death-bed confession."

"The damn sap!" snapped Trixie, her face coloring.

"What a fool he was to waste his time on a hunk of peroxide like you," observed Kennedy. "And what a dirty write-up I'm going to give you, sister."

"Rats for you, buddy," she gave him.

"Here's hoping you become a guest of the state. Don't forget to primp up and look pretty when the tabloid photographers get around. I don't even see what the hell Bonelio saw in you."

"Damn you, shut up!" she cried fiercely.

"Now, now," cut in MacBride, "that'll be enough. You, Shanz, are under arrest, and your trial won't come up till the new administration's in."

"Where's Krug?" he grumbled.

"Still looking for him," said MacBride. "He slipped out at three this morning. Moriarity was over to his house and saw signs of a hasty departure. Krug got cold feet when he heard we had Bonelio. He knew he couldn't help Bonelio, because the wop staged a gunfight with us. And he knew that if Bonelio knew Krug couldn't help him, then Bonelio would squeal. As a matter of fact, Bonelio has squealed. You'll go on trial in connection with the killing of Bedell. The net is out for Krug."

Even as he said this, the telephone rang. He picked it up.

"Hello," drawled a voice. "I want MacBride."

"You've got him."

"Well, MacBride, this is Duveen. I was sore as hell because you picked up Hess and the other two guys. They were on the way to blow up one of Bonelio's warehouses. Say, I hear you're looking for Krug."

"Yes, I am. He's wanted—bad."

"I've got him. I'm calling from up-State. He ran into me a little while ago with his car. I nabbed him. I'm sending him in with a State trooper. That's all, MacBride."

"Thanks. Drop in for a drink some time."

"I might, at that."

That was all.

MacBride rubbed his hands together. "And now we've got Krug," he said. "Krug, Shanz, Bonelio. And thank God, they'll go on trial when Anderson is State's Attorney."

Shanz groaned. A little man, a tool of others, he had tried to barter honor for power.

The three of them, including Trixie Meloy, were marched out and locked in separate cells.

The commissioner came in, a large, benign man, mellow-voiced, steady-eyed.

"Congratulations, MacBride," he said, and shook warmly. "It was great work. You've broken up an insidious crowd in Richmond City, and there's every possibility you'll be made inspector and attached to my personal staff."

"The breaks helped me," said MacBride. "I got a lot of good breaks toward the end."

"That may be your way of putting it. Personally, I attribute your success to nerve, courage and tenacity."

With that he left.

MacBride sighed, sat down and felt his head. It hurt, there was a dull pain throbbing inside. He would carry a three-inch scar on his cheek for life. He felt his pockets.

"Thought I had a smoke...."

Kennedy looked up, grinned, pulled a cigar from his pocket. "Have one on me, Mac."

MacBride eyed him for a moment in silent awe. Then he chuckled. "Thanks, Kennedy. I see where I have to buy you a box of Montereys."

"See they're good and moist, Mac," said Kennedy.

Law
Without
Law

Chapter I

KENNEDY chuckled. "So you're back in the Second, Mac."

"See me here, don't you?"

"Ay, verily!"

The old station-house, blown up during the last election, had been rebuilt, and the office in which Captain Stephen MacBride sat and Kennedy, the insatiable newshound, stood, smelled of new paint and plaster. Something of the old atmosphere was lost—that atmosphere which it had taken long years to create: dust, age-colored walls decorated with news clippings, "wanted" bulletins, likenesses of known criminals.

Two days ago MacBride had been suddenly and inexplicably shifted from the suburban Fifth to the hectic Second. He was surprised, more than a little incredulous; and he suspected some ulterior motive behind the new Police Commissioner's leniency.

So did Kennedy. And Kennedy said, "This is funny, Mac."

"As a crutch."

"Now, if you'd asked me a week ago, I'd have said you were stuck in the Fifth for the rest of your term—or shoved farther out in the sticks. What did Commissioner Stroble say?"

"Said we ought to get on well."

"Was he nice?"

"Gave me a drink and asked about the health of my family."

"Hot damn!" Kennedy clasped his hands and with a serio-comic expression stared at the ceiling. "O, Lord what hath come over the powers that be in this vale of iniquity, Richmond City?"

"You jackass!"

"Mac, poor old slob—"

"Don't call me a slob!"

"Mac, my dear, what's up now? Why did the Commissioner suddenly put you in the precinct nearest your heart's desire?"

"Out of the pure and simple goodness of his heart."

"Amen!"

Kennedy sagged limply and supported himself with one extended arm against the wall.

"Of course, Mac," he said, "you know and I know that this is one awful lot of liverwurst."

"Then why ask?"

"Kidding you."

"Ho!"

"Getting your goat."

"Ho! Ho!"

Kennedy left the wall, crept dramatically across the floor and slid silently upon the desk. And in a hushed voice, with mock seriousness, he said, "Mac, somebody's trying to make a boob out of you!"

"How do you know?"

"I suspect, old tomato—I suspect. It's too sudden, Mac. Stroble has got something up his sleeve. He's brought you back into the town for a purpose."

"How big do you think he is?"

"Pretty big."

"Big enough to be the Big Guy?"

"Almost—and yet, not quite."

"Who is?"

"Beginning to get a faint idea. If I'm right, the Big Guy has been behind it all from the very beginning. The gangs have come and gone, but the Big Guy has succeeded in remaining hidden. If it's the bozo I think it is...."

"Yes?"

"I don't think you'll reach him."

"Oh, go to hell, Kennedy! Listen, I'll get to him. Man alive, I *couldn't* lay off now! The thing's got in my blood. I've got to see it through. And I'm going to."

"Well, Mac, so far you've surprised me. Why you aren't occupying a snug grave in somebody's cemetery, is beyond me. But you've still got lots of opportunity of following in Jack Cardigan's footsteps. He was a poor slob."

"A martyr, Kennedy."

"Well, dignify it." Kennedy put on his topcoat. "I'm going places, Mac. Good-luck."

He wandered out, trailing cigarette smoke.

MacBride creaked back and forth in his chair, stopped to light a cigar, went on creaking. Damn new chairs, the way they creaked! The whole room was strange, aloof. Not like the old one, not as dusty—as intimate. Those three chairs standing against the wall—mission oak, bright and shiny, like the desk. Everything trim and spic and span— on parade. Even the clock was new, had a fast, staccato tick. He remembered the old one, a leisurely, moon-faced old chronometer, never on time.

A noise in the central room roused him. He raised his eyes and regarded the door. It burst open. Rigallo and Doran and a third man weaved in. The third man looked like a Swede, and was a head taller than either of the detectives. He slouched ape-like, great arms dangling, and his sky-blue eyes were wide and belligerent. He wore corduroy trousers, a blue pea-jacket.

"What's this?" asked MacBride.

Rigallo said, "Know him?"

"No."

The two detectives steered the man across the room and pushed him into one of the three chairs. He looked more the ape than ever—an ape at bay—sitting there with shoulders hunched, jaw protruding, huge hands dangling across his knees.

"Who is he?" asked MacBride.

"Says Alf Nelson," clipped Rigallo. "Me and Tim here were poking around the docks. We caught this baby trying to set a Tate & Tate barge adrift. He'd slipped the bow line and we caught him as he was on the stern."

"H'm," muttered MacBride. "That right, Nelson?"

"It ain't."

"He's a lousy liar!" snapped Rigallo.

"We saw him," supplemented Doran.

MacBride said, "Come, Nelson, why did you do it?"

"I tell you, I didn't do nothin'." His Scandinavian accent was barely noticeable. "These guys are tryin' to frame me."

"Ah-r-r!" growled Rigallo. "Can that tripe, buddy! D'you think we waste time framin' guys? Come down to earth, you big white hope!"

"Look here, Nelson," said MacBride, rising. "This is damned serious. It's a rough night on the water, and that barge would have caused a lot of trouble. Riggy, was anybody on the barge?"

"Yeah, guy sleeping. We woke him up. Scoggins. He was scared stiff, and I'll bet he doesn't sleep a wink the rest of the night."

MacBride took three steps and stood over Nelson. "Did you have a grudge against Scoggins?"

"No. I tell you, I ain't done nothin'. I found the lines loose and was tryin' to fix 'em."

"Cripes!" spat Rigallo.

"Who's he work for, Riggy?"

"Dunno. Frisked him for a gat. Here it is. Thirty-eight."

MacBride said, "Who do you work for, Nelson?"

Nelson growled, pressed back in his chair. MacBride reached down toward his pockets. Nelson raised a hand to block him. Doran caught the hand and knocked it aside. MacBride went through the man's pockets.

"H'm. Badge," he said, "of the Harbor Towing. This guy's a barge captain. Here's his Union card. Name's right. Thirty-five. Unmarried, citizen. Listen, Nelson, come across now. Why the hell did you try to cut that barge loose?"

"I told you I didn't try to cut no barge loose," rumbled Nelson.

MacBride turned on Rigallo. "You're sure he did, Riggy?"

"Ask Tim."

"Sure he did, Cap," said Doran.

MacBride put Nelson's belongings in the desk and said, "Tim, plant him in a cell. I'm going down to the river. You come along, Riggy. There may be something in this, and there may not."

Chapter II

IT was cold and windy on the waterfront. The pier sheds loomed huge and sombre, and overhead the sky arched black as a cavern roof. And there was not a solitary star afield, not a vagrant moonbeam, not a patch of color against the black inverted bowl.

The river was a dark mystery moving restlessly toward the sea, and fringed sparsely with pierhead lights which probed its surface with thin, tremulous needles of radiance. And here and there, between the fringes, other lights—red, green, white—marked black shapes that moved through the thick gloom. The sound of bells, rung intermittently, skipped across the water with startling clarity.

MacBride and Rigallo strode down Pier Five and came to a barge moored at the end. Beneath them the water gurgled among the piles, and the barge thumped dully against the wharf. The tide was high, and they leaped to the barge without difficulty.

A man was standing in the doorway of the small, lighted cabin, smoking a pipe.

"Scoggins," said Rigallo.

"Hello, Scoggins," said MacBride. "Let's go inside."

They entered and Scoggins closed the door and leaned back against it. He was a small man, knotty in the framework, weather-beaten, steady-eyed.

MacBride said, "You know Nelson?"

"Yeah, years—from seein' him around the docks and in the lunch-wagon sometimes. Works for the Harbor Towin'."

"Ever have a scrap with him?"

"Nope."

"Sure?"

"Yup. But I got a scare tonight, though!"

"You figure he tried to cut you loose?"

"Says he didn't. I ain't never had a line slip on me yet, and I been twenty years on the river."

"Well, look here, can you think of anything that might cause him to do it?"

Scoggins frowned thoughtfully and rubbed his jaw. "Gosh, I dunno. Of course, Tate & Tate, the comp'ny I work for, had a split with the Union, and they ain't hirin' Union men 'less they can help it. The Harbor Towin''s all Union. Guys get in scraps over that sometimes. Day before yest'day Bill Kamp, who's on Number Three Barge, got in a fight with a Harbor Towin' guy. The guy called Bill a scab and Bill poked him."

"What caused this split with the Union?"

"Dunno. Just know they split. Young Mr. Tate was sore as hell over somethin'."

"Do you know what barge Nelson is on?"

"Number Three. Up at Pier Twelve now."

MacBride turned to Rigallo. "Come on, Riggy, let's snoop around."

They left Pier Five, reached the cobbled street and walked north. Fifteen minutes later they turned into a covered pier, met a watchman, flashed their shields and passed on down the vast interior.

On the south side of Pier Twelve they found a lighter flying a metal pennant numbered Three. A light shone in the little cabin. They leaped down from the wharf, pushed open the door and walked in.

A girl sat on the bunk. She was a large girl—not fat, but large, broad in the shoulders, wide at the hips. Her skin was fair, her hair light brown; and her cheekbones were high, prominent; her mouth wide with lips full and frankly sensuous. Her clothes were cheap and not precisely in the mode, and she regarded the two intruders with a dull stare.

Rigallo smiled. "Hello, girlie."

"Hal-lo."

"Where's Alf?" asked MacBride.

"Ay don't know."

"H'm. We were supposed to meet him here tonight," lied Rigallo.

"Yes," nodded MacBride.

She shrugged her broad shoulders. "So vas I. Dat Alf iss neffer on time."

"Ah, he's a good guy, though," said Rigallo.

She regarded him stolidly for a moment, then grinned, showing large white teeth. "Yah, Alf iss good fal-ler. Ay vait. You fal-lers vaiting for Alf?"

"Sure," nodded Rigallo. "We're his friends. Eh, Mac?"

"You said it, Riggy."

"Alf's some guy," said Rigallo.

"Yah," nodded the girl, shedding some of her reserve. "Alf iss good fal-ler." She paused, meditated heavily, then laughed and slapped her knee. "Ay tal you, Alf is vun big guy. Dis Meester Braun he likes Alf much."

"Sure," said MacBride. "Mr. Braun's a good guy, too. But he should treat Alf better."

Still more of the girl's reserve vanished, and she leaned forward, waxing confidential. "Yah, like Ay tol' Alf. But Ay t'ank dis Meester Braun iss be sqvare by Alf. Alf he tal me he vill get lots dol-lars."

"Well, it's no more than right," put in Rigallo.

"Yah. Alf vill be rich fal-ler some day."

MacBride and Rigallo grinned at each other. Then they grinned at the girl, and MacBride said, "Gosh, miss, Alf's been holding back on us. Never told us he had a nice girl like you."

She dropped her eyes. "Yah, Ay t'ank Alf luffs me lot. Ay luff Alf lot."

"He'll invite us to the wedding, though, I hope," said MacBride.

"Sure," nodded Rigallo.

"Yah," said the girl.

MacBride tried, "When did Alf say he would be back?"

"Vun hour ago. But Ay vill vait."

"Yeah," said Rigallo. "Alf said something about a job down on Pier Five. I wondered what he meant."

"Vass it Pier Five?" asked the girl.

"Yeah," said Rigallo.

"Ay vill go."

"No. You stay here," put in MacBride. "We'll look him up and tell him you're waiting. What did he say he was doing?"

"Alf didn't say. Alf ain't tal me much, but he say he be very busy dese nights soon."

MacBride stood up. "Well, if we see him, we'll tell him you're waiting. What did you say your name was?"

"Hilda. Hilda Yonson. Ay come from Oslo two year' ago."

"See you again," said MacBride.

"Yeah, see you again," said Rigallo.

"Yah," said Hilda Yonson.

MacBride and Rigallo climbed back to the wharf and strode through the pier-shed.

"Who is Braun?" asked Rigallo.

"Don't know. Probably one of the bosses. Well ask the night watch-man."

In a little office at the far end of the pier they found the watchman, and MacBride asked, "Who is Mr. Braun?"

"Manager. Yeah, he's the manager."

"Good-night," said MacBride, and steered Rigallo into the street.

"What now, Cap?"

"Nothing, until I see Braun."

"It looks as if Nelson is somebody's dope."

"What I think, Riggy. Flag that taxi."

MacBride went home that night, pounded his ear for eight hours and was back on the job at eight next morning. In plain clothes, he left the station-house and went down to the general offices of the Harbor Towing Company, which were located over Pier Nine.

Braun had evidently just arrived, for he was going through the morning's mail. He was a fat, swarthy man, nervous and shifty, with a vague chin.

"Oh, Captain MacBride," he said. "Ah, yes. Won't you sit down? Won't you have a cigar?"

MacBride sat down but refused the cigar. "You probably know," he said, "that I've got one of your barge captains over at the station-house."

Braun's eyes squinted, and he licked his lips. "Why, no! That's too bad. Likely a drunken brawl, eh? Well, I suppose I'll have to bail him out—mark against his salary."

"Not quite," said MacBride. "He was caught trying to cut a barge adrift last night. Pretty serious."

"Well, I should say so! Can you imagine! Humph! You never know what these drunks will do."

"But Nelson wasn't drunk."

"Well, that *is* strange! Now why do you suppose he tried to do a fool thing like that, Captain?"

"Search me. Thought maybe you might know."

"Me?"

"Uhuh."

"But, Captain, I'm surprised, how should I know why these fool Swedes—"

"Aboveboard, now, Mr. Braun!"

"Why—um—why, what do you mean?"

"Don't make me go into detail."

"But I tell you, Captain, I don't understand—"

"Aboveboard, Mr. Braun!"

Braun pursed his lips, his eyes dilated. He looked amazed. "Really, Captain—"

"Oh, for God's sake, cut out this stalling!"

"I tell you, Captain, I'm in the dark. I don't know what you're driving at."

MacBride's lips curled. "There's something crooked somewhere."

"Well, if there is, I'd certainly like to know about it. If Nelson has been going wrong, I'll certainly fire him. Tell you what, I'll go down to the station-house and give him a talking. Let's see. It's nine now. I'll be there at ten, Captain."

MacBride stood up. "I'll be waiting there."

"Good! Won't you have a cigar?"

"No."

MacBride's exit was like a blast of wind.

Chapter III

TWENTY minutes later he walked into the offices of Tate & Tate, and a boy piloted him into the sanctum of Hiram Tate, the younger and executive member of the firm. Tate was a lank, rock-boned man of forty-odd, with flashing dark eyes.

"I came over," said MacBride, "about that bit of business on Pier Five last night."

"Oh, you did? Good! I'll go right over with you and prefer charges against this bird you've got."

"What is your opinion?" asked MacBride. "Why do you suppose

he tried to cut that barge loose?"

"Captain, my answer will be heavily prejudiced. You want to know what I think? I think that the Harbor Towing is trying to intimidate me. We're non-Union. I'll tell you why. Mike Tate, my old man, was double-crossed. And keep this under your hat. The Harbor Towing and Tate & Tate have always been rivals for the river trade.

"We've had more damned inspectors on our tail than I thought were in existence. What for? For little things. Unsanitary lavatories. Doors that opened in instead of out. Electric wiring. Unsafe barges. Condemned tugs. Ever since we kicked the Union in the slats.

"And what started it? The municipal pier at Seaboard Basin. It was offered for sale, and we wanted it. The Harbor Towing wanted it. We claimed it should come logically to us because we had no uptown terminal and did a lot of uptown business. The Harbor Towing carried it right to the Union. I was out of town. The old man represented us, and he's known for a convivial old souse. They got him tight at the board meeting, and he signed all the dotted lines he could find.

"Well, we couldn't retract. The whole mess was attested by a notary, and when the old man came to he discovered that the Harbor Towing owned the municipal pier. When I came back to town I found him raving mad. I got sore, too, and we told the Union what we thought of it, and dropped. What's the use of catering to an outfit that kowtows to big money? The Harbor Towing is a big outfit, and they get all the court decisions, too. It's damned funny. When we get a square deal, get at least one section of the municipal pier to unload and load freight, we'll go back into the fold. That's my story. Believe it or not."

"I'll think it over. If you want to press a charge against Nelson, we'll indict him."

"I'll press charges, all right!" Tate rose and put on his overcoat. "Have a cigar?"

"Go good. Thanks."

They drove to the station-house in Tate's private car, and as they entered the central room, they found Rigallo pacing up and down in something akin to rage.

"Hell, Cap, where have you been?" he snapped.

"What about it?"

"Bower came down from Headquarters and took Nelson up for a quiz."

MacBride tightened his jaw. "Why'd you let him?"

"How could I stop him. I'm only a dick."

"What's this?" put in Tate.

MacBride said, "Nelson's at Headquarters."

"I want to place that charge."

"All right," said MacBride; then to Rigallo, "You go along with Mr. Tate, Riggy."

They went out, and MacBride banged into his office. Kennedy was parked in his chair before his desk, immersed in solitaire.

"Out of my throne, Kennedy!"

"Just a minute, Mac. I've almost got this."

MacBride grabbed the back of the swivel chair, hauled it and Kennedy away from the desk, slid another into its place, and sat down. He studied the cards for a moment, made several swift moves, filled the suits and said, "Learn from me, Kennedy."

"That was good, Mac. How about two-handed poker."

"No. Busy."

"What doing?"

"Thinking."

"Bower came down and got Nelson."

"Don't I know it!"

Kennedy chuckled. "Bower's the Headquarters 'yes' man. Guess the Commissioner wanted to see Nelson, shake his hand, and tell him to go home."

"H'm." MacBride stood up, put on his coat and strode out.

Ten minutes later he entered Police Headquarters.

Commissioner Stroble regarded him through a screen of excellent cigar smoke.

"How about Nelson?" asked MacBride.

"We let him go," said the Commissioner.

"Let him go!" echoed MacBride.

"Why, certainly. No case at all, MacBride. We had a chap named Scoggins here, too. I weighed both testimonies. Scoggins was asleep. Nelson saw that one of the cables had slipped and was trying to fix it. Scoggins was vague. Don't bother with such small change, Mac-Bride."

"Small change!" MacBride curled his lip. "If it was so small, why did Bower take Nelson from the precinct, and why did you bother with it?"

Stroble's eyes narrowed. "Remember, MacBride, I took you out of the Fifth, gave you another chance. Don't be a fool!"

"You're trying to make a fool out of me! I know the situation on the waterfront, and it's not small change. That guy Nelson is guilty as hell. And the outfit he works for is a damned sight guiltier!"

Stroble leaned forward, pursing his lips. "MacBride, I said it was small change. Now don't hand me an argument. Go back to your roost and forget about it. This interview is over."

MacBride went out with a low growl. He walked back to the station-house, certain now that trouble was breeding on the river. Small change! He cursed under his breath. He was very near the end of his tether. Time and time again someone in the machinery, of the city government had tried to balk him.

In his office that day he had moments of black depression. He wondered if after all he were not beating his head against a stone wall. What was he? Only a common precinct captain, with strong ideas of his own. How could he hope to carry out his own straightforward plans when the Department sidetracked him?

Yet there was the strain of the hard in his blood. To give up now, to fall in line with the long column of grafters, would be a tremendous blow to his conscience—and to his stubborn pride. Rigallo and Doran would razz him. And Kennedy! And a lot of other men who were aware of his single-handed struggle against graft and corruption.

No, there was no backing out now. He had built a structure of two-fisted justice, escaped death, release from the Force, by the skin of his teeth. The game at this stage was far too interesting. He had wiped out some of the most notorious gangs in Richmond City, had made the political racketeers squirm, had driven some right out of office.

But still he had not got to the roots. Had the Commissioner before his appointment, been the drive wheel in the racket? And now, being in a position of vital importance, would he rebuild all that MacBride had knocked down? How big was he? How far could MacBride push him? Why had he permitted Nelson's release on such short notice?

Small change! Hell!

It was strange that a month should pass without an untoward murmur on the river. At times MacBride wondered if after all Nelson had been innocent. But then it wasn't like Rigallo to make such a raw blunder. He was not a detective who usually went in for small game.

An interesting and significant bit of news drifted in one morning. Kennedy, the inevitable, walked in on MacBride and said:

"What do you think, Mac?"

"What?"

"A Tate & Tate barge sank last night. One of their oldest. Just foundered, so the report goes, off the coast. Sprung a leak. Went down with one hundred thousand dollars' worth of copper wire. The barge captain was saved. The tug *Annie Tate* was towing, and saved him. Read what the *News-Examiner* says."

He scaled a newspaper on the table, and MacBride conned a terse editorial:

> Last night the Tate & Tate barge Number Two sank off the Capes. It is evident that this barge was sadly in need of repair. The sea was only moderately rough and the tug *Annie Tate* had good steerageway.
>
> A cargo valued at $100,000 was lost in fifty fathoms, and the barge captain, Olaf Bostad, is in the City Hospital suffering from exposure. It seems to us that there is a deplorable lack of efficiency somewhere. Why the Number Two, one of the first barges built for Tate & Tate, was allowed to go to sea, is beyond us.
>
> It seems incredible that a reputable company should place a man in jeopardy by sending him on a coast-wise voyage in a barge of such ancient vintage. The company, of course, does not lose. The underwriters do. We no longer wonder why marine insurance is at such a premium, and why many underwriters refuse to insure coastwise barges.

"H'm," muttered MacBride.

"I wonder who paid for that," said Kennedy. "Tate & Tate are in hot water now, for sure. Watch the insurance company go into action!"

"And the waterfront bust wide open," said MacBride.

Indeed, the first rumble came on the following day, when not a single tug or barge of Tate & Tate moved. Captain Bower, of Head-quarters, boomed into the station-house with orders from the Commissioner.

"MacBride, you've got to patrol the river," he said. "Use all your available men. Two cops on each pier where there's Tate & Tate shipping. The insurance company has refused to allow Tate & Tate to move until every barge and tug has been inspected. The city is also sending its own inspectors, and there's a complete tie-up."

"All right," nodded MacBride.

He called on his reserves, dispatched them to six different piers, and himself went down to the Tate & Tate general offices.

Young Hiram Tate was in high heat. "What do you think of this, MacBride? By God, can you beat it? That barge was overhauled only two months ago and the underwriters O.K.'d it. Now we're tied up. Not a thing allowed to move. We've got thousands of dollars' worth of freight that has to move—has to make trains, ships—and some of it's perishable. Hell, we'll go bankrupt!

"What happens now? Consignees and consignors are bellowing. But we can't move. We lose our contracts, and the movement of freight is taken over by other companies. And what company mainly? The Harbor Towing. God, what a blow below the belt this is!"

"We're putting men on the piers to prevent trouble," said MacBride.

But trouble broke. When a Harbor Towing tug and three lighters warped into Pier Eight to move perishable freight from a Tate & Tate shed, a fight started. Fists flew, and then stones and canthooks. The police joined, and shots rang out, and one man was wounded before the outbreak was quelled.

But the feud had taken root and spread the length of the waterfront, and MacBride was here and there and everywhere, struggling for law and order.

The Commissioner called him and said, "Clamp the lid, MacBride. It looks as if Tate & Tate employ a lot of hoodlums. This can't go on. Pitch 'em all in jail if you have to."

MacBride had been up most of that night, and he was weary. "If you'd get the inspectors on the job and make that insurance company snap on it, this would stop. I'm doing the best I can."

"Keep up the good work, MacBride!" was Stroble's parting shot.

MacBride slammed down the receiver, whirled and stared at Rigallo. "Now I know why I've been shifted here! I'm getting a beautiful kick in the slats! I'm told to ride Tate & Tate, and, Riggy, way down in my heart I believe Tate & Tate is the goat!"

"Mac, I'm with you, you know. So is Doran."

"Thanks, Riggy. It's good to know."

Reports came in continually from the river. All the reserves were out. Fights occurred every few hours—uptown—downtown.

MacBride slept at the station-house that afternoon, awoke at six, had hot coffee and a couple of hamburgers sent up, and prepared for another night. Tate & Tate were at the breaking point. The inspectors were taking their time, and the first barge that was looked over was held up for some minor detail that was not yet settled among the inspectors.

On the other hand, the Harbor Towing Company was reaping a harvest, taking over all the freight that Tate & Tate could not handle. And the Union men of the Harbor Towing, old enemies of the non-Union crowd of Tate & Tate, took every opportunity to bawl insults at the men whom circumstances had forced to a stand-still.

Hiram Tate called MacBride on the telephone and yelled, "Look here, MacBride! You've got a good name in this lousy burg. What am I going to do? These pups from the Harbor Towing are getting away with murder. You can't blame my men for fighting. I've bailed twenty out already. If this keeps up, if my floating equipment isn't allowed to move, we'll go bankrupt. It's dirty, MacBride. There's some underhand work somewhere. I tell you, if it keeps up, I'm going out on the river myself and bust the first Harbor Towing bum that opens his jaw!"

"Sit tight, Tate," said MacBride. "I've got to maintain law and order."

"Law and order, hell!" exclaimed Tate, and hung up.

Rigallo asked, "What's the matter, Cap?"

"Tate's sore. Can you blame him?"

"No."

"Riggy, this is getting worse. There's big money in it, and between you and me it looks as if the Harbor Towing is trying to wipe out Tate & Tate, their biggest competitors. And how they're doing it! That sunken barge was just what they needed. Graft all around. Ten to one the underwriters were bribed. The *News-Examiner* was bribed. The city is being bribed."

"D' you ever stop to think, Cap, that the barge might have been monkeyed with?"

"You know, I wonder!"

The hours dragged by, with more reports coming in, and at midnight came a staggering report from one of the patrolmen stationed at Pier Fifteen.

"We just found a stiff, Captain."

"Who?"

"Guy named Nelson. We heard a shot and ran down the dock and found him dead in his barge. Right through the heart."

"Hold everything, Grosskopf. I'll be over."

MacBride hung up and looked at Rigallo. "Riggy, somebody plugged Alf Nelson of the Harbor Towing."

"God help Tate & Tate!"

"Let's go!"

Chapter IV

OFFICER TONOVITZ met MacBride and Rigallo at the entrance of Pier Fifteen.

"Grosskopf's on the barge," he said.

They strode down the covered pier, came out in the open, and saw Grosskopf standing outside the cabin door. MacBride and Rigallo jumped down to the barge.

Nelson was lying on the floor, flat back, one arm flung across his chest, the other extended straight from his shoulder. A chair was overturned.

"Fight," ventured Rigallo.

"Maybe not," said MacBride. "He might have been sitting on the chair, and jerked up when he was hit."

"Door and windows were closed," put in Grosskopf.

"Didn't find anything?"

"No."

MacBride went out and up to the dock, and found a knot of men hovering nearby, expectantly.

"You guys knew Nelson, didn't you?"

Most of them did.

"See anybody around here tonight?"

One replied, "I seen Gus Scoggins."

"Going or coming?"

"He must have been goin' to the barge. I seen him on this dock. Was about nine o'clock. He said, 'Hello, Joe.' And I said, 'Hello, Gus.'"

"You didn't see him go back?"

"Well, no. I didn't hang around. I was on the way to my own barge when I saw Gus."

"Who do you work for?"

"Harbor Towin'."

"Sure you're not tryin' to frame Scoggins?"

"Who? Me? No. I'm a' old timer. I know Gus for years. I don't figger he did anything."

"He might have," said another voice. "Him and Nelson ain't been good friends since Scoggins claimed Alf tried to cut him loose."

MacBride left the group and called Grosskopf. "Ring the morgue and have them get Nelson. Tonovitz, you stay on this barge. Riggy, come with me."

MacBride and Rigallo went to the float dispatcher for Tate & Tate and got from him the position of Scoggins' barge. It was at Pier Four, and ten minutes later they found it. No lights shone. MacBride boarded, tried the door, found it padlocked from the outside.

"He should be on board," remarked Rigallo.

"He should," agreed MacBride. "Cripes, if Scoggins did this, Tate & Tate will be swamped!"

They climbed back to the pier and accosted the patrolman on duty, O'Toole.

"You know Scoggins? Have you seen him?"

"Saw him about eight-thirty, Cap, leaving."

"When he comes back, hold him and ring the station-house. If he doesn't show up by the time you leave, call me and tell your relief to watch for him, too."

"O.K."

MacBride and Rigallo shot back to the station-house. Rigallo went home, and MacBride hauled out a blanket and curled up on a cot in one of the spare rooms.

By morning he had the medical examiner's report. The bullet had gone through Nelson's heart aslant and lodged in his spine. A thirty-two.

O'Toole had rung in with no word of Scoggins. MacBride called the patrolman at Pier Four, and found that Scoggins was still absent. He hung up, went down to the pier, picked up the harbor master for Tate & Tate, and had him open the door to the little cabin. Everything was in order. Scoggins' suitcase, clothes, and other odds and ends, were still there.

MacBride went back to the pier, and found Hiram Tate, just arrived.

"What do you think about this killing, MacBride?"

"Looking for Scoggins. Somebody saw him around Nelson's barge last night."

"This is a rotten break, MacBride! Do you think it was Scoggins?"

"It looks as if it might be. He hasn't showed up all night."

They walked back to the street, and then MacBride made for the barge that had been Nelson's home. Officer Pallanzo was on duty, and he was having his hands full.

"I can't get rid of her, Cap," he complained.

MacBride stood with arms akimbo and stared at Hilda Yonson, who sat on the dock beside the barge. Her hands were clasped about her knees, and she was rocking back and forth and moaning. Her yellow hair blew in coarse wisps across her hueless face. Her hat was askew.

"Alf… Alf.…"

She was dazed. When MacBride spoke, it seemed she did not hear him. She rocked on—and on, staring with red-rimmed eyes.

"Look here, Hilda," MacBride said, bending down. "Come on. Don't sit around here. I'll take you home."

He shook her. She looked up, and her lips quivered. "You—you said you vass Alf's friend. All de time you had Alf in de station-house."

"Forget that. I was doing my duty. Come on, Hilda, I want to get the man who killed Alf. I want you to help me get him."

"Ay vill keel him!" She doubled a fist and squared her jaw.

"No, you leave that to me. Let's go." He took her arm, urged her.

She rose and permitted MacBride to lead her from the barge. She walked with a steady, purposeful tread, her face grim.

MacBride found a room at one corner of the warehouse, and they entered it, Rigallo close behind.

"When did you last see Alf, Hilda?" asked MacBride.

"Ay see Alf last night."

"What did he say?"

"Ay didn't talk. Ay go down by de dock und Ay see Alf iss playin' cards vit two fal-lers. So Ay don't go in. Ay go home."

"You know the men?"

"No. Vun vass dressed like vat you call sheik. Ay looked in by de vindow. De odder vun vass dat fal-ler Scoggins."

"About what time?"

"Vass maybe half-past nine."

MacBride turned to Rigallo. "This looks queer, Riggy—Nelson and Scoggins playing cards."

"With another guy—yeah."

"Ay vill keel him, whoever it vass dat keeled Alf. O-o-o-o, my poor Alf!" she moaned, rocking on the chair.

"Listen, Hilda," put in Rigallo, "buck up. And don't do any killing. Leave that to us. We'll get this bum and he'll burn for it."

"Ay vill bet it vass dat Scoggins."

They took her home, where she lived with an elder sister, and then went over to the station-house.

"The Commissioner's been calling you, Cap," said Sergeant Flannery. "Wants to talk to you."

MacBride took the phone and called Headquarters, and the Commissioner said, "That Scoggins is a good lead, MacBride. Tail him and get him. He's the guy we want, all right."

"I'm not so sure," said MacBride.

"Get him, MacBride. Grill young Tate. Maybe Tate knows a lot about it. Maybe he knows where Scoggins is."

Hanging up, MacBride swore softly. "Riggy, they're sure out to crush Tate & Tate, and making no bones about it."

Sergeant Flannery knocked and came in. A little boy accompanied him.

Flannery said, "Kid just came in with a note."

MacBride took a rumpled piece of brown wrapping paper, and read:

> *For Cap. MacBride, Second Police Precinct. I been took here and held. Looks like these guys are going to kill me or something. Get me out of it. I can't write more now. Gus Scoggins.*

MacBride looked at the boy, who was standing on one foot, twisting a cap which he held in his hand.

"Where'd you get this, son?"

"I picked it up in the gutter on North Street."

"You know just where?"

"Yes."

MacBride stood up and put on his overcoat. "Come on, Riggy. Where's Doran?"

Flannery said, "Playing poker with the reserves."

"Call him."

MacBride and Rigallo pushed out into the central room, and a moment later Doran appeared and joined them.

"We're going places, Tim. You heeled?"

"Yup."

"Then let's go. Come on, sonny."

Chapter V

MacBRIDE flagged a taxi, and they all piled in. Ten minutes later they alighted and walked down North Street.

"It's on the next block," said the boy, "on the other side of the street. See that red brick house? I found it right in front of that, in the gutter."

"All right," said MacBride. "Here's a half-dollar. Run home."

The boy ran off and MacBride stopped. "Riggy, Tim, we've got to get Scoggins. The Commissioner wants him."

"I wonder if he really does," said Rigallo.

MacBride grinned. "I'll be doing my duty. He told me to get him."

They walked on, crossed the street and drew near the red brick house. An empty store was on the street level, windows soaped and pasted with *To Let* signs. Above this ranged two stories. North Street is a mongrel street. There are warehouses, garages, poolrooms, a few tenements.

"There's an alley," said Doran, pointing a few doors further on.

"Good idea," said MacBride. "We'll go around to the back."

They entered the alley, followed it to the rear, vaulted a couple of board fences and eventually found themselves in the yard back of the red brick house. A door that apparently led into the back of the store barred the way. There were two windows.

"We don't want to make any noise," said MacBride. "Cut the putty away from that top pane and we'll pry it out."

They used jack-knives, succeeded in removing the pane with a minimum of noise. MacBride reached in, unlocked the window, pushed it up. Then he crawled in. Doran and Rigallo followed, and they stood in an empty room littered with paper and old boxes.

"Upstairs, I guess," said MacBride, and opening a door, stepped into a musty hallway.

Each man carried one hand in his pocket, on his gun.

MacBride led the way up a flight of stairs. He stood on the first landing, looking around. Doran and Rigallo joined him. There were four doors along the side, and one at either end of the corridor.

MacBride whispered, "You guys park on the next stairway and watch. Quiet, now."

They nodded and cat-footed off.

MacBride stood alone, deliberating. Now that he was here, what should he do? The situation presented some difficulties. Where was Scoggins? What room? How much of a gang was here? Where was the gang? Why hadn't Scoggins been more explicit?

Questions? The answers would be arrived at only through action. He shrugged. Couldn't stand here all day. Suppose he picked a door at random and knocked?

Well, try it. He did. Squared his shoulders, assumed an innocent expression and rapped on the nearest door. Whom should he ask for?...

The door opened and a man in an undershirt and trousers looked out.

"Hello," said MacBride.

"Hello," grunted the man.

"I'm a tenement-house inspector," said MacBride. "I'd like to look through the rooms. Won't take long."

"What do you want to look for?"

"Just see about lights, fire exits. Won't take long. Few minutes. Hate like hell to bother you, but the boss has been riding me."

"Well, come in, then," grunted the man.

MacBride entered, wondering what tenement-house inspectors were supposed to do. He took out a pencil, however, and a batch of old envelopes from his pocket. He made a few lines, looked very thoughtful, went to each of the two windows in the room, opened and closed them. The man in the undershirt watched him closely.

"Well, this room's all right," said MacBride. "Now the next."

"Wait a minute," grumbled the man, and entered the next room, closing the door behind him. MacBride heard subdued voices during the brief moment the door was open.

He stepped to the hall door, swung it open, caught Rigallo's eye, and put a finger to his lip. Rigallo, hiding with Doran on the staircase, nodded and grinned. MacBride closed the door softly.

A second later the other door opened, and the man in the undershirt came back. With him was another man, a tall, slim, saturnine man smoking a cigarette through an ivory holder. He eyed MacBride with a cold stare.

"Who sent you here?" he clipped.

"My boss."

"Well, come around some other time."

"Can't. I'm taking this block today."

"Well, take this dump some other day."

"What's the idea?" shot back MacBride. "What do you suppose the boss will say if I take all the houses on this street except this one?"

"That's your lookout. Here's twenty-five bucks. Mark this place as okey."

"Sorry," said MacBride.

"Then clear out."

MacBride didn't know how tenement-house inspectors acted in such a case, but he knew how a cop acted. "Now look here, mister," he said. "My job is to look these places over, and I'm going to look it over. Don't get snotty, either, or I'll condemn the damned joint right off the bat."

"You will, eh?"

"You said it."

"Who cares?"

"I don't," shrugged MacBride.

"And neither do I. Can that crap and on your way, buddy."

"Well, all right, then, if you want to get mean about it," said Mac-Bride. "I'll hand in a bum report."

"Sure. Go ahead. I don't care."

MacBride put away his pencil and paper and pulled open the door, shoved his hand into his pocket, and stood there.

"Now I'll get mean," he ripped out. "Just like this!"

His gun jumped into view, and the two men gasped.

"Raise 'em high!" snapped MacBride; and over his shoulder, "Come on, boys."

But Doran and Rigallo were already beside him. "Frisk 'em," said MacBride.

Rigallo entered the room and approached the man in the undershirt, relieving him of an automatic. The other man snarled:

"What the hell kind of a stunt is this?"

"Shut up!" said MacBride. "Get your hands up."

He snatched a gun from the man's pocket and put it into his own.

"It's a frame-up!" yelled the man.

"Damn you, close your trap!" barked MacBride.

The door to the next room swung open. He caught a momentary glimpse of a group of startled faces. Then the door banged, as Doran leaped toward it and tried to keep it open.

"Hold everything, gang!" yelled the saturnine man.

A shot crashed, splintered the door.

Doran stepped back, leveled his gun and put three shots through the lock.

Rigallo handcuffed the two men together. MacBride took another pair of manacles and secured them to a water-pipe.

"You guys are dicks!" cried the saturnine man.

"God, but you're bright!" chuckled MacBride.

Somewhere below, glass crashed. Doran reloaded his gun. Rigallo fired a couple of shots through the door.

Footsteps were pounding up the stairway. MacBride jumped into the hall, his gun leveled. Two policemen appeared, guns drawn.

"Take it easy, boys," called MacBride. "Stay here in the hall. We've got some bums bottled up."

Even as he said this a door further down the hallway burst open and men rushed out. Revolvers blazed, and one of the policemen went down. MacBride fired and Doran joined him. Eight men swept down upon them like an avalanche. Rigallo came hurtling out of the room.

Doran sank under a blackjack. MacBride put two shots through the head of the man who had wielded it. A clubbed revolver skimmed along his skull and thudded on his shoulder. He twisted and clubbed his own gun, and broke a man's nose. Blood splashed over him.

Somebody reeled, balanced on the balustrade, and then pitched down into the hallway below. Somebody else kicked MacBride in the stomach while he was trying to reload. He doubled and fell to the door, and another foot cut open his left ear.

Rigallo, holding the doorway of the room wherein the two men were manacled, put a slug in the back of the man who was kicking MacBride's head. The man fell over the captain and never moved once, until MacBride shoved him over and staggered to his feet.

Two men rushed Rigallo, and one swore in Italian. Rigallo snarled,

"As one wop to another, back up!" The man struck with his blackjack. Rigallo dodged and blew out the man's stomach.

"Cripes!" choked the other.

"Stay back," warned Rigallo, "or I'll spill your guts, too."

Two more policemen rushed up the stairs, met two gangsters at the head, forced them back. Suddenly the shots ceased, and the hallway was strangely quiet. Six men, one of them a policeman, lay on the floor, dead. Three gangsters stood with their backs against the wall, disarmed, breathing thickly, one with a broken and bloody nose.

Rigallo still stood in the doorway. MacBride lifted up Doran, shook him.

"You all right, Tim?"

"Yeah—sure," mumbled Doran.

"Hold him," MacBride said to one of the policemen.

Then he turned toward the door, laid his hand on Rigallo's shoulder. "Riggy, this was a hell of a blow-out!"

"Sloppy," nodded Rigallo.

MacBride entered the room and looked at the two men manacled to the water-pipe.

"Well, you satisfied?"

The man in the undershirt said nothing. The other said, "No, are you?"

"Not yet."

MacBride entered the other room. A table was littered with bottles and glasses. He looked around, rubbing his jaw. He crossed and opened another door, looked into a bedroom. It was empty. He backed up, called Rigallo.

"You and Doran hunt for Scoggins. He must be hidden somewhere. Go right to the roof, if you have to."

They went out, and MacBride sampled a bottle of Three Star Hennessy. It was good stuff, warmed him up. He noticed a closet door, and with the bottle still in his hand, walked over and grasped the knob. He pulled, but the door resisted, yet it was not locked. He dropped the bottle and drew his gun. Someone was in that closet, holding the door shut.

"Come out!" MacBride called.

There was not a murmur.

"Out, or I'll riddle the door!" said MacBride.

Still no answer.

"I'll count three," said MacBride. "Ready. *One!*" He marked time. "*Two!*" His gun steadied. "*Three!*"

His finger tightened on the trigger. He aimed low.

Bang! Bang!

Rigallo and Doran came in, with Scoggins between them.

"Found him, Cap," said Rigallo.

"Just a minute, Riggy," said MacBride. "I've found something else."

He waited. He saw the knob move.

"Atta boy!" he called. "Open it or I'll shoot higher. Ready!"

The door burst open and a wild-eyed man tottered out.

"Well!" exclaimed MacBride. "Greetings, Mr. Braun!"

"G-God!" stuttered Braun.

A new voice penetrated the room— "Is that Braun of the Harbor Towing, Mac?"

MacBride pivoted.

Kennedy of the *Free Press* was leaning in the doorway, tapping his chin with a pencil.

Chapter VI

BRAUN, that short, round, dark, nervous man, seemed to be swallowing hard lumps.

MacBride spoke to a policeman, "Ed, you shove those three bums in the hall into the next room with the other two."

"Right-o, Cap."

"Riggy and Tim, you stay in here with me," went on MacBride. "Kennedy, you can stay here on the condition that you don't publish anything unless you have my consent."

"Suits me, Mac."

MacBride rubbed his hands gingerly. "This will be interesting. Make yourselves at home, men—you, too, Braun, and you there, Scoggins. There's a bottle and glasses. Let's get clubby."

Braun was not in a clubby mood. He was emphatically nervous, and kept biting his thin red lips.

MacBride said, "Now, Scoggins, what happened?"

Scoggins had taken a drink. He wiped his mouth. "Gosh, I was scared. T' other afternoon me and Alf Nelson met in the lunch-room across from Pier Ten. I said, 'Hello, Alf.' And he said, 'Hello, Gus.' Then I said, 'Look here. Alf, we know each other for years. We worked together. What's the sense o' bein' mean? I know you tried to cut me loose t'other night, but I'm willin' to forget it.' And Alf said, 'I been a big bum, Gus.' And I said, 'You been a fool, Alf. You never had much brains. You're lettin' some big guys talk you into doin' things. You'll get in trouble, Alf, if you don't look out.' So Alf looked kinda guilty, and he said, 'Yeah, I been a big bum, Gus. I been wantin' to get some money ahead, so me and Hilda could get hitched. You and me been friends for years, Gus.' And I said, 'We sure have, Alf. And like one friend to another, I'd warn you to look out for them big guys. If you get in Dutch, they ain't goin' to help you.' So he said, 'I guess you're right, Gus. I been a dumb-bell.' I said, 'You sure have, Alf.' And he nodded and then said, 'Gus, come over my barge tomorrer night and have a game of pinochle like old times.' So I said I would, and I did.

"So I went over. We played for an hour, and then some guy came in, and Alf said, 'This is a friend, Gus. Call him Pete.' So I called him Pete and he called me Gus, but I didn't like him. He wasn't a water-front man. Along about 'leven o'clock I figgered I better go, and Pete said, 'Me, too. I got a motorboat out here. I'll take you up-river.' I said, 'Thanks,' and we went.

"There was another guy waitin' in the boat, and when we got out in the river they jumped me. I was knocked out. When I come to I was in a room upstairs. I was sore. I wonder if Alf double-crossed me."

"Alf is dead," said MacBride.

Scoggins squinted. "What!"

"Was killed about an hour after you left."

"Dead!"

"Uhuh."

"But who did it?"

"I don't know—yet." MacBride turned to Braun. "Maybe you know."

Braun started. His eyes blinked. He moistened his lips. "Captain, I seem in a peculiar position. Unfortunately, circumstances are against me. I believe I'll not say anything until I've thought things out more."

"Until you've seen a lawyer?" sneered MacBride.

"Until he's seen the Commissioner," sliced in Kennedy.

It was like dropping a bomb. MacBride swung on him. Braun

shuddered, clenched his hands, pursed his lips. Rigallo tapped the floor with his toe. A long moment of silence enveloped the room. Kennedy smiled whimsically, one eyebrow slightly arched.

MacBride said to Rigallo, "Bring in those guys we hitched to the pipes inside."

Rigallo grinned, entered the adjoining room, returned a minute later with the saturnine man and the man in the undershirt. The saturnine man had tightened his dark face, and his eyes were two black slots of malevolence, his lips were flattened against his teeth.

Scoggins said, "That's the guy we played cards with. He's the guy took me for a motorboat ride."

"The guy that killed Nelson, eh?" put in Kennedy. "Know him, Mac?"

"Not yet."

"He's from Chicago, if I've got my mugs right. Pete Redmond."

"Well, what about it?" snarled the man.

"Soft pedal," said MacBride. "I'm going to plant you for a long while, buddy."

"Like hell you are!" snapped Redmond.

"Sh!" put in Braun.

Redmond turned to him. "What's the matter with you? You look yellow around the gills. Come on, tell this guy who we are. I can't hang around here all day. I got a date. Call the Commissioner on the telephone."

Braun turned a shade whiter. "Sh! Don't be a fool, Redmond!" he gulped.

"Well, then, let's go. He can't hold us. Telephone the Commissioner. I tell you, I got a date."

MacBride said, "Braun, do you want to make a telephone call?"

Braun shifted nervously, wore a pained look.

"Go ahead," urged Redmond. "Call him up."

Braun went over to the telephone, called a number. "Hello, George," he said. "Listen, George.... Huh? You know.... Well, what are you going to do?... Yeah, Pete is here.... Well, how could I help it?... Well, don't bawl *me* out, George.... All right."

He hung up, said, "He'll be right over."

Kennedy licked his lips. "Hot diggity!"

Braun was pale. Redmond scowled under MacBride's steady gaze and said, "Think you're wise, eh? I get a great kick out of you, big boy. I didn't think they came that dumb."

"You'll find how dumb I am," said MacBride.

"Wait till the Commissioner comes," smirked Redmond.

"Ah, just wait," said Kennedy.

So everybody waited. Thirty minutes passed, and then an hour.

Braun said, "I wonder what's keeping him."

"He'd better hurry," said Redmond. "I got a date."

"Oh, damn your date!" cried Braun.

"Yeah?" snarled Redmond.

MacBride took a drink and said, "Pipe down."

The telephone rang. Rigallo was nearest and took the call. When he hung up, he said, "We should all go over to Headquarters."

"Now why the hell should we go to Headquarters?" snapped Redmond. "I'm not going."

"Let's go," said MacBride.

"I don't savvy this at all," complained Redmond.

"It will be all right," soothed Braun.

"It better be," said Redmond.

MacBride called the morgue, said, "There are a lot of stiffs at 46 North Street. Better come up and collect 'em."

He went into the next room, and told one of the policemen to remain with the dead until the men from the morgue arrived. To the others he said, "We're taking the rest over to Headquarters."

MacBride, Rigallo and Doran and the three policemen gathered the six gangsters together and marched them down the stairs. All were handcuffed, including Braun, who stumbled as he walked. MacBride hauled him along roughly. Scoggins walked beside Kennedy.

Below, a crowd of people swarmed on the sidewalk outside the door. MacBride chased them as he led the way. Rigallo and Redmond were behind him. They marched down the street, two by two.

"I don't like this," complained Redmond. "I don't see why the hell we have to go to Headquarters."

"Be quiet," called back Braun.

"I tell you, guy, if—"

Bang!

Chapter VII

REDMOND sagged, belched blood.
Bang!

Braun stopped in his tracks, buckled, groaned.

"Duck!" yelled MacBride, and dragged Braun into the nearest hallway.

Rigallo lugged Redmond into a fruit store.

Four shots rang out, and the four gangsters behind crumpled.

Kennedy and Scoggins dodged into a hardware store as a shot smashed the window beside them.

MacBride had disengaged himself from Braun. Braun was dead.

Rigallo joined the captain and said, "Redmond's cooked, too. What the hell do you suppose happened anyway?"

"God knows, Riggy! Those shots came from that store across the way. Come on!"

He rushed into the street, blew his whistle. Doran came on the run, followed by the policemen. Doran said, "Every guy was picked off, Cap, and there was some straight shooting! That store—"

"Yeah. Let's go," clipped MacBride, and crossed the street on the run.

The store was empty, but they broke through the door and cascaded into the interior. The men bunched around MacBride.

"They've cleared out—through the back! Come on!" he said.

He led the way into the rear, and they found a back door open and thundered out into a yard. A fence barred the way, but they vaulted over it, crashed through the back door of another house and milled in a dark hallway.

MacBride rushed headlong, came to another door, yanked it open and looked out upon Jackson Street. He started to step out, when a machine gun stuttered and the door-frame splintered. Rigallo yanked him back, slammed the door.

"Don't be a fool, Mac!"

They heard the roar of a motor. It diminished in a few seconds. MacBride again opened the door, stepped out, looked up and down the street, said over his shoulder, "Come on."

His men came out warily. The street was empty—not a car, not a person in sight.

"Dammit!" muttered MacBride.

"Well, why worry?" asked a policeman. "One gang against another. That's a good way of getting rid of rats."

"It sure is," said another cop.

MacBride grumbled.

Kennedy said, "Come on, Mac. I've got several ideas."

"I'm going to Headquarters," growled MacBride. "Riggy, you and Doran go back to North Street and see the morgue bus gets those bums."

He turned on his heel and strode down the street. Kennedy fell in step beside him.

"Mac, we're near the end. It won't be long now. I figure you're just outside the Big Guy's doorstep."

MacBride made no comment. His jaw was hard, and his eyes glittered.

They entered Police Headquarters. Kennedy lingered at the desk while MacBride went on to the Commissioner's office. But the Commissioner was not in. MacBride rejoined Kennedy at the desk, prodded him and marched out.

"What's the matter?" asked Kennedy.

"He's not in?"

"Where'd he go?"

"Left no word."

They stopped on the wide steps outside, and MacBride lit a cigar.

A big black limousine drew up, and Commissioner Stroble alighted. He stood speaking with someone who remained in the tonneau behind drawn curtains. Then he suddenly spun around and saw MacBride and Kennedy standing on the steps. He spoke hastily in an undertone and stepped back to the sidewalk.

The car started off. Kennedy ran down the steps, called, "Hey, how about a lift?"

The Commissioner looked startled. Kennedy jumped to the running-board, but the car jerked ahead, and he slipped, fell, rolled into the gutter.

Stroble mounted the steps, eyes narrowed. "What do you want, MacBride?"

"Just wanted to see you."

"Come up to my office."

As MacBride followed Stroble in, he turned and saw Kennedy standing on the sidewalk, grinning.

In the Commissioner's office, a tenseness became apparent. Stroble took off his overcoat and sat down.

"Well, MacBride."

"I thought you were coming over to North Street."

"I was. But when I reached the street there was a gunfight going on. I'm too old for gunfights, MacBride."

"Braun was killed. He was a friend of yours."

Stroble sighed. "Poor Charlie. Yes, he was a friend of mine, from school days. What kind of a mess did he get into?"

"I'm sure I don't know," said MacBride. "I caught him with a bad gang. A bird named Pete Redmond, from Chicago, and some other guns."

"My!" exclaimed Stroble. "That was strange. Charlie shouldn't have done that."

"He was sure you could help him," gritted MacBride.

"Yes, for old times' sake. Months ago he came to me and said Tate & Tate were riding him. Trade was falling off. He wanted more police protection. Well, I tried to make it easy for him. You'd do the same, MacBride, for an old friend. I didn't know he'd gone bad."

MacBride restrained himself with an effort. Deep in his heart he knew that Braun had been double-crossed, yet what could he do? There was no evidence.

Stroble was saying, "It was strange, too, how that other gang popped up. Why do you suppose they committed such wholesale slaughter?"

MacBride blurted out, "It looks to me like a double cross."

Stroble blinked. "I say, now, do you really think so?"

"Yes."

"H'm. That is possible. Poor Charlie! He was a good chap, MacBride, but a bit of a fool. No clue to who did it?"

"No. All the cops ran to North Street when the shooting started. The gang, after they killed Braun and the others, beat it through to Jackson Street and made a clean getaway. We tried to follow, but I damned near got plastered by a machine-gun. We had to hide."

"Sensible, MacBride—very sensible. Personally, I believe that in such a situation, you should be careful. Gangs often destroy each other, and take that task off a policeman's hands. Of course, we must spread an alarm. But poor Charlie! I didn't think he'd take advantage of me—of a good thing, MacBride."

"Scoggins, you know, was kidnaped and held by Braun's gang."

"Goodness. Now why do you suppose they did that?"

MacBride leaned forward, barbed every word—"So that we'd think Scoggins killed Nelson. So that red tape would tie up Tate & Tate a little longer, drive them nearer to bankruptcy, give the Harbor Towing a big lead."

"Could that be possible!" exclaimed the Commissioner. "And there I was trying to do Charlie a good turn, for old times' sake! It wasn't fair of Charlie. Do you think so, MacBride?"

"I don't know."

"H'm. Well, run along. I've some work to do. File the report on this when you find time. Good luck."

MacBride almost lost control of himself. His fingernails dug into his palms. A grunt escaped his lips.

The Commissioner looked up. "Eh?"

MacBride snapped, "Good day," and banged out.

In the street he found Kennedy, and the reporter said, "You look fit to be tied, Mac."

"I am! I'm stumped!"

"Mac"—Kennedy took his arm and steered him down the street— "Mac, buck up. Before very long you're either going to get the Big Guy—or he'll get you."

"What do you mean, Kennedy?"

"I know things. Come on over to the station-house."

They tramped into MacBride's office. Kennedy closed the door and locked it. He rubbed his hands together, smiled his tired, whimsical smile. He slid upon the desk, and tapped the blotter in front of MacBride.

"Get this, Mac, and think it over," he said. "I've been keeping a few things under my hat. Yesterday I made a discovery. Why do you think Stroble was giving the Harbor Towing all the breaks?"

"Braun was a friend of his."

"Nonsense! Stroble is a big stockholder—silent one, you know— in the Harbor Towing."

"How do you know?"

"I found out. I went to that lousy brokerage firm of Weber & Baum. They used to handle Stroble's business, but he broke with them, and they got sore. In confidence Baum told me that Stroble practically owns the Harbor Towing. And look here. The Mayor owns the Atlas Trucking Corporation—under cover—and the one is practically linked with the other.

"I've got the whole thing doped out, Mac. Pete Redmond was head of Stroble's private gang, and Braun had to move as he was told. When they balled things up that way, and when you flopped on their big parade—and I turned up at the right moment—the Commissioner knew that he was cooked.

"You had Braun and Redmond cold. Even Stroble, with all his power, couldn't get them clear. So what did he do? Wiped them out! Double-crossed them! Got another gang to kill every one of them as you marched down the street."

"Good God!" groaned MacBride. "I believe you, Kennedy. I'm sure you're right. But the Mayor—man—the Mayor! You're sure he's mixed up in it?"

"I'll say this, Mac. I'll bet my shirt that the gang that wiped out Redmond was the Mayor's own. Stroble went to him, told him the fix he was in. The Mayor knew that if Braun and Redmond were caught, they'd squeal on the Commissioner and that Stroble would yap on the Mayor. So he lent Stroble his gang."

"But who is the Mayor's gang?"

"That's for you to find out."

"And you think the Mayor is the Big Guy?"

"If he isn't, I'm all wrong."

MacBride snorted. "Hell, Kennedy, it's incredible. I never thought much of him, but—"

"Look here, Mac," cut in Kennedy. "The Atlas Trucking Corporation has been having hard sledding, too. The Harbor Towing will have to shut up. Tate & Tate will get that concession at Seaboard Basin. But the Colonial Trucking Corporation is a subsidiary of Tate & Tate, and I'll bet that before long this trade war will be carried toward that end."

"If it is, Kennedy—"

"You'll find a hard nut to crack."

"I'll crack it or croak."

Kennedy lowered his voice. "I didn't tell you, Mac, who was in that limousine I tried to hop."

Their eyes met, MacBride's wide and blunt, Kennedy's narrowed and smiling.

"Who, Kennedy?"

"Don't you know?"

"You mean, the…"

"Sure," nodded Kennedy. "The Mayor!"

Graft

Chapter I

POLICE CAPTAIN STEVE MacBRIDE, elbow on desk, chin on knuckles, looked down along his nose at the open dictionary, and concentrated his gaze on the word "graft." Now graft is a word of various meanings, and the definitions, as MacBride discovered, were manifold. But the definition that attracted and held his eyes longest was clean-cut, crisp and acutely to the point:

> Acquisition of money, position, etc, by dishonest, unjust, or parasitic means.

His lips moved. "Parasitic. Humph! That's what they are, parasites!"

He sighed, creaked back in his swivel chair, and stared absently at the night-dark window. Cold out. The panes rattled. The wind hooted through the alley. More distant, it keened shrilly over housetops, whinnied through the complicated network of radio aerials. Even the poor had radios—bought tubes and what-not and went without shoes.

But graft. Parasitic. Parasites in the Town Hall. Hell, why hadn't he taken up plumbing, after his father? You could straighten out a bent pipe, plug a leak. But, as a police captain, with a wife and a daughter to support, and three thousand still due on that new bungalow in Grove Manor....

He banged shut Webster's masterpiece with a low growl, got up and took a turn up and down the room. Straight was MacBride—morally and physically. Square-shouldered, neat, built of whipcord, hard bone, tough hide. His face was long, rough-chiselled, packed well around cheek and jaw. His mouth was wide and firm, and his eyes were keen, windy—they could lacerate a man to the core.

He ran the Second Police Precinct of Richmond City. His frontiers touched the railroad yards and warehouses, plunged through a squalid tenement district and then suddenly burst into the bright lights of

theatres, hotels, nightclubs. It was the largest precinct territorially in Richmond City. It was also the toughest.

Beyond the rooftops, a bell tolled the hour. Midnight. MacBride looked at his watch. Home. He could catch the last street car out to Grove Manor. Stifling a yawn, he walked to a clothes tree and took down his conservative gray coat and his conservative gray hat. He had one arm in his coat when the door opened and Sergeant Flannery, bald as a billiard ball, poked in.

"Just a minute, Cap. Girl outside pestering me—"

"Why pass the buck?" MacBride had his coat on. "I'm going home, Sergeant."

"But I can't get rid of her. She wants to see you."

"Me? Nonsense. You'll do for a sob case, Flannery. I mind the last sob sister you pawned off on me. Was hard up for a drink, the little tramp. Widowed mother and all that crap. Bah!"

"This one's different, Cap. Married a little over a year. Left her kid, three months old, home with her old lady. Name of Saunders. Lives over on Haggerty Alley. Damn near bawling. Wants to see you."

"Well"—MacBride started to put on his hat, but changed his mind and flung it on the desk—"send her in."

Overcoat partly buttoned, he dropped into the swivel chair and sighed after the manner of a man who has to listen, day in and day out, to tales of woe, of stolen cats, strayed dogs, blacked eyes, and broken promises. Well, another wouldn't kill him....

The girl came in timidly. She wore no hat, and her coat was a cheap thing, and she looked cold and forlorn and afraid. Pity—MacBride claimed there was not an ounce of it in his make-up—prompted him to say:

"Take that chair by the radiator. Warmer."

"Thank you."

Pretty kid. Young, pale, brown-eyed, hatless, and hair like spun copper. A mother. Haggerty Alley. God, what a draughty, drab hole!

"Well?"

"I came to you, Captain, because Jimmy—he's my husband—because Jimmy always says, 'MacBride, the gent runs the Second, is one reason why there ain't more killings in this neighborhood.'"

MacBride was on guard. He hated compliments. But, no, this wasn't salve. Her lower lip was quivering.

"Go on, madam."

"Well, I feel funny, Mr. MacBride. I feel scared. Jimmy ain't come home yet. I've been reading things in the newspaper about some trouble in the trucking business. Jimmy drives a big truck between Richmond City and Avondale—that's thirty miles. He leaves at one and gets back to the depot at nine and he's always home at ten. He's been carting milk from Avondale, you know—for the Colonial Trucking Company."

MacBride's eyes steadied with interest. He leaned forward. "What makes you afraid, Mrs. Saunders?"

"Well, I was reading the paper only the other night, about this trouble in the trucking business, and Jimmy said, he said, 'Wouldn't surprise me if I got bumped off some night.' You know, Mr. MacBride, only last month one of the drivers was shot at."

"H'm." MacBride's fingers tapped on his knee. "Don't worry, Mrs. Saunders. Everything's all right. Truck might have broken down."

"I phoned the depot, and they said that, too. But the drivers always phone in if they're broke down. Jimmy ain't phoned in. The night operator was fresh. He said, 'How do I know where he is?' So I hung up."

"Listen, you go right home," recommended MacBride. "Don't worry. They don't always break down near a telephone. Run home. Want to catch cold chasing around the street? Go on, now. I'll locate Jimmy for you, and send a man over. Got a baby, eh?"

Her eyes shone. "Yes. A boy. Eyes just like Jimmy's."

MacBride felt a lump in his throat, downed it. "Well, chase along.

I'll take care of things."

"Thank you, Mr. MacBride."

She passed out quietly; closed the door quietly. Altogether a quiet, reticent girl. He stood looking at the closed door, pictured her in the street, rounding the windy corner, with shoulders bunched in her cheap coat—on into Haggerty Alley, dark, gloomy hole.

Jerking himself out of the reverie, he grabbed up the telephone, asked Information for the number of the night operator at the Colonial Trucking Company's River Street depot. He tapped his foot, waiting for the connection.

"Hel-lo-o," yawned a voice.

"Colonial?"

"Yup."

"That driver Saunders. Heard from him yet?"

"Cuh-ripes!" rasped the voice. "Who else is gonna call about that guy? No, he ain't showed up, and he ain't called, and if you wanna know any more, write the president."

"I'll come down there and poke you in the jaw!" snapped MacBride.

"Aw, lay off that boloney—"

"Shut up!" cut in MacBride. "Give me the route Saunders takes in from Avondale."

"Say, who the hell are you?"

"MacBride, Second Precinct."

"Oh-o!"

"Now that route, wise guy."

He picked up a pencil, listened, scribbled, said, "Thanks," and hung up.

Then he took the slip of paper and strode out into the central room. Sergeant Flannery was dozing behind the desk, with a half-eaten apple in his pudgy hand.

"Sergeant!"

Flannery popped awake, took a quick bite at the apple, and almost choked.

"Chew your food," advised MacBride, "and you'll live longer. Here, call the booth at Adams Crossing. We're looking for a Colonial truck, number C-4682, between Avondale and here. Call the booths at Maple Street and Bingham Center. Those guys have bicycles. Tell 'em to start pedaling and ring in if they find any trace. Brunner—you can locate him at the Ragtag Inn. He hangs out there between twelve and one, bumming highballs. Tell him to fork his motorcycle and start hunting."

He paused, thought. Then, "Where's Doran and Rigallo?"

"Stepped out about eleven. Down at Jerry's, shooting pool. Should I flag 'em?"

"No."

MacBride turned on his heel, entered his office and kicked shut the door. He sat down, bit off the end of a cigar, and lit up. He hoped everything was all right. Poor kid—baby three months old—Haggerty Alley—eyes like Jimmy's. Bah! He was getting sentimental. Did a man get sentimental at forty?

The door opened. Kennedy, of the *Free Press,* drifted in. A small, slim man, with a young-old face, and the whimsical, provocative eyes of the wicked and wise.

"Cold, Mac. Got a drink?"

MacBride pulled open a drawer. "Help yourself."

Kennedy hauled out a bottle of Dewar's and poured himself a stiff bracer—downed it neat. He slid on to a chair, coat collar up around his neck, and lit a cigarette. The cigarette bobbed in one corner of his mouth as he said:

"Anything new about this trucking lead?"

"Not a thing."

Kennedy smiled satirically. "The Colonial Trucking Company versus the Atlas Forwarding Corporation. Hot dog!"

"Take another drink and breeze, Kennedy."

"Cold out. Warm here. Say, Mac, look here. What chance has the Colonial against the Atlas when the Atlas is owned—oh, privately, sure!—by the Mayor? Funny, how those inspectors swooped down on the Colonial's garage last week and condemned five trucks as unfit for service and unsafe to be on the public highways. Ho—protecting the dear, sweet public! D'you know the Atlas is worth five million dollars?"

"Shut up, Kennedy!"

"Funny, how that driver was shot at last week. He was going to tell something. Then he turned tail. Who threatened him? Or was he paid? The new State's Attorney, good chap, could get only negative replies out of him. Hell, the guy got cold feet! Then he disappeared. This State's Attorney is ambitious—too clean for this administration. He'll get the dirty end, if he doesn't watch his tricks. So will a certain police captain."

MacBride bit him with a hard stare. Kennedy was innocently regarding the ceiling.

"Some day," he went on, "or some night, one of these drivers isn't going to get cold feet. I pity the poor slob!"

Sergeant Flannery blundered in, full of news.

"Brunner just rang in. Found the truck. Turned upside down in a gully 'longside Farmingville Turnpike. Milk cans all over the place. Driver pinned underneath. Brunner can't get him out, but he says the guy's dead. He's sent for a wrecking crew, nearest garage. Farmingville Turnpike, two miles west of Bingham Center."

MacBride was on his feet, a glitter in his windy blue eyes. Haggerty Alley—eyes like Jimmy's. Hell!

"Haul out Hogan," he dipped, "and the flivver." He buttoned his coat, banged out into the central room, fists clenched.

Kennedy was at his elbow. "Let's go, Mac."

"It's cold out, Kennedy," said MacBride, granite-faced.

"Drink warmed me up."

No use. You couldn't shake this newshound. Prying devil, but he knew his tricks.

Outside, they bundled their coats against the ice-fanged wind, and waited.

The police flivver came sputtering out of the garage, and the two men hopped in.

MacBride said, "Shoot, Hogan!"

Chapter II

HAVE you ever noticed how people flock to the scene of an accident, a man painting a flagpole, or a safe being lowered from a ten-story window?

MacBride cursed under his breath as the flivver rounding a bend on Farmingville Turnpike, he saw up ahead dozens of headlights and scores of people. A bicycle patrolman was directing traffic, and the flivver's lights shone on his bright buttons and shield. Automobiles lined either side of the road. People moved this way or that. One pompous old fellow, with a squeaky voice, remarked that truck drivers were reckless anyhow, and served him right for the spill.

MacBride stopped on the way by, glared at the man. "Did you see this spill?"

"No—oh, no, no!"

"Then shut your trap!"

The captain was thinking of Haggerty Alley, and his tone was bitter. He moved on, and Motorcycle Patrolman Brunner materialized out of the gloom and saluted.

"Right down there, Cap. Guy's dead, and the truck's a mess. Can hardly see it from here."

"How'd you spot it?"

"I went up and down this pike twice, and the second time I noticed how the macadam is scraped. The guy skid bad, and you can see the marks. Closed cab on the truck, and he couldn't jump."

"Wrecker here yet?"

"No—any minute, though. Hoffman's handling traffic."

"Give me your flashlight. Go out with Hoffman and get these cars moving."

"Right."

MacBride took the flash and started down the embankment. Kennedy, huddled in his overcoat, followed. The way was steep, cluttered with boulders, blanched bushes; and as they descended, they saw turned earth and split rocks, where the truck had taken its headlong tumble.

Then they saw the truck, a twisted heap of wood and metal. A ten-ton affair, boxed like a moving van. But the truck had crashed head-on into a huge boulder, and the radiator, the hood, the cab and the cargo were all jumbled together. And somewhere beneath this tangled mass lay the driver.

Kennedy sat down on a convenient stump and lit a cigarette. MacBride walked around the wreck, probing with his flashlight. The beam settled on an arm protruding from beneath the snarled metal. Bloody—the blood caked by the cold.

He snapped out the flash, stood alone in the chill darkness, quivering with suppressed rage. The wind, whistling across the open fields, flapped his coat about his legs. Probably that girl was still sitting up, with her slippered feet in the oven of the kitchen stove, and her wide, sad eyes fixed on the clock. Brutal thing, death. It not only took one, but stung others. He wondered if there were any insurance, and thought not. Good thing, insurance. He carried twenty thousand, double indemnity, in case of accident. Could a guy in the Second Precinct die any other way but through an accident? Or was getting a slug in your back by a coked wop, death from natural causes?

A broad beam of light leaped down into the rocky gully.

"Wrecker," said Kennedy.

MacBride nodded, watched while several men came weaving down the slope.

"Cripes!" muttered one, upon seeing the wreck.

Another said, "Hell, Joe, we can never haul this out. Need a derrick."

"Well," said MacBride, "you've got axes. Hack away enough junk so you can get the man out."

MacBride stood back, hands in pockets, chin on chest. Axes flashed, rang. Crow-bars heaved, grated.

Brunner came down and said, "Morgue bus just came, Cap."

They got the body out, and one of the men became sick at his stomach. Another—case-hardened—chuckled, said, "Hell, buddy, you should ha' been in the war!" War! This was war—guerrilla warfare! War of intimidation!

They put a blanket over the dead man, laid him on a stretcher, carried him up over the hill and slid him into the morgue bus.

"I want the report as soon as possible," MacBride said to the man from the morgue.

The bus roared off into the night.

MacBride and Kennedy climbed into the police flivver. It was a bleak, cold ride back to the precinct.

The captain, without a word, went straightway into his office, uncorked the bottle of Dewar's and downed a stiff shot. He rasped his throat, stood staring into space.

Kennedy drifted in, espied the bottle, rubbed his hands together gingerly. "B-r-r! Cold out."

MacBride turned, eyed him, then waved toward the bottle. "Go ahead."

"Thanks, Mac."

Alone, MacBride went out into the black, windy street, turned a corner, crossed the street and entered Haggerty Alley. He stopped before a drab, three-story dwelling. Aloft, one lighted window stared into the darkness. He drummed his feet on the cold pavement, then suddenly pushed into the black hallway, snapped on his flash, and ascended the worn staircase.

Third floor. One lighted transom. He knocked. The door opened. That pale young face, wide, questioning eyes. Shoulders wrapped in a plaid shawl.

"Come... in."

MacBride went in. Yes, the kitchen, and an old woman sitting before the open oven of the stove, and clothes drying on a line above the stove. Faded wallpaper, hand-me-down furniture, warped ceiling. Cracked oilcloth on the floor. Neat, clean—poverty with its face washed.

The girl knew. Oh, she knew! Her breath, bated for a long moment, rushed out.

"Is he...?"

MacBride stood like an image of stone. "Yes. Bad wreck."

She wilted, like a spring flower suddenly overcome by an unexpected frost. The old woman moved, extended a scrawny arm.

"Betty!"

The girl reeled, spun, and buried her face in her mother's lap. The mother cradled her in ancient arms.

MacBride wanted to dash out. But he held his ground, and something welling from the depths of him melted the granite of his chiseled face. The old woman looked up, and though her eyes were moist, there was a certain grimness in her expression. Age is strong, mused MacBride. It meets fate with an iron jaw.

The old woman, looking at him, shook her head slowly, as if to imply that this was life, and we either died and left others to mourn, or mourned while others died.

MacBride put on his hat, backed toward the door, opened it softly. He bowed slightly, and without a word, departed.

He was a little pale when he reached the station-house. Doran and Rigallo, his prize detectives, and four or five reserves were hanging about the central room, and Kennedy, his coat collar still up to his ears, was leaning indolently against the wall and blowing smoke circles.

MacBride nodded to Doran and Rigallo, and strode into his office. Kennedy tried to edge in but MacBride closed the door in his face. Doran hooked one leg over a corner of the desk and Rigallo stood jingling loose change in his pocket.

He said, "Trouble, eh, Cap?"

"Plenty!" MacBride bit off.

"Was the guy shot?"

"No telling yet. Too messed up to see. That's the morgue's job. We'll get news soon. But I'm willing to bet my shirt the guy's been done in. If he has, I'm going to bust loose and drive the Atlas Corporation to the wall."

Doran grunted. "Fine chance, with that bum of a Mayor back of it. How the hell did he ever get in?"

"Don't be dumb," said Rigallo. "That last election was a farce. All the polls in the Fourth and Fifth wards were fixed. Guys voted twice, and the polls committee scrapped a lot of votes for the opposition because of some lousy technicality—illegibility, unreadable signatures, and all that crap. Who votes in this city? The better element yap at conditions and turn up their noses and don't even go near the polls. The bums, the bootleggers, the blockheads and gunmen vote! And the New Party sends loud-mouthed guys to ballyhoo the mill and river bohunks during lunch-hour, and under-cover guys go around near the employment agencies, the bread-lines, and the parks. They find guys out of work and up against it, and they slip 'em a ten-dollar bill to vote. The Atlas Corporation employs eight hundred men, and they vote right or lose their jobs and their wives, mothers and the whole damned family are dragged to the polls. Now d'you wonder why we have this bum of a Mayor?"

MacBride said, "Sounds like Kennedy."

"It is," replied Rigallo. "Kennedy and I have the whole thing thrashed out."

The telephone rang. MacBride picked it up, muttered his name, and listened. When he put the instrument down, he sucked in his breath and curled his lip.

"Poisoned," he said. "Saunders, the driver, was poisoned. A stuff that he could drink and it wouldn't have any effect for an hour. Then it hits a man like a stroke of paralysis. That's how it hit Saunders."

Doran said, "Must have stopped at a roadhouse for a snifter and got poisoned liquor."

"Just that," nodded MacBride. "I'll find that roadhouse. Some pup is going to hang for this, just as sure as God made little green apples!"

"Remember, Cap, the Mayor," put in Doran.

MacBride doubled his fist. "I'll bring it right to his doorstep if I have to, and I'd like to see the bum try to can me. I'm sick and tired of these conditions! I'm going to put a dent in the Atlas Corporation, and wipe out this graft, this dirty, rotten corruption."

"They'll bump you off, Mac."

"I'll take the chance! I'm insured for twenty thousand, and my plot in the cemetery is paid for!"

It took a tough man to run the Second.

Chapter III

NEXT day the noon edition of the *Free Press* gave the wreck and the death of Saunders a front-page column. It recited the details in its customary offhand manner, giving the place, the approximate time, name of the deceased, and financial loss. It wound up with the non-committal statement that the police were investigating the matter, but did not say why.

MacBride, reading it over his coffee, at his home in Grove Manor, was a little disgruntled at its apparently disinterested attitude. But, turning the pages, his eye rested on the editorial columns, and particularly on an item labeled,

CRIME—CORRUPTION.

Crime. We've always had it. It is a disease, recurring every so often, like smallpox, diphtheria, and scarlet fever. It lays waste, like any and all of these diseases, and causes suffering, misery and despair.

And on the other hand, wealth, affluence, power. To whom? Why, to those, quite often in high place, who like parasites, feast avidly upon the meaty morsels gathered by vultures who swoop in the dark, kill from behind, and crow at the dawn.

What we need is a crusader. Not a preaching, scripture-quoting, holier-than-thou sort of fellow. Not an altruist, nor a gavel-thumper. But a Man, and we capitalize that symbolically. A man somewhere in the rusty machinery of this municipality, who cares not a whoop for authority and is willing to stack the possibility of losing his job against the possibility of sweeping out the unclean corridors of intrigue and corruption, and satisfying the ego of his own morals and ethics.

A two-fisted, slam-bang, tougher-than-thou sort of man! The streets of Richmond City are more sordid than its sewers. They smell to high heaven. We need a chunk of brimstone to sterilize them. Amen.

"Whew!" whistled MacBride. "This will cause apoplexy in the Town Hall. The *Free Press* is out to ride 'em."

He was back in his office at the precinct at one, and Kennedy was sound asleep in the swivel chair. He kicked it, and Kennedy awoke.

"Hello, Mac."

"Hello. Pretty ripe, that editorial."

"Thanks."

MacBride looked at him. "You didn't write it."

"Yup. My name'll go down in posterity."

"If the Big Gang knew you did it, it would go down in the Deceased Column. Get out o' that chair."

Kennedy got out and sat on the desk, swinging his legs.

MacBride said, "I see, now, that you were shooting in my direction. Humph. Crusader!"

Kennedy smiled. "Would you, Mac."

"I am," snapped MacBride, "but there's nothing of the crusader about me. I'm sore, and I'll bust up this racket if it's the last thing I do. That poor kid, Kennedy—her name's Betty.... God Almighty! Government of the people, by the people and for the people! What a bromide!"

He pulled an empty cigar box from his desk, took a pen and a piece of paper, and on the paper printed, in large letters:

SPARE CHANGE, BOYS,
FOR A HARD-HIT NEIGHBOR

This he pasted on the cover of the box, and said, "Dig down, Kennedy."

He himself dropped in a couple of dollars, and Kennedy added another and some odd change. Then MacBride carried the box into the central room and placed it on the desk, where none might pass without seeing it.

Still in plain clothes, he shook Kennedy, and walked down to River Street. He found the Colonial depot, and from a number of drivers learned that, on cold nights, they usually stopped at the *Owl's Nest*, out beyond Bingham Center, on the pike, for a shot of rum. Reasoning that Saunders had lived, driven and drunk similarly, he took a trolley car to the outskirts of the city, alighted where Main crossed Farmingville Turnpike, and boarded an outbound bus.

It was a long ride, and they passed the shattered truck on the way. It still lay in the gully, but a derrick was at work, and one of the Colonial's trucks was gathering up the remains. At four-thirty he left the bus, and stood regarding the *Owl's Nest*. It stood well back off the highway, a low, rambling casino with many windows. The main entrance was decorated with colored light bulbs, but on one side was a sign, *Delivery Entrance*, and MacBride judged that this also was the logical entrance for truckmen in quest of a drink.

He pushed this door open and found himself in a hallway that turned sharply to the left. But directly in front of him was an open door leading into a small, shabby room containing two tables and a half dozen chairs, and a fly-specked electric light hanging from the ceiling.

MacBride sat down, and presently a man in shirt-sleeves entered.

"Rye highball," said MacBride.

The man, large, beetle-browed, hairy-armed, looked him over, then shook his head. "No drinks here, buddy."

"Tripe! I know."

"Not here, buddy."

"You the boss?"

"No."

"Flag the boss."

The man disappeared, and a few minutes later a short, fat, prosperous-looking man entered with a frown of annoyance. But the frown disappeared like a cloud and sunlight beamed.

"Oh, hello, Mac."

"Didn't know you ran this dump, Hen. Sit down."

Hen sat down, cheerful, twinkle-eyed, and said to the hovering waiter, "Make it two, Mike." And a moment later, to MacBride, "What you doing out this way, Mac?"

"Poking around."

"I mean—really, Mac"

"Trailing a clue. Hear about that truck smash-up?"

"Sure. Tough, wasn't it?"

"You don't know the half of it. And that's why I'm up here, Hen."

Hen's eyes widened perplexedly. He started to say something, but the drinks arrived, and he licked his lips instead. The waiter went out, and the two men regarded each other.

MacBride jerked his head toward the door. "How long has that guy been working here? What's his name?"

"A month. Mike Bannon."

"He serves all the drinks?"

"Ye-es."

"All the truck drivers stop in this room, I guess?"

"Sure."

MacBride took a drink and let it sink in. "Good stuff," he nodded, and then leaned across the table. "You're a white guy, Hen, and you're sensible. Fire that man."

"What's the matter?"

"Fire him tomorrow. If he gets sore, tell him the cops are tightening down on you, and you're cutting out the hooch for a month or more. I'm doing you a turn, Hen. You want to keep your hands clean, don't you?"

"Cripes, yes, Mac!"

"Then bounce him—tomorrow at noon."

"Okey, Mac."

MacBride was back in the precinct at seven. He picked up Rigallo and Doran and they all went over to Headquarters and sought out the Bureau of Criminal Identification. This was a vast place, lined with rows of card indexes, and on the wall were several huge metal books, attached by their backs, so that a man could swing the metal pages back and forth and scan the photographs of those men who, having stepped outside the law, were recorded therein, with further details of their crimes recorded in the surrounding files. MacBride, turning page after page, suddenly grunted and pointed.

"There's the guy, boys," he said.

He noted the number, gave it to the attendant, and while waiting, said to his prizes, "Working at the *Owl's Nest*."

The attendant reappeared with a card and handed it to MacBride. MacBride scrutinized it. "H'm. Michael Shane, arrested for criminal assault against Rosie Horovitz, June 12, 1924. Indicted, June 13th. Acquitted July 2nd. Lack of evidence. And again: Arrested October 5, 1925. Charge, felonious assault with attempt to rob. Charge preferred by Sven Runstrom. Indicted October 6th. Sentenced October 15th, sixty days, hard labor."

"Lets go out and nab him," said Rigallo.

"No," said MacBride. "He's working as Mike Bannon. Come on."

They returned to the precinct, and in the privacy of his office, MacBride said, "This guy poisoned Saunders' liquor, but I'm after bigger game. He's a tough nut, and he'll hold his tongue until some shyster, retained by the gang, gets him out of our hands on a writ. What we want to know is, who's the boss of the gang, the Mayor's right-hand man. *That* is the guy we want. We've got more to do than apprehend the actual murderer of Saunders. We've got to grab the mob and their boss, and prevent further killings, and when we do this we'll have the Mayor against the wall. Shane is a stoical bum, and a rubber hose wouldn't work him. We've got to get the big guy—the one with the most brains and the least guts."

"What's your idea?" asked Rigallo.

"Just this. At tomorrow noon Shane gets his walking papers from Hen Meloy. You go out there tomorrow morning in a hired flivver, and when this guy gets on a bus headed for town, tail him. He'll head for his boss, to report. Tail him that far and then give me a ring."

MacBride went home early that night, slept well, and was back on the job at nine next morning. He took the cigar box from the desk in the central room, went into his office, and counted out forty-two dollars and fifty cents. This he shoved into an envelope, with the brief message, "From the bunch at the Second Police Precinct." He called in a reserve, gave him the envelope and the Haggerty Alley address, and then, sitting back with a sigh, started his first cigar of the day.

Kennedy dropped in on his way to Headquarters, and said, "The municipal inspectors condemned two more Colonial trucks. Said Saunders' death was caused by a faulty steering gear. Nobody knows the details? What did the morgue say, Mac?"

"Run along, Kennedy."

"Keeping it under your hat, eh? It's all right, Mac. I can wait. Here's another tip. The Colonial people aren't dumb, and there's a guard riding on all their night trucks now. They're die-hards, Mac. These guys liked Saunders, and they're primed to start shooting first chance they get."

Kennedy went out, and MacBride cursed him in one breath and complimented him in the next.

At two o'clock the telephone rang and MacBride grabbed it.

"Cap? Rigallo."

"Shoot, Riggy."

"Tailed him okey. Two-ten Jockey Street. I'm waiting in the cigar store on the corner. Come heeled."

MacBride hung up, slapped on his visored cap, and strode into the central room. "Six reserves, Sergeant! Ready, Doran!"

A windy look was in his eyes, and his jaw squared.

Chapter IV

JOCKEY STREET is hell's own playground. You enter it from the theatrical center, and all is glittering, blatant and intensely alive. But as you bore deeper, riverward, the street lights become further apart, the chop suey joints disappear, and the houses, losing height, likewise lose color.

It was cold that afternoon, and fog smoked in from the river, damp and chill. The din of upper Jockey Street died to a murmur, and on its lower reaches few men were afield. Here or there you heard footsteps, and soon, dimly at first, then clearer, a pedestrian materialized out of the fog, swished by and gradually disappeared again, trailing his footsteps. Up the man-made causeway came the muffled, rhythmic tolling of a pierhead fog bell.

Down it rolled a black, inconspicuous touring car, with drawn side-curtains. Nearing a side street, the door to the tonneau opened, and MacBride leaped out. The car rolled on, was swallowed up by the wet gray clouds.

MacBride strode toward a cigar store. Rigallo came out, smoking a cigarette, looking unconcerned. They fell in step and strolled down the side street, leisurely.

"He hasn't come out, Riggy?"

"No. Came on the bus to Main and Farmingville. Took a taxi from there. Got off at Main and Jockey. Walked. I left the car there and walked, too. Saw him go in 210. There's a gray touring car parked outside—powerful boat."

"I'll crash the joint."

"They'll never open the door. Bet you need signals."

"Try my way."

They circumnavigated the block, and came out upon Jockey Street a block nearer the river. Here the police car was parked, the men still hidden inside. MacBride stood on the edge of the curb, spoke to the curtains.

"I'm aiming to get in 210. Two minutes after I leave here you boys get out and surround this block. It may be messy."

"Okey," came Doran's low voice.

MacBride said, "Come on, Rigallo," and they walked up the street. He explained. "We'll both climb the steps to the door. I'll knock. Somebody will come, but if he doesn't get the proper signals, he won't open. But he'll listen. Then you walk down the steps, hard as you can, and walk away. He may open then and peek out. I'll crash it."

"What then?"

"Hell knows!" MacBride's fists clenched. "Just let me get in that dump!"

They reached the four stone steps that led to the door of 210. They mounted them, and MacBride, one hand on the gun in his pocket, knocked with the other.

They waited, looking at each other. Presently they heard the padding of footsteps, then silence. MacBride knocked again, insistently. No, that wasn't the signal. He nodded to Rigallo. Rigallo nodded back, stamped heavily down the steps and walked off.

MacBride flattened against the door-frame, breath bated, gun half-drawn. The latch clicked. A hinge creaked. The door moved an inch, another inch. A nose appeared. Then two beady eyes, and a pasty, pinched face.

MacBride cannoned against the door, and knocked the lookout sprawling. The door, working on a spring, slammed shut. The captain was bent over the prostrate, speechless form, with the muzzle of his gun screwed into a sunken chest.

"Chirp and I'll bust you!"

The man writhed under the firm pressure of the gun. His mouth worked, gasping. His eyes popped.

"Cripes!" he moaned.

"Pipe down! Quick, now. What's the lay? Where's the gang?"

"Cripes!"

"Spill it!"

"Cripes!"

Desperate, MacBride rapped his jaw with the gun barrel.

"Ouch!"

"Then talk!"

"Second floor, door t' back o' the hall. Cripes!"

"Open?"

"Uh—yup."

"How many?"

"Tuh-ten."

"Get up!"

MacBride hauled the runt to his feet, dragged him to the front door, opened it. Rigallo was on the curb. MacBride motioned to him, and Rigallo skipped up.

"Take this, Riggy!"

Rigallo grabbed the lookout, clapped on manacles. "Should I get the boys?"

"No. I'll start the ball. There are ten guys upstairs, and I feel ambitious. Besides, if we all crash it, it will be a mix-up and the boys might get hurt. One man can crash a room better than six. I'll blow when I need you. You hang here, and then blow for the boys."

"It's a long chance, Cap!"

"I carry heavy insurance. Don't let this door close."

MacBride turned and re-entered the hall. Gun drawn, he went up the stairway, paused at the first landing, listened, and then ascended the next flight. He was wary, alert, dangerous. There were captains on the Force who directed operations from the outside, smoking cigars on street corners, at a safe distance. MacBride was a man who never sent his men into a trap before first examining the trap himself. One reason why his wife lay awake nights, thinking.

Door in the rear. He stood at the stair-head, muscles tense, gun pointing toward the door. He advanced, straight, light-footed, primed to go off. He stood before the door, the muzzle of his gun an inch from the panel.

His left hand started out, closed gently, carefully, over the knob. Some said you should turn a knob slowly, bit by bit, until you could not turn it any more; then heave and rush. But sometimes you never got that far. A knob might creak. A wandering gaze on the other side might see it turning.

Turn, heave and rush all at once—that was it. MacBride did it. The door whanged open and he crouched on the threshold, poised and deadly.

A woman, alone, looked up from the depths of an overstuffed chair. She had been trimming her fingernails with a steel file, and she sat there, apparently unperturbed, the file, in her right hand, poised over the thumb of her left. She wore a negligée, pink and sheer. Her hair was peroxide treated, bobbed and fuzzy.

MacBride reached back and closed the door. The woman, with a shrug, went on trimming her nails, and said, in an offhand manner,

"Got your nerve, Cap, busting in on a lady."

"What's wrong with that sentence, Gertie?"

"Well, rub it in."

"Get dressed."

"I'm not going out."

"No?" He leaned back. "I'm waiting."

She rose, running her hands down her sides and lodging them on her hips, thumbs forward.

"Suppose I yell?"

"You'll be the first woman I ever killed."

"You would?"

"I sure would."

They stood staring at each other, the lynx and the lion.

"Think I can get dressed with you in the room?"

"I'm not particular. If you're too modest, put on that fur coat."

"I'm not modest. *Particular,* guy."

"Put on the coat."

She tilted her chin, cut MacBride with a brassy, withering look. Then she sauntered over to the coat, picked it up and slipped into it. She thrust her hand into a pocket.

"Careful!" warned MacBride.

She laughed, drew out a handkerchief, touched her nose and then shoved the handkerchief back into her pocket. A split-second later flame and smoke burst through the fur, and hot lead ran up MacBride's gun arm. His gun clattered to the floor.

The woman leaped for the switch, threw off the lights. With his left hand MacBride, gritting his teeth with pain, recovered the gun. Another burst of flame slashed through the darkness, and a shot whanged by his ear. He dived, headlong, collided with the woman and knocked her over. Again her gun went off, wildly, and the shot banged through the ceiling.

With his wounded hand MacBride groped for hers—found it, wrenched away her gun, groaned with the pain of it. He heaved up, rushed to the door, shot home the bolt. Then he dived for the light switch, snapped it, and a dazzling radiance flooded the room.

The woman, on her feet, flung a Chinese vase. MacBride ducked and the vase crashed through a mirror. She crouched, quivering in every muscle, her breath pumping fiercely from her lungs, eyes wide and storming with anger.

"You—lousy—bum!" she cried.

"Pipe down!"

Fists hammered on the door, feet kicked it. Voices snarled.

The woman laughed hysterically. "The Gang! The Gang! They'll riddle you! They'll cut your dirty heart out!"

"Will they?"

MacBride drew his whistle, blew it.

Chapter V

ABRUPTLY, the scuffling and pounding stopped. A moment of silence, then retreating footsteps.

MacBride stood with his cap tilted over one ear and a slab of hair down over one eyebrow. His right arm hung down, blood weaving a red tracery on his hand, then dropping to the floor. His hand felt heavy as lead, dragging at wounded muscles. A thought struck him, and he shoved the hand into his coat pocket.

Footfalls sounded again, hammering up the stairs. Cops' shoes—heavy-soled, thick-heeled. Now they were out in the hall, moving about, whispering hoarsely. MacBride backed against the door, unbolted it, pulled it open.

Rigallo came in. "Hell, Gertie!" he chuckled, sarcastically.

Gertie thumbed her nose and wiggled her fingers.

"You trollop!" snapped Rigallo.

"Pst, Riggy," said MacBride. "Where's the lookout?"

"Doran's got him in the machine."

"Jake!" He looked into the hall. Six cops out there and two closed doors. They had the doors covered. "Take her downstairs, Riggy."

"Who's her boy friend?"

"That's what we'll find out. She's not talkative just now. Grab a dress, sister, and take it along."

"If you think I'll spill the boy friend's name, MacBride, you're all wet," she snapped.

"Take her, Riggy."

Rigallo grabbed a dress from a hanger and flung it at her. It draped across her shoulder. She left it there.

"Get out," he jerked.

She put one hand on her hip and sauntered leisurely. Rigallo took a quick step, gripped her by the arm and propelled her out not too gently. She cursed and added something relative to his maternity. He trotted her down the stairs.

MacBride joined his cops. "Let's bust this door."

Seven guns boomed, and seven shots shattered the doorknob and crashed through the lock. Patrolman Grosskopf, one-time leader of a German mud-gutter band, hurled his two hundred and twenty pounds of beef against the door and almost ripped it from its hinges.

MacBride waved his men back and stepped in. The room was empty. His right hand was still in his pocket. His men did not know he was wounded. He came out in the hall and nodded at the other door.

Bang! Seven shots sounded as one.

"Now, Grosskopf."

Grosskopf catapulted, and the door capitulated.

The room yawned empty. It showed signs of some having made a hasty departure. Bureau drawers were pulled out, a chair was overturned. Glasses, some of them still containing liquor, stood on the table. A chair, also, stood on the table.

"Up there," said MacBride, pointing to a skylight. "To table, to chair, to roof."

He led the way up to the roof, and they prowled around, from one roof to another. Wind, fog, and emptiness. They came to a fire-escape in the rear.

"They skipped," he said. "Come on back."

Below, in the hall, they found Rigallo and the woman, Doran and the lookout. MacBride looked at the woman but addressed his men. "We've got an ace-in-the-hole now. Let's go."

They went out into the foggy street, and MacBride said to the lookout, "Thought you tricked me, eh? Ten men in the back room!"

The woman laughed. "Ten! That's headquarters, Cap, not the barracks. What a joke! There was only three—in the front."

Rigallo said to the lookout, "Boy Scout, we will entertain you a while at the precinct. I have a nice new piece of rubber hose."

They piled into the police car. Its motor roared. It turned about and purred up Jockey Street, and at Main Rigallo got out and picked up his flivver, and the two cars proceeded toward the Second.

The prisoners were locked up in separate cells. Then MacBride, alone, went out and walked several blocks and entered a door above which was a small sign bearing the legend, Dr. O.F. Blumm, M.D.

"Oh, hello, Mac."

"Hello, Doc. Fix this." He drew his blood-soaked hand from his pocket, and the doctor frowned, murmured, "H'm," and added, "Take off the coat, shirt."

The bullet had struck just above the wrist, sliced open three inches of the forearm and lodged in the hard flesh just short of the elbow. MacBride, teeth clamped, his eyes closed, shed streams of sweat while the doctor probed for the bullet and finally removed it. Then MacBride sank back, a little pale, very grim.

"It might have been worse," remarked the doctor.

"Sure," said MacBride, and breathed quietly while the wound was cauterized, stitched and bandaged.

"Most men take a little dope for this, Mac."

"Uh!" grunted MacBride through tight lips.

Through the fog, he returned to the station-house, his hand concealed in his pocket, his wound throbbing.

Kennedy was lounging in the office. "You look yellow around the gills, Mac."

"Liver," clipped MacBride, and took a drink.

"Hear you got Gertie Case and Midge Sutter."

"Um."

"How long do you suppose you can hold 'em?"

"Watch me."

"There'll be a writ of release here before you know it," said Kennedy. "How come you didn't get the gang?"

"Breeze, Kennedy! Dammit. I'm not in the mood!"

Kennedy shrugged and went out.

Alone, MacBride drew out his hand, laid it on the desk. God, how the arm throbbed! He heard a voice outside the door and slipped the hand back into his pocket. The door opened and a big, bloated man, with a moon-face, large fishy eyes, and an air of pompous importance, sailed in.

"Hello. Mac."

"Hello."

Captain Bower, plainclothes, a Headquarters "yes man," and the Mayor's bodyguard. MacBride drew into himself, wary, on guard.

Bower deposited his indecent bulk in an armchair and sent a tobacco shot into the cuspidor. "This latest business, Mac. The Jockey Street fizzle."

"Fizzle?"

"Well, whatever you like. Anyhow, it's out of your district, and Headquarters is going to handle it. Another thing. We're also handling the case of Saunders. Of course, there's nothing to it, and we'll dispose of it right off."

MacBride's jaw hardened. Graft again! Nothing to it! Bah! They knew he was out to riddle their racket. They were cornered, and playing a subtle game. They could not fire him immediately, could not shove him out in the sticks while this thing was hanging fire. But they *could* take a case out of his hands. Could they?

"It's my case, Bower," he snapped. "My men got the clues, did the tailing, and we've got Midge Sutter and that Case broad salted."

"On what charge?"

"Suspicion. That's enough for any cop."

"We'll work it out at Headquarters," said Bower, very matter-of-fact. "I'll take the pair along with me, now."

Color crept into MacBride's face. "Not before I indict 'em—tomorrow."

Bower frowned. "Don't be a goof. What can you indict 'em on?"

MacBride was in his last ditch, his back to the wall. He had hoped to conceal this, but—

He drew out his wounded arm, placed it on the table. "This, Bower. The woman potted me."

Bower's face dropped, and his mouth hung open. He stared at the bandaged hand. Then he drew his face back into place and got up.

"Good-bye," he sniffed, and pounded out.

MacBride waited a few minutes, then called in Rigallo. "Riggy, take Sutter in the sweat room. Sweat him."

"Right," nodded Rigallo, and went out.

MacBride sat back in his chair and lit a cigar. The pain pounded furiously, shot up and down his arm, reached his neck. Sweat stood out on his forehead, and muscles knotted on either side of his wide, firm mouth. An hour dragged by.

Then Rigallo came in, brushing his hands together. His hair, ordinarily neatly combed, was a bit disheveled.

"Well?" asked MacBride.

Rigallo shook his head. "No go. The guy is little but tough. He's been through it before. Knows if he squeals the gang will crucify him."

MacBride held up his wounded arm. Rigallo clicked his teeth.

"Hell, Mac. I didn't know!"

"The broad got me. Look here, Riggy. You're the whitest wop I've ever known. My back is to the wall, and I need a guy who's willing to kick authority in the slats and play this game to a fare-thee-well."

"Shoot, Mac."

"Take the broad and bounce her around from one station to another. They'll have a writ out for her, or some trick. The idea is, the writ mustn't find her. When they come here, I'll say she's over at the Third. Then I'll ring you and you take her to the Fourth and so on, and the guys at the Fourth will tell the runner you've taken her to the Fifth. Keep ahead of the runner. The precincts will play with us. They're good guys. Keep moving until tomorrow morning. Judge Ross will be on the job then, and he's the only judge we can depend on. He'll indict her. We'll get hell, Riggy, but we'll crash this racket."

"Right!"

Five minutes later Rigallo was headed for the Third, with Gertie Case.

Ten minutes later a runner appeared with writs for Gertrude Case and Midge Sutter.

"Sutter's here," said MacBride, "and you can take him. But the Case woman's over at the Third."

And he telephoned the Third.

A little later a doctor from the Medical Examiner's Office, accompanied by Captain Bower, entered, and the doctor said:

"I'll look at your wound, Captain."

Grim, stony-faced, MacBride allowed his wound to be looked at. The doctor said, "Bad, Captain. You can't carry on."

"The hell I can't!"

"Nevertheless—" The doctor sat down and affixed his signature to a document, scaled it across to MacBride. "You're released from active duty until I sign a health certificate of reinstatement. Signed by the Commissioner and attested by me. Go home and rest."

MacBride saw through a red haze. Vaguely, he heard Bower's words, "Your lieutenant will take charge until a captain can be sent over."

MacBride's heart sledge-hammered his ribs. The men went out, and he sat alone, like a man in a daze. Alone against graft, corruption and the very Department to which he had given eighteen years of his life! The blow should have crushed him, sent him storming out of the station in rage and righteous indignation. It should have driven him to ripping off his uniform, throwing his badge through the window, and cursing the Department to the nethermost depths.

But tough was MacBride, and a die-hard. He heaved up, swiveled and glared at the closed door. His lip curled, and challenge shone in his eyes.

"Home—*hell!*" he snarled.

Chapter VI

BUT he went out, his slouch hat yanked over his eyes. Night had closed in, half-brother to the fog. And both shrouded the city. Street lights glowed wanly, diffusing needle-like shafts of shimmering radiance. Headlights glared like hungry eyes. Autos hissed sibilantly on wet pavements. Faces appeared, palely afloat, and then disappeared.

Cold and wet and miserable, and MacBride tramping the streets, collar up, hands in pockets, pain pumping through his arm. In minutes he aged years. Why not let things slide? Why go to all the bother? What reward, what price honor? Let Headquarters take 'em. Let Bower frame their getaway. Cripes, but Bower would get a nice slice of graft out of this! How could a single precinct captain hope to carry his white plume in this city of graft?

He dragged to a stop at an intersection. Well, Rigallo was standing by him. And the State's Attorney was a square-shooter.

"H'm."

He suddenly flagged a taxi, climbed in and gave an address. Out of the dark of the street another figure appeared, got into a second taxi.

Ten minutes later MacBride alighted in a quiet, residential street, told the driver to wait, and ascending a flight of brownstone steps, pushed a bell-button. A servant appeared and MacBride gave his name. A moment later he was ushered from the foyer into a spacious library.

State's Attorney Rolland, thirty-eight, lean, blond, clean-cut in evening clothes, extended a hand. MacBride shook with his left, and though Rolland's eyes flickered, he said nothing.

"You look worn, Captain. Sit down. Cigar?"

"Thanks—no. Am I keeping you?"

"No. Dinner at eight." He leaned against the edge of a broad mahogany table, arms folded loosely, eyes quizzical.

MacBride detailed, briefly, the fight in Jockey Street, the apprehension of Gertie Case and Midge Sutter; the release of Sutter on a writ, the game of hide and seek even now being played by Rigallo.

"I'll pick up Rigallo and the woman around dawn," he went on. "I'll get her indicted. I thought if you could be around there, to take her in hand before her lawyer gets to her— Hell, we've get to get the jump on these pups!"

"Don't know her man, eh?"

"No. That's why we've got to hold her. If she's faced with twenty years for shooting an officer, she'll think. She's thirty now, and no guy is worth enough in her eyes to take a twenty-year rap for him. She'll come across. Ten to one her boy friend realizes this."

"And you believe that Saunders chap was poisoned?"

"Yes. Bannon did it. He's been lying low for a couple years. Always lone-wolfed. That's why we can't connect him with the gang he must have hooked with. If the Case woman squeals, we'll get the gang, and getting the gang means—"

"Ah, yes," nodded Rolland.

It was politic, in the State's Attorney's rooms, not to mention the name both men had in mind.

Then Rolland said, "Good you have the woman. These gangsters laugh at a prison sentence. But a woman—and especially one of her type—looks upon prison as death. I'll be there in the morning. Take care of your wound."

They shook, and MacBride departed. The Regime thought they had picked soft clay in Rolland. What a shock when they had discovered cement instead, unpliable!

Entering the taxi, MacBride drove off, and further back, another taxi began moving.

He left his taxi at the Fourth, and discovered that Rigallo and the woman had gone on to the Fifth ten minutes before. He hung around, saw the runner with the writ rush in and start broadcasting to the desk. The sergeant told him where the woman had gone, and cursing, the runner went off and out like a streak.

MacBride followed from station to station, and at the Seventh, just after the runner had gone on, he met Bower.

"Look here, MacBride. What's your game?"

"What's yours, Bower?"

"Cut that boloney."

"Then cut yours."

Bower scowled. "You'll get broke for this. Stop that guy that's got the dame."

"I don't know where he is. What's more, Bower, I'm off duty. Got nothing to say. You find him—and try stopping him. Your job depends on that, Bower."

Bower worked his hands. He started to say something, but bit his lip instead and stormed out.

A game was being played on the checkerboard of Richmond City's police stations. Rigallo moved from one to another, doubled back, moved across town, uptown, downtown. Midnight passed, and dawn approached, and still Rigallo kept the lead; and Bower blundered in his wake, fuming and cursing; and the man with the writ, worn to a frazzle by the chase, now tottered at Bower's heels.

MacBride, weary, haggard, sapped by the pain in his arm, sometimes dizzy, met Rigallo in the Eighth at four a.m. Gertie cursed and protested at such inhuman treatment, but no one paid her any attention.

MacBride and Rigallo formulated plans, and then MacBride took the woman and carried on the game. When Bower caught up with Rigallo, the latter wasted half an hour of the other's time by stalling, kidding and then finally telling Bower that the woman was probably uptown. Bower saw the trick and bowled off in high heat.

When he caught up with MacBride, he discovered that the woman had again changed hands and was now probably downtown. Bower cursed a sizzling blue streak and was indiscreet enough to call MacBride an untoward name.

With his one good hand, MacBride hung a left hook on Bower's jaw and draped him over a table. Then he went out into the wet gray dawn, and felt a little better.

At half-past eight he met Rigallo in the Third, joined him and the woman in Rigallo's flivver.

"Cripes, I'll never get over this!" rasped Gertie.

"You said something, sister," nodded MacBride.

"You're a big bum, MacBride," she stabbed. "And you're another, Rigallo."

Rigallo spat. "Three of a kind, eh?"

"And your mother's another," she added.

Rigallo took one hand from the wheel and with the palm of it slapped her face.

She laughed, baring her teeth, brazenly.

A block behind, a taxi was following.

Ahead yawned the entrance to Law Street, and halfway down it loomed the Court.

"Here's where you get indicted, sister," said MacBride.

"I'm laughing."

"You don't look that way."

On one side of the entrance to Law Street was a cigar store. On the other corner was a drug-store. As the flivver crossed the square, a man sauntered from the drug-store, and at the same time another sauntered from the cigar-store. They looked across at each other, and both nodded and shoved hands into pockets.

Bang!—bang! Bang—bang!

Chapter VII

RIGALLO stiffened at the wheel. Gertie screamed, clutched her breast. MacBride ducked, and the flivver leaped across the square, slewed over the curb and crashed into the drug-store window.

Pedestrians stopped, horrified, frozen in their tracks. The two well-dressed men who had stood on either corner joined and walked briskly up the street toward a big, gray touring car.

The taxi that had been trailing the flivver stopped, and Kennedy, leaping out, ran across to the demolished flivver. He reached it as MacBride, streaked with blood, burst from the wreckage.

"There's the car, Mac!" He pointed.

"Where's another?" clipped MacBride.

Kennedy nodded to the taxi, and they ran over.

"Nossir," barked the driver, "I ain't chasin' them guys." He climbed out. "You guys go ahead."

"I'll drive," said Kennedy casually.

"Kennedy," said MacBride, "you stay out of this."

"What! After tailing you all night! Coming?"

He was beside the wheel, shoving into gear. MacBride clipped an oath and hopped in, and the taxi went howling up the street.

He muttered. "Pups—got—Riggy! Step on it, Kennedy!"

"The broad?"

"Dead."

"They made sure you wouldn't indict her."

"Pups! *Watch that turn!*"

"Yu-up!"

Kennedy took the turn on two wheels, knocked over a push-cart full of fruit, and jammed his foot hard down on the gas.

"Applesauce!"

"And crushed pineapple!"

Bang!

A cowl-light disappeared from the taxi.

Bang—bang—bang! went MacBride's gun.

People scattered into doorways. Moving cars stopped. Heads appeared at windows.

The gray car swung into a wide street set with trolley tracks. It weaved recklessly through traffic, heading for Farmingville Turnpike, where speed would count. It roared past red traffic lights, honking its horn, grazing other cars, swerving and swaying in its mad, reckless flight.

The taxi hurtled after it no less recklessly. MacBride was leaning well out of the seat, twisting his left arm to shoot past the windshield. Kennedy swung the machine through startled traffic with a chilling nonchalance.

MacBride fired, smashed the rear window in the tonneau.

"Lower, Mac. Get a tire," suggested Kennedy.

"Can't aim well around this windshield."

"Bust the windshield."

MacBride broke it with his gun barrel. He dared not fire again, however. People were in the way, darting across the street in panicky haste. A traffic cop was ahead, having almost been knocked over by the gray touring car. MacBride recognized him—O'Day. He leaned out, and as they whanged by, yelled:

"O'Day—riot squad!"

The gray car reached Farmingville Turnpike, a wide, macadam speedway, and its exhaust hammered powerfully. The taxi was doing sixty miles an hour, and Kennedy had the throttle right down against the floor boards.

"Faster!" barked MacBride.

"Can't, Mac. This ain't no Stutz!"

Bang! No shot that time. The rear left had blown, and the taxi skidded, bounced, and dived along like a horse with the blind staggers. Kennedy jammed on his brakes as a big powerful car slewed around him and slid to a stop ten yards ahead. It was a roadster, and out of it jumped Bower.

"Well, MacBride, see what you done!"

"Pipe down, Bower!" clipped MacBride, starting for the roadster. "Come on, Kennedy. This boat looks powerful."

Bower got in his way. "MacBride, for cripes' sake, lay off! You'll get broke, man!" His voice cracked, and he was desperate.

"Out of my way!" snapped MacBride.

Bower tried to grasp him. MacBride uncorked his left and sent Bower sprawling in the bushes. Then he ran toward the roadster and Kennedy hopped in behind the wheel.

"Step on it, Kennedy!"

Kennedy stepped on, and whistled. "Boy, this is *my* idea of a boat!"

Inside of three minutes he was doing seventy miles an hour. Mac-Bride's hand dropped to the seat, touched a metal object. He picked it up. It was a pistol fitted with a silencer. Kennedy saw it out of the corner of his eye. MacBride opened the gun. A shell had been fired.

"Now," said Kennedy, "you know how we got a flat."

MacBride swore under his breath.

Soon they saw the gray touring car, and Kennedy hit the gun for seventy-five miles an hour. They were out in the sticks now. Fields, gullies, occasional groves of sparse timber flashed by. Curves were few and far between. The road, for the most part, ran in long, smooth stretches.

The roadster gained. MacBride screwed open the windshield, fired, aiming low. He fired again. The touring car suddenly swerved, its rear end bounced. Then it left the road, hurtled down an embankment, whirled over and over, its metal ripping and screeching over stones and stumps.

Kennedy applied his brakes, but the roadster did not stop until it was a hundred yards beyond the still tumbling touring car. MacBride reloaded his gun, shoved the one with the silencer into his pocket, and started back. Kennedy was beside him. As they left the road and ran through the bushes, they saw two figures staggering into the timber beyond.

MacBride shouted and fired his gun, but the figures disappeared in the woods. Kennedy brought up beside the shattered touring car. Four broken, twisted men were linked with the mangled wreckage.

"They're done for, Mac," he said.

"You stay here, Kennedy. I'm going after the others."

"So am I."

"Kennedy—"

"Let's go, Mac." He was off on the run.

MacBride galloped past him, dived into the timber. Somewhere ahead, two men were thrashing fiercely through the thickets. Five minutes later MacBride caught a fleeting glimpse of one. He yelled for the man to stop. The man turned and pumped three shots. Two clattered through the branches. A third banged into a tree behind which MacBride had ducked.

Kennedy, coming up at a trot, raised his automatic and blazed away. MacBride saw the man stop, throw up his arms, and buckle.

"Come on," said Kennedy.

They plunged ahead, reached the fallen man.

"Bannon!" muttered MacBride. "You finished him, Kennedy."

"Good."

Bang!

Kennedy and MacBride flung themselves into a convenient clump of bushes. They lay still, back to back, until they heard the sounds of continued flight up ahead.

"Let's," said MacBride, heaving up.

"Sure—let's."

MacBride started, hunched way over, darting from tree to tree, bush to bush. He stopped, to listen. Kennedy puffed up behind him.

"Come on," said MacBride.

"Sorry, Mac...."

MacBride pivoted. Kennedy was sitting on the ground, holding his right leg.

"Hell, Kennedy!"

"Hell, Mac!"

MacBride bent down.

"Go on," grunted Kennedy. "Get the slob!"

"I'll get him," said MacBride, and started off.

Dodging from tree to tree, he finally came to the edge of the timber. Before him lay a wide, marshy field, and the wind rustled in blanched weeds and bushes.

Bang!

MacBride's hat was shifted an inch, and the bullet struck a tree behind his head. His teeth clicked and he fired three shots into the weeds, then ducked. He crouched, breath bated, and listened.

The weeds crackled, and he heard a groan. Warily he crawled out into the weeds, worming his way over frozen puddles. A groan, and a rasped oath reached his ears. Sounded a bit to the right. He wriggled in that direction. He stopped, waiting. Five, ten minutes passed. Half an hour.

Then, ten yards from him a head appeared above the weeds, then a pair of shoulders. MacBride stood up.

"Drop it, guy!" He leaped as he said it.

With a snarl the man spun, but not completely. MacBride jabbed his gun in the man's side, and the latter regarded him furiously over one shoulder.

"Hello, Sciarvi."

Black and blue welts were on Sciarvi's face. He was hatless, and his overcoat was ripped in several places.

"Where'd I pot you?" asked MacBride, snatching his gun.

"In the guts," grated Sciarvi.

"Didn't know you had any."

"Get me to a doctor. Snap on it, and can the wisecracks. You don't worry me, MacBride."

"Get going." MacBride prodded him. "And lay off the lip, you lousy dago! You're the guy I've been looking for, Sciarvi, and I'll see you to the chair!"

"Yeah? Laugh that off, MacBride. I got friends."

"I'll get your friends, too."

"That's a joke!"

"On you, Wop."

They passed into the timber, and came upon Kennedy leaning against a tree and smoking a cigarette.

"Sciarvi, eh?" he drawled. "Spats Sciarvi, the kid himself, the Beau Brummell of crookdom, the greasy, damn dago."

"Yeah?" sneered Sciarvi. "When I get out of the doctor's care I'll come around and pay you a visit."

"Tell me another bed-time story, Sciarvi!"

They moved along, Kennedy limping in the rear. They came upon Bannon, alias Shane, lying face down, quite dead. They walked past, rustled through the bushes, and came out near the wrecked car.

Half a dozen policemen and a sergeant looked up, and then Bower appeared, red-faced and bellicose.

"Oh," grumbled MacBride, "the riot squad. What did you do, come around to pick souvenirs?"

"We'll take the prisoner," rumbled Bower.

"You'll take hell!" said MacBride.

"Damn you, MacBride!" roared Bower.

MacBride pulled the gun with the silencer from his pocket, held it in his palm, looked at Bower. "Don't you think you'd better pipe down?"

Bower closed his mouth abruptly, stood swaying on his feet, his bloated face suffused with chagrin.

"Come on, Bower," snarled Sciarvi, "do your stuff."

Bower caught his breath, glared at Sciarvi with mixed hatred and fear. Then he stamped his foot and pointed a shaking finger at MacBride.

"You'll see—you'll see!" he threatened, but his tone was choked and unconvincing.

MacBride chuckled derisively, turned to the sergeant and said, "There's a stiff back in the woods. Better get him."

Then he pushed Sciarvi up the slope toward the road, and Kennedy limped after him. They reached the roadster and Kennedy eased in behind the wheel.

"Your leg," said MacBride.

"It's the right one, Mac. I'll use the hand-brake."

Sciarvi was shoved in and MacBride followed, and the roadster hummed back toward Richmond City.

"Now the big guy," said Kennedy.

"Now the big guy," said MacBride.

"Jokes!" cackled Sciarvi.

Chapter VIII

THE MAYOR paced the library of his opulent, fifteen-room mansion. He wore a beaver-brown suit, a starched, striped collar, a maroon tie and diamond stick-pin. He was small, chunky, with a cleft chin, a bulbous nose, and shiny red lips. He wore pince-nez, attached to a black ribbon, and this, combined with the gray at his temples, gave him a certain *distingué* air. He was known for a clubable fellow, and a charming after-dinner speaker; and he went in for boosting home trade, sponsoring beauty contests, and having his picture taken while presenting lolly-pops to the half-starved kids of the South Side, bivouack of the bohunks.

He was not his best this morning. There was a hunted look in his usually brilliant eyes, and corrugated lines on his forehead, and he'd lost count of how many times he'd paced the room. He stopped short, to listen. There was a commotion outside the door, a low, angry voice, and the high-pitched, protesting voice of Simmonds, his man.

Perplexed, he started toward the door, and was about to reach for the knob when the door burst open. He froze in his tracks, then elevated chest and chin and clasped his hands behind his back.

MacBride strode in, kicked shut the door with his heel. He was grimy, blood-streaked, and dangerous. A pallor shone beneath his ruddy tan, and dark circles were under his eyes. He was weary and worn and the hand of his wounded arm was resting in his pocket. His coat collar was half up, half down, and his battered fedora, with Sciarvi's bullet hole in the crown, was jammed down to his eyebrows.

"Well?" said the Mayor.

"Well!" said MacBride.

And they stood and regarded each other and said not a word for a whole minute.

"Who are you?" asked the Mayor.

"MacBride. A common precinct captain you never saw before. But you know the name, eh?"

"Humph," grunted the Mayor. "I shall refer you to my secretary. I'm not in the habit of receiving visitors except by appointment."

MacBride lashed him with windy blue eyes, and a crooked smile tugged at his lips. "Mister Mayor, Spats Sciarvi's dying. He wants to see you."

The Mayor blinked and a tremor ran over his short, chunky frame. "Sciarvi? Who is Sciarvi?"

"Better come along and see."

"I don't know him."

He turned on his heel and strode away.

MacBride put his hand on the knob. "Remember, Mister Mayor, I carried a dying man's wish. He's at 109 Ship Street."

The Mayor stopped, stood still, but did not turn.

MacBride left the room, and as he went out through the front door he ran into Bower. They stopped and stared at each other.

Bower snarled, "Where's Sciarvi? What did you do with him? He ain't at Headquarters. He ain't in none o' the precincts. He ain't in the hospitals."

"Ask the Mayor," said MacBride, and passed on.

He got into a taxi, sank wearily into the cushions, and closed his eyes. Twenty minutes later the taxi jerked to a stop. The driver reached back, opened the door and waited. After a moment he looked around.

"Hey," he called.

"Um." MacBride awoke, paid his fare and entered a hallway.

The room he walked into was electrically lighted. Sciarvi lay on a bed, his face drained of color. Kennedy sat on a chair while a doctor was bandaging his leg. Another doctor hovered over Sciarvi.

"MacBride…?" a question was in Sciarvi's tone.

MacBride shook his head. "Your friend wouldn't come. Never heard of you."

Sciarvi stared. "You're lyin', MacBride!"

"God's truth, Sciarvi!"

Their eyes held, and in the captain's gaze Sciarvi must have read the awful truth.

He closed his eyes and gritted his teeth. Then he glared. "Damn your soul, MacBride, why are you hidin' me here? Why didn't you take me to a hospital?"

MacBride said, "You started yelling for a doctor. This was the first M.D. plate I saw."

"Why the hell didn't you turn me over to Bower?"

"You're in my hands, Sciarvi, not Bower's. I've got two doctors here. You wanted your friend, and I went for him. He said he didn't know you. You've gotten a damned sight more than you deserve already. Quit yapping."

"Cripes, what a break!" groaned Sciarvi, relaxing, closing his eyes.

MacBride sat down, stared at Kennedy's bandaged leg. Kennedy looked sapped and drawn. But his cynical smile drew a twisted line across his jaw.

"I needed a vacation, Mac," he drawled.

"Hurt?"

"Hell, yes!" And still he smiled, eyes lazy-lidded, features composed.

The one doctor left Kennedy and joined the other doctor and the two doctors put their heads together and conversed in undertones. Then they looked at Sciarvi, examined his wound, took his temperature. After which they went back to the window, put their heads together again, and mumbled some more.

The upshot of this was quite natural. One doctor said, "Captain MacBride, we have come to the conclusion that, for the sake of everyone concerned, this man should be removed to the City Hospital."

"Gawd!" groaned Sciarvi.

"Huh?" said MacBride.

"Gawd!" groaned Sciarvi.

All eyes looked toward him. He glared at the doctors. "City Hospital, eh? Why the hell don't you come right out and say I'm done for? I know the City Hospital. You saw-bones always send a dyin' guy there. It's just a clearin' house for stiffs. Come on, mister, am I done for?"

The doctor who had spoken before, spoke again. "I will tell you frankly—you have one chance in a hundred of living."

"What odds!" cackled Sciarvi, sinking again. Then a shocked look came into his eyes, and he stared with the fierce concentration of those who are outward bound.

"MacBride!" he choked.

Kennedy drew a pencil and a couple of blank envelopes from his pocket.

MacBride stood at the bedside. "Yes, Sciarvi?"

"The Mayor—the pup! He hired me, at a thousand a month to wage a war of—whaddeya call it?—intimidation?—against the Colonial Trucking. He promised absolute protection in case I got in a jam. For the killing of Saunders—Bannon did it—I got a bonus of fifteen hundred. The Mayor supplied that special kind o' poison. He got it from the City Chemist. When you got Gertie, I wised him and he started working to nip an indictment in the bud. His right-hand man is Bower. Bower flopped, and two this mornin' I told the Mayor that if Gertie was planted in the State's Attorney's hands, we were done for. He turned white. He was in a hole, and he asked me what idea I had. I told him we could block off Law Street and get rid of Gertie. He said go ahead. We went ahead. Huh—and now the pup says he don't know me! Ugh.... Get a—ugh...."

"Get an ambulance," said one doctor.

"He wants a priest," said MacBride, understanding.

"He won't die for half an hour," said the doctor. "And if we get him to the hospital—"

"He'll burn in the chair eventually," said MacBride.

"That's not the point," said the doctor, and took up a telephone.

When he put it down, Kennedy said, "I wrote it down, Mac. I've signed as a witness. You sign and then the doctors."

All signed, and then MacBride stood over Sciarvi. "Want to sign this, Sciarvi?"

"Read it."

MacBride read it. Sciarvi nodded, took the pen and scrawled his signature.

"Get a... ugh...."

Five minutes later an ambulance clanged to a stop outside. Two men came in with a stretcher, a hospital doctor looked Sciarvi over briefly, and then they carried him out, and the ambulance roared off.

Kennedy hobbled out on MacBride's arm, and they entered a taxi. Twenty minutes later they drew up before an imposing mansion. Kennedy hobbled out and with MacBride's assistance climbed the ornate steps.

MacBride rang the bell and a servant opened the door. MacBride brushed him aside and helped Kennedy into the foyer.

The Mayor was standing in the open door of his library, and his face was ghastly white. Toward him MacBride walked and Kennedy hobbled, and the Mayor backed slowly into the room. MacBride closed the door. Kennedy sat down in a comfortable chair and lit a cigarette. The Mayor stood with his hands clasped behind his back—very white, very still, very breathless. MacBride looked around the room, and then walked toward a table. He pointed to the phone.

"May I use it?"

The Mayor said nothing. MacBride picked up the instrument and gave a number. A moment later he asked, "That Sciarvi fellow. What about him?" He listened, said, "H'm. Thanks," and hung up.

Then he drew an envelope from his pocket and handed it to the Mayor. The Mayor read, and moved his neck in his stiff collar, as though something were gagging him. His hand shook. Then he laughed, peculiarly, and scaled the letter on the desk.

"His dying confession," said MacBride, picking up the envelope.

"Confessions made at such times are often worthless. This Sciarvi was a little off. A dead man makes a poor witness."

MacBride nodded. "Yes. But, you see, Mister Mayor, he is not dead. He had one chance in a hundred, and he got it. They just told me he'll live. Of course, it will mean the chair."

The Mayor drew a deep breath. MacBride bit him with keen, burning eyes, and nodded toward Kennedy.

"This," he said, "is Kennedy, of the *Free Press*. Of course, this confession will appear in the first edition."

He said no more. He shoved the envelope into his pocket and turned to Kennedy. "Come on."

They went out, arm in arm, and left the Mayor standing transfixed in his ornate library.

MacBride went home that night, and his wife cried over his wounded arm, and he patted her head and chuckled and said, "Don't worry, sweetheart. It's all over now."

He had his wound dressed and went to bed and slept ten hours without so much as stirring once. And he was awakened in the morning by his wife, who stood over his bed with a wide look in her eyes and a newspaper trembling in her hands.

"Steve," she breathed, "look!"

She held the paper in front of him, and he saw, in big, black headlines, three significant words:

"Mayor Commits Suicide."

New Guns for Old

Richmond City tries to reform.

Chapter I

POLICE CAPTAIN STEVE MacBRIDE was on leave. He had it coming to him. As one of the main factors in the scouring of Richmond City's corrupt municipal government, he was due some little respite from the shield and the gun. With the passing of a self-seeking Mayor and a Police Commissioner who had played with him, the city was in a position to recuperate from a long siege of political disease. It all depended, however, on how the convalescent municipality was nursed back to normalcy.

It was spring, merging into summer. MacBride had passed two weeks of his long-promised vacation at his bungalow out in Grove Manor. He had puttered around in his garden, painted the white picket fence and the screens that enclosed the latticed veranda. He planned to spend the last two weeks in the mountains with his wife. They had a car, and it was their intention to drive up and camp out, and call it a kind of second honeymoon. For MacBride was only forty—lean, clean-clipped, with the spark of youth still in his blood.

He was busy packing on the day before their impending departure, when a boy rode up on a bicycle and handed him a telegram. He carried it up to the veranda, sat down and tore it open. The message was brief and to the point:

> *Report at Headquarters tomorrow morning.*
> *Collins.*

Collins was the Police Commissioner.

"Hell," muttered MacBride, and went into the house.

He showed the message to his wife. She read it slowly, and then looked at him.

"What does it mean, Steve?"

"That I'm to report, Anne."

"I know, but—"

He cracked fist into palm. "Something rotten in the wind, else Collins wouldn't have taken the trouble to wire me."

"Oh, I hope our little trip won't fall through!"

"Looks as if it might."

"Oh, Steve!"

He patted her on the shoulder. "What I get for ever having taken up the shield. If they call me back, I'll raise hell."

When he walked into Collins' office next morning, he suspected the worst. Collins sat behind his desk wearing a strained and somewhat worried look. Inspector O'Keefe was there. Captain Hamlin, Detective-Sergeant Brunner, Detectives Morina and Stein.

"Sit down, MacBride," said Collins. "The Mayor will be here any moment."

"What's up?" asked MacBride.

"Let the Mayor tell you." Collins smoked his cigar and stared at the desk.

Mayor Burkhart came in ten minutes later. He was a large, well-groomed man, who held his head well back and looked at the world through rimless spectacles. His gaze was direct and piercing, his lips wide, thin and determined. He put aside his hat and stick, clasped his hands behind his back and stood silhouetted against the window.

"Men," he said, "I've had you come here this morning for a purpose. As you know, I'm a reform Mayor. I demand reform, and my psychology is that of taking the offensive. Also, to strike quickly and brook no opposition."

He paused, flexed his lips against his teeth, gave each man a brief, penetrating glance.

He proceeded, "I have studied your methods and do not approve of them. I do not approve of halfway measures. Since Richmond City experienced one of the worst crime waves on record, it seems to me to be a case in point that your methods were not altogether efficacious."

The men, outstanding arms of the law, listened in silence.

The Mayor's voice was sharp, incisive. He bared his teeth over certain emphatic words, delivered them neatly clipped, his chin raised.

He said, "Remember the horrible gang wars, the blood-shed, the insidious corruption, against which the department fought like men in the dark—"

"Pardon, Mr. Mayor," interjected Collins. "I was not Commissioner. The men who took their jobs seriously were hampered by a crooked Mayor and Commissioner."

"But lax police methods permitted such conditions to gather impetus. Reform can only be acquired through stringent methods. You must take the bull by the horns. Now listen to me." His eyes flashed about the room. "I intend to rip out the root of crime. Within the next twenty-four hours I want every speakeasy in Richmond City closed. I want every nightclub raided. There are at least a dozen barber shops in this city where liquor can be purchased. I want them raided, too, and their business licenses revoked. There are a dozen more delicatessen stores selling liquor. I want those establishments raided and their business licenses also revoked. Understand! Every nightclub, every restaurant, every back-alley speakeasy, every barber shop and every delicatessen store. Within twenty-four hours." His teeth snapped shut.

The men looked at one another. MacBride looked at Collins, saw the Commissioner's lips tighten.

MacBride stood up. "Mr. Mayor, I still have two weeks' leave coming—"

"That will have to be postponed. Your record in the recent clean-up is outstanding. You will affect plainclothes and attend to the closing of the nightclubs. Any place where ginger ale is sold, you can be sure that liquor is sold also."

"It can't be done," said MacBride.

He was known for a holy tenor among the criminals. He was also known for a captain who had loose ideas about authority.

"It can," said the Mayor.

"Too sudden," insisted MacBride. "Try to close all these places in twenty-four hours and there will be hell to pay. The crime wave has died down. Why stir it again? I've handled crime for twenty years. I know there are some things we've got to tolerate. A certain amount of liquor traffic is one of them. If we crash the places that we know exist, places will open whose existence we'll never know about, and they'll breed crime. Crime doesn't breed in a place that is known to the police. It's the other places."

The Mayor rocked on his feet and thinned down his lips. "MacBride, do you presume to tell me my business?"

"Not at all. I'm airing my own business—which has to do with a sensible handling of crime. And—this is not presumption—I think I know crime a little better than you do. I've handled it in the raw."

"Tut, tut!" said the Mayor. "Please be quiet until I have finished. There are other places to be closed."

Collins creaked in his chair.

The Mayor went on, "These Jewish pawnbrokers and jewelers. These so-called fences. You know many of them—you men?"

Heads nodded somewhat reluctantly.

"So!" clipped Burkhart. "Another medium for crime. Jewels, silks, merchandise, furs are stolen. The criminals dispose of them through the fence. If there were no fences, there would be no market. Is that not logic?"

"No," said MacBride.

Collins flung him a worried look. The other men shifted. They all knew MacBride—knew what a tough egg he was, a man who held opinions of his own and stood by them; a man who often injured his own chances with the powers-that-be by saying just what he thought, regardless of circumstances or cost.

"No?" asked the Mayor, restraining his annoyance.

"No," reiterated MacBride vigorously. "I know every fence in Richmond City. Some of them are my friends. It was through a fence that I nailed Red Hennessy, the guy that killed Barbour three years ago in a stick-up. A fence is an unofficial intelligence department for the police. Look it up and see how many men have been trailed through them."

"But if there were no fences—"

"If," said MacBride, "there were no fences in Richmond City, there would still be fences in New York, Chicago, every other city in the United States. By doing away with the fence here we would sever what contact we have with the underworld. And the underworld can't be snuffed out in a day. It's an institution, the same as the police department.

Burkhart knocked the ash from his cigar. His voice lowered. "Mac-Bride, I know what sort of man you are. You take things in your own hands a lot. You're stubborn. Well, maybe I'm stubborn too. You have your orders. That goes for all of you men. Close up every place that sells liquor. Bar the doors of every known fence. Tighten the bolts on these doors of crime, and watch the grand exodus of criminals from Richmond City. Remember!" He raised a forefinger. "Within twenty-four hours."

He picked up his hat and stick, strode to the door, pulled it open. "Gentlemen, I bid you good-day."

Chapter II

THE news clicked through Police Headquarters. It fell like a bomb-shell in every police station. Precinct captains, who had gritted their teeth under the lash of the late regime, gritted their teeth again. From extreme measures used by a corrupt administration, they found themselves in the hands of an extreme reformist, a man fired by ambition, a man who believed he could thwart destiny itself.

Even as they had been bound by orders before, so they were bound by orders again. Though many of them believed that reform had to be coaxed, not driven, they were of necessity forced to drive. They were all cogs in the tremendous wheel of municipal government, and each cog had to move with the wheel. Strictest secrecy was demanded by the Mayor. Each precinct captain was told of the plans that day by a sealed letter from the Mayor. Each captain was warned to say nothing until the appointed hour. After eight o'clock that night he was ordered to be prepared for any emergency call.

At four that afternoon the men detailed to close the delicatessen stores known to sell liquor, started out, the idea being that in such establishments more gin is bought between the hours of four and six than at any other time—the cocktail time. At seven the men detailed to close the barber shops, left Headquarters. At the same time, a detective-sergeant and two plainclothes-men, were dispatched to handle the known fences.

At eight MacBride was eating in a small restaurant, a block from Headquarters. Kennedy, of the City *Free Press,* wandered in, spotted him and came over.

"What the hell, Mac?"

MacBride went on eating, said, "Well, what the hell?"

Kennedy sat down. "I mean, you being around here. Thought you were going to the mountains."

"So did I."

"Well?"

"Changed my mind."

Kennedy grinned. "Or did somebody change your mind for you?"

"Go to hell," said MacBride, casually.

Kennedy chuckled. "Poor old Mac."

"On your way, Kennedy. This is one of the times when you get on my nerves."

"Something's up, Mac."

"My temper, if you don't breeze."

"Now, Mac—"

"Kennedy—" MacBride put down his fork and sat back. "Kennedy, there are times when I like you. There are times when I don't. I've got a touch of liver tonight. Now get the hell out of here."

Kennedy shrugged. He rose, a lazy-eyed, whimsical young man. "All right, Mac." He put on his hat, lit a cigarette, grinned. "Poor old Mac. They can't even do without you in peace, eh?"

MacBride ignored him. Kennedy sighed, turned and wandered out. MacBride stared after him. They were old friends, these two. Too bad he had met Kennedy then, mused MacBride. Kennedy was no fool. He suspected that something was in the wind.

At ten MacBride blew into Headquarters and went straight to the office that had been given him. Moriarity and Cohen, the two detectives allotted him, were playing poker dice. They had been attached to the Second Precinct during the reign of crime and had been MacBride's best men.

"Any news?" asked MacBride.

Cohen said, "Brunner busted into ten barber shops and nailed them up. He just phoned in. O'Keefe got eight delicatessen stores.

Hamlin is still working the fences. Cripes, this is my idea of a burlesque show. But it ain't even funny."

"Keep your ideas to yourself, Ike," recommended MacBride.

He still was loyal to his shield.

"But, cripes, Cap," said Cohen, "you know yourself it's a lunatic's idea."

"Never mind, Ike," said MacBride. "We've got a job to do. We'll close every damned joint in this town. That's our orders."

"And see what happens," chimed in Moriarity. "It can't be done, Cap."

"We'll close 'em all," said MacBride. "It can be done."

"But what will it start? I'll tell you what it'll start—"

"That's another matter, so don't worry about it. The first place on the list is The Palm Club—at eleven-thirty. Incidentally, the guy that owns it, George Clark, is a good friend of mine. He runs the cleanest place in town."

"Good old George," nodded Cohen. "He gave three thousand berries to the City Poor House."

At eleven MacBride and his two aides walked out of Police Headquarters and climbed into a taxi. At eleven-thirty sharp they walked into The Palm Club, in the heart of the theatrical district.

An after theatre crowd was already there. The orchestra was playing. Huge imitation palms and colored lanterns lent a tropical atmosphere. A fountain sparkled in the center of the parquet dance-floor. It was a high-class rendezvous, a place that had never given the police a bit of trouble.

MacBride, hands thrust into his pocket, met the headwaiter and nodded.

"Where's George?" he said.

"Busy now, Captain. What can I do for you?"

"Get George."

"But—"

"Get George."

Puzzled, the headwaiter moved off. A few minutes later George Clark appeared. He was a large, well-poised man, with a benign smile. He thrust out his hand.

"Well, well, Mac!"

"Hello, George," said MacBride, and shook. "We're in a hurry. Now don't get sore. You've just got to close up. You know and I know that there's a highball on every table. Padlock, George."

Clark looked incredulous. "For God's sake, Mac, you don't mean—"

"That's just what I mean, George. No fuss. Do it quietly. I won't hang around. I'll depend on you to be shut tight in fifteen minutes.

"Orders, George." MacBride turned to Moriarity and Cohen. "Come on, boys."

They walked out and left Clark like a man in a trance.

A block farther on they entered The Three Aces, run by Billy Kildane. Kildane met them at the door, and MacBride said:

"Hello, Billy. Just dropped in to tell you that I'm staging a padlock act."

"A—what!"

"Lock and key. Chase out the boys and girls and lock up tight."

"But, Mac, look at the crowd!"

"I know, that's tough. I'm merely relaying orders. So long, Billy."

MacBride and his men went out. Inside of an hour they closed seven of the most famous supper clubs in the theatrical district. Everything went along smoothly. There were no arguments. MacBride carried out orders with a minimum of words.

At twelve-thirty he led the way into The Jungle, a colored night-club run by Max Lebowitz. A bizarre, garish place, with a howling orchestra and dark-skinned entertainers tap-dancing and moaning blue melodies. Lebowitz bobbed on the scene grinning and rubbing his hands together.

"Max," said MacBride, "you've got fifteen minutes to chase out the crowd and close up—tight."

"How's this?"

"Padlock."

"Come now, Mac—honest?"

"Honest. Stop the band, clear the place and lock it up. Orders."

Max frowned. "Hell d' you suppose I can chase all these people out? What's the meaning of this, anyhow?"

"Now don't let's go into detail, Max. Be nice. I'm trying to be. You've got to close down."

"Ah, that's a lot of nonsense, Mac. What the hell kind of a game you trying to hand me?"

MacBride sighed. "If you want me to close it up personally, I'll do it."

"But I don't see—"

"Never mind what you see, Max. You heard me. Now don't hand me an argument. Close up."

Max snarled, "I thought you were my friend, Mac. This is a fine thing—"

"Ike," broke in MacBride, "go down and stop that band."

"No—no," urged Lebowitz. "I'll do it. I'll close up. All right, Mac, I won't forget this. It's a lousy trick."

"Good-night, Max," said MacBride, and started out. "Come on, boys."

As they went down the scale in night life, they found each succeeding place more difficult to close. They had to close The Parrot themselves, had to drive the crowd into the street. And when they left it darkened and with barred doors, Cohen wagged his head.

"There will be hell to pay, Cap," he said.

"Number twelve is The Blue Moon," said MacBride.

The Blue Moon was in the heart of Bohemia, a cellar club, low-ceiled, fantastically decorated, patronized by a mixed crowd. Lew Gates ran it.

"Well, Mac, what the hell are you doing down this way?" asked Gates.

"Poking around, Lew. Do you think you can close this place quietly in fifteen minutes?"

"No."

"Well, close it."

Gates peered keenly. "What's that?"

"Ask the gang to go home, Lew, and lock up."

"I don't get you, Mac."

"Now, Lew, of course you do. You're closed for business."

"Who said so?"

"I did."

They regarded each other steadily. Then Lew shrugged. "That's a lot of crap, Mac. I ain't heard anything about it."

"You just heard me."

"You're kidding."

"I'm in earnest, Lew. Close up."

Gates turned away. "Ah, be yourself, Mac. You ain't that kind of guy."

MacBride caught him by the arm. "Look here, Lew. Use your head. I mean what I say."

Gates pivoted sharply. "I'm damned if I'll close!"

"Want me to close it for you?"

"Try"—Gates pointed to the crowd—"try to clean that bunch out."

MacBride turned to Moriarity and Cohen. "Let's start."

He strode across the dance-floor and stopped at the orchestra stall. The leader was on the point of swinging into a new number.

"Wait a minute," said MacBride. "The music's over."

The leader lowered his hand. "Huh?"

"Pack up. You've got ten minutes." He left them and returned to the center of the floor; raised his voice—"Ladies and gentlemen, you will have to leave. This place is being closed by the police. You've got ten minutes."

A low murmur of surprise rose, followed by a rumble of disapproval. A few rose.

A man shouted, "Hold your seats. This is funny."

"It will be funnier," said MacBride, "if I take you by the neck."

"Yeah?"

MacBride flung over his shoulder, "Moriarity, collar that wiseacre."

"Yup," clipped Moriarity, and made a beeline for the man.

The man rose, a little more than three sheets in the wind. He made a pass at Moriarity, but Moriarity grinned, ducked, and catching hold of him, dragged him across the floor. His companion, a flamboyant woman with blonde hair, began shouting:

"I call this a nerve, I call this a damned shame. I and Ken weren't harming no one. I ain't going to let no man make no fool out of Ken." With a grand gesture she swept plates and glasses from the table, stood up, glared, and jammed her arms akimbo.

"Madame," said MacBride, "sit down and shut up."

She stamped her foot. "That for you!"

Lew Gates appeared on the floor. "Hey, you, what the hell you mean by busting that stuff?"

"Well, Lew, these guys—"

"Aw, pipe down!" snapped Gates. "Park your hips, Katie, and sign off." He turned to MacBride. "All right, Mac, I'll close, but that's what I call a rotten deal."

"Think hard, Lew. We've always been friends," said MacBride.

"And this ends it."

"Have it your own way, Lew. Be sure you're closed in ten minutes."

He turned and walked off the floor. Moriarity had deposited the girl's companion in the cloak-room. He joined MacBride on the way out and Cohen followed. In the street, they breathed with relief.

"That's all for tonight," said MacBride.

"Thank God," said Cohen. "The beginning of the end. I see another reign of terror, Mac, and I don't mean maybe. If all these guys hadn't been friends of yours, there'd been some trouble—and some gun work on the side."

Moriarity nodded. "Yeah. But I've got a hunch, Cap, that you've lost some of those friends."

MacBride walked on in silence. He had carried out the Mayor's orders. He had done a neat, bloodless job—bloodless because those men knew him. Some had argued, but that was natural. He had expected worse.

And by the time he reached home he had definitely put thoughts of a vacation out of his mind. For the ear of his mind heard the distant rumble of another conflict with the shield and the gun.

THE press howled.

The *Times-Courier*, a colorless sheet, patted the Mayor on the back. It said that Providence had sent him to Richmond City, that within six months the city would be the cleanest in the East. The writer waxed eloquent, used every complimentary adjective he could call to mind, wound up by calling the Mayor a high-minded patriot.

The *Free Press* was more subtle. It said, in part, "We were surprised, but not pleasantly. We approve of reform, as every sensible citizen should, but the ways of reform are manifold. We recommend, however, a gradual pressure. Richmond City has been ill with crime. It was recovering. In our opinion it has suddenly been ruptured, and we believe a rupture rarely heals completely."

The *News-Examiner*, a frankly blatant sheet, laughed out loud and wanted to know what peculiar disease of the mind had fallen upon the Mayor.

The *Post-Express* was hopeful but refused to commit itself one way or the other. It leaned tentatively toward the Mayor. The writer seemed chameleonic.

TWO days later MacBride sat in his office at Headquarters. The day before he had closed fifteen speakeasies, and he had made more enemies. This, perhaps, was due to the fact that he refused to take each man aside, tell him that it was the Mayor's orders and that personally he, MacBride, had other ideas. Of course, personally he had other ideas. But he was loyal to his badge and in some measure loyal to his Mayor. Wherefore he held his tongue and closed one place after another with brevity and dispatch. Many claimed that he had become self-seeking, that he was looking for promotion under the new regime. This was a blow to MacBride's pride, but he swallowed it, albeit hard.

He also had a premonition of disaster. It was undefined, but it persisted in his policeman's mind. He did not venture to predict in what manner the whip of crime would crack over Richmond City. But privately he held that it would crack.

Kennedy said, "Burkhart may even be murdered. His ideals don't jibe with logic. He thinks he's hard-boiled. His methods are centuries old. Time has passed him by."

"We'll see," muttered MacBride.

"What are your own opinions, Mac?"

"They don't matter."

"But they do."

"And no matter what they are, they're not for publication."

Kennedy chuckled. "Good old, loyal old Mac. Bet it hurts, though. Well, well, hell is simmering. Every club bolted, every speakeasy barred, twelve barber shops run by wops out of business, ten delicatessen stores shut tight, every fence in town closed. Air-tight, you say? My eye, Mac, my eye! It's like a balloon blown up to the bursting point. Somebody'll prick it. Watch it bust. Reform is predicated on intelligent administration. Reform can be brought about by tightening the screws bit by bit, but you can't suddenly walk into the ring, haul off and kick prevailing conditions out into the cold. New York, Boston—even Boston!—and Philadelphia, are pulling a tremendous horse laugh. And so are some of us right here. I am. So are you."

MacBride scoffed. "You think you know more than you do, Kennedy. Go out and cool off."

Kennedy leaned forward, tapped the desk. "I know this, Mac. I know that under the skin you agree with me. But I know, too, that you've got a queer sense of loyalty, and that you'll carry out a command even if you break your neck doing it. And you'll never chirp. Oh, I know you, Mac."

"You know hell, Kennedy." MacBride stood up, jammed his hands into his pockets and paced the floor. He stopped short, spun, stood spread legged. "I've closed those places and they'll stay closed so long as I have anything to do with it."

"Sure. You're on orders. You've got to back up the Mayor, whether you like it or not. Listen, there are other guys in the Department giving free voice to what they think. Why the hell do you have to go around close-mouthed? You're a fool, Mac—a poor fool!"

Days swung by. Night life was at a stand-still. Petitions reached the Mayor day after day, imploring a sensible compromise. Some of these petitions were signed by men prominent in business and professional circles. But the Mayor was adamant. And by way of reply he closed five lunch-wagons suspected of traffic in liquor. He made his own laws.

Possessed suddenly of an idea that a certain dairy company was surreptitiously moving liquor in their trucks, he sent out a special squad of plainclothes-men, had all the company's trucks stopped and searched and also their dairies. No liquor was found, but the milk trucks missed fast night trains, much milk went bad and a lot of money was lost. The company protested vigorously, but the Mayor was undaunted. Lawsuits were instituted against the city. Municipal spies were sent out and many private residences were searched. A little liquor was found, but it did not compensate for the hard feeling that was thereby aroused.

And MacBride, faithful to his badge, continued to carry out orders. One of the closed speakeasies had dared to open, and on express orders of the Mayor, MacBride was sent to close it. He went, alone, walked into the place and found six men drinking whiskey. Tony Morilla, the owner, stood stock-still, a cigarette between his lips. He was a hard case, but he had always called MacBride friend and during the last crime wave he had kept his hands clean and aided the police in the apprehension of a coked gunman.

"You know why I'm here, Tony," said MacBride.

"I got an idea, Mac."

"I told you to stay closed."

"I know."

"And here you're open."

They faced each other, silently. In Morilla's eyes smoldered dark fire. The cigarette was motionless between his lips.

MacBride jerked his shoulder. "Clean these men out."

Morilla turned to the men. "You'll have to go boys. Pay me some other time."

Muttering, the men went out.

"Now, Tony, you'll have to come along."

Morilla shrugged. "That a clean break, Mac?"

"No. Quietly, now, Tony."

Morilla's lips tightened. "All right."

An hour later Morilla was behind bars.

Next morning MacBride was called into the Mayor's office. Burkhart looked expansive. He grinned broadly and shook MacBride's hand with keen warmth.

"MacBride you're doing wonderful work," he said. "You haven't fallen down on a single job. You've done everything with a neatness I admire. Have a cigar."

MacBride took a cigar and lighted up. After the first puff he said "I've merely carried out orders."

"Merely!"

"And look here, Mr. Mayor. Take a tip from me: you're headed for a fall. This business can't go on."

"But, MacBride, look how successful we've been!"

"I'll give you one reason why. I know all those men I've jumped on. They gave in because they knew me, and now many of them are bitter against me. It was so sudden—no warning, no compromise—"

"Which is why we've been successful."

"Look farther. We're not successful, and I don't approve of your methods. You're paving the way for another reign of terror. You're making Richmond City fertile ground for criminal exploitation. Please take a little advice from a man who knows his business. I know mine. I've given twenty years of my life to it, and if I say it myself I've got a damned good reputation."

"Which is why I like you, MacBride," smiled the Mayor. "At first we had a little argument. I know how you feel. It's hard on you, telling old friends that they must close shop, but if you have the interest of the city and the Department at heart, you'll forget that. I need you, MacBride. You're the best man I have. Carry on and inside of a year

I'll put you in plainclothes for good and"—his voice lowered, and his smile spread—"I'll make you an inspector!"

"It doesn't stir me. Put me back in uniform right now and plant me in my old Second Precinct. I'm a precinct man, Mr. Mayor. I could very well use an inspector's pay, but not at that price. And don't think I've carried on as I have through any thought of promotion."

"I know, MacBride. You're a modest man."

"No. I'm not modest—"

The Mayor chuckled. "MacBride, if I had more men like you—But no matter. Think things over. You are now attached to my personal staff."

"What!"

"My personal staff, MacBride. Now pardon me. I have another engagement in a few minutes. Good luck."

MacBride left, boiling. *Personal staff!* He had not anticipated this, did not want it. It meant that now he was closer to the Mayor than before, and that the Mayor would rely on his honesty to a greater degree. The news spread through the Department.

Captain Hamlin met MacBride next day and almost sneered. "I guess you're the Mayor's right-hand man, Mac. And you were the guy who talked so big at that first meeting."

"Pipe down, Hamlin."

"I guess we all know how you stand now."

"Easy, Hamlin."

"Easy hell, Mac. What are you doing, getting ambitious too? Is there an inspector's job around the corner?"

MacBride's windy blue eyes cut Hamlin sharply. "You close your jaw, Hamlin, or I'll close it for you."

"Hurts, eh?"

MacBride's fist doubled. "Another crack out of you and I'll cave in your nose!"

Hamlin stared hard, but after a moment his eyes wavered. He forced a weak laugh, turned and moved off. MacBride continued on his way, banged into his office and brooded over his pipe.

He was the only man of that group who was elevated to the Mayor's personal staff, and the sudden coolness with which they treated him was clearly apparent. It hurt MacBride to have them think that he was cheek and jowl with Burkhart. They were fools, and perhaps they were a little envious too. But he believed that they despised him more than anything else. Hence he became more or less a lone wolf.

Kennedy, who was more discerning, chuckled and said, "Poor old Mac."

And MacBride barked, "Damn you, shut up!" But secretly he regretted the outburst, for Kennedy and he, though always bickering, understood each other perfectly. And Moriarity and Cohen showed no change toward him. They were good men, and they had on more occasions than one gone through gun-smoke and flame with the hard captain, and they knew his worth, his honesty, his rough courage.

At the end of six weeks the Mayor was still holding his own. He was always on the lookout for loopholes in what he termed his airtight campaign. He closed two famous restaurants and another barber shop and he circulated a large amount of spies throughout the city. He ignored complaints, and presently finding time heavy on his hands, he passed an ordinance that made all restaurants and dancing casinos close at midnight sharp. Then he closed a popular burlesque house and banned presentation of three plays which he considered slightly off color. The *Post-Express* screamed at this, because two of the plays had had successful runs in Boston.

MacBride came in late one morning and the clerk said, "Kennedy dropped by. He wants you to meet him for lunch at the Brown Coffee Pot."

The Brown Coffee Pot was only four blocks away, and at noon MacBride walked in. Kennedy was waiting for him and led the way to a table in the rear. The reporter was grinning. He rubbed his hands gingerly. He chuckled.

"Well, spill it," said MacBride.

"I knew it," said Kennedy. "I knew it."

"Knew what?"

"That it would happen."

MacBride leaned on his elbows. "Come on, Kennedy."

Kennedy laid down his cigarette. "Chick McTurk is in town."

"He's in Chicago."

"He's in Richmond City."

MacBride sat back. His eyes narrowed. "I gave McTurk his walking papers three years ago."

"But he's back again. And he's worth dough. I saw him hurrying through the railroad station. With him was Jazz Millio."

"Another rat!"

"Sure. And why do you suppose they're here? Why would Chick leave a normal racket in Chicago to come to Richmond City? Because there are good pickings here. The place is ripe for a guy like Chick. And ten to one all his gunmen are pouring into town, too. There's liquor here—gallons of it lying idle—and Chick is going to do a bit of hi-jacking. He always was a nervy hi-jacker, and at this time Richmond City certainly is meat for him."

"I told him never to show his face here again. I warned him, Kennedy. He's a damned trouble-maker, and that Millio would kill a guy for two cents."

Kennedy quickened his voice. "Look here, Mac. Lie low. Don't make a move. Burkhart has come to the end of his tether. He brought this on. Nobody else. It's not your fault—no one's but the Mayor's."

MacBride's eyes were narrowed. "I told McTurk not to come back. It's my game, too. He raised hell here three years ago. I could have sent him up, framed him, but I gave him a break. He promised never to come back. If he thinks he can kick me in the slats this way, he's dumb."

"Think, Mac. It's a glorious opportunity to show how futile the Mayor is, to show that his ideas of reform are rotten. It will crush him. For cripes' sake, stay out of it and show the guy up. Don't be a fool all your days, Mac."

MacBride flattened his lips. Kennedy was hard, but he was also in some measure right. Yet his plan soured in MacBride's mind.

"Kennedy, it's not square. I know Chick is here. I'd be a lousy bum to pretend ignorance and let hell bust loose."

"Nonsense, Mac! For the love o' God—"

MacBride shook his head. "No, Kennedy. I'm going to land on McTurk like a ton of brick."

Chapter IV

MacBRIDE returned to Police Headquarters. There was something keenly purposeful about him. A new snap was in his movements. It was simple: he had something to do, something definite, something tangible against which to release his accrued vigor.

He breezed into his office and found Moriarity and Cohen waiting for him. Both were sound asleep, their feet on the desk. MacBride heaved the feet off.

"Snap out of it, boys."

They yawned awake.

"Quick!" clipped MacBride. "Wake up. Peel your ears and listen to this. Chick McTurk and a dago named Jazz Millio are in town. I want McTurk."

"Where is he?" asked Cohen.

"That's what we've got to find out. Kennedy saw him coming through the railroad station this morning. McTurk's here for a purpose. I'm going to railroad that baby out of town, and if he yaps I'll frame him."

Moriarity asked, "What did the Mayor say about it?"

"He doesn't know. And he's not going to know. He'll ball up the works. All this is between you and me, and don't breathe a word to anybody. If we let McTurk get a head start on us, he'll pitch the city into a new gang war, mark my words. He's a hi-jacker and he's here for big money. I'll give you copies of his handwriting. Fan the hotels. I'll do the same."

Moriarity and Cohen went out. MacBride started a fresh cigar and followed a few minutes later. On the way out he ran into Hamlin, and Hamlin said:

"You and your two little boy scouts seem to be doing a lot of running around."

"If you did a little more, Hamlin, you wouldn't be so fat," clipped MacBride.

He did not stop, but continued on, leaving Hamlin with a dark scowl. He visited six hotels that afternoon, and returned to Headquarters unsuccessful. Moriarity and Cohen came in a little later and shook their heads.

"We've got to find him," said MacBride, "at any cost. And we've got to find him in a hurry. Look everywhere. Pay a stoolie, I don't care what. If you find a guy you think knows something, make him talk—frame him—anything. We've got to nail McTurk before he starts the ball rolling."

"Right," said Cohen.

"Right," said Moriarity.

And they left with a businesslike air.

MacBride sat thinking, looking back, recalling incidents relative to his old case against Chick McTurk. It was a bit hazy. After a while he went out to the Bureau of Criminal Identification and began running through the files. While he was doing this, Hamlin wandered in.

"Oh, you here, Mac?"

"See me, don't you?"

Hamlin chuckled. "What the hell are you and those two gumshoes up to?"

"Just a little diversion, Hamlin."

"Secret work for the Mayor, eh?"

"Hell, no!"

"I'd like to believe it."

"I'm not asking you to, Hamlin, and I don't care."

Hamlin sighed. "Tell me, Mac. What kind of work do you have to do to get on the personal staff?"

"Nothing."

"And to slip into a soft inspector's job?"

MacBride looked up from a metal file box. "Are you trying to crack wise, Hamlin?"

Hamlin laughed softly. "You're not kidding anybody, Mac."

MacBride started to say something, but shrugged, snorted. "Go 'way, Hamlin. You're a nuisance." He proceeded to ignore the man and continued looking through the files. Presently he drew out a card and read it. His lips tightened. He slipped the card back into place and replaced the file box.

Then he strode out, passing Hamlin as if the man did not exist. He went to his office, picked up his hat and left Headquarters. A block farther on he hailed a taxi and giving an address, jumped in.

He alighted before a small apartment house in a street that was otherwise flanked by old brownstones. He entered the lobby and instead of going to the desk, approached the elevator man.

"Miss Kelsey's apartment."

"You'll have to telephone up first," said the man.

"No I don't." MacBride flashed his shield. "Up we go."

He entered the elevator and it slid up to the third floor, then stopped.

"Number thirty-two, chief," said the man.

"Thanks," nodded MacBride, and proceeded down the corridor.

He pressed the electric button at 32. He listened, received no answer. He pressed it again. Presently a woman's voice—"Who is it?"

"Telegram."

"Slip it under the door."

"It's collect."

There was a pause. Then the door opened on a crack. MacBride jammed his foot in the opening and then shoved. He muscled into a small ante-chamber.

"Hello, Clara," he grinned.

"What the hell do you want, MacBride?" The woman, a henna haired beauty, glared at him. "Is this nice, busting in this way?"

"No." MacBride strolled past her and into the salon. He looked around. "You alone, Clara?"

"Of course I'm alone," she snapped.

MacBride sighed and sat down. "Oh, I just thought Chick might be around."

"Chick! He ain't in town."

"No?"

"No."

"Hell, I thought he was. See you're dressed for dinner."

"What about it? Can't a girl dress for dinner? I'm going out. I'm in a hurry too, MacBride."

"I'm not. Sit down and take life easy. You look nervous, Clara."

She put her hands on her hips. "Say, I'll tell the world you got one hell of a nerve! You get out, MacBride!"

"Now, Clara, be a nice girl. I'm in no hurry. I was looking up old records and saw that you testified once in Chick's favor, four years ago. I just dropped around to say hello."

"Well, you've said it. Now get."

MacBride chuckled and settled back more comfortably into the chair. Clara raved on. She paced the floor. She stamped. She heaped abuse upon MacBride's head, but he answered with nothing more than an occasional chuckle.

Suddenly the telephone rang. She stopped short and caught her breath.

MacBride was on his feet. He muttered, "Don't answer it!"

Her eyes blazed. "A frame-up!"

"Don't answer it!"

"Damn you!" She turned and dived for the telephone.

MacBride caught her by the wrist, spun her from her feet, dropped her into a chair.

"You heard me, Clara!"

She panted hoarsely, her cheeks flaming, her lips quivering with inarticulate abuse.

The bell rang insistently. Clara stared at the instrument. MacBride watched her. He stood spread-legged, calm, determined. Silence. And then another series of rings.

Clara sprang to her feet, tense and desperate.

"Damn you, MacBride, let me at it!"

"Sit down."

"I won't! You're a dirty louse, that's what you are! You're a snake! I—I'd like to brain you."

"Shut up."

"I won't—"

He caught her again, clapped his hand over her mouth, held her firmly. "Now listen to me, sister. I've got work to do. Close your jaw."

She struggled, kicked, clawed. MacBride tightened his grip, stifled her curses.

A bell rang. It was the door bell.

Clara stiffened.

Still holding her, MacBride pulled his gun with his free hand and dragged her to the door. He turned the bolt. The door clicked open and he stepped back.

"Come right in, Chick," he said.

Chick McTurk gasped. He was a tall man, dark-skinned, black-eyed. He wore evening clothes. His fists clenched.

"In quick, Chick!" snapped MacBride. "Keep your hands clear or I'll drill you."

Chick came in, and MacBride kicked the door shut. Then he flung Clara away and covered both of them.

"Raise 'em, Chick." MacBride frisked him and drew forth a small automatic. "Now sit down—both of you."

Chick dropped into a chair, sighed. "Well, MacBride, what the hell's the meaning of this?"

"I told you once, Chick, not to show your mug in Richmond City again."

"Well, I've shown it."

"And you're going to do an about face and fade away—you and that greaseball playmate of yours—Millio."

McTurk sneered. "Trying to run the town again, eh?"

"On my own, Chick. I guess I've just about nipped you in the bud. We won't talk here." Manacles clinked in his hand. "You and I will leave quietly, Chick. Get up."

McTurk got up. MacBride clicked one of the bracelets on his own wrist, the other on McTurk's. McTurk turned to Clara.

"Sit tight, Baby. This ain't going to last long. Mac's got a screw loose again."

"He's a big bum," said Clara.

"Better look for another meal ticket, sister," recommended Mac-Bride.

He took McTurk out. He hailed a taxi and they climbed in. The street lights were just going on.

"You pulled a fast one, MacBride."

"I told you not to come back, Chick."

"Headquarters will seem like old times."

"But," said MacBride, "we're not going to Headquarters."

"I don't get you."

"Be patient."

Fifteen minutes later the taxi drew up in a dark, deserted street. MacBride hauled Chick out and they entered a dark hallway. He knocked on a door. A face appeared in the gloom.

MacBride said, "Charley, give me a room. I'll take the key here. You don't have to go up."

"Sure, Mac." A moment later the face reappeared. "Number twenty."

"Thanks."

MacBride took Chick up two flights of stairs to room twenty and opened the door. He found the lightswitch and turned it. They were in a small, bare room, that contained nothing more than a chair, a bed and a washstand. MacBride removed the manacles from his wrist.

"What does this mean, Mac?"

"Your room for a while."

McTurk frowned. "You've got no right to pull this!"

"I'm taking the right," said MacBride.

He manacled Chick to the bed post. McTurk snarled, "I'd like to know what the hell you're up to!"

"You'll find out, later. I'll see you get food and water."

McTurk cursed him as he went out. MacBride locked the door, went down the stairs and out into the street. A few blocks farther on he caught a cruising taxi.

When he walked into his office at Headquarters Moriarity and Cohen were there. They shook their heads.

Cohen said, "Not a trace, Cap."

" 'S all right," said MacBride. "I've got him."

They looked at him, grinned.

"Good old Mac," said Moriarity.

But MacBride was not smiling. He looked thoughtful.

"But it's only the beginning," he replied.

He sank into a chair, an abstracted look in his eyes.

"Ike," he said, "go over and hang around in front of Number 12 Murdock Street. Clara Kelsey lives there. You and Moriarity work shifts. Watch the place. Watch her. We want Millio."

"Okey, Cap."

"And, Ike. If you get him, take him to Charley's place. I've got McTurk bottled in room twenty. Take Millio there and then ring me." He added, "We've got to jump this game while it's hot."

Cohen left. MacBride and Moriarity went out for a bite to eat in the Brown Coffee Pot. Hamlin was there and he came over to join them.

"You guys sure seem in be working overtime," he said.

"What makes you think so?" asked MacBride.

"Hell, you're never in Headquarters. Let us in on it, Mac. What's up?"

MacBride grinned. "Remember, Hamlin, I'm on the personal staff."

"Mayor's little poodle dog, eh?"

"Sure," chuckled MacBride. "What's the matter, you sore?"

"Kind of, Mac. But we all are—when a guy plays poodle dog to his boss. Here's hoping you get that promotion."

"Here's hoping I paste you on the jaw some day."

Hamlin moved off, and MacBride said to Moriarity, "That guy's just dumb enough to get in my way. If he balls up my parade, I'll put him in the city hospital. You relieve Ike at midnight."

"Yeah."

They went back to Headquarters and to pass the time away, played two-handed pinochle. At eleven the phone rang and Moriarity grabbed it He listened and then shoved it across the desk.

"Ike, Cap."

MacBride clamped the receiver to his ear. "Shoot, Ike.... Eh, what's that.... *Good!* Be right over."

He slammed down the receiver, said, "Ike's got Millio."

"Cripes," grinned Moriarity. "Where's my hat?" He leaped up.

MacBride had his and was already on the way out. Moriarity bounded after him and they caught a taxi in the street below.

"What luck!" chuckled Moriarity.

"But it's only the beginning. It all depends on—"

"On what?"

"On tomorrow."

A little later they walked into Charley's place and went up the dark staircase two steps at a time. MacBride had his key out. He poked it in the keyhole, but Cohen opened the door and grinned. MacBride pushed in, and Moriarity closed the door.

Millio was sitting on a chair. There was a black-and-blue welt on his face and dark murder in his eyes. He was small, dapper, deadly-looking.

"Tried to get wise," explained Cohen. "Tried to pull his smoke and I slammed him."

"Yeah, you lousy Jew!" snarled Millio.

"Pipe down you spaghetti-bending pup," clipped Cohen.

"I'll pipe down hell—"

MacBride barked, "You'll pipe down.—D'you frisk him, Ike?"

"No."

MacBride stepped forward and went through Millio's pockets. He produced a wallet, letters, various papers, threw them on the wash-stand. Then he examined them. Finally he opened one sheet of paper, scanned it, tightened his lips.

"Look at this, boys!"

Cohen and Moriarity looked. They saw a typewritten list of addresses:

46   Jockey St, Cellar, 30 Cases Scotch

20	River Road, 2nd Floor, 40 Cases Scotch
6	Bell Street, Cellar, 50 Cases Gin
38	Western Road, Barn, 150 Cases Gin
92	Farmingville Tpke, Barn, 200 Cases Scotch
88	Old Stone Road, Cellar, 210 Cases Gin
11	Princess Street, 3rd Floor, 90 Cases Rye
75	Starlight Blvd., House, 400 Cases Scotch
9	MacAllister Alley, Cellar, 350 Barrels Wine
25	Rock Street, Cellar, 380 Barrels Wine

"Cripes!" muttered Moriarity.

MacBride said, "Eleven hundred and seventy cases of booze, and seven hundred and thirty barrels of ink. What a haul—if they get it." He turned to Millio. "Where'd you get this list, wop?"

"Try and find out."

MacBride folded the sheet of paper and tucked it away in his pocket. "You'll warm your slats here for a while, Millio, same as your boy friend."

He manacled Millio to the other end of the bed. Then he left with Moriarity and Cohen. And as they walked down the street, Cohen said:

"But how the hell did he get that list?"

"I don't know," said MacBride.

"What next?" asked Moriarity.

"I have an appointment with the Mayor—tomorrow."

Chapter V

AT ten o'clock next morning MacBride walked into the Mayor's office. Burkhart sat behind his desk smoking a Corona and looking pleased with himself.

"Well, MacBride, I guess my campaign is working out smoothly, eh? City is quiet as a tomb. Have a seat."

MacBride sat down. "Don't you believe it," he said.

"What's the matter?"

"Richmond City is primed for another gang war."

"Oh, nonsense!"

MacBride shook his head. "I know. I've been poking around, and I'm in a position to forestall it."

The Mayor leaned forward. "Why haven't I known about this before?"

"It wasn't necessary. I'm going to dicker with you, Mr. Mayor."

"Dicker with me! How dare you propose such a thing? Remember, you are in the employ of the city, bound by duty to have its interest at heart."

"Just that. I have its interest at heart, and that's why I'm here to dicker."

"I detest that word. I refuse to dicker."

"Call it compromise."

"I refuse to compromise." Burkhart's lips thinned against his teeth, and his chin went up. "I am serving the people."

"So am I, and dammit, you've got to listen to me. I don't give a rap if you are the Mayor. I'm here to strike a bargain. You don't know, evidently, that at present there's a gang in Richmond City—from Chicago. A gang of hi-jackers headed by two notorious gunmen. This gang is here to take advantage of the conditions that prevail. They're here to raid.

"I ask you to open every place that you've closed, because there are places open now, I'm sure—places we know nothing about. The barbers' union is rising against you, because you've put barbers out of work. That milk company will beat you in the damage suit. The league of restaurant owners is fighting the midnight closing order, and they have the citizens behind them. Lift the ban and I'll meet you half-way. I'll nip this gang war in the bud. I'll railroad the leaders out of Richmond City."

"But first you must get the leaders."

"I have got them!"

"I heard nothing about it."

"I have them in a hideout of my own—two of them—the leaders."

Burkhart stood up. His eyes narrowed. "And you told me nothing about it. This is treason, MacBride! I won't have it! I shan't bargain with you. You are self-seeking!"

"God Almighty!" exploded MacBride.

"You worked on your own. You excluded me, when I made you an attaché on my personal staff and promised you the position of inspector."

"I didn't ask for the personal staff—didn't want it! And I don't want an inspector's job. I'll refuse it if you offer it to me."

"Don't worry, I shan't offer it to you!" clipped the Mayor. "What's more, I demand the information that you possess regarding this new gang."

MacBride was on his feet, too. "At my price!"

"There is no such thing as price!"

"There is! I have the city's interest at heart. Put me back in my old precinct when it's over. I don't want any return. I've given my life to this job, and I hold the whip-hand. If you fall down on me, the city will be thrown into a reign of blood and you'll be the laughing-stock of the country. You are now—"

"Careful, MacBride!"

"Careful hell! I was never known to be careful and I'm not starting now. Open these places. Lift the ban. Stop making a fool of yourself, and I'll stop this impending trouble!"

Burkhart wiped his lips. He had paled. "I demand that you place your two prisoners in the hands of the Commissioner so that I may deal with them according to law."

"This gang is big, I tell you. Chuck those guys in jail and their gang will bust loose on general principles."

"We have a police department, MacBride."

"Yes, and if this war breaks we'll have a large funeral list and many non-combatants will be killed. I'm trying to prevent blood-shed. Can't you see?"

He was trying hard to put over his point. Sincerity was in his eyes, in his voice, in every gesture. Sweat gleamed on his face. He was a man fighting alone, fighting against the will of a mad zealot.

Burkhart stood motionless. The light, flashing on his spectacles, hid his eyes.

"MacBride, I am a man for the law as it is written. Produce those two men and let the responsibility rest on my shoulders."

MacBride groaned. His fists knotted. He shook them. "Will you go in the streets and fight this gang? Will you pack a gun and meet cars armed with machine-guns and bombs? No. The cops do it, and when they're dead they get medals and nice funerals and flowers and they're called heroes. Bah! I'll bargain with you. You've got to meet my terms if you call yourself a sane man. You can't go on running this town like a maniac! I refuse to produce those men until you meet me halfway."

"And I refuse," said the Mayor. "I'll strip you of your shield. I'll throw you in jail."

"You try it. Throw me in jail, and within two days Richmond City will be a bloody field!"

"We'll see." The Mayor smoothed down his coat "I'll call my sergeant in and have him put you behind bars."

"Call him in!" snapped MacBride. "You can't buffalo me!"

The Mayor leaned forward to press a button. MacBride jumped and caught his hand. "Let that go!" he snapped.

"Let go of my hand!" gritted the Mayor.

MacBride looked up, muttered, flung the Mayor away. He pivoted and jumped for the door, flung it open and dashed out. In a minute he was in the street. At the next corner he jumped into a taxi, dropped to the seat, breathless. The blood was pounding in his temples, and anger boiled in his heart. The cab rolled on. MacBride drew forth the typewritten list he had taken from Millio. He studied it. His lips pursed and he muttered an oath.

The car ground to a stop and MacBride leaped out, paid the fare and entered Charley's place. He raced up the stairs, the key already in his hands. But as he bumped against the door it swung open and he almost fell in. Then he stopped short.

McTurk and Millio were gone. The revelation staggered him. He cursed bitterly. There would be no way possible for him to prove to the Mayor that, by way of vengeance, he had not let these men go. Even now, no doubt, the Mayor had issued an order to apprehend him.

He hurried downstairs and burst in upon Charley.

"Who went in that room, Charley?"

"Huh? Nobody, so far as I know."

MacBride crashed fist into palm. "Those birds got away!"

He left Charley standing open-mouthed, and rocked out into the street. He strode along in a daze. The world seemed to be crashing down about him. He stopped in at a small lunch-room and ordered coffee. He tried to formulate some plan. That gang war would break now—no doubt about it—and the Mayor would be in a position to send him up for ten years.

Desperate—he had a wife and a daughter out in Grove Manor— he swung out of the lunch-room. He was more the lone-wolf than ever. He looked at the list of addresses again. He was near 46 Jockey Street and hurried to that address. It was a three-story building, and when he rang the bell a man opened the door. MacBride pushed his way in.

"I want to talk with you," he said. "Now don't get scared. You've got some Scotch downstairs. Get in touch with your boss and tell him to remove it. There are a lot of hi-jackers in town and this place is booked for a raid."

"How do you know?"

"Never mind. Do what I tell you, and then clear out. I don't care where you put it, but get it out of this cellar."

"Cripes."

MacBride left and walked around to 20 River Road. He delivered a similar message there and then hurried on to the next address. There was no time to waste. He had to hurry. At five o'clock he walked in on George Clark, owner of The Palm Club.

"Listen, George," he said. "You've got two hundred cases on Farmingville Turnpike, haven't you?"

Clark was suspicious. "You on the prod again, Mac?"

"No. Take a tip. Chick McTurk and his hi-jackers are in town. Your hideout is known. Shift that stuff, George. Do it quick, and leave nobody out there after you've moved."

"Is this straight goods, Mac?"

"Have I ever framed you, George?"

"No."

"Then snap on it. I'm trying my damnedest to prevent a gang war."

He left Clark and hastened to the next address. In all cases he was brief and to the point, and since many of the men knew him, they did not doubt his word. By ten o'clock he had covered all the addresses. It was the only thing he could have done, and he thanked his stars that those men believed in him sufficiently to count his word as gold.

And then he proceeded to disappear into the dark heart of the city. He called his wife from a telephone booth and said that he would not be home, and that if she should not hear from him in a couple of days, not to worry. She pressed him for details, but he reassured her that everything was all right and then hung up.

He slept that night in a Greek boarding house near the river. He stayed in all of next day, and went out when night had fallen. He bought a newspaper and was relieved to find that nothing unusual had happened. Another night passed, and another day, and still MacBride trod the ways of a hunted man.

He was on his way back to the Greek rooming-house that night when a taxi skidded to a stop and a man jumped out. MacBride whirled, ready to fight, when he recognized Kennedy. Kennedy gripped his hand.

"Mac!"

"Well, Kennedy?"

"What the hell happened?"

"How should I know?"

"Headquarters is looking for you. Hamlin has been detailed to run you down—"

"That rat!"

"But what happened? Why should you be hunted?"

"You'll find out soon enough, Kennedy."

"There's something queer somewhere. Some house-breaking went on last night. A place on Jockey Street, one on River Road, a farmhouse out on Starlight Boulevard. Are you mixed up in that?"

MacBride grinned. "Of course, not."

"Give me a break, Mac. Tell me."

"I've told you."

"I mean, the truth. Look here, Mac. I wised you that Chick was in town. I told no one else."

MacBride gripped Kennedy's shoulder. "Kennedy, we're old timers. I've never put one over on you yet. When there was news to tell, I gave you first crack at it. But there were times when I held news back till the last. This is one of those times."

"Hell, Mac, if you weren't so damned honest you'd get somewhere. You always insist on fighting a crowd—"

MacBride chuckled. "Forget it you newshound. Omit the bouquets. I'm running along. G'-night."

He grabbed Kennedy's hand, shook it and strode off. He knew that Kennedy would say nothing in regard to their having met. He turned into the next block, walking rapidly, his heels re-echoing in the deserted street. It was a strange sensation to be hunted, after having hunted men for twenty years.

Another day swung by, and when MacBride went forth into another night he was satisfied to know that the papers carried no startling headlines. He even glowed a trifle, for it was obvious that his plan had worked, and there was some little reward in knowing that he had succeeded even while being hunted. He had remained loyal to the tradition which he had built around himself. He had defied the highest city authority for an ideal of his own, and thus far that ideal was not in vain.

He ate at a lunch-room near the docks, sitting back in the corner, watching the door. It was raining, and the rain hammered against the windows. Men rocked in, their rubber coats swishing, gleaming wet. Plates banged. A big nickel percolator whistled. The cash register jangled.

His meal finished, MacBride put on his hat, turned up his coat collar and went out. A man stepped in front of him.

"All right, MacBride. I've been waiting."

Drops of rain trickled from the turned-down brim of Hamlin's hat. A street light played on his wet chin. His hands were in his slicker pockets, and one pocket bulged.

"Took you long enough to find me," said MacBride.

Hamlin smirked. "No matter. I've got you. You're in for it, Mac."

"Makes you feel big, pinching me—doesn't it?"

"Not at all. Duty."

"Personal vanity, Hamlin. You don't know the meaning of duty."

"Let's get along."

Hamlin flagged a taxi and they climbed in. MacBride leaned back in the seat and puffed on his cigar. The red end glowed with each inhalation, revealing his grim, sardonic mouth; flickered in his eyes. The taxi rolled off, its tires swishing on the wet pavement.

"You may get ten years," said Hamlin.

"Don't let it worry you."

"It's not."

"Then shut up."

They rode on in silence. The taxi turned into a dark side street, narrow and deserted, walled in by black faced houses. It cruised leisurely. Suddenly another car thundered alongside, cut sharply in front. With an oath the taxi driver tugged on his wheel, jammed his brakes and screeched to a stop halfway across the sidewalk.

"What the hell!" clipped MacBride.

Hamlin shoved his hand into his pocket.

Even as he did so the door of the cab was yanked open, and a voice snapped, "Easy, you guys!"

A gun glinted.

Other men piled out of the touring car—four of them—and closed in around the taxi. Hat-brims were flapped down low over their eyes.

One said, "Out, you—lively!"

Hamlin started to say, "Cripes, Mac—"

But MacBride climbed out. The situation possessed some measure of irony. Hamlin fumbled out of the taxi and someone ripped his hand from his coat pocket. Hamlin half-spun, in anger.

"I got your gun, Hamlin," said the man.

Three men gripped MacBride, and a fourth took his gun also. MacBride grinned his hard, tight grin.

"What's the joke?" he said.

"D'you see a joke?" The voice was harsh, brittle.

"Millio," drawled MacBride, and added, "Yeah, you." And then he chuckled.

"You'll laugh the other way any minute," grated Millio.

"Lay off," came another voice "Snap on it, guys!"

"Oh, you Chick," said MacBride. "All here, eh? All you nice little boy scouts."

A cigarette end glowed under McTurk's nose.

The men rough-housed MacBride and Hamlin into the touring car. Millio paused with his foot on the running-board and looked back.

He mused aloud, "That taxi guy...."

McTurk said, "Well?"

Millio reached into the car, drew out a long-barreled pistol to which was attached a silencer.

"Hey, you!" barked MacBride

Hamlin sat quite still, pale breath bated.

Crash!

It was not the gun that made that noise. It was the windshield on the taxi. The driver fell sideways.

"Didn't have to bust the glass," observed McTurk.

Millio chuckled and climbed into the touring car.

MacBride was straining at the three men that held him. "You—lousy—pups!"

The roar of the exhaust, the crashing of gears, drowned his protest. The car slewed back into the street and hissed on through the rain. The curtains were closed. Millio and McTurk and the chauffeur sat in front. MacBride and Hamlin and the others were jammed in the rear.

"Tough on you, Hamlin," said MacBride.

Hamlin had been so cocky when he collared MacBride. He was not so now. His lips seemed to have been sealed. He sat in stony silence, like a man petrified.

The car sped on. MacBride could not tell what course they were following because of the curtains. He was mystified. Why did they want him now? He supposed that eventually they would kill him. But something else first. If it were just a matter of killing, they could have done that in the street. But why drag in Hamlin?

Smoother going, with fewer stops, indicated that they were well out of traffic. But soon there were many turns, much shifting of gears. Then presently the car rolled to a stop. Millio jumped out and pulled open the rear door. MacBride and Hamlin were jostled out into a narrow, deserted street in the darker depths of the city.

They were rushed across the sidewalk and into a black hallway. One of the men snapped on a pocket-flash. The others followed in and the door was closed. The man with the light moved toward a staircase and went up backwards, throwing the light down upon the others.

At the first landing he waited. McTurk took a key from his pocket and opened a door, reached in and pressed a light button. Light flooded the room.

MacBride and Hamlin were pushed in.

McTurk said, "Come in, Millio. You other guys wait in the other room, and don't get tight."

Millio entered, closed the door, bolted it. He covered MacBride and Hamlin while McTurk took off his hat and slicker.

"All right, Jazz," he said, fingering his gun gingerly.

Millio shrugged out of his wet clothes and lit a cigarette.

"You guys park," clipped McTurk.

Hamlin and MacBride sat down. Millio took another chair and sat with his gun lying across his knee. McTurk remained on his feet, spread-legged, a drawn and deadly gray look on his face. Millio hummed to himself.

"Can it!" muttered McTurk.

Millio shrugged and puffed his cigarette in silence.

Hamlin sat quite rigid, his arms straight, his hands braced on his knees. He stared at the floor with an abstracted look. Neither fear nor thought nor challenge shone in those eyes. He seemed dazed. His face looked like an inanimate mask of dough.

MacBride looked quizzical. His eyes were narrowed, alert; thin chips of living steel. He was primed for anything; his brain tense but his body at ease.

"Somebody's got to come clean," said McTurk.

"What I say," supplemented Millio.

"Pipe down," recommended McTurk. "I'll say what's to be said."

Millio smiled and conceded the floor to his companion.

McTurk went on, "I want to know where that booze is. One of you palookas know."

"Not me," said MacBride. "And I'm sure Hamlin doesn't."

Hamlin pursed his lips.

McTurk clipped, "Come on, Hamlin."

"I—don't—know."

"You don't know!" snarled McTurk.

"Ha!" chimed in Millio.

McTurk shot him a lacerating glance.

Millio looked innocently at his cigarette.

"Of course he doesn't know," said MacBride.

McTurk's jaw squared. "Hamlin, don't you know?" His voice was barbed.

"No," murmured Hamlin.

"You slob!" McTurk's hand tightened on his gun. "I paid you two thousand bucks for a tip! And what kind of a tip did you give me? Tell me that!"

MacBride's scalp contracted. He looked at Hamlin. The man was wilting. His breath, long held, was pumping through lips that fluttered.

"Spill it, Hamlin!" barked McTurk. "Come across! You know, you bum."

"No—no," choked Hamlin. "I don't." It seemed as if he wanted to look at MacBride, but fear, shame held his eyes to the floor.

Millio stood up, fingering his gun. He eyed McTurk, a twisted spectre of a smile drawing at his lips.

"Hamlin—" McTurk stepped forward. He stood before Hamlin, tight, murderous lines on his face, his body taut. "Hamlin, you double-crossed me! I paid you two thousand in cold cash for certain addresses. I went to those addresses and every joint was dry as a Baptist church. Now where the holy hell do you think you get off?"

Hamlin squirmed. He looked at the door. He seemed to be choking and gasping for air.

"I didn't—double-cross you," he muttered. "Something went—wrong."

MacBride's lips were flat against his teeth. Vertical lines were on his cheek, and muscle lumps bulged at either side of his jaw.

McTurk said, "You get the works, Hamlin." He spun on Millio. "Jazz, get the iron with the silencer."

Millio grinned. "Betcha, Chick!"

Hamlin's eyes bulged with fear. He held his throat.

MacBride clipped, "Hold on, Chick. Hamlin didn't double-cross you. Nobody did."

"What do you know about it?" snarled McTurk.

"Lots. You let Hamlin go and I'll tell you something. I'll tell you what happened to the booze."

"Let him go so he can come back with a gang of cops—"

"Chick," smiled MacBride, shaking his head, "you know he won't came back."

Hamlin bowed his head. In that sentence MacBride had literally called him a coward.

"You mean it?" bit off McTurk.

"I'll tell you what happened to the booze," nodded MacBride.

McTurk backed up. "Hamlin, beat it, and forget you ever came here." As a final derisive gesture he returned Hamlin's gun.

Hamlin heaved up. He swayed, stared at MacBride, his mouth working. He extended his hand.

"Mac—"

MacBride smiled at the hand. "Hang it up, Hamlin. Breeze."

Hamlin sagged out, groaning.

MacBride chuckled. "Well, Chick, I'll tell you what happened to it. It was removed. Know why? Because I went around and tipped off all the addresses that they might be raided."

"Yeah? Go on. Where is it now?"

"Dunno," shrugged MacBride.

"What!"

"I told you what happened to it, didn't I?" droned MacBride.

McTurk's lip curled. "So that's your trick, eh? Clever guy, eh? Well, you bum, *you'll* get the works! Millio, go out and get the smoke. We can't afford any noise."

Millio needed no urging. The door banged behind him.

MacBride stood up. His jaw was squared. "You're a fool, Chick. You'll hang for this."

"Stay back," snapped McTurk.

MacBride grinned and moved closer. "There's a cop on beat somewhere near, eh? That's why you're afraid of noise."

"Stay back!"

Unexpectedly MacBride dived for him, a quick, elastic leap. McTurk dodged, holding his fire.

"By cripes. I'll blow—"

MacBride grabbed his arm, twisted it.

"Shoot, Chick!" he snapped.

He rushed McTurk across the room. They stopped at the window. MacBride caught a fleeting glimpse of two patrolmen talking beneath a street light. He crashed the window.

"Damn you!" snarled McTurk.

In desperation he fired. The bullet tore through MacBride's coat There was a sharp sting in his side. He plastered McTurk against the wall, sank a fist in his face. The gun went off again, as MacBride ripped it from McTurk's hand.

McTurk broke loose, lunged for the door.

"Stop, Chick!" barked MacBride.

The door whipped open and Millio broke in. His breath hissed. His gun belched. The bullet grazed McTurk and slammed into the wall. MacBride crouched. His gun burst into flame and Millio bent over. He fell forward. McTurk tried to grasp the gun as it fell. He got it as it hit the floor.

"Chick—don't!" called MacBride.

McTurk fell and twisted as he fell. He fired twice, and the shots went wild. Somebody fired from the hall and put a hole in MacBride's hat. But the hat stayed on, and MacBride cut loose. One shot hit McTurk as he was rising. He fell down again, screaming, and MacBride put another shot through the doorway.

Somewhere a whistle blew.

MacBride shot out the light.

Feet pounded in the hallway. Blood was soaking MacBride's shirt. He felt dizzy. Pain ripped from his side up to his shoulder. The running feet sounded farther away. He groped for the door, reached down and felt the bodies of Millio and McTurk. In McTurk's pocket he found a flashlight. Somewhere in the farther regions of the house he heard doors banging. The gang was clearing out.

Below, nightsticks were banging on the front door. MacBride found the stairway. He dared to snap on his flash. He went down the steps, sagging. As he neared the bottom a face appeared in the white beam—a hand—a gun.

"It's me, Hamlin," said MacBride. "Careful."

Hamlin's face looked like a death mask.

"Me—MacBride, Hamlin. Open the hall door. Can't you hear the cops?—"

Bang!

MacBride fell against the banister. He cursed bitterly. Damn Hamlin! Another shot cracked. The bullet whistled by.

"Me, Hamlin! MacBride, you—"

Bang!

MacBride groaned, tumbled down the stairway. His flashlight fell from his hand, clattered down ahead of him. It stopped near the bottom, and its beam again shone on the white, deadly face of Hamlin.

Hamlin fired at the light, smashed it.

MacBride, sliding down on his back, fired at the gun flash, the last shot in the gun.

Hamlin screamed.

MacBride fell to the bottom. He tried to stand up. He swayed, reeled, fell heavily—fell across Hamlin, who was lying on the floor, whimpering.

WHEN MacBride came to he was in a hospital bed, and the first thing he saw was his right arm swathed in bandages. Then he knew that his face was bandaged, and that his side was stiff. He felt like cursing.

"How are you, Mac?"

MacBride's eyes shifted. He saw Collins. Standing beside Collins was the Mayor. Burkhart looked haggard. On the other side of the bed was a doctor.

Burkhart leaned forward. "How do you feel, MacBride?"

"Lousy," said MacBride.

"You've been unconscious for twenty hours," said Collins.

"Hell, I must have missed a lot," muttered MacBride.

Burkhart said, "Your wife is in another room, sleeping. She practically collapsed, but is all right now, though the doctor suggests keeping her there. Your daughter is attending her."

Collins leaned over the bed, holding a newspaper. "Can you read that, Mac?" MacBride squinted.

> Captain Stephen J. MacBride, attached to Police Headquarters, is again in the limelight. Last night he effected the capture, single-handed, of Chick McTurk, notorious hi-jacker, and Jazz Millio, Chicago gunman. He killed Millio and wounded McTurk. McTurk died five hours later in the City Hospital, leaving behind a confession which incriminates Captain Peter Hamlin, also attached to Headquarters.
>
> According to the confession, Hamlin supplied McTurk with a list of addresses at which various quantities of liquor were stored. For this information McTurk paid Hamlin two thousand dollars.
>
> The confession goes on to say that McTurk and Millio, who had been hidden in a rooming-house by Captain MacBride, were released secretly by Captain Hamlin who apparently had trailed MacBride there.
>
> The confession continues with the assertion that when McTurk and his men raided the addresses given by Hamlin, no liquor was found and no opposition met with. McTurk, assuming that he had been double-crossed by Hamlin, sought vengeance. Quite by accident he saw Hamlin and MacBride enter a taxi on River Road. He and Millio, in a touring car with several other gangsters, followed and captured MacBride and Hamlin in Hector Street. McTurk declared that Millio shot the taxi driver with a silenced pistol, after which they took MacBride and Hamlin to a hideout in Race Alley, intending to kill two birds with the proverbial single stone.
>
> At this point the confession becomes jerky, due to McTurk's failing breath. He writes that Hamlin said the liquor had been at the addresses, but that something must have gone wrong subsequently. He then goes on to say that MacBride spoke up, declaring he knew what had happened to it, and demanding Hamlin's release for such knowledge. McTurk let Hamlin go.
>
> Further details must be got from MacBride and Hamlin, since McTurk died at that point in the confession. Both MacBride and Hamlin are recovering from gunshot wounds at the City Hospital.
>
> There can be little doubt in the minds of disinterested, sane observers that this action of MacBride forestalled the inception of another

of the bloody gang wars which were common in Richmond City not so long ago.

MacBride nodded and Collins stepped back.

Collins said, "What perplexes us, Mac, is why Hamlin was still in the building when McTurk claims to have released him. He was shot in the right hip. The cops found you and Hamlin lying together at the foot of the stairway. And about this liquor, too."

MacBride was staring abstractedly into space. "About the booze, I tipped off the owners that a raid was in the making. They simply removed it from those addresses. About Hamlin—" He paused. "Well, it looks pretty bad for Hamlin, doesn't it?"

"About ten years," nodded Collins.

"H'm," mused MacBride. "Well, I don't know why he was still in the house. I guess maybe he wanted to try getting me out. Too bad he was wounded. There was—some—mean shooting in the hallway."

Inwardly MacBride cursed himself for giving Hamlin such a clean break. He knew—oh, he knew!—that Hamlin had tried to kill him, to seal his lips. Well, anyhow, Hamlin had ten years of bars ahead of him. That would break him. Disgrace....

The Mayor was saying, "MacBride, it has been a nightmare to me." He turned and asked Collins and the doctor to leave the room. When they had gone he went on, in a low voice, "I've been a fool, MacBride."

"You have," nodded MacBride.

"Yes, I have. And I need you more than ever, now. I want your advice on several things—particularly about revising—"

"Are you talking of compromise, Mr. Mayor?"

Burkhart bit his lip. "Yes, I am."

"Then here's my price. When I'm better, put me back in my old precinct—the Second."

"But, MacBride, an inspector's job—"

"Don't want it. I hate Headquarters. You're a good guy, Mr. Mayor, even though you've been a fool. We both stand for law and order, only you had a cock-eyed notion of what law and order means. I'm with you to the last ditch, if you'll meet me halfway."

"I'll meet you halfway."

"That's all I ask—that and my old job in the precinct."

Burkhart smiled. "MacBride, you're white. You're not bitter."

"The hell I'm not. When I get better I'm going to punch Hamlin's nose all over his face!"

Burkhart reached down and gripped MacBride's hand.

"When you do, Mac, let me know, so I can watch you."

Hell-Smoke

A new racket hits Richmond City.

Chapter I

WELL, he was back. Back in the Second Precinct. Back in the raw maw of Richmond City, where on one frontier the railroad yards sprawled toward the river, and on the other the bright lights bloomed, and traffic rolled like thunder. The hard-boiled Second where many a gang boss had risen to fame and then suddenly had seen the blaze of a gun in his face.

Pete Redmond—gone the way of all criminal flesh; and Sciarvi, private gunman for the late and not lamented Mayor, shot to death in a duel with MacBride, tough captain of a tough precinct; and others—Jazz Millio, premier Chicago gun artist who considered shooting a man in the back the highest example of sportsmanship—and his boss Chick McTurk, national bootlegger, who met his doom in the hell-howling Second.

And so MacBride was back in the precinct nearest his heart. Plainclothes and Headquarters had known him for a while, following the downfall of a corrupt city administration. And toward the end, that gunfight with Millio and wounds that had put him in the hospital for a month and a promise from the Mayor that he would be put back in the Second.

So another month rolled by, and crime lay low in the Second, because MacBride ruled with an iron hand, even while he regained the crisp health and swift vigor which weeks in the hospital had in some measure taken away. Spring was upon the city, and flowerpots were prominent on tenement fire-escapes, and children played in the streets and danced to the raggedy tunes of itinerant hurdy-gurdies, light opera of the alleys.

MacBride was lounging in his swivel chair, feet planted on his desk. His coat was unbuttoned, his white-topped cap on the back of his head, and a seasoned briar in his mouth. His hands were interlocked at the nape of his neck, and he was idly creaking his chair to the rhythm of street music that was not far distant.

Well-tanned he was, from working in his garden at Grove Manor—lean in the face and the framework, straight-nosed, wide-lipped, his hair clipped close and a muscled hardness around his jaw. He was relaxed—but you somehow knew that in the short space of a split-second he could spring to action, with all his faculties ready to his touch. No man had ever run the Second with a drawl, a yawn or a drawing-room accent.

Quietly, casually, like Spring itself, Kennedy, of the *Free Press,* strolled in, helped himself to a chair, and to a cigar from MacBride's humidor. Sighing, he lit up.

MacBride, still slowly creaking his chair, said, "About high time you bought some cigars, Kennedy, instead of bumming mine."

" 'S all right, Mac. I don't mind. Besides, you get 'em at cut-rates. How's your liver?"

"Fine. How's yours?"

"Don't know. Nice day."

"Fine."

"In the Spring—tra-la—young man's fancy and all that crap. Which has nothing to do with the case. The case, Mac, old tomato!"

"What case?"

Kennedy chuckled and settled back more comfortably in his chair. These two were friendly enemies, eternally bickering, but underneath it all they respected each other after the manner of men who are chary of showing emotion.

Now Kennedy dropped his bantering air and was suddenly, intensely serious. "Look here, Mac, old boy. This is news—and for a while I've a hunch you're not going to see much of Grove Manor. Headquarters will get it soon—may have it now. The Street Railways, the Subway, are going on a strike—and that is only the beginning of it. We're in for hell, mark my word. The strike fever is on, and it will spread. It is a new kind of crime, damned near legalized, and it's ten times worse than a gang war."

"Where'd you hear it, Kennedy?" MacBride had stopped creaking.

"We've had scouts scouring the agitators' hang-outs. It's straight goods. Last night, in the Hotel Burnham, Lachowsky, the big poo-bah, met his lieutenants. Stiles, our man, was in the next room with a trick detector on the wall, and heard the whole shooting-match. You know

this Alex Lachowsky, the palooka who some years ago was behind
the strike in Winnipeg, Canada. The same guy. Mixture of Jew, Polack
and a few Balkan countries to boot. A hellion, and a trouble-maker.
Wears a blue workman's shirt, hobnailed shoes, chews tobacco and
spits like a longshoreman. But eloquent! Cripes, in his rough, slam-
bang way he can swing any mob—and seventy-five percent of the
guys on the Street Railways and the Subway are wops, Jews or Polacks,
and they like his line. With him are Mike O'Sleary, the wild Mick,
and Nick Palazzo, the ambitious dago.

"Tonight, at five sharp, the rush hour, the guys leave their jobs,
leave trains standing, and howl for a twenty percent raise. They warn
strike-breakers. Every trolley car, every subway train, stops at five. A
magnificent gesture—and, take my word, the biggest thing that's
popped in years.

"Lachowsky is no dumb-bell. He's an almighty grafter, and he sees,
if you ask me, a way to make a fortune. No, the companies will not
raise twenty percent. They couldn't afford. But this baby—this Balkan
wiseacre—knows his tricks. He'll let the thing come to a head, and
then—I'll bet my soul on it—he'll quietly speak with the company,
get a nice slice of graft, and then go back, work up his oratory, and
tell the bohunks that a five percent raise will be ample—and they'll
fall for him. He's cursed with eloquence that swings the men of the
streets!

"Now wait—hold on—don't interrupt. Get this: think of the un-
employment situation here. Think of the men on the streets, the daily
bread-line at the South Road Mission, the guys who play harmonicas

outside theatres at night, holding the hat, so they can catch odd pennies, get a meal and bed. Watch them, any day, grouped in front of employment agencies, staring at the ads. Take a look at the park benches at night. Enough unemployed in Richmond City to run all the trolley cars and all the subway trains we've got. Many of them have run subway trains, many have applications with the subway; and any man with the brains of a twelve-year-old kid can learn to run a trolley car in an hour.

"All right—what does this mean? It means that we have men desperate for jobs, willing to fight in order to make a living wage. It means that, despite threats, they will go for those jobs, and there'll be wrecks, shooting, bloodshed. Gangs will be born overnight—the city will split. No professional gangsters, but amateurs—and when amateurs start they're just as deadly.

"And the Second Precinct is in the heart of it all. Here are your subway terminals, here all your trolley cars come in from the subways—here, in the tenements on the South Side, live your motormen and conductors. And here, Mac, are you—meditating on the beauties of spring. Sweet cripes!"

MacBride hauled out a bottle of Scotch and poured two drinks. Kennedy took one, and MacBride the other. And MacBride, hard-bitten campaigner of a dozen sensational gang wars, raised his glass.

"Watch my smoke, Kennedy."

Chapter II

AN hour later Collins, Police Commissioner, called up from Headquarters.

"Mac, get this. Hell's primed to bust loose. We've got wind of a walk-out—subway and trolleys, and it looks as if the Second were in for it. Call out all your reserves, and I'll shoot down some extra squads from Headquarters and drag in some reserves from the sticks. Keep a tight lid, Mac. Bust up anything that looks like a row. We're putting a cop on every subway platform and in the trains, and we're calling the recruits for work on the trolleys. It looks bad, Mac, but I'm relying on you!"

"Right," said MacBride, and hung up.

And he went to work. Skipping over the first details with a crowd of policemen in the central room, he added, "And I'm behind you. Get that! Permit no troublesome-looking groups to gather on street-corners. If any guy starts to make a speech, grab him and lock him up. Use your nightstick if you have to, and be tough. Reserves will be coming in here soon, and we'll have the Second pretty well covered."

It was four o'clock. In ones and twos he dispatched them. The station-house, which that afternoon had been a drowsy place, was now electrified with excitement, suspense, action. New groups of reserves came in, and MacBride gave them brief, quick orders. A riot squad from Headquarters drove up in a powerful touring car, and the sergeant in charge advised MacBride that they would be roving the neighborhood all night.

Out of all the bivouacs of the law, policemen appeared. You saw them on street-corners in pairs, keenly on the lookout. In pairs they appeared at subway kiosks, and others went down to the platforms. Mysteriously they appeared on the South Side, conned the ragtag streets, the pool-parlors, the known speakeasies. Small, black flivvers were observed patrolling the trolley lines; and large touring cars, filled with policemen, cruised through the precincts. Every available officer was on the walkabout—called suddenly from leaves, from homes, from tables, from bed, and strung out strategically to cope with an impending strike-wave that promised to have all the frenzy of a rebellion, all the bitterness of a professional gang war.

And MacBride paced the office of his station-house, and Moriarity and Cohen drank Scotch.

"It won't be long now," clipped MacBride. "And you boys stick here."

"Tough," said Cohen. "I had a date with the swellest-looking frail that ever got a divorce."

"Hell for you, Ike!" grinned Moriarity.

Cohen looked at his strap-watch. "Cripes, Cap, no chance of me keeping this date? Honest, this broad is got Vilma Banky skinned—"

"Now, now," horned in MacBride, "cut out the bed-time talk. You, Ike, warm your heels. Go over around the South Side—make it the Three Points—and keep your eyes peeled. Ring in if anything looks wrong. You, Mory, fan Railroad Avenue and pop in and out of the speakeasies—and for God's sake, don't get drunk."

"Me—drunk?"

"Ha! Ha!" chortled Cohen. "Mind the time, Cap, you told him to sit in Louie's and wait for that fence? Plastered he got—the souse-pot! What a fine gumshoe—"

"Breeze, Ike," said MacBride. "Let me see the stern of your pants fading through the doorway. Come on. No—no, I don't give a good damn if this broad has got Vilma Banky stopped—you breeze, and you keep on the job!"

"Ah," sneered Moriarity, "and the nice little boy got a shave and an earwash—"

"You, Mory!" clipped MacBride. "You waylay your tongue and give your legs a chance. Out! Railroad Avenue and—don't—get—drunk."

MacBride sighed and dropped into his chair. He looked at the clock on the wall. A quarter to five. He puffed on his pipe. He felt responsibility heavily upon him. The clean, efficient-looking office irked him. He was a Captain of Police, paid to direct men, to give orders from his chair, to wait and receive reports. And yet he yearned for the fight in the rough and the raw, to be with his men in the maw of trouble. Twenty years of police work had not tamed him, had not made him want to sit back and grow fat, to take the comparative leisure and freedom from danger which his position offered. No, he did not think his men incapable. He knew that Moriarity and Cohen, whatever they might appear to be on the surface, were innately good dicks, ribbed with courage, rough on rats, the one willing to stop a gangster's slug to save the other. And others—plain men, with families and mortgages and flivvers; Germans, Jews, Italians, Irishmen, Polacks, Swedes—all banded together under the sign of the shield and the nightstick. Men who laughed one day, and on another night met death violently and unafraid. Proud he was of them—this rugged, tart-tongued Captain who called them fools, drunks and old women—and quietly, shyly, went to comfort the wives of those who had died in the line of duty. And they liked him—for his blunt courage and his blunt tongue and his squareness.

He got to his feet, muttering under his breath.

Five o'clock!

A bird singing outside somewhere, and nearby, too, children laughing—a woman singing in a tenement not far away; and the sun slanting through the window, and the mellowness of a spring evening beginning to creep in....

And yet, trouble brewing! Men worked to a fever pitch by the misdirected eloquence of a mongrel trouble-maker who claimed to work within the law. Other men, half-starved, aching for work and willing to risk a broken neck to get in. And blood waiting to be shed in the mad frenzy of ill-conceived "rights."

"Good God!" MacBride asked the wall. "Can't men ever be satisfied? Is crime—in all its new forms—a disease?"

And he answered himself, "Yes—damn it!"

And he longed to be out in the rowdy streets, smelling for trouble, eager to prevent it with the swift, fierce ruthlessness that had made him a terror among the lawless. But his job was in the station-house—waiting.

An hour passed—two hours and then a third. He took a drink and rasped his throat. He breathed deeply. Perhaps the deadlock of the law was working. A patrolman drifted in and reported that the South Side trolley line, which had been stalled for an hour, was again running—with strike-breakers on the job.

MacBride nodded. He called up several subway stations, got in touch with the policemen on duty.

"All quiet," came the report. "The Metro Line is running on reduced schedule—but running."

He telephoned police booths where he knew trouble would be most likely to break—and the reports were favorable. Short lines had been temporarily suspended, but the main lines were running, and the trolley company, eager to keep up some sort of service, and running short on motormen, had thrown into service buses with which they hoped to fill up the gaps. The transportation arteries of the city were moving however, slowly; and they were moving doggedly.

MacBride felt a thrill in his blood. His men—the badge and the nightstick—were maintaining order. No fights. No violence. At ten he had a patrolman fetch him something to eat from a nearby lunch-room, and he ate at his desk. At eleven he peacefully smoked a cigar. At eleven-thirty Kennedy walked in.

And he said, "Just dropped in for a drink. This dago hooch is getting lousy."

MacBride drew forth the bottle and they had a drink.

"All quiet on the front," said Kennedy, eyeing his empty glass.

"Yes," breathed MacBride.

"Cops as thick as fleas on a mutt. The papers waiting. The presses marking time. Right-hand columns left blank for a last crack-up."

"Blood-thirsty sheets! City editors will cry like babies if nothing happens!"

"City editors never cry. They curse like hell."

"What do you think?"

"About the strike?" Kennedy shrugged. "Takes time for a fuse to get to the works. This sudden show of police has given them a shock. However, a shock wears off and— Mind if I take another snifter?"

"Drink yourself blind. I've got a case of it."

"Glad you told me. I'll drop in oftener."

MacBride swung up and down the room. Kennedy slouched back in his chair and tipped his hat over his eyes, sighed contentedly and drowsed.

Midnight crept by. MacBride's body longed for a bed. He yawned despite himself. The jangle of the telephone bell broke off his yawn. He picked up the receiver.

Cohen was shouting, "Cap, listen! Get this! Cripes! The Morris Street car was coming down the hill—past the paper factory. Some guys jumped out of the alley—you know the alley—and heaved bricks. The motorman was knocked down. A milk truck came out of Hocker Street, and the car hit it. The motorman got a fractured skull. Listen! Yeah—and some people hurt. Listen! I picked up two cops and we lit out for the gang. One of them heaved another rock—and Brunner's got a busted nose. Kline fired his gun in the air to stop them, and they split up, and a Polack went nuts and pulled his gat and started smacking shots all over the place. One knocked down a pedestrian—and Carney needs a new hat—he got his aeriated. Listen! This Polack was shooting mad, or crazy, but, hell, we had to do it. I smacked him in the leg with a shot and he fell down and his brother or somebody let out a whoop and came for me with a knife. Carney hopped for him and cracked his knob with the nightstick.

"Cripes—but wait! Some of the other guys thought it necessary to collect the wounded and they came for us—ten of them—with clubs and knives and a lot of yells. So Brunner—with his busted nose all over his face—and me and Carney and Kline we told these babies to back up—but—hell's bells—there was no stopping them and they piled in! I had to blow one guy's guts out because he was trying to stick a knife in Carney's throat. We—kind of—broke them up—you know, gave them hell-smoke and all the trimmings. But, listen—I'm calling from a drug-store, corner Waller and Jane Streets. Listen, Mac—I'm kind of all in—if you know what I mean— For cripes' sake—listen, Waller and Jane—drug-store—"

There was a groan, and then silence.

MacBride slammed the receiver into the hook. He grabbed his hat and bumped into Kennedy, who looked mildly inquisitive.

"Out of my way, Kennedy! It's started! Hell's broke, and it's the beginning of more hell. My job's in the streets!"

He crashed into the central room. "Lieutenant Hoyt—you're in charge! Use your head! Stick here! I'm bound for the South Side!"

And he cannoned through the door, into the street. And Kennedy sailed after him.

Chapter III

MORRIS STREET was blockaded. The trolley car that had collided with the milk-truck was derailed athwart the tracks, and the truck itself was twenty yards farther down the hill, lying on its side, with milk and milk cans cluttering the street. Behind the derailed car was a string of others, unable to proceed. The motormen looked apprehensive, and there was a uniformed policeman on every car and more on the sidelines.

The street was packed with people, and people hung from windows, and there were cat-calls, threats flung to the strike-breakers, and the tension of a drumhead, with beneath it electric waves of unrest. A big black touring car from Headquarters was pulled up near the derailed tram, and riot guns were visible. Policemen walked about purposefully, their nightsticks swinging gingerly in their hands. And people made faces at them—behind their backs, of course—people who were supposed to be law-abiding citizens. And sometimes a mocking voice—"Brass buttons, blue coat, couldn't kill a nanny goat!" Hidden somewhere in the crowd, or shouted from some dark tenement window.

MacBride came booming down upon the center of trouble, his white-topped cap slanted over one ear, his shoulders squared, his feet swinging with sureness of purpose. He looked tough, he felt tough, and as a matter of hard-boiled fact, he was tough. Sergeant Slade, in charge of the riot car, stopped him.

"Looks quiet enough now, Cap."

"Don't like the looks of this crowd. That the trolley?"

"Yeah. A wrecker's coming out to shove it back on the rails. Ambulance just took a couple of cops and some strikers to the hospital."

"Ike Cohen too?"

"No. Ike's down in the Rex Drug Store. He wouldn't go."

MacBride nodded and rolled off, and Kennedy followed. In the Rex Drug Store they found Cohen sitting with his coat and shirt off while the druggist was bandaging his arm. He looked pale, but he grinned, and a cigarette bobbed in one corner of his mouth.

"You go to the hospital, Ike," clipped MacBride.

"Like hell I will. Listen, I had a date with the swellest broad that ever rolled her socks—"

"Now don't bring that up. You're—"

"Oh, I'm all right. Billy, here, gave me a good drink and the arm was only scratched by a dago knife. Brunner—you should see his nose—went to the hospital, and Carney had to go too, 'count of a bust on the dome and a kick in the guts."

"No prisoners?"

"Give a guy a break, Mac—"

" 'S all right, Ike. I know."

"We had the whole stinking bunch on our necks. When Kline finally blew his whistle they scattered. Cripes, I got the sweetest crack in the jaw with a number ten Polack boot that you ever saw. My eyes—honest, Mac—my eyes waltzed all over my head and I hit Kline by mistake. I wonder if my pal Moriarity is still sober. The Mick and I fight good together. He hits 'em first and then I hit 'em again as they fall—and the morgue bus usually collects 'em. Man alive!" He chuckled recklessly.

MacBride left him in the hands of the druggist and returned to the streets. Back on Morris again, he saw that the wrecker had arrived and was attempting to swing the derailed car back on to the rails. The low murmur of the crowd was ominous.

MacBride picked up Sergeant Slade again and said, "Look here. We've got to clear away this crowd. It's growing in size and it's getting nasty. Spread the word among your men that Morris Street is to be cleared. Snap on it, Sergeant!"

And MacBride, pivoting, went down the lines and passed the word to the men from his own precinct, and the push began. The crowd muttered. It was stubborn.

"Back!" roared MacBride. "No one allowed on this street. Go home. Get off the street— *You,* there, don't look so tough! Go on, keep your mouth shut And *you,* in the derby, you heard me! Start pedaling.

Breeze! I said breeze, or do you want to warm your pants in an unpadded cell?... Come on, now, everybody on your way. Back—back.... Hey, you, get off the street, back on the sidewalk. I said *back!*... Everybody home and to bed.... What's that remark? I think I'm tough, eh? Right, and ten times tougher than you are, so get wise to yourself.... Never mind any lip or I'll run you in.... Who the hell threw that stone?... By God, I'll— Back! Off this street, I said! Back—*back!*"

It was slow work, gruelling work. They hated the uniform, these people who were supposed to respect it. They cursed it and looked upon the officers of the law as a martial enemy. They gave ground slowly, smoldering with anger, and a spark would have ignited them.

Slowly, but definitely, the policemen cleared Morris Street, drove the mob down side-streets, into tenements from which many of the quarrelsome had issued. And then a patrolman was stationed at the corner of each street that ran into Morris, for a distance of eight blocks, the heart of the South Side.

"That's that," clipped MacBride.

He stood with Sergeant Slade and watched the wrecking-crew that was slowly swinging the derailed car back on to the tracks.

"This neighborhood is full of bad actors," said Slade. "Hot blooded guys, with no sense. A hot-bed of blockheads who think the State is going to the dogs and should be run differently, and that they are being persecuted. Of course, they never thought of this until a lot of soap-box orators started telling them."

"Lachowsky and his crowd," nodded MacBride.

"Yes. If somebody accidently killed that guy Richmond City would breathe easier—and these poor sapheads would throw a big funeral and weep over a lost saviour. A lot of brains in this city stopped growing at the age of ten. I tell you, Mac— What's that?"

They listened, and looked up Morris Street.

"Sounds like a drum," muttered MacBride.

And then they saw the lurid glow of a sulphur torch, and a string of automobiles—touring cars and light trucks—coming down the hill. MacBride's jaw tightened. He started off on the run. He saw some policemen running out into the street, holding up their hands to stop the procession. He saw the leading car swerve, gather speed, and saw one policeman knocked sprawling into the gutter. He shouted.

The leading car boomed by, packed with yelling men, and on the back MacBride saw a sign, *The Loyal Brotherhood of Railway Employ-*

ees. He jumped to stop the next, a truck, but it swerved out of his way, and rumbled by, and in it a drum was booming and torches were flaring. Policemen came on the run.

"Stop them!" MacBride yelled. "By God, they'll start a riot!"

He leaped full into the glare of the third car, raised his hand, shouted at the top of his lungs; and when the car did not stop he drew his gun, blazed away, and flattened the two front tires. The car rolled onto the sidewalk, and men piled out, screaming, "Murder! They're tryin' to murder us!"

The other cars, coming down the hill, overran curbs. One hurtled by with a policeman on the running-board, fighting with the driver, commanding him to stop. The car skidded, banged across the sidewalk and drove crashing through the plate-glass window of a hardware store. Pots and pans and wash boilers and kettles clanged and gonged out into the street, and men bellowed, and shots barked, and glass sliced to the pavement.

"Murder! Murder!" rang through the street.

"Oh, God!" breathed MacBride, gray-faced.

Whistles blew, the call of the law. Policemen came on the run, from up the street, from down the street. They came pounding out of alleys, nightsticks drawn, eyes keened—these men who put their lives up for sale at forty dollars a week. And whistles still blew, the call creeping from street to street, out toward the very frontiers of the Second Precinct.

There was Detective Ike Cohen, his wounded arm thrust into his pocket—swanky man in the way of dress, reckless in the face of the danger. There he was, racing up Morris Street, with his gun drawn. There was Patrolman Grosskopf, who had a wife and three kids, and who was getting on in years—Grosskopf lumbering up to the call, grim determination on his fat face. And Patrolman Nils Swansen, big and blond, about to be married. And small, dark Patrolman Pagliano, two days a father, and the prize tenor of the Second—bounding along to the call of the shield and the nightstick. And others sweeping into the red face of danger—Eilstein, Maloney, Shanzenbach, Harrigan, Mstibovsky, Honickberg, Malloy, Lindendorf.

Mob hysteria broke. MacBride saw it break when that car crashed through the plate-glass window. He ran and bellowed for the other cars to turn around and go back up the hill. But the men, many of them inspired by liquor, billowed out of the cars, shouted and stormed down the street.

MacBride caught hold of Sergeant Slade. "We've got to bunch our men and stop this. No use trying to talk sense. We've got to be rough. We've got to give 'em hell-smoke. Break them up, Sergeant!"

"Right, Cap!"

And MacBride galloped off, collected patrolmen, drove on toward the mob that was trying to gather into formation.

And cries of, "Murder! Murder! The cops are tryin' to murder us!"

MacBride ran into Cohen and barked, "Ike, get out of this!"

"Rats! I've got no place to go and that broad will give me hell! Let's crash this merry-go-round!"

The policemen, bunching, swept down upon the mob, holding their gunfire but waving their nightsticks. And the mob broke, scattered, but regathered as others, those who recently had been driven from Morris Street, poured into it again from alleys and doorways.

A policeman went down under a blow to the ear, and his partner turned, cursed, and wielded his nightstick, bringing down the first aggressor. He was pounced upon by three others and borne to the gutter; mauled, kicked, cursed, until two policemen came sweeping down and struck left and right, savagely, with nightsticks.

"They're murderin' us!" rose the terrible cry—terrible because it incensed mob blood that was already boiling.

And a gun belched flame and bitter lead—a mob gun, fired by a towering Pole whose eyes blazed and who was crazed with a twisted fervor.

He looked dazed, then. And oddly enough, he stood, a giant of a man, with his back to a store window, and his gun seemed to go off automatically, and each time it went off his lips jerked and he looked more dazed. One of his shots brought down Patrolman Pagliano—two days a father, prize tenor of the Second. Another shot, blindly delivered, broke the neck of a man who was on the point of attacking Grosskopf.

And MacBride, seeing the dazed killer, swung his gun—paused. Then he leaped, clubbed the man to the sidewalk. The man rolled over, crawled up, roared, stood swaying and swept his gun toward the Captain. And MacBride shot him—finished him and choked as he saw the man roll into the gutter.

Rocks, bottles fished from ashcans, hammers, wrenches, flew indiscriminately. More policemen came tearing into Morris Street, and the law fought bitterly and drove the mob down the hill, fighting for every inch of ground. Wild shots smashed tenement windows, and flower pots sailed down from fire-escapes. Screams and oaths re-echoed, and then came a full riot squad, and riot guns began to bark.

MacBride was in the thick of it, his cap gone, his hair wild, wind in his eyes, blood on his face, one eye blacked, his collar ripped off and a fierce, hard set to his jaw. The riot guns hammered. The mob retreated faster. Then it broke, and the law swept after it—fifty-odd policemen, leaping on the violators, bringing them down, clamping on handcuffs. But many got away. The fight was out of them, and they fled like men possessed of the devil—into alleys, over fences, out and madly away from Morris Street. And tenement windows closed, and the din and clamor died, and presently the law stood getting its breath and viewing the spoils. And three ambulances rolled into view, and then the morgue bus for those who no longer needed an ambulance.

MacBride, ragged and torn, stood with his hands jammed against his hips, eyes steeled and hard jaw level.

"Boys, lock these babies up. Help load the wounded and pile in the stiffs. Ike, you get the hell to a hospital—or home. Sergeant Slade, that was good work. Have a drink with me at the station-house. Double patrol on this street till further notice. I see you're here, Kennedy. I hope to cripes your paper will feel satisfied. All you boys who were stationed on trolley cars, go back to them. You boys from other beats, go back to them. Telephone me personally if anything looks wrong. I'll be camping at the station-house till this thing blows over—and it hasn't yet. Kennedy, give me a butt."

Chapter IV

RICHMOND CITY bled.
Headlines ran wild in the morning papers, and there were pictures of Morris Street, some showing the dead lying as they had fallen. There were other reports. A trolley car, rolling in late from Grove Manor, was boarded by six men as it moved slowly up Wyndham Hill. It was stopped, and motor-man and conductor were beaten insensible, the windows were smashed, the gear box wrecked. Another car was attacked on Railroad Avenue, and the motorman was taken to the hospital with a fractured skull.

MacBride read—and smoldered.

Kennedy sat on the desk, dangling his legs.

"You must admit, old onion, that my story is colorful," he said. "And notice how often I mention Captain Stephen J. MacBride."

"Oh, you're a big-hearted slob!" MacBride was bitter. "The world's going crazy. I'd like to get my hands around the neck of the guy who started this!"

"Lachowsky, of course, lies low. He's planted the seed and now he steps out for a while."

MacBride struck the desk with his fist. "Yes, he planted it! And he could unplant it!"

"The boss sent Rogers to interview him, but he's not to be found. He'll let the thing get nice and ripe, then talk terms."

"And in the meantime people get killed! It's rotten! That bum should be shot! There's Ike Cohen, my best man, laid up. Pagliano dead and his wife hysterical! Mstibovsky dead! Oh, God, Kennedy, I feel like going out and finding Lachowsky and giving him a bit of hell-smoke on my own! I'll not be losing good cops! They're my men, my gang!" He banged the desk violently.

Kennedy said, "Don't get too ambitious on your own. This is beyond you. The only thing you can do is carry on, direct your men, bust up riots, and mark time till it blows over. You've tried a lot of things on your own, and you've succeeded—but this is bigger than you are. You can't touch Lachowsky—even if he turns up. He didn't tell the mob to kill anybody. Of course, he knew what would happen. But—actually—he didn't say, 'Go out, my children, and derail cars, throw rocks at scabs, shoot a few policemen by way of diversion and bring home the dear old bacon'."

"No," muttered MacBride, "he didn't."

That afternoon the drivers of milk wagons walked out, and the jobless, the men desperate to make money at any cost, flooded the offices of the dairy companies. The insidious strike fever was spreading, and more policemen were called out. And that night the Union of Longshoremen gave notice that a fifteen percent raise was required, and the men left their jobs.

At ten o'clock an Italian was picked up in a subway station on the outskirts of the city. The patrolman on duty had noticed him idling on the platform and letting several trains go by. The man was found to be in possession of a bomb. At midnight a subway train of six cars was derailed between the Maine Avenue and Carlton Square stations.

No one was killed, because the train had been moving slowly. Someone had walked the tracks, thrown a switch the wrong way and evidently escaped with the crowd of passengers who stumbled along to Carlton Square Station. At the same time a riot broke out on Railroad Avenue. One policeman was wounded, six prisoners were taken, and a bystander was killed.

The city was in a state of war.

Brief rows on street corners crackled throughout the second night like electric sparks. They were not tremendously significant as compared to the larger riots, but they helped to keep up the dreadful strain of hysteria that was seeping into the pores of the city like poison. In a poolroom on Jockey Street a crowd gathered and an agitator, starting to make a speech, was stopped by a policeman. Somebody threw a billiard ball and broke the policeman's neck. The gang cleared out and the proprietor could not say who threw the ball. Jockey Street was a hard-boiled street.

Martial Law! shouted the *Morning Observer.* Call out the militia! But Headquarters tightened its jaw and called out more reserves, more recruits.

And then, like carrion, came a new menace.

The noon edition of the *Free Press* had another headline:

GREAT SILK ROBBERY

And Kennedy sailed into MacBride's office. "Hell's bells and hot dogs, ain't this rich!"

MacBride flung down the paper, bit the end off a cigar and snapped a match on his fingernail.

"Kennedy, this thing is just about growing to my size." And he lit up.

"Seventy-five thousand dollars worth of silk, Mac, old onion! From the warehouse at Pier Fifteen. I knew this would happen—oh, I didn't foresee this particular robbery. I mean I knew that if this strike was rich enough, crime—real crime—would follow as naturally as the night follows the day. A gang has been formed—all the guys who've been lying low since that Millio-McTurk fizzle—and I'll bet many of Millio's guns are in on it. They hadn't the price to go back to Chicago, so they stuck around—and now they're in on something big. Oh, there'll be a hot time in the old town! Hot sizzling hell, we haven't had such beautiful headlines in years!"

"All you think about—headlines," snapped MacBride. "Look here, Kennedy—I'll bet you'll croak of remorse if something else doesn't happen tonight. Damn my stars, if I only had someone I could lay hands on. This waiting—this marking time, and old Peters killed in that poolroom!"

The tough Captain was like a dog on a leash. He had implored Headquarters to spring a net for Lachowsky, to get him and frame him and make him try his eloquence toward stopping the mania which he had started. But Headquarters was conservative. It had not the wild, untamed blood of MacBride.

Later that night he was pacing his office when there was a commotion in the central room. He looked toward the connecting door and as he did so it burst open and a man skidded in, propelled by Detective Moriarity.

"I nailed this palooka proper," clipped Moriarity.

"It's Artie Sloane," said MacBride.

"Yes, it's Artie Sloane," nodded Moriarity. "I caught him down on the pier talking to a gang of dock-wallopers—talking trouble, telling 'em how persecuted they were."

Sloane slouched against the wall, a cigarette drooping from his mouth, a scowl on his face. "Yah, you're a tough egg, you are, Moriarity! You think you're tough!"

"Close your jaw, you bum, or I'll put my fist through it! There's the rod he was packing, Mac."

MacBride looked at an automatic pistol. Then he looked at Sloane. "Last time I saw you was when you came out of stir after a four-year stretch for shooting up a drug-store. What the hell's the idea now of talking cheap politics to strikers?"

"That's my business. And what about it? You got nothing on me. I ain't done a thing that the law can touch me for."

"You're right," nodded MacBride. "I was never so cheap to hold a yegg for packing a rod, but I'll be cheap this time. We'll board you for a while, guy."

Sloane snarled, "You'll what!"

"You heard me. What gang are you running with?"

"Gang? I ain't with no gang. Who the hell says I'm with a gang?"

"Why not talk turkey?" said MacBride. "You damned well know you were in on that silk job. Now what's behind this business?"

"Ah grow up, Mac! Silk job! Cripes, I'd laugh if I wasn't so lousy sore at you guys. You especially, Moriarity."

MacBride flexed his lips. "Mory, I've got a strong hunch that we've had a good break tonight. This bum knows something. He wasn't trying to work those dock-wallopers up out of the goodness of his heart. There's a reason behind it. Take him"—MacBride jerked his thumb—"take him in the other room, get a couple of cops and—sweat him."

Sloane recoiled and his eyes widened. "You ain't gonna sweat *me!*"

"Unless," said MacBride, "you want to sit down here with me, have a drink, and spin us your yarn."

"I ain't got no yarn! Listen, you guys lay off me! Let me ring my lawyers, O'Shay and Finkleberg. Gimme that phone."

MacBride blocked him. "Lay off. You talk here or you get rough-housed in the other room."

"Cripes, Mac, I tell you I'm on the level. I was just telling those guys things—"

MacBride looked at Moriarity. "Take him, Mory."

"Right," grinned Moriarity, and gripped Sloane's arm.

Sloane tried to fall down. Moriarity held him up. Spun him around and dragged him through the door.

MacBride sat down and took a drink.

Half an hour later Moriarity came in, brushing his hands. "He passed out."

"Say anything?"

"Lot of dirty names. Nothing else."

MacBride said, "I'm sure he's crooked. I'm sure he can tell us something worth while."

In the morning a runner from the firm of O'Shay and Finkleberg appeared with a writ to release one Arthur Sloane who was arrested for "disturbing the peace."

MacBride said, "Take that scrap of paper back and burn it up."

"But, look here, Captain, the law demands that you—"

"And get out of my office. I'm holding Sloane for carrying a gun, and I don't give a rousing damn for you, your firm or that writ. I'll apologize to Judge Williamson, later. On your way, buddy."

At noon Moriarity appeared after another session with Artie Sloane.

"Mac, he sprung a lead! Not much. He said he was running with Lou Katz."

"Katz!" echoed MacBride. "The self-styled boss of Jockey Street last year. Is he back in town?"

"Must be."

MacBride cracked fist into palm. "We want Katz, Mory!"

"For the silk job?"

"To hell with that. Incidentally, yes, but"—his eyes keened and his lip curled —"I've got a hunch, Mory. I've got a queer little hunch in the back of my head. We may even—man, we may even bust up this strike!"

"Not through Katz, Mac?"

"Through Katz!" gritted MacBride.

Moriarity scratched his head. "Don't get you."

And MacBride clipped, "Then get Katz."

Chapter V

BUT Lou Katz was not an easy man to lay hands on.

Eager, impatient, MacBride joined the hunt himself. He was to be observed, late next night, slipping out of the station-house in plain clothes. He faded into the wilder back alleys of the city.

He stopped for a drink in a speakeasy that was run on the third floor of a loft building. Tony Pigalli, the owner, knew him of old, and Tony came over and sat down while MacBride ran his eyes over the men gathered there.

"Strange, Mac, you being around here. I ain't done anything, have I?"

"Of course not, Tony. I came out for a bite to eat and thought I'd finish up with a drink. Anything strange about that?"

"No—no, of course not. I've got some good stuff, anytime you want a case."

Pigalli was a man who played with the law, ran his joint as squarely as he knew how, supplied captains and inspectors with liquor, and sometimes knew where a certain gunman might be found. He valued the patronage of the law above that of the crook, and he was discreet.

"Moriarity was in here," said MacBride.

"Yeah," said Pigalli, turning a diamond ring on his finger.

"Now I'm here."

"Yeah," nodded Pigalli.

"I hear Lou Katz is back in town."

"So they tell me."

"Ever come in here?"

"No."

"Never?"

"No," said Pigalli.

"Where does he go?"

Pigalli shrugged. "Maybe any place."

"Lots of places in town, Tony; that's right."

"Yeah."

"Joe Kelly's. Burt Henson's. Charlie Dyer's."

"Yeah," nodded Pigalli, turning his ring. "And Bud Thompson's—sure, lots of places."

"Thanks," said MacBride, and stood up. "Good-night, Tony."

"Good-night, Mac."

MacBride descended to the street, knowing that Lou Katz was an habitué of Bud Thompson's.

Bud Thompson's was on Jockey Street, on the frontier of Richmond City; a narrow, dim-lit street that started in the bright lights of Maine Avenue and descended slovenly to the waterfront. And at its lower end it was most dangerous, and where it was most dangerous, was Bud Thompson's speakeasy.

"Hello, Bud," said MacBride as he drifted in.

Thompson was an ex-pug, and his joint was a rough layout. A dozen men were drinking, and some were playing poker.

"Ain't seen you in ages, Mac. Have a drink."

"No thanks, Bud." MacBride looked around. "See Lou Katz lately?"

"Is Lou in town?"

"Come, now, Bud. We're old friends," chided MacBride.

"Honest, Mac—is he?"

"Sure he's in town. Where, Bud?"

"Aw, Mac, I don't know. Jeeze, if I knew I'd tell you."

"Well, thanks, Bud. Thought you might know. Good-night."

"Good-night, Mac. Drop in again."

"Sure."

Bud went to the door with him, and the lookout let him out. The door closed and MacBride started walking. But suddenly he turned around, retraced his steps and knocked at the door. The lookout opened it on a crack. MacBride pushed it, and the lookout tried to say something.

MacBride brushed him aside, hurried across the room, reached another door that was partly ajar and pushed it open quietly. Bud Thompson was at a telephone, snapping:

"City 465. Open your ears! I didn't say 469. I said 465."

"Hang up, Bud," said MacBride.

Thompson's chair scraped as he spun. His face blanched.

"It's all right, Bud. I know how you feel about it. Give me the phone."

He took the instrument from Thompson's hand and rang central. He said, "Look here. This is Captain MacBride, Second Precinct. Never mind calling that number. But get me the address of it and ring me back."

The operator snapped, "I can't do it. I don't know if you really are Captain MacBride."

"All right, give me Police Headquarters." And when he got Headquarters he asked for Lieutenant Ballinger and said, "Jake, this is MacBride. Ring the telephone people and get me the address of City 465. Ring me back at Jockey 402. Thanks, Jake."

He hung up and looked at Thompson. "That was a fast one, eh, Bud? Tough. But I mean business. If I was a sorehead I'd close you up for spite. But I'll have a drink with you."

"Cripes, Mac, you know how it is. I hate to squeal—"

"Sure, I know. Make it rye."

Ten minutes later Ballinger called back and gave MacBride the address. And MacBride left, with an offer of a case of rye from Thompson—which he refused.

Thompson saw him to the door, and MacBride paused. He regarded Thompson steadily. "You want to keep open, Bud, don't you? You want us to be nice to you?"

"Well cripes, Mac, I was in a hell of a fix—"

"Forget that. If you want to stay out of trouble, don't do any more telephoning tonight."

Thompson stared at the floor, his brows knit.

MacBride clipped, "You get me, Bud?"

"Got you."

Without another word MacBride passed into the street.

The address given him by Ballinger was in Moon Street, and Moon Street bites into the western frontier of the Second Precinct. It is a street of many shades, undecided yet as to just what status it chooses to hold. There are garages there, a church, some warehouses, some wholesale twine and paper companies, and thrown in at intervals are apartment houses—not high-class, and yet not extremely low.

MacBride rang the janitor's bell at Number 40. The door automatically clicked open and he walked in to a plain, narrow lobby. At the rear of the lobby was a door marked Janitor, and on this he knocked. A man opened it, yawning, pulling suspenders over his shoulders. MacBride flashed his badge, and the man stopped yawning.

"Is City 465 the house telephone or an apartment phone?"

The janitor said, "Apartment. Woman named Crosbie. I can ring her—"

"No. What apartment?"

"Eight, fourth floor."

"All right. Thanks. You can go to bed, old timer."

The janitor scratched his chin. He eyed MacBride quizzically. Then he shrugged.

"All right, chief."

And he backed in, closing the door slowly, reluctantly.

MacBride climbed the stairway, and stopped on the fourth floor. There were apparently two apartments on each landing. He stared at the door that bore on its panel a graceful brass 8. He took his gun from its holster and slipped it into his pocket. He rang the bell.

Chapter VI

A LONG moment passed before the door opened.

A woman looked out—a woman of, say, thirty, with brown shingled hair and a cigarette between her fingers.

"Wrong flat, I guess," she said.

"No," said MacBride. "May I come in?"

"Come in? Hell, mister, don't you think you pack a hell of a lot of nerve? On your way."

She slammed the door, but MacBride's foot jammed it and the door rebounded, swinging wide.

"Listen here, stranger!" snapped the woman.

But MacBride pushed in, saying, "It's all right, sister. I'm from the station-house. MacBride's my name, and I won't keep you long. In fact, you don't interest me a bit."

They were standing in a small entrance hall, and a couple of feet beyond was an open door from which streamed the light of a room into which it led. MacBride nodded toward it.

The woman seemed to have lost power of speech. Her lips moved, but she said nothing. Chagrin probably stayed whatever words groped for expression, and she kept flicking the end of her cigarette.

MacBride moved past her and looked into the room. It was a sitting-room with furniture of Grand Rapids Renaissance and a lot of chintze curtains and an old-rose reading lamp. It was empty. There was another room beyond, apparently a bedroom—darkened.

The woman strolled in, puffing on her cigarette. She flounced into a chair.

MacBride looked at her. "Where is Lou Katz?"

Smoke drifted from her nostrils. "On second thought, old boy, don't you think you've got the wrong apartment?"

"No. Where's Lou? Come on, girlie. I haven't got all night."

"There's nobody keeping you."

"If I were you, I wouldn't get fresh."

"Why shouldn't I, when you bust into my flat?"

She was cool now.

MacBride looked around the room. "Lou's living here, of course."

Her lips twisted. "What do you think I am?"

"That's beside the point," he droned; then snapped, "Light up your bedroom."

"Listen here!" She jumped up and planted a hand on her hip. "Since when is a cop allowed to come into a woman's flat and—?"

"Sister, I mean business! Cut out the small talk. Do as I told you. There's a cigar in that ash-tray—still smoking!"

She almost gasped. But then she shrugged. "If you want to see my bedroom, turn the lights on yourself."

"Turn 'em on!" snapped MacBride.

She chuckled and dropped back into a chair. "Not me, old boy."

His hand knotted over the gun in his pocket. He swivelled and stepped to one side of the door.

"Come out!" he barked. "You—in that room, come out!"

There was no answer.

MacBride said, "This window is open. If I blow my whistle, a dozen cops will be here in a couple of minutes. Now come out!"

Presently there was a movement. The next moment a man stood in the doorway—a big man, with his hands in his pockets. He eyed MacBride levelly, and then grinned.

"Hello, Mac."

"Oh, it's you, Chuck."

"Yeah. Seems you're makin' a hell of a stink, Mac."

Chuck Turner rolled into the room. Once upon a time MacBride had sent him up for pirating on the river.

"Why were you hiding, Chuck?"

"Huh. That's a funny question, Mac." He winked and grinned at the woman. "I figured maybe it was her boy friend. You know how it is, Mac."

"Oh, I see," nodded MacBride. "Little affair going on, eh?"

"Yeah," smirked Chuck. "Have a drink, Mac?"

"No, thanks."

There was a moment of silence. MacBride rocked on his feet, smiling tightly. The woman lit another cigarette and looked embarrassed. Chuck rubbed his ear and looked sheepish. His jaw worked slowly. He spat out of the window.

"Know anything about that silk job, Chuck?"

Chuck looked up. "Huh?" And then he shook his head. "Nope."

A strange, elusive tension hung in the room. MacBride's eyes were narrowed, steel-keened, reflecting sharply the glow of the lamp on the table. Taut muscles were becoming tighter about his jaw.

The woman looked at him and stopped puffing. Chuck Turner stopped chewing, and a perplexed frown grew between his eyes, and his hands hung motionless at his sides. Slowly, imperceptibly almost, the fingers began to close.

MacBride's hand jumped from his pocket, and the blue steel of his revolver shone dully.

Chuck's hands bunched, and his jaw squared. The woman twitched in the chair.

MacBride moved swiftly, until his back was to the open window. His other hand produced a police whistle.

"Now get this!" He spoke loudly. "There's somebody else in that room! You're not a cigar smoker, Chuck. Besides, you wouldn't be chewing tobacco and smoking a Corona too. I remember Lou Katz favored Coronas." He raised his voice. "Lou, if you're in there, come out. If you don't, I'll blow this whistle." He flung to Chuck. "You raise your hands and keep 'em up."

No sound came from the other room.

"Come out!" yelled MacBride.

The woman was quivering with fright and rage now. Chuck was transfixed—and yet deadly.

"You—you—damn you—" the woman was complaining.

"Shut up," MacBride told her, and then put the whistle to his lips, looking at Chuck.

"F'r Gawd's sake, Mac—"

Bang!

Flame belched from the bedroom and the table-lamp was shattered, the rooms pitched into darkness.

MacBride blew his whistle.

The room was not so black that he could not see a shape hurtling toward him—Chuck Turner. The tough Captain fired to wound, and Chuck crashed against the window frame—would have gone out and headlong to the street had not MacBride grabbed him and rolled him aside.

The woman let out one terrific scream and then became silent.

"Switch on the lights!" shouted MacBride.

"Go to hell!" snapped the woman.

MacBride weaved warily from side to side. He looked into the darkened bedroom.

Then something hard banged against his head and he reeled, fell over a chair and crashed to the floor. He flung off the chair, blinking, shaking his head, heaved to his feet, staggered against the table, but steadied himself. He caught a fleeting glimpse of a man's leg disappearing up the fire-escape.

He lunged for the open window. The woman blocked him. He pushed her aside and she clawed at him, tried to bite his hand. He flung her away, and she toppled over an armchair. Then he was on the fire-escape, and climbing upward, three more stories to the roof. The night wind cleared his head. He snorted and felt primed again. Again he blew his whistle, signaling whatever policemen were in the neighborhood to surround the block.

Before him lay a desert of roofs—skylights, chimneys, low dividing walls. He crouched in a shadow, listening, peering keenly about him. The wind hummed gently in a tin ventilator nearby. A bird was disturbed and flew up and away.

A dark form sped across a bar of moonlight. MacBride raised his gun to fire, but the form was again lost in the shadows. MacBride followed swiftly, vaulted over a low wall, followed the pounding footsteps of the pursued. When the sounds suddenly ceased, MacBride stopped behind a chimney and waited.

A long moment passed. Then there was a scuffling sound on the roof—then footsteps pounding again, and a figure scaling the wall beyond. MacBride fired and missed, and the echoes of the shot hammered across the rooftops. As MacBride cleared that wall a burst of flame split the darkness ahead and a bullet chipped a brick beside his hand. He dropped to his knee and fired at the flash, but his shot snapped through a tin ventilator.

There was a sound like the bang of a door. MacBride raced on and brought up against a door that led to regions below. He turned the knob, but the door was locked. He yanked at it. It resisted. He put three shots through the lock, heaved again, and the door rasped open.

He felt his way down a narrow, winding staircase, black as pitch. Then he reached another door, opened it, and found himself in a dimly lighted hallway. Faintly he heard the hammering of footsteps, far below. He followed, noticing that the halls were wide and dusty. Then suddenly all the lights went out, and MacBride groped down through darkness again, feeling his way along the banisters.

This—he mused—was some sort of storehouse. You can't mistake the smell. Hides had been stored here recently. He found himself soon with no more stairways to descend, and decided he must be on the ground floor. He heard—close by—the roar of a powerful automobile engine; sounded as if it were in the next room.

He probed the darkness for a door. He lit a match and squinted. He was in a store. There was a long counter in the rear, and a heap of empty barrels and packing cases. Obviously the place was not in use. In the front were broad windows with shades pulled down. He ran toward the door. He had to shoot the lock away.

And as he burst into the street he saw a low touring car sweep out of a garage next door and go thundering down the street. He would have fired—but he had to reload, and he galloped as he reloaded.

Two policemen came trotting around the next corner. They saw him and one yelled:

"Hands up, you!"

"Never mind me," barked MacBride. "We want that car!"

He flashed his badge and then one of them recognized him. "What's up, Captain?"

"I'm tailing that silk job. Is there a machine handy?"

"No. We've got the block surrounded, and Grosskopf just pinched a broad and Chuck Turner in a flat up the street."

The other policeman said, "Hartman's down the street with his motorcycle."

"Show me," clipped MacBride. "There's that car swinging into River Road!"

In two minutes he reached Motorcycle Patrolman Hartman and said, "I'll take this, Hartman."

He forked it, cranked it. The exhaust exploded violently, then roared, and MacBride swept off down the street. He lost his hat as he skidded into River Road, and then he opened the throttle wide and cannoned after a red tail-light that shone faintly in the distance.

He hadn't ridden a motorcycle in five years, but that didn't cramp his style. He streaked up River Road at sixty-five miles an hour, and realized that the car ahead must have been doing the same. He swayed, he bounced, but somehow he retained his seat and somehow the motorcycle held the road. The wind thundered and clapped and screamed about his ears. His hair tugged at his scalp and the wind hammered his eyes, fought with his breath. He squared his jaw against the wind. The thunder of the exhaust boomed among the huge pier-sheds.

Then the red light disappeared—the car swung off River Road. MacBride followed it into Dane Street; hooted down between rows of blank-faced houses; saw the red light turn left; got close enough to catch the license number; had to brake suddenly to avoid hitting a pedestrian, and in so doing skidded against the curb and upset. But he was up in a minute, his knee through his pants, but his determination still strong.

Far ahead he saw the red light turning again, and howled after it;

lost it for a while. Five minutes later he was rolling along when he saw a car stopped against the curb. The number caught his eye and he pulled up. The car was empty.

He looked up at the street sign on the corner. He was on Low Street. The one that crossed it was Jockey. He cracked fist into palm, hopped back on to the motorcycle, swung into Jockey and coasted down the grade for three blocks, then he swung into the curb, jacked up the 'cycle and took a long breath.

Bud Thompson's was halfway down the next block.

He caught sight of a policeman strolling toward him. He beckoned, and Patrolman Shanzenbach came up. He was surprised to see Mac-Bride in plainclothes, with a motorcycle to boot. But then you never knew what this captain would do.

MacBride said, "Shanzey, there's going to be some hell-smoke tonight. I've tailed the silk job, I'm pretty sure—right to this street, and the guy we want is in Bud Thompson's, and ten to one he's got his gang. The welcome sign will not be hung over the door. I've got a hunch that if we get Lou Katz, we crimp this strike. Round up the other cops on this beat—quick."

"Here comes Maloney now."

Maloney was surprised, too.

MacBride said, "You walk along, Maloney, and stand opposite Bud Thompson's. I'll see you in a minute. I've got to ring the station-house."

A block away was a police telephone. Even in a tight moment like this he wanted to know how the rest of the precinct was getting on.

Sergeant Schneider puffed, "Cap'n, we been looking all over for you. Where you been? Uh—here, Moriarity—"

Then Moriarity's voice. "Come on home, Mac. Cripes, we've got him! Yeah, I picked him up three hours ago in a cigar store on Maine Avenue—"

"Wait, wait, Mory! Who'd you pick up?" broke in MacBride.

"Lou Katz!"

"What!"

"And how! Kennedy's playing blackjack with him now. Come home, Mac."

"Okey, Mory. Good work."

MacBride hung up, a little dazed. Three hours ago! Just about the time MacBride had first walked into Bud Thompson's. There was something wrong—and yet....

He walked briskly toward Jockey Street, and found Shanzenbach coming up with five patrolmen. He joined them and they continued down Jockey Street.

Maloney stepped out of a hallway.

"Cap, a guy looked out of Bud Thompson's. I was just passing under that street light. He saw me and dived back in again."

"When?"

"A minute ago."

MacBride said, "Gang, let's go in."

Chapter VII

THEY crossed the street and stopped in front of the door.

"There is no back-way out," said MacBride.

He knocked, and waited. He knocked again, but the only answer was an echo.

He looked around at his men. "Shanzey, you've got lots of beef. Let's you and me ram it."

They backed away, looked at each other, nodded and then let drive. The door creaked as three hundred and eighty pounds of hard beef and bone crashed against it. They stepped back, swayed, then drove against the door again. A panel split.

"Again," said MacBride.

"Right," said Shanzenbach.

Another panel split. Shanzenbach rubbed his shoulder. But they drove again, and with a crackling sound the door gave 'way. Darkness yawned inside, and not a sound was there.

"Give me a spotlight," said MacBride.

Maloney gave him one, and without a word MacBride passed in through the door, flattened against the wall and groped for a partition which he remembered jutted out on the way into the main room. He found it and snapped on the spotlight.

Nothing happened. He threw the beam along the walls, swept it down over the floor. He stopped its progress—because the white shaft had picked up the body of a man lying on the floor. It was Bud Thompson, and a streak of blood was on his forehead. MacBride sent the shaft of light farther afield. The tables were deserted. Nobody was in the room.

He found the light switch, snapped on the lights. His men were standing about him, guns drawn. Maloney moved forward and bent over Thompson.

"Unconscious," he said. "Been beaned."

"Yeah," said Shanzenbach. "He'll take at least six stitches."

They stood around the man, looking at one another, listening, then looking toward MacBride.

MacBride was peering at the door that led into the room where Thompson sometimes slept. One of the patrolmen was pouring a pitcher of water over Thompson's face.

Shanzenbach caught MacBride staring at the door, and Shanzenbach moved toward it.

MacBride said, "Back, Shanzey. I carry heavier insurance."

He moved slowly, quietly toward the door. He laid his hand on the knob. He turned the knob. The door was locked. He stepped back, looked at his men, nodded.

"All right, boys. A little target practice. All together now—bust the lock."

Eight guns boomed and eight bullets smashed the lock. The smoke curled upward slowly, fell back, rolled toward the street entrance. MacBride walked toward the door, kicked it, and it swung open. Police guns bristled.

"Come out!" snapped MacBride.

Only silence came out.

"Of course," went on MacBride, "we can wait you out, but it will only make us nasty. Whoever you are, you're a rat, and I've trailed you here from Moon Street. Now get wise to yourself."

A minute passed, and then a dark, sputtering object sailed through the door, bounced off MacBride's shoulder, hit the floor and rolled under a table.

"My God! A bomb!" shouted Maloney.

"Throw it!" yelled MacBride.

"Where is it?" yelled another.

"Under that—" said Shanzenbach, and hurled aside a table.

Maloney dived for the bomb, picked it up, his face white, his eyes popping. He ran toward the street.

"My God, throw it out!" yelled Shanzenbach.

Maloney threw it. It burst as it passed through the doorway. The building billowed, heaved. Red and white flame ballooned mightily, and glass crackled. The floor lurched and split open. The walls careened and a beam, shattered, whanged through space and knocked Maloney sprawling. Plaster rained and the ceiling came down with a deafening boom.

MacBride was lifted from his feet and slammed against the wall. He lost his gun, was blinded by the ghastly glare, shocked to the core by the awful holocaust. Plaster and broken wood and twisted metal crashed upon him, and dimly he saw Shanzenbach reeling about and trying to disentangle his head from the chandelier which had fallen upon him. There was Maloney, lying on his side and waving one hand after the manner of a man trying to brush away mosquitoes. The gesture would have seemed ludicrous if it weren't so terrible. Another policeman was sitting against the back of an upturned table, his cap on one ear, blood streaming down his cheek, and a dazed, blank look in his eyes, and a wrinkle on his forehead, as though he were trying to reason out some difficult problem. Another—oddly enough—was lounging in a chair, his hat gone, his head lying on his chest and his hands crossed on his stomach. He seemed to be dozing peacefully.

Smoke was billowing, and flames were crackling, and another part of the wall fell reluctantly. A piece of plaster two feet square hit the man who seemed to be dozing and knocked him off the chair. He woke up, sat erect, looked about him and then his lips said, "God Almighty!"

He tottered up and tried to help Shanzenbach get rid of the chandelier.

MacBride stumbled away from the wall. There was a cop lying on the floor with a table on top of him, and MacBride hauled it off, and the man said, "Thanks, Cap," and then closed his eyes. MacBride bent down to shake him. The eyes rolled open and stared as only the dead stare.

He stood up, grimaced, while the heat of the flames rolled around him and their red glow smeared the shadows. He saw a man leaping across the ruins—hatless. He dived after him, stumbled over Maloney, got up again and saw the man hurtling through the flames, toward the street.

"Hey, you!" he yelled, and lunged after him.

Flames snapped at his legs, singed his cheeks, crackled in his hair. He leaped over a fallen beam. His heel touched it and chipped off a shower of sparks. He reached out for the man, caught hold of his coat, and the coat ripped off. He leaped and reached again, grasped his shirt, and the shirt came off.

The man half turned to beat MacBride, and MacBride caught hold of his flying hand, gripped it, held on doggedly and then closed in. Hot coals crunched beneath their feet, and shoe-leather smoked, and smoke slithered about them like a suffocating fog.

MacBride struck, and then caught the man's hand even as the gun boomed and a shot went wild into the razed upper regions of the house. They twisted and lurched and heaved, and their feet roasted in their oven-like shoes.

The man, gagging, broke loose and fought for the street, for clean, cool air to breathe. And MacBride, choking, too, lurched after him and caught him on the sidewalk, his eyes burning and half-blinded from the smoke, but his purpose still clear in his mind.

He struck savagely, and his hard fist was gashed against teeth that gave 'way. The man struck back and laid open MacBride's jaw. He struggled to free himself. He wanted to get away. MacBride held on and struck while he held on, and they carried the fight into the gutter. They fell down, rolled over and over, and MacBride's fists worked like pistons.

Dimly he heard the clanging of bells—fire-bells—and the roar of a siren. Then he became aware that he was pounding a man who was limp and unconscious, and he sat back, gasping for breath, as a fire-engine clanged to a stop.

He stood up and reeled back toward the flames. He saw Shanzenbach staggering out with another policeman in his arms. Then came Maloney, also bearing a man. MacBride tried to go in again, but two firemen stopped him, as others plunged in through the flames.

"Shanzey," said MacBride, "a drink would go good. If we can get a car we'll all go over to the station-house. I've got a bum parked in the gutter. It looks mighty like Lachowsky."

Chapter VIII

KENNEDY and Lou Katz were playing blackjack in the central room of the station-house. Moriarity had reversed a chair and was straddling it, with his arms on the back and his chin on his arms. Sergeant Schneider at the desk, was eating a Limburger sandwich and drinking a bottle of home-brew.

Katz was a sleek, dark-haired man, well-dressed, thin-cheeked and slant-eyed.

He was saying, "The police of this here town is getting on my nerves. Here I've been away for a long time, and as soon I come back to the old home town, they invite me over to the station-house. Such a kind bunch of guys that they insist on me spending the night with them!"

Moriarity said, "You're funny as a crutch, Lou."

"And," added Katz, peeling off a card, "they don't even know how to treat a guest. Insult him. Your play, Kennedy."

At this juncture the street door flew open and MacBride walked in looking very much like a man who has been through something rougher than a tea-party.

"Cripes!" said Kennedy. "He's been up to something again."

Lou Katz puffed on his cigar. "If he hasn't, advise me by mail."

Four policemen, no less battered, followed on the heels of the captain, and among them was a tall, red-haired man, with his under-shirt in ribbons, welts on his face and a look of terror in his eyes. He espied Katz and snarled:

"*You!*"

"H'm," murmured Katz. "This isn't so funny."

"*You!*" bellowed the red-haired man. "You double-crossed me, you insufferable puppy!"

"Hey," said Katz, waving his hand. "Keep what's left of your shirt on. I didn't double-cross nobody."

"You did! You were supposed to meet me at the flat—"

Katz sprang up. "Watch your tongue! Where's the brains you're supposed to run over with?"

"Brains! Brains I have, Katz—many brains! But you played the foul sneak, deserted me. You failed to appear at the flat. You failed to appear at our other rendezvous, in Jockey Street. And when I asked for protection from that friend of yours—that Thompson person—he refused, saying he had no desire to become involved in anything so dangerous that it would cause him trouble with the police. I—yes, dear God, I had to strike him! Oh, you low person, Katz! You essence of filth, of all that is—"

MacBride barked, "You, Lachowsky, shut up!"

"I have been tricked by a foul—"

"*Shut up!*" MacBride snapped; then went on, "And you are slated for the chair. The bomb which you threw, you damned idiot, killed one of my men. Oh, I suspected this combine. My hunch was right. You've started your last strike, Lachowsky, and when the papers get this, when the men you've urged to strike, read what you've done tonight, that you're up for *murder,* they'll turn tail.

"Brains? They deserted you, didn't they? You knew, even in that flat, that if I saw you there, in company with Chuck Turner, a known gunman, you'd be done for. I suspected your game when we nabbed Artie Sloane on the river. You hired Katz and his men to maintain the mob hysteria, to do a little shooting now and then, to keep up the blood of the strikers. Yes—and now I've got you cold."

Katz sighed. "Lachowsky, I guess you sure balled up things. I guess you sure did."

And Lachowsky snarled, "I? It was you, when you carried away that silk! That was what the police were after!"

Katz narrowed one eye. "You big bum! Here I've been sitting pretty, and you come out and spill the works. MacBride was after you first— Hell, I'd like to blow you up, you louse!"

"I was paying you to work for me, yes," said Lachowsky. "But I made it clear in the beginning that it was for me alone."

Katz walked up and down, stopped, shrugged. "It's in the blood. There was a warehouse loaded with silk so easy to swipe it was child's play. With the cops busy over strikers—hell, it would have been an insult to my reputation to let that stuff lay there. And, anyhow, Lachowsky, I didn't kill anybody. I'll take a stretch for robbery—but you, big boy, you're up for *murder.* Now try your brains on that."

"Oh, you cur!" groaned Lachowsky. "You double-crossed me!"

Katz snapped. "Listen here, I didn't! I never double-crossed any guy. Moriarity—this Mick here—nabbed me in a cigar store when I was on my way to the flat, and I've been here ever since. If you shoot the works when I'm not around to wet-nurse the rough end, that's your tough luck. Make another crack like that and I'll wrap a chair around your head!"

Lachowsky raised his arms and started to be eloquent—but Mac-Bride made a gesture, and two policemen dragged him off.

MacBride sagged into his office and dropped into a chair. Kennedy drifted in and leaned against the wall, smiling.

"Mac, old onion, that was good work," he said. "You've fooled me again. This will be a sensation in the first editions, and you're right—the mob will get scared when they see that their idol is up for murder. And with this yarn, we'll rake up other ones about him—his work in Winnipeg and out through the Middle West. He's done for. This strike will die a natural death. It seems to me, Mac, that you're one damned good cop."

MacBride pulled open a drawer and drew forth a fresh bottle of Scotch. He cut away the seal, twisted in a corkscrew, clamped the bottle between his knees and yanked. The cork popped.

"For which bit of applesauce," he said, "I suppose you expect a drink."

"It's good Scotch. But I'm sincere, old onion. Someday you'll get finished—they'll get you in a dark alley when you're not looking—oh, not these guys—but some other gang, and they'll sing your swan song."

"Pleasant thought," mused MacBride, pouring out two drinks.

"Hard facts."

MacBride gave a brittle chuckle. "I die hard, Kennedy. What I lack in brains, I make up for in guts. And that's the catch—when you get right down to it, a bum is yellow—got a streak a foot wide and a yard long down his back."

They clinked glasses.

"But," said Kennedy, "that's just what it takes to finish you off—a yellow bum with a gun some night in a dark alley."

MacBride grinned through his bruises. "Kennedy, that thought is just what keeps me young and kind of pepped up. It's what keeps my stomach down and my head from growing bald—and it's what still makes me able to get in two shots even after I've been hit."

"To you," said Kennedy.

"To you," said MacBride.

And the Scotch went down neat.

Tough Treatment

And that was what the tough town called for.

Chapter I

MacBRIDE sat in a rocker in his room on the fifth floor of the Braddock Hotel. It was winter, and a thin layer of ice masked the window and a ragged border of snow surrounded it. But closed as it was, the rattle of a trolley car over switches in the street below, and the hoot of a locomotive whistle penetrated the room. A radiator hissed industriously.

Kennedy, fully dressed, even to his overcoat, lay on the bed, smoking a cigarette and staring at the ceiling. He looked tired—but then he always looked tired.

MacBride said, "Kennedy, you're dropping ashes all over my bed."

"Sorry, Cap. Thought I was dropping them on the floor." He sat up and scratched his head. "Play you some penny ante."

"I wish you'd go down to your room, so I could go to bed. It's midnight."

"Is it? I don't like the beds in this dump, anyhow. Play you some marbles, then."

"Go to hell."

"That's right. We've got no marbles. But we can pitch pennies, though."

MacBride snorted.

Kennedy chuckled. "Poor old Cap is sore. Well, as a matter of fact, I don't blame you. This city of Millboro is certainly not my idea of paradise, either. It's a shame, Cap. There you go and clean up Richmond City, and before you know it the governor of the State requests you to come down here and wipe up."

"Listen, Kennedy, I'm going to wipe up."

"Yeah, s' I suppose."

"I've been eating Christmas dinner with my wife for twenty years and I'll be damned if I'm going to miss the next one."

"Then you'll sure have to step on it."

"I am stepping on it. But so help me God, I never saw such a worn-out police department as this town has! These guys wouldn't know enough to get in out of the rain."

Kennedy said, "The main thing is, Cap, that they're sore. They're sore because you've been drafted down here to show them how to run their business. They don't like it. The sorest of all is Chief Herman. He's been sitting pretty for ten years and he doesn't like the idea of somebody being put over his head. Take it from me, old tomato, he's not going out of his way to play house with you."

"Hell, Kennedy, do you think I wanted to come down here? Richmond City suits me. My wife's cooking suits me, and I never liked a hotel anyhow. I talked straight to Herman. I said I was here to clean up and the sooner he played ball with me the sooner I'd be out. But that guy's a lousy sorehead."

"Granted," nodded Kennedy. "Cap, this is a wild town. She's ripe with vice. Of her population of thirty thousand, three-fourths are bohunks who work in the steel mills and the coal yards. They've grown up but they left their brains behind in the process. They're meat for suckers. Mill Street has more vice joints to the square yard than any street in Richmond City. *The Barn*, up on the hill, is a damned sight worse than any honkatonk of a frontier city in the old days, and Kildeen, the guy that runs it, is making a fortune. There are more grifters in this burg than in all of Richmond City, more bootleggers and more gamblers.

"The trouble with this city is that it's an overgrown small town. When Central Steel put up its mills here five years ago the population doubled. Lowbrows in the town then saw a way of getting money and started making hooch and running illicit houses. They're old inhabitants, and many of them are related to the men who are on the Force. If not related, then they're old friends. It's simply a city with small-town habits. Nobody wants to step on his neighbor's toes. I don't say there is graft here, Cap. I don't think there is. But the police and the town are too closely interwoven. The methods are antiquated, there's no new blood on the Force. The cops like to keep on good terms, from the Chief right down.

"You come here, a disinterested party, with one aim in view: to suppress vice and the exploiting of the bohunks, to clean out the crooks that were naturally drawn here by the easy pickings. You thereby incur the enmity of the vice crowd and the sullen envy of the police.

"This Kildeen—he's no small cheese. He's popular—in fact, he's so popular that there is no need of graft. He's buffaloed the Police Department. They're afraid of him. They're afraid that if they pick on him they'll rile his followers, and it doesn't take much for these bohunks to start a riot.

"Cap, old horse, we have in this city a situation typical of many cities of its size in America. It is a case of the skeleton outgrowing the body. The town has grown, and law and order have not kept pace with it. It is a civic problem difficult to overcome. Gentle measures cannot turn the trick. It needs to be ruptured—sudden, swift and tough treatment.

"I wouldn't take your job for ten thousand berries. You've got a fight on your hands—not only against the lawless, but against the grooved methods of the law. This Police Department is in a rut, and a rut it is satisfied to be in. And your life is about as safe as that of a man sitting on a case of dynamite on the Fourth of July. Take it from me—Kildeen and these brain-shy bohunks are dangerous."

MacBride puffed on his pipe. "Kennedy, I came here mainly to advise Herman. He's acted on my advice about as fast as a guy with infantile paralysis. Now I'm through giving advice. I'm going to act. I know some guys would like to see me pushing up daisies. As a matter of fact, I've had two blackhand letters in the past week. Oh, I didn't tell you? Well, I didn't think they were important."

Kennedy sighed. "Poor old Cap."

"Pipe down. I'm not crabbing." He stood up, lean, straight, chisel-jawed. "That Kildeen—he can't buffalo me. I'm going to close *The Barn*, Kennedy, and I'm going to tie Kildeen up in a knot. I didn't come down here to use mainly brain power. God knows I don't run high on brains, but I know how to paste a guy in the jaw."

"Only don't leave your back exposed in dark alleys, old boy. There are a lot of guys, I imagine, who think you've lived too long already. What's that?" he suddenly broke off, looking toward the window.

"Police whistle—trouble call, wasn't it?"

"Yeah, I think so."

MacBride pivoted and strode to the window. It opened hard, due to the frost. Chips of ice and lumps of snow fell away as he jerked it up, and a blast of cold air struck him in the face, cold as a bar of ice.

From the roof of the house across the street burst a dagger of flame. A bullet slugged the window sash an inch from MacBride's head. Glass rained down upon him as he flung himself to the floor. Another shot cracked on the frosty air, spat through the window and shattered a mirror hanging on the opposite wall.

"Pups!" muttered MacBride.

Kennedy made a long dive and snapped out the lights. A shot barked and demolished the globe a split-second later, and Kennedy slid into a corner on all fours.

"Lousy shots, Cap!"

"Yeah," came MacBride's voice through the dark. "That's what I call a dirty trick. Those babies knew that if I heard a police whistle I'd open the window."

"You're sure a burr in somebody's sock, old tomato."

"Yeah, and I'm going to be a boil on somebody's neck."

Chapter II

CHIEF OF POLICE HERMAN had grown fat on his job. He had one too many chins, as much hair as a billiard ball, and thick-lensed glasses that seemed to distort his pale blue eyes. In so enormous a hulk of man his thin, petulant voice seemed oddly incongruous. He sat behind his desk in Millboro's Police Headquarters, fidgeting with a pen.

"I know, I know, MacBride. I know how you feel. No man likes to get shot at. You're a marked man, seems. Your reputation has preceded you, and I suppose there are a few persons in this city who want to get rid of you. But—but, look here, Cap—I hope you don't mind if I call you Cap—look here, Cap, we can't dynamite out these conditions, not in this city. Conditions are far different than those in Richmond City. This is an industrial city—steel and coal and the type of men who go to produce steel and coal. Now—man to man, Cap— they must have their sport. What of it if Mill Street is full of improper women— And Kildeen's *Barn?* What of it? I'll admit a lot of things go on there, but it can't be helped. We must be broad-minded in affairs of state, Cap, and realize the weaknesses of human nature, the vanity, the—"

"Now wait a minute!" MacBride took a measured turn up and down the floor. He stopped, squared off, and jammed his hands against his hips. "You're on the wrong tack, Herman, if you think you can change my ideas of right and wrong. Your argument, ever since I came to this town, a week ago, has read like a 'Spring Song.' The greatest weakness I see in this town is the Police Department.

"I know bootlegging is inevitable. It's tolerated all over, if it's kept quiet. But in this town, Herman, vice is flaunted like a banner. You and your department are being buffaloed. You're being laughed at. You're licked and you, Herman, are assuming this tolerant air to try hiding the fact that you are licked."

Herman looked shocked. "Why, Captain MacBride, this is almost an insult!"

"If the truth is an insult, all right—"

"MacBride. I won't be talked to that way. I've handled law and order here for twelve years, and I think—"

"You think you ought to know something about it. As a matter of fact, you don't know anything."

Herman flushed, and his lips moved silently. The direct attack of this hard-bitten captain from Richmond City staggered him. He should have known that MacBride was not the man to decorate his words with honey.

MacBride braced his arms on the desk. "I've come to tell you, Herman, that I'm through giving advice. From now on I am going to act. To begin with, I'm going to close *The Barn*. I'm going to wipe out Mill Street. I'm going to wipe out the bootleggers. I'm going to do all of this merely to show them that they can't buffalo the law. I was sent down here to help rid this town of filth. It seems as if I have to do it alone— Well, that's all right by me."

"Cap, you can't do it."

"Watch me, Herman!"

"It's suicide!"

"Don't be melodramatic. I want papers necessary to close *The Barn*. Meantime you can twiddle your thumbs."

Herman argued. He was reluctant to recommend such papers as MacBride demanded, until MacBride finally threatened to call upon the Mayor and have a meeting of the City Council. In consequence of which, Herman capitulated, and secured a padlock order.

MacBride took along with him a sergeant named Connolly, and they drove out toward *The Barn* in a battered police flivver. *The Barn* stood halfway up a hill back of the city. It was a huge, rough-board structure of two stories, painted red. It overlooked the mills.

They parked out front. MacBride led the way into a dusky interior. There was a long lunch counter, an array of coffee percolators, bottles of ginger ale stacked on shelves behind. There were two dozen or more oilcloth-covered tables. Off to the left loomed a large, crude dance-hall. Colored streamers, soiled by smoke and coal-dust from the mills, hung in a fantastic net-work from the rafters. The whole interior was rough, unfinished and—like its name—had the appearance of an overgrown barn.

Two men stood behind the counter. They wore dirty white aprons. At one table sat four men with bottles and glasses. They were not men of the mills. Their clothes were flashy, and they lounged.

Sergeant Connolly stood just inside the door and MacBride made a beeline for the counter.

"Where's Kildeen?" he asked.

One of the counter men said, "Ain't been down yet."

"Get him."

The man blinked. "Who are you?"

"MacBride's my name. Get him."

The man slouched off and disappeared. When he came back he said. "He'll see you in an hour."

"Yeah?" said MacBride. "Is that a wisecrack?"

"Jeeze, it's just what he told me!"

"All right. Now you lead me to him." MacBride went around to the back of the counter. "Come on, don't look so surprised."

"Well, hell, guy—"

"To you, buddy, I'm Captain MacBride. Get moving."

The man grumbled and scowled and led the way down a corridor. He then ascended a flight of stairs and knocked at a door. A voice snapped, "Who's there?"

"MacBride," clipped the captain.

There was a moment of silence. Then the door opened and a huge, rock-jawed man stood there.

"I said, MacBride, that I'd see—"

"You're seeing me now, Kildeen," said MacBride as he pushed in. "Where the hell do you rate that crap?"

He kicked the door shut with his heel. He flung a quick look about the room. A girl, attired in a dressing gown, was sitting on a sofa. A thin, pale young man, with jet-black hair and tight, hueless lips, stood by a window.

"So you're Kildeen," said MacBride.

"That's me."

"And I'm MacBride. I suppose you know why I'm down here."

"Yeah, I heard."

"Good. Now I have a court order here, Kildeen. This dump of yours is padlocked."

"Joke?"

"I've got no sense of humor."

"This is a good time to get one."

The girl shifted her position. The pale young man looked at the floor. MacBride produced the paper and laid it on the table.

"There it is, Kildeen."

Kildeen chuckled and hooked his thumbs in his belt. "You can't ride me, MacBride. I don't care what the hell kind of a reputation you got."

"Read that, Kildeen, and use your head. This is just the beginning. I'm not fooling. Some guy tried to plug me last night, and I'm sore. Millboro is in for a clean-up. If you think I'm a lot of noise, try me out."

He turned and pulled open the door. "Get me. This dump is closed from now on."

He passed out and slammed the door behind him.

Chapter III

LIKE a withering blast the hard-boiled captain descended upon Mill Street. Innately he knew the weaknesses of human nature, and was no holier-than-thou man in the matter of accepting them. But since his job was the carrying out of the law, it naturally followed that Mill Street should come under his hammer. What he demanded was that the law be respected. It had been laughed at for too long a time in Millboro.

He visited more than a dozen houses, and his talks were distinctly brief and acutely to the point. He carried a railway schedule with him, and suggested early and fast trains, outward bound. He was derided, scorned, cursed. He was called a bible-preacher, a sky-pilot, and other names far more derogatory. He merely tightened his lips a little harder, keened his windy blue eyes, and repeated the departures of early trains.

At noon he met Kennedy and they walked into a one-arm lunch-room.

"Busy, Cap?"

"Yeah. I just had a talk with a lot of wisecracking frails in Mill Street."

"See Kildeen?"

"Yup. That dump is closed. I've got more rounds to do this afternoon. Oh, I'll be busy for days. I've got a list of twenty speakeasies here, and, Kennedy, every one is going to be padlocked."

"Cap, you're in for hell."

"Who cares? I'm going to close this town tight as a safe-vault. When it's closed, when these hard guys wake up to the fact that the law is no fool, then we'll open up a bit. A few speakeasies never hurt any town. But first they've got to accept the fact that the law is boss. It took me a year to put that over in Richmond City. I'm working over-time here."

After lunch he left Kennedy and blasted his way through the back alleys in his customary whirlwind manner. He walked into Nick Ricardo's *Fandango Club,* a large, low dive that took up the entire second story of a building near the railroad yards. A couple of dozen men were in there, drinking, and every one of them looked like a rat.

Ricardo was a soft, obese figure of a man, with a cast in one eye and a drooping, sullen face, dark as oiled leather. MacBride was led to him by a waiter, and the latter, fearing trouble, beat a fast retreat. Ricardo was sitting at a table with a small Italian who catered to loud clothes and smelly hair-oil. Ricardo squinted, for he did not know the captain.

"You Ricardo?"

"Yeah, I'm Ricardo."

"I'm temporarily in charge of this burg's police department. Just dropped in to padlock you."

"Yeah?"

"Yeah. Here's the order." He flung a paper on the table. "Read that and pay attention to it."

"Oh, so you're this MacBride that's been raising hell over in Richmond City."

"The same. You notice that says this place is to be closed immediately. Broadcast now."

"I'll close tonight, MacBride."

"You'll close right now."

Ricardo scowled. "You trying to be tough?"

"I don't have to try. I was born that way. Snap on it."

Ricardo shrugged and stood up. He strolled over among the tables. The men stood up, reluctantly. They looked at MacBride and growled. They slouched out, and MacBride waited until the last had gone.

"Thanks, Ricardo," he said.

Ricardo remained silent, his hands thrust into his pockets.

MacBride carried on, from street to street. Wherever he went he was met with sullen looks. But he drove on with the relentless persistence of a machine. He gave no quarter.

When the last on his list had been closed, he walked into the station-house of the Second Police Precinct and called all the men into the central room. He could see that they did not favor him. They hated to have an outsider running them, and they were not backward in showing it.

But he said, "Men, we have come to a crisis. We've come to the point where we must prove that what the law says goes. I'm not down in your city because I want to be. The governor sent me, because he thought that my work in Richmond City was the sort of stuff that this city needed. If all you boys will work with me, give me your best, we can clean up. If you don't, we can't. One man can't do everything. I've started the ball rolling. You've got to help me keep it rolling. I ask for the best in you."

He did not find ready acquiescence. They did not look at him. They nodded, but indifferently. He found the same attitude in all the precincts he visited, and his blood began to boil within him. And he thought, what would have happened to Richmond City if he'd had such men under him during the last fierce crime wave.

But he did not weaken. If anything, he became stronger, more determined, and, yes, bitterer. At first the job before him had seemed a big one. Now it seemed colossal. It was starkly evident that the police, even as the vice crowd, resented him.

And he mused, such was the reward of having gained a reputation.

Chapter IV

IT was snowing. The flakes were small and hard, and the night was cold. MacBride strode along Front Street towards his hotel, after a belated supper. His overcoat collar was up around his ears and his breath shot out in white clouds. The newly fallen snow crunched beneath his feet.

He was swinging into his hotel when Kennedy, coming from the other direction, met him. They stopped in the entrance and Kennedy grinned.

"That laugh looks dirty, Kennedy."

"Not at all, Cap. Thought you closed *The Barn?*"

"Go on."

"Open. Making whoopee."

"Yeah?"

"Yeah."

MacBride turned on his heel. "See you later, Kennedy."

Kennedy came after him, fell in step. "Going places, Cap?"

"And doing things."

"Hot dog!"

"Better go home, Kennedy."

"I want to go places, too."

"You would."

MacBride swung into the garage where the flivver was kept and cranked it up. Kennedy climbed in and they shot out into Front Street. MacBride drove fast, his jaw clamped.

Kennedy said, "So Kildeen thinks you're a lot of wind?"

"Did he say so?"

"Actions, Cap."

"I'm going to blow that baby to a buggy ride. Dammit, Kennedy, if only I could rely on this louse-livered police department. Those guys hate me like poison."

"I told you so."

"By God, if I only had Moriarity and Cohen and a couple of good cops like Brinkerhoff and Abati I'd kick this whole town in the pants. Why ever the hell was I sent down to this dump anyhow? The food is rotten, the beds are like cement, and you can't open your window without getting a mug-full of coal dust."

"Orders. Same as me. My paper sends me anywhere you go. I go where you go. Wasn't that a song?"

"How the hell do I know?"

"I heard a good story tonight, Cap. Traveling salesman in the lobby—"

"Why bring that up?"

Kennedy pointed. "See the lights. *The Barn* is open for business—and how!"

MacBride cursed.

The wind drove the snow into their faces, piled it against the windshield. The car slewed from one side of the road to the other. MacBride shoved back into second gear and the motor labored crankily. As they drew nearer *The Barn*, they could see cars parked out front. They heard the bleat and blare of a jazz band, and lights streamed through the many windows out upon the snow.

Kennedy said, "Just like a frontier camp, Cap. At least like what I've read about. And this, my dear tomato, in the effete East."

MacBride pulled up, yanked on the emergency and turned off the ignition. His overcoat flapped about his legs as he strode toward the entrance. He pushed open the door and rocked into *The Barn*. His chilled clothes, coming in contact with the warm interior, shed clouds of vapor.

Kennedy, drifting in casually behind him, closed the door with a kick of his heel.

The place was crowded with a hundred-odd men and a handful of women. There was ginger ale on all the tables, but more than ginger ale was in the glasses. The men were rough, swart men, for the most part, crudely dressed. Poles and Hungarians and Italians making whoopee.

MacBride did not see Kildeen, hence he crossed the hall and ran up the stairway. He remembered the door and tried it. It was locked. He pounded on it. He was still pounding when it flung open. He lunged into the room.

At a table were seated Kildeen, the small, pale-faced man MacBride had seen with him that afternoon, and two huge, dull-looking Slavs. Chips and cards were on the table, and a lot of money which Kildeen was attempting to thrust out of sight.

"Never mind that, Kildeen," rapped out MacBride. "This is a pinch, guy!"

"Yeah, is it?" Kildeen towered up, his fists knotted, his brows bent.

MacBride looked at the Slavs. "How much have you guys lost?"

One said, "I lose wan hundred bucks, I be just learnin' de game."

Kildeen looked as if he could have brained the man.

"Thought that was your game, Kildeen," bit off MacBride. "Sucker layout, eh? I came here with a court order this afternoon. You kept open in defiance of that. Now, big boy, you're going to warm your pants in jail for contempt of that order."

"Am I? Listen here, MacBride, you can't come down to this town and raise hell! We won't stand for it!"

"You won't, eh? Boy, I'm here to raise holy hell with any palooka that tries to whitewash me. Now shut your mouth and put on a coat. When I get you cooped up I'll come back and close this dump for keeps."

"I won't go!" roared Kildeen.

"I'm damned if you won't!" roared MacBride. His gun leaped into his hand.

Kildeen's face tightened. He gritted his teeth, then said out of the side of his mouth, "Mike, look after things while this flatfoot takes me down. I won't be long."

He shoved into an overcoat, slapped on a cap and strode out. MacBride followed him through the door and then went up beside him. He put his gun back into his pocket. Down the stairs they went and across the hall. MacBride took Kildeen out so rapidly that hardly anyone saw them.

He pushed him toward the car, piled him into it and climbed in behind the wheel. Kennedy, drifting up, climbed into the back. Men were gathering at the door, looking out. MacBride howled the motor, shoved into gear and swung the car down the hill.

Kildeen chuckled, "Jeeze, you're a joke, MacBride."

"Yeah?"

"Yeah."

"Well, laugh your ribs loose, big boy."

"How long d'you suppose I'll stay in jail?"

"Longer than you think. You're going to stay in jail until I've brushed this town up. No bail, buddy—no writ. The governor of the State is behind me, and you can't say you were framed. You pulled a bone, Kildeen, when you defied that writ. Think it over. Then let me hear you laugh."

At Police Headquarters Kildeen was put in a cell. When that had been done, MacBride was just warming up.

To the lieutenant he said, "I want a squad of reserves. I'm going back and chase those bohunks out of *The Barn*."

The lieutenant wagged his head. "Lord, Captain, there'll be hell to pay."

"There'll be worse than that if I don't get a little coöperation here!"

The lieutenant swallowed his tongue and called out a squad of silent, slouching policemen. MacBride stood with his arm jammed akimbo. He had a withering eye and he sent it slashing across them.

"We are going up to *The Barn*," he said, "to close it. Carry your nightsticks in your hands. No guns, unless I say so."

He pivoted on his heel with a military snap and strode out. The policemen straggled after him, a weedy and ill-assorted crowd. Kennedy was waiting in the flivver, his coat collar almost over his head.

The squad car drew up and the policemen climbed in. MacBride told them to follow him, then jumped into the flivver and pounded down the street.

When they reached *The Barn* the music had stopped. MacBride, the first to enter, saw a lot of groups talking and gesticulating, and he knew that they were discussing the arrest of Kildeen. A few saw him enter, and the news clicked throughout the hall. The uniformed policemen filed in and hung back of MacBride.

He commanded the attention of every eye, a tall, lean, chisel-jawed man, emanating a distinct air of capability. He raised his hand and said, in a loud, clear voice:

"This place is closed by police order! Everybody must leave at once!"

Grumbling stuttered down the hall. A huge, ape-like Pole came lunging toward MacBride, shaking his rock-like fist.

"You take 'way our frien' Kildeen! Why?"

MacBride batted not an eye, nor did he budge an inch, even though the fist waved at the end of his nose.

He said, "Kildeen defied the law. I arrested him. And let me tell you something, you bohunk, if you go shooting that fist around my direction I'll jug you, too. *Get back!*" he barked, his eyes a blue blaze.

The Pole stood dumfounded for a long moment, his mouth agape, his low forehead wrinkled, his great arms hanging limply at his sides.

"Back!" clipped MacBride.

The man looked around sheepishly, then backed up and joined half a dozen cronies who had been looking on maliciously. They muttered under their breath.

MacBride waved his hand. "All out!"

A few started for the door. Others followed, at first slowly, then rapidly and in large groups. But they went scowling, muttering. Twenty-odd hung back, among them the huge Pole and his little clique of six.

"Come on, boys, all out," said MacBride.

The Pole came forward again, rolling from side to side like an ape. He stuck out his jaw and bared his teeth. He shook his tremendous fist.

"You take 'way our frien' Kildeen!"

MacBride turned to the policemen. "We'll have to herd these guys out. Up and at 'em."

The policemen spread warily, not in sympathy with their job. The others saw this and began to babble. The Pole, looking about like a caged animal, struck MacBride and sent him sprawling across the floor.

MacBride rebounded, blood on his cheek, took a flying leap and laid a hard overhand shot flush on the Pole's nose. The Pole sat down on the floor heavily, his face ludicrous with surprise.

"Snap on it!" MacBride yelled at his men. "Make these guys respect you!"

One of the policemen, stung by this derision, waved his club. The bohunks charged, and nightsticks began to work in earnest. MacBride lunged for the door and bolted it. Then he came back, clubbing his gun, diving into the middle of things.

He was knocked down by a flung bottle but came up again, boiling mad. He waded in like a battering ram. He saw his men being beaten back. They covered up, bunched together for protection.

"Split!" he shouted. "By God, what's the matter with you?"

They acted like men who never had been in a fight. They gave ground, and MacBride himself was getting the worst of it. Two of the policemen were knocked down. They jumped up and scampered to the rear.

Those outside were trying to break down the door. MacBride knew that if they broke in, his men would be beaten to a frazzle and tramped under foot. He lunged clear and fired a shot through the ceiling.

"Guns!" he yelled.

The policemen looked at him as if they doubted him.

"Guns!" he roared.

The guns came out, and before them the rioters fell back. MacBride, at the head of his men, stood spread-legged.

"Now get out, or I'll cut loose with this and blow you apart!"

Sweating, snarling, the men broke and scuffled toward the door. MacBride opened it and drove back the crowd that was trying to break in. The others filed out.

MacBride looked around and saw the pale-faced man whom Kildeen had called Mike. Small, slight, his lips almost as colorless as his face, his eyes large and dull and steady. MacBride went toward him.

"What's your name?"

"Morio."

"What are you hanging around here for?"

"I know Kildeen."

"That's no answer."

"Isn't it?"

"No."

"That's the only answer I got." His voice was low, quiet.

"Something tells me I've seen your face somewhere before. Anyhow, you breeze with the rest of the gang. Anybody else upstairs?"

"Kildeen's woman."

"Tell her to breeze, too. I'll give you five minutes."

"Thanks."

He turned and strolled off. A couple of minutes after he had gone Kennedy appeared in the hall. MacBride, who was standing by the entrance smoking a cigar, had not seen him enter.

"Where'd you come from, Kennedy?"

"I've been cruising around upstairs."

"Didn't see you come in."

"I got in the back way. Come up, Cap. I want to show you things."

MacBride followed him upstairs. Kennedy led the way into what looked like a comfortable sitting-room. There were some easy chairs, a table, warm-looking rugs, and a baby grand piano.

Kennedy leaned against the wall and grinned. "Nice cosy little place, eh, Cap?"

"That what you brought me up here for?"

"No. Brought you up to listen to me play the piano. What will you have?" He drifted over and sat down before the piano.

"You're drunk, Kennedy."

"Hell, I wish I was. Listen!" His fingers ran over the keys, but nothing happened. Chuckling, he swiveled on the stool.

"Well?" asked MacBride.

Kennedy stood up and opened the top of the piano.

"Bright, eh?"

MacBride looked and saw a fancy roulette layout.

"Hell!" he grunted. "How'd you find it?"

"Was just roaming in the gloaming and tapped the keys in passing. No sound. Tapped some more. Opened top. Found this."

"Sucker game."

"Yeah."

"Come on, Kennedy. I owe you a box of cigars."

"I take Coronas."

"Funny how you lowbrows get ritzy tastes."

In the hallway they met Morio and the woman. The latter was furious.

"You're sure a pain in the neck, MacBride," she said.

"Try liniment, sister."

"Get wise that I'm taking only an overnight bag."

"You get wise and take a trunk."

She laughed and headed for the stairway. Morio followed her, carrying his own bag.

MacBride and Kennedy made a tour of the upper regions. They found two more obvious card-rooms and six small bedrooms, each containing nothing more than a bed, a chair and a washstand.

They went downstairs and found the janitor, an old, weather-beaten Irishman. MacBride permitted him to stay. There was a furnace to attend to, and Kildeen's property to be watched, even though he was in jail.

Outside, MacBride walked to his car under a barrage of low oaths and catcalls. *The Barn* was closed—lights out and doors locked. He climbed into the flivver and looked at it as he started off, the crowd hissed and then roared derisively.

The squad car shot past him, and was soon lost to sight.

"Those guys are in a hurry," chuckled Kennedy.

"Yeah. Cripes, what a bunch of lemons!"

Chapter V

THERE were a lot of wiseacres in Millboro who must have had an idea that MacBride was a lot of noise. It is difficult to distinguish between a braggart and a man who is by nature forceful in speech and action.

MacBride was by nature forceful. True, he talked a lot, but he also acted. He was not the man to bottle up his emotions, therefore he rarely, if ever, held a grudge for long. When he got mad, his safety valve popped and steam roared. And he could get almighty mad.

Next morning he rose and shaved and whistled. He was in good spirits. He had put the lid on Mill Street, closed *The Barn*, and thrown Kildeen in jail. The hidden roulette wheel was another count against Kildeen, and MacBride felt that he was sitting on top of the world.

But he did not sit back and rest. He prowled the streets religiously. He made another tour of Mill Street to make sure that his orders had been obeyed. He went back over the string of speakeasies, too, and wound up by throwing three offenders in jail. He inspected the station-houses and kept pumping the men full of the psychology of law and order.

His reputation spread through the city like wildfire. His picture was published in the papers and he was pointed out on the streets. The Civic Committee, at whose insistence the governor had sent him to Millboro, entertained him at luncheon and assured him they were behind him to the last man.

Three days after Kildeen's imprisonment a gang of one hundred or more bohunks paraded through the city with placards demanding the release of Bud Kildeen. And that night they marched again, bearing torches that incarnadined the snow. Two policemen were beaten up on general principles.

When MacBride walked into Police Headquarters next day he found Chief Herman in a state very closely akin to apoplexy.

"Take it easy," he said.

"Easy!" cried Herman. "By Godfrey, MacBride, I have just been visited by a committee of six policemen who represent the entire force. They gave me notice that if you were not recalled by the governor within twenty-four hours, they would strike!"

"Strike!" boomed MacBride.

"Yes, strike!"

"They can't! A policeman is duty bound—"

"They did it in Boston. They'll do it here. For God's sake, MacBride, go back to Richmond City! Let us run things here."

For a long moment MacBride was speechless. A police strike! It seemed incredible that men who had taken up the shield should desert it in a crisis. Blood rushed to his head. He struck the table with his fist.

"This is treason, Herman! And, by cripes, you're willing to see it go through!"

"No, Cap—no. I merely ask you—"

"You ask me to throw in the sponge because this gang of old women you call a police department is yellow! You like to sit in a chair and not worry a solitary damn whether you're respected or not! You don't care if vice runs free in the streets, if *The Barn* runs wide open like the old Haymarket in New York years ago, before Gaynor! What the good holy hell do you suppose you're being paid for?"

"MacBride, I merely—"

MacBride interrupted him fiercely.

"You merely! You merely what? You merely want me to go home like a nice little boy. *You* don't seem to care that you've been buffaloed for years. So long as you're not made uncomfortable personally, it's all right by you. But *I* care. I didn't get my reputation by polishing the seat of my pants in a swivel chair all day long. And I'm not going to pitch in the sponge now, when I've got a strangle-hold on conditions in this city. You relay that message of your committee to the governor and I'll wire him mine.

"And I warn you, Herman, if your men strike, if they show that they don't care to bust up vice, this city will be hell's own playground. They can't strike! By God, they can't! It's treason!"

He banged out. He went up to see the Mayor. The Mayor was old and easygoing. He was not pleased, either, at the actions of MacBride, and he admitted that he was unable to cope with the situation. He added that since the Civic Committee had taken the matter over his head to the governor, it was up to the governor now.

Boiling, MacBride left and slammed his way through the precincts. He became eloquent in his appeal for loyalty. He spoke of the shield and what it stood for. He asked the men on their honor to stand by. He tried to show them what would happen if they walked out and left the city at the mercy of the vice crowd. He frankly admitted that he would be unable to run the city alone. He needed them. It was disloyal to desert the shield. But nowhere did his eloquence seem to go over. They simply resented him and his methods.

It was a hard blow—not only to his pride, but to his faith in manhood at bedrock. Because he was himself innately loyal to his calling, it was difficult for him to conceive of men who, having taken up the shield, would throw it away in time of stress. When it became evident that pleading to their sense of honor was futile, he flayed them, cursed them, compared them with rats that ran in the gutter and snakes that crawled in the mud. He damned them to the nethermost depths of hell.

One spokesman said, "We'll strike, Captain. That's the only way we can get what we want, and we don't want an outsider running us."

"Of course you don't!" he snarled. "In the first place, you joined the Force to get an easy job. As soon as there's work to be done, you get sore. You guys shouldn't be in the Department. You should be out in some home for old men."

Having wired the governor, he waited anxiously for a reply. And the reply came—and told him to carry on. The Commissioner received instructions to tell his men that if they walked out they would forfeit their jobs. They laughed. It is no easy matter to fire an entire police department.

The news clicked throughout the city. The lawless got wind of it and howled with delight. There were more parades through the streets that night, demanding the release of Kildeen—and also the ousting of Captain MacBride.

The entire city was in an uproar.

The Civic Committee met. They foresaw disaster, and tried to talk reason with the committee for the policemen. The latter would not talk reason.

MacBride's talk to the Civic Committee was brief. "Depend on me. I'll pull this city together somehow."

"Do you think they'll really strike?" asked the chairman.

"Yes," said MacBride.

And they did—at noon next day.

Chapter VI

MacBRIDE had been up most of the night doing a lot of telegraphing and some long-distance telephoning. Never the man to follow precedent, he had appealed to the governor to forget precedent also and meet a logical demand. For twenty minutes they had talked on the telephone.

The result was that at noon next day, as the entire police force walked out, MacBride was down pacing the railway platform. Far distant, he heard the hoot of a locomotive whistle. He stopped pacing, keened his windy blue eyes, and smacked fist into palm.

When the train pulled in—it was a special—many hands waved to MacBride from the windows. When it stopped, eighty uniformed policemen alighted—among them four sergeants and a lieutenant. Trim, capable-looking men, out for business.

MacBride stood spread-legged, with his hands jammed against his hips. His eyes sparkled. He grinned. He was proud of these men—his men—the pick of the Force of Richmond City. There were Abati, Brinkerhoff, Stein, McArdle—to name a few. Lieutenant

Banner—Sergeants Meloy, Schmidt, Davidson and Roco. And two plainclothes men—Moriarity and Cohen—MacBride's right-hand men.

"Where's the house-party?" asked Moriarity.

"Yeah, Cap," said Cohen, "where's the picnic? Let's step on it. I got a date with a broad Saturday night."

They went up to Police Headquarters in machines. Chief Herman looked haggard.

"Cap, there's over a hundred citizens downstairs wanting to see you. Why—"

"Simple," said MacBride. "I was up all night doing it. They're citizens come to be made deputies. Most of them have had in applications for the Force. We'll be taking in loads of applications from now on. You need new blood here, Herman, and you're going to get it. I've got eighty crack cops from my own city. Besides tying this town up, they're going to train the deputies in their spare time. I'll show you, Herman, how to put law into a city."

Herman was aghast. The monumental energy of this tough captain astounded him. He slumped back in his chair.

MacBride's voice lowered. "And if you aren't careful, you're going to be out of a job. The head of the Civic Committee is also head of the Great Eastern & Central Railway's Police, and he may look for your job."

"You mean Tulley? He's not fit—"

"He's fit enough to head a Civic Committee. Just take hold, Herman. You have a bare chance of hanging on."

MacBride had a stiff task before him. To begin with, he distributed his handful of eighty men throughout ten precincts that hitherto had boasted three hundred. When he ran out of sergeants, he made sergeants of patrolmen. He kept Lieutenant Banner and Moriarity and Cohen at Headquarters. One hundred citizens were given deputy shields and told to report in the morning. Ex-service men were picked first.

Other citizens, not caring to be in active service because they held good positions, volunteered to answer any call for help. They were supplied with blue bands to wear on their sleeves, and were asked to report immediately any infraction of the law.

In the heat of all this preparation MacBride was visited by Morio, that pale, hueless lipped man.

"Want to see Kildeen," he jerked out. His eyes darted about. He looked worn and fretful.

"Why?"

"Well, he's my friend. Can't I see him?"

"No. He's out in the jail."

Morio's face twitched. His eyes darkened. "I got a right to see him!"

"You can't, Morio." MacBride leaned forward. "Unless I go alone and stand beside you."

Morio shrank. "You gotta do that?"

"Look here, wop. I don't know whether I've seen you before or not. Take a tip from me and blow this town. If you don't, I may decide to lock you up and see if maybe I haven't seen you before."

"I want to see Kildeen."

"Nothing doing. That guy stays cooped up until this thing blows over. I'm taking no chance on having him give you orders for the outside."

Morio sprang to his feet and clenched his fist. His lips writhed against his teeth.

"Damn you, MacBride! You're crazy! Why can't I see him? He ain't committed murder. It ain't law. You're over-stepping the law—"

"I sure am, Morio—I sure am. What this town needs."

"Cripes, you think you're wise. You're just a big bum—a lousy bum—"

"Get out!"

"You're—"

"Get out!"

Morio quivered with rage. His eyes blazed with hatred, and his breath pumped from his lungs. He kept baring his teeth. He seemed eager to leap, to strike, to tear MacBride apart. His face was the face of an animal—fierce, lustful, vicious.

MacBride was deadly cool. "Out, Morio."

With a hissing intake of breath, Morio spun and ran out.

Chapter VII

A LOT of people must have underrated MacBride and the cops he brought down from Richmond City.

The next night another anti-MacBride parade was started. It was started at Twelfth and Broad Streets. It got as far as Thirteenth.

Parolmen Kline and O'Shay, coming up Thirteenth Street, heard the shouting and saw the glare of the torches. They hopped to it. They reached Broad Street as the leaders swung into view. They went right into the street and held up their hands. The leaders laughed uproariously.

In less time than it takes to tell it five of the leaders went down beneath Kline's and O'Shay's nightsticks. Then Kline took a breath to blow his whistle and started using his stick again. Three policemen came galloping to the scene. Half a dozen wandering deputies appeared. The men's hearts were in their work. They were joined by a number of citizens wearing blue bands on their sleeves.

Inside of ten minutes the parade was broken up. Five more minutes and the street was empty, except for those who had been knocked out. They numbered an even dozen of picketers and three who stood for law and order.

They were carried or dragged to the nearest drug-store and patched up. After which the twelve were marched to the county jail.

Some persons in the street began to remark that perhaps MacBride meant what he said, after all.

He did. He worked long hours, examining applicants for the Force, suggesting that Herman accept them. Herman was merely an automaton by this time. He did whatever MacBride said. And MacBride inaugurated a police school, talked to the rookies, chose the best of his own men to teach them the ways of a policeman. And his own men worked overtime, too, because they knew him and liked him and gave him their best.

Moriarity and Cohen ferreted out dives that no one seemed to know about. They scoured the streets mostly by night. They raided a gambling joint and arrested the owner. They suddenly appeared in a vice dive down near the railroad and wiped it out. There was a new law in Millboro, touched with a bit of brimstone. And the seed of it all lay in the courage and perseverance of one man who never knew when he was licked.

Kennedy said, "Cap, I've got to hand it to you. You're certainly some tomatoes. By the way, as I came in I saw that dago Mike Morio hanging around out front."

MacBride went to the window, opened it and looked down into the street. "Not there now." He closed the window and stood rubbing his jaw. "Kennedy, I've seen that greaseball somewhere—before. Ike Cohen saw him passing here this morning too. I think I'll pinch that guy. I told him to blow the town, but I see he didn't. I gave him a break. He's got no cause to yap when I pinch him. We'll mug him and send the pictures around. I've got an idea that baby's dangerous."

He told Ike Cohen to find Morio.

The cops were working in long shifts. The city was under-policed, and success lay in constant vigilance and an ability to strike quickly when trouble loomed. A riot broke out that night downtown, because Patrolman Brinkerhoff stopped a soap-box oration delivered by a mill boss on behalf of Kildeen. The orator's imagination ran away with him and he pictured Kildeen being starved and persecuted in a dungeon in the county jail. Brinkerhoff pulled him off the box and somebody else hit Brinkerhoff with a rock. The rock keeled him over, but he got up and cut loose with his nightstick. He was joined by two more patrolmen and a few deputies. The riot lasted fifteen minutes, after which the bohunks scattered.

At about the same time MacBride was paying Kildeen a visit. Kildeen had been reading the papers, and he knew in some measure what had taken place. He seemed to have thought things over.

"You sure surprised me, MacBride. When does my trial come up?"

"Pretty soon. And when it's over, if I were you I'd clear out. I don't know what kind of a sentence you'll get. You may get off with a heavy fine. At any rate, you're through in this city."

"Am I?"

"And how."

"We'll see."

"We sure will."

MacBride went back to Headquarters. At midnight he was still at his desk examining a mass of applications that had come that afternoon.

And at midnight there was a rap on the door and Patrolman Abati came in.

"Cripes, Cap, McArdle's been shot!"

"What!"

One of his own men brought from another city to give a respect for the law in this. The news hit like a blow.

"Stein and me were cruising around in the flivver up near *The Barn*. McArdle was stationed around there, you know. We saw a couple of guys out front and stopped. The janitor there was holding up McArdle. They got him in the guts. Seems he was walking past there when he saw a quick flash of light in one of the upper windows, like as if a guy was walking with a flashlight. He woke the janitor and the guy let him in. McArdle went up alone. The guy must have heard him. But they met in a dark hallway upstairs. McArdle tried to collar him and the guy cut loose with his gat and breezed. We took McArdle to the hospital. He's in bad shape. He caved in on the way down."

"What did the janitor say?"

"Nothing. He had been sound asleep. He didn't know anybody was in the place."

"God!" muttered MacBride. He reached for his hat and coat. "What hospital, Tony?"

"City."

MacBride went out into the winter night and hopped a taxi. When he reached the hospital they told him that McArdle had just died. He stood with his hands in his overcoat pockets, knotted into fists. His face turned to granite. He swung on his heel and strode out and walked back to Headquarters through dark, windy streets, his shoes crunching on the packed snow.

"Murder!" he muttered. "Murder."

Chapter VIII

COHEN said, "I've turned this town upside down. I can't find this guy Morio."

"Find him," clipped MacBride. "You too, Moriarity. Some guy was in *The Barn* last night looking for something."

He went down to see Kildeen.

"Kildeen," he said, "a cop was killed last night by somebody in *The Barn*. The cop saw a light in one of the windows and went in. He got it in the guts."

Kildeen's lips tightened. His eyes narrowed and glinted. He cursed.

"You got any jack up there?" asked MacBride.

"Yes. In the safe. About two thousand bucks."

"I'd better take it out and put it in the bank. You give me the combination. What's your bank here?"

"State Bank."

"I'll put it there and send over your deposit slip."

"O.K." He wrote the combination on a slip of paper.

As MacBride tucked it away he said, "This wop Morio. How long has he been with you?"

"I've known him about a year. What do you mean—*with* me? He just used to hang out there."

"Yeah, I know. He just used to help you flimflam the bohunks. Anyhow, we're after that guy, Kildeen. He's been wanting to see you like hell—for something. I wouldn't let him."

Kildeen scowled at the floor. He turned away.

MacBride said, "All right, I'll tuck that jack away for you. I've got a sneaking idea that maybe you wouldn't be so happy if we caught Morio."

Kildeen spun around. "Do you think I told him to kill the cop?" he snarled.

"I didn't say he killed that cop," said MacBride.

Kildeen stared, and his jaw fell.

MacBride chuckled. "So you think Morio killed that cop."

"I didn't say so!"

"Not exactly. Cripes, what a hint that is. You thought, though, that Morio was after something. You thought of him first when you heard that some guy had busted into your dump. Now didn't you?"

"Aw, hell! I did not! You went and accused Morio yourself."

"*I* did? Where do you rate that crap? I said we were looking for him. I didn't say why."

Kildeen growled, and sat down.

MacBride said, "Yeah, you're all balled up, big boy. You put your foot in it that time. Boy, you may get deeper in this thing than I thought."

MacBride went out, with a brittle chuckle.

At Headquarters he found Kennedy and a man named Small.

"Jack Small," said Kennedy, "of the New York Evening *Express.*

They've been getting interested in you, Cap, and sent up Jack to cover the city."

Small said, "The paper'd like an exclusive picture of you. I've got a photographer, outside, if you'll sit at your desk."

"Sure," said MacBride.

They took a time exposure of him, and he grinned. "The wife likes to collect 'em. Wherever I'll walk at home now I'll see my mug pasted on the wall."

"It ain't a bad mug, as mugs go," said Kennedy.

"Yeah," said MacBride, "I've seen a couple worse."

Kennedy was lighting a cigarette. "Where?"

"You would have to spoil it," MacBride clipped.

Small chuckled, said, "Kennedy always did have a sense of humor."

And MacBride wanted to know, "Oh, you call that a sense of humor?"

"Old tomato!" grinned Kennedy.

"Old louse!" growled MacBride, but with the ghost of a smile.

Two days rolled by, with Morio still at large. Moriarity and Cohen worked tirelessly to discover his hiding place. But the streets were quiet. Rookies were put on patrol. Not a speak-easy was open, and those that had been closed were watched by day and by night. A number of policemen who had gone on strike drifted back and wanted to be reinstated. They were turned away. MacBride was building a new force out of raw material and told them that they had forfeited their jobs and any claim to reinstatement.

"You men, all of you, deserted in a crisis," he said. "I wish there was a law whereby I could arrest you. You, just as much as the vice crowd, thought that you could buffalo me. Get out. There are no soft jobs in this department."

Nor did he lessen pressure. He kept the clamps tight, ranged the city's streets himself. The City Council, inspired by his comparative success, called a special meeting. Chief Herman was summoned, and the chairman, after a brief speech pertaining to Herman's decline as an official of the city, asked him pointedly to resign. This was followed by a similar suggestion on the part of the Mayor.

Herman gave up without a struggle. MacBride was then termed Acting Commissioner, and the Mayor asked him to suggest a likely man to succeed Herman. MacBride suggested Tulley, police head for the Great Eastern & Central Railway.

A night of wind and sleet found him plowing along toward his hotel. It was ten o'clock, and it was the first night in a long while that he had left Headquarters so early. In his room, he called up Kennedy.

"Play you some cards," he said.

"Sure. Be right up."

Kennedy came in whistling a popular tune. MacBride was stuffing his pipe.

"Home early, eh, Cap?"

"Yeah. About time."

"Yeah. You've been looking fagged lately. Five hours sleep a night is no good for any guy. Got cards?"

"Uhuh."

They sat down in shirt-sleeves. The radiator was hissing, and the room was warm. Wind and sleet hammered against the window, howled across the roof. It was a good night to be in. MacBride dealt.

Kennedy said, "How about Morio?"

"Nothing. Ike's been running his pants loose looking for him. Moriarity too."

"He might have blown the town."

"Maybe. I sent out notices to most of the cities. I sent the bullet that killed McArdle along with the one that missed me here in this room to a gun expert."

"Think Morio tried for you, too?"

"Dunno. Possibility."

"Then he's Kildeen's gunman."

"Dunno. Kildeen didn't tell him to kill McArdle. There's a slight possibility that Morio was after the jack in Kildeen's safe. He got scared off when he fired that shot. He didn't get it. But there's something funny about it. You open?"

"Yeah. For two reds."

"Stay. Cards?"

"Give me three."

"But Morio was damned eager to see Kildeen. When I said I'd let him see him if I stood alongside, he pulled out. Queer duck. Dangerous."

"I bet two reds. But if he's in town, he sure must be keeping well under cover, because Moriarity and Cohen could find a needle in a haystack. Those guys are hot stuff."

"You said a jawful, Kennedy. I bump you. But if we get Morio, I'll bet my shirt Kildeen gets a belly-ache for keeps. If we can prove that Morio was his gunman—"

The telephone bell interrupted him. He laid down his cards, got up and walked over to the wall. He took down the receiver.

"Hello.... Yeah, this is MacBride, Harry.... *What!*... Good cripes— I'll be right over! Get two squads ready!"

He hung up and dived for his coat.

"That was Lieutenant Harry Banner, at Headquarters," he clipped. "There was a call from the jail. A big gang of bohunks are trying to break in. They want Kildeen released."

"Hell!"

"Hell is right!"

He blew out of the hotel like a mean wind.

Chapter IX

THERE was action at Headquarters. Two squads of rubber-coated policemen were in the Central room when MacBride banged in.

"Hello, gang, Sergeant Meloy, you'll go with us. We'll take riot guns. Harry, get in touch with all the precincts and have them stand by. Come on, guys."

His rubber coat flapped and crackled as he strode out into the street. Two big police cars were drawn up beside the curb. The men piled in, Kennedy among them. MacBride got into the front car, beside Abati, who was to drive.

"Let's go," he clipped.

The cars shot off. The tires hissed through slush. The wind drove the sleet at a slant. They roared through the city, through traffic, out of it and on to a winding macadam road. The night was black as pitch, bitterly cold. The sleet thrashed against rubber coats. The cars skidded and slewed but kept on.

"I heard a shot," called out Kennedy.

"So did I," said MacBride.

He peered through the wet windshield, kept wiping it with his hand.

"Step on it, Tony."

"I'm doing fifty-five now, Cap."

"There it is," said Kennedy, pointing to some lights glowing in the darkness ahead.

MacBride leaned out and looked back. The second car was not far behind. He had his gun out, gripped in his hand.

The lights on the dash threw a glow up into his face. His jaw was squared, his mouth tight, his eyes keened hard. His face gleamed with sleet.

The prison loomed darkly, a squat mass of brick surrounded by a heavy iron fence. They heard shouting and soon they could see the flashes of guns—flame slashing through the wet darkness. The first car roared up to the gate. MacBride jumped out and his men lunged after him. The second car skidded to a stop and Sergeant Meloy came at the head of his squad.

Somehow the gate had been opened. In the hollow square formed by the buildings men were fighting. MacBride trotted beneath an archway and into the hollow square and into a mass of milling, swearing bohunks. A crack from a club downed him. He rebounded and saw Abati tearing into the mob, his nightstick working mightily.

MacBride cannoned his way to the nearest door and burst into a room filled with bohunks and guards fighting desperately. Warden McAllister saw him.

"God, MacBride, there must be a hundred here! They want Kildeen!"

"How'd they get in?"

"Blasted the gate open."

"Kildeen's cell guarded?"

"I'm damned if I know!"

MacBride fought his way onward. He won to a corridor and raced down it. Prisoners were looking through bars. He found Kildeen's cell and stopped before it.

"What the hell?" asked Kildeen.

"The bohunks have come down to get you out."

"Cripes!"

"They're going to have a tough time."

"Listen, MacBride, what the hell am I supposed to do? I didn't tell 'em to come down."

"You stay right where you are, mister."

There was a rush of feet and two policemen came pounding down the corridor.

"You stay here, boys. If they try to take Kildeen out, shoot—and shoot to kill. But warn 'em first—give 'em a break."

He left them and ranged through the building. There was a terrific explosion that rocked the floor beneath his feet. He heard the snarl of wrenched timbers and the roar of falling plaster. He turned into another corridor and was met by a rush of smoke. He plowed through it and found himself in the midst of a mob. A few of them had guns, and one fired. The bullet slapped through MacBride's sleeve and he fired a split-second later and lunged through as he fired again.

In the hollow square the riot guns were crackling. Another blast went up and caved in the side of the building containing the offices. Brick and plaster sailed skyward and then thundered down. Smoke billowed and flames licked through the sleet.

Stumbling through the ruins, MacBride ran into Ike Cohen. Cohen's face was bloody.

"These pups are loaded with dynamite!" he snapped.

"Yeah. We've got to get the fire department, if I can find a telephone. Where's the warden?"

"Hell knows. I picked him up a couple of minutes ago. That poor old guy's been floored so many times it ain't funny."

MacBride cruised around and found the warden staggering down a smoke-filled corridor. He gripped his arm.

"Where's a phone?"

"The offices are wrecked. Try the kitchen. This way."

Bloody and soot-smeared, the warden led the way. In the chef's office they found a phone that was working. MacBride called Headquarters, told Banner to send out some fire engines and some more cops.

Out in the hollow square again, he found Kennedy drifting around in a daze.

"What's the matter with you?"

"I was beaned by a couple of rocks, I guess."

"You better get out of this."

"What, and miss the fun?"

"You're crazy."

"*Watch it!*"

He dragged MacBride down as a rock sailed over their heads.

"That big bum threw it, Mac."

MacBride caught sight of the man who had argued with him in *The Barn.* He made a beeline for him, and the man waited, hefting a club. MacBride dodged the blow and struck out with his gun. Inside of a few seconds he had a mob on top of him. He went down under an array of kicks and wielded clubs, and somebody stepped on his face. A group of policemen saw him go down and waded in. The riot guns burst loose again, and yells of anger and pain thundered in the hollow square.

Then MacBride was up again, his hat gone, his hair pasted down over his forehead.

"Try to run 'em into that building on the left!" he shouted. "Bottle 'em up!"

Flames were writhing through the building containing the offices. As yet the building housing the cells was untouched, but in imminent danger. It stood to the right of the burning building, while to the left stood the one which MacBride had pointed out to his men.

He ran about gathering his men together. And while he was doing this another squad arrived from Headquarters in charge of Lieutenant Harry Banner himself. He detailed Banner to drive all those inside the cell building, out into the square. He went in himself and bludgeoned his way to Kildeen's cell. A gang of ten were there, held back by the guns of the two policemen on guard.

"Back up!" roared MacBride. "Get the hell out of this corridor! Snap on it!"

"We want Kildeen!" one of them yelled, and the others roared approval.

"Get back!" shouted MacBride, and started for them.

He fired a shot over their heads. They screamed and broke and fell away. He pressed into them, the muzzle of his gun still smoking. A shot burst from their midst. It slammed through his right arm and his gun fell to the floor. The mob rushed him, swept over him. The guns of the two policemen bellowed. Two of the mob went down howling, and the others stopped. Gun-smoke writhed over their heads.

MacBride, groping through a tangle of legs that stumbled over and about him, recovered his gun with his left hand. He managed to reach his feet as Banner and the new squad hove into sight.

"Hell's bells, Cap!" gritted Banner.

"Plaster those guys, Harry!"

"You winged?"

"Yeah, kind of."

"Slobs!"

The mob, seeing the new force, bolted. They tore down the corridor, and MacBride placed Banner at the head of his men. They drove the gang into the hollow square. The flames roared and the square was luridly lit. A few dead and wounded lay about, and something akin to a chant was rising from the mob. They were wild-eyed. The sleet drove down upon them, and the fire crackled behind them. The heat, thrown down upon the flags in the square, melted the ice, and the policemen slushed about.

"Drive 'em in!" roared MacBride.

His men were concentrated. Riot guns and revolvers bristled in the fire's glow. Rubber coats crackled and swished, and shields shone on visored caps. They waited.

"Up and at 'em!" sang out MacBride.

The cops advanced. The mob rumbled and growled. They had no leader now. Someone had floored the big fellow. They milled about in perplexed indecision, at least seventy strong.

"In that building!" commanded MacBride.

Blood was oozing from his cuff. Pain pumped through his arm, and it dangled at his side, powerless. He sent two shots over their heads. Banner did likewise. So did Moriarity and Cohen. The mob broke. Now they fought one another to get through the entrance of the building. They clawed and kicked and hammered with their fists.

Fire bells clanged across the night.

The cops pressed hard. They closed in and threatened with their guns, and the mob flowed through the door, into the building, into the trap. There was no other exit. The last men lunged in as a hook and ladder swung into the yard, its engine thundering, its spotlight sweeping the square.

"Now hold 'em in there, Harry," said MacBride to Banner.

He turned and ran towards the gate, out through it to the squad cars. There was a first aid kit in each car. His arm was bleeding badly. Another fire engine howled by and rumbled through the gate.

MacBride picked up a searchlight from the seat and snapped it on. The beam leaped into the night. The end of it touched for a bare split-second a face on the opposite side of the road, above the edge of the bushes. Then the face disappeared.

"Morio!" roared MacBride.

Chapter X

HE forgot the kit, forgot his bad arm. He grabbed his gun and galloped across the slippery road, plunged into the bushes. Ice-caked, they snapped and rattled against his rubber coat. He caught a fleeting glimpse of Morio and yelled, "Hey, you, stop!" But Morio tore through the bushes.

MacBride fired, and his shot went wild, snarling through the thickets. Flame burst from the thickets and lead whistled past his head. He fired at the flash, paused, breathless; heard Morio crashing onward.

Slush ice slopped beneath his feet. The wind whipped sleet against his face. He spat the sleet from his lips and weaved through the darkness. Hatless, his wet hair freezing on his head, he toiled mightily. Blood caked on his hand. He felt weary and dizzy, but his mouth was clamped like a vise.

Suddenly he came upon an old barn, at the edge of the thickets, and paused. He knelt down and crawled along until he came to an open door. He muscled in through the door and sat against the inner wall. He listened in the darkness.

Faintly he heard a man breathing. He moved down along the wall a distance of six feet. He stopped and sat still.

"So you're in here, Morio." The words were hardly out of his mouth when two shots flamed in the dark and the bullets whistled through the open door. Instantly MacBride fired at the flashes. The bullets slugged something solid, and MacBride flung along the wall. Two more bullets crashed against the wall where he had sat an instant before.

"Lousy, Morio!"

Another shot searched him out, missed; then he heard the click of a hammer on an empty chamber. He jumped up and lunged toward the last gun-flash. He fell over something—a huge barrel; toppled and felt something yield beneath him.

"Damn you!" screamed Morio.

He struck and hit MacBride's wounded arm. The captain sucked in his breath and struck with his gun.

"Oh!" cried Morio.

MacBride struck again—missed and smashed his gun on a plow. He let the remains go and groped with his hand. Morio twisted and writhed beneath him. MacBride found his throat and gripped it in spring-steel fingers.

"Oh!" choked Morio.

He kicked and clawed. MacBride's head reeled. Spots flashed before his eyes, but he held on, exerting pressure, closing his eyes and gritting his teeth. Waves of darkness darker than the night seemed to rush over him. Melting sleet dripped from his face. He pressed harder—harder. The world spun around. A final wave of darkness, greater than the others, cascaded over him.

Chapter XI

HE woke up in a clean white bed. A neatly dressed nurse was standing at the bedside, and next to her stood a white-coated man pawing his beard.

"Greetings, Captain," he smiled.

MacBride looked at his arm, swathed in bandages. His head was swathed in bandages.

"What's wrong?" he asked.

"Wounded arm, six scalp wounds inflicted by a blunt instrument and a few other scratches. Outside of that, nothing."

MacBride reflected. "Say, I was lying in somebody's barn—"

"About four hours ago."

"Was I out that long?"

"Indeed."

"What happened to Morio?"

The doctor coughed. "Perhaps the gentlemen outside could tell you."

He opened the door and beckoned. In filed Lieutenant Harry Banner, Moriarity and Cohen and Kennedy.

"Hell," said Kennedy, who had a patch over his eye, "Cap's in bed again."

Banner looked serious. "How you feeling, Cap?"

"Lousy. How are you?"

"O.K."

Moriarity had a black eye and Cohen had three black and blue bumps on his forehead.

"You guys have been fighting," said MacBride drily.

"Yeah," grinned Cohen. "Look at Mory's shiner. What he gets for trying to stop a rock with his head. He ain't that tough."

"Look at your own kisser, guy," said Moriarity. "You ain't been playing handball, either."

MacBride said, "Well, what's the news?"

"Plenty," said Banner. "They got the fire out, for one thing, and the jail's jammed with bohunks. Four were killed. Abati was killed, and Brinkerhoff is wounded. We found you in that barn, passed out, with your mitt around Morio's neck. He wasn't lively, either. Did you know he was a coke?"

"No."

"Yeah. He's limp as a dish-rag right now. One of the bohunks up and admitted that Morio got them to go down to the jail and try to get out Kildeen. He's been living in the woods since he disappeared.

"He's gone to pieces. He wants some dope. This guy Kildeen was supplying him with it. He says Kildeen has about fifty thousand dollars worth of it hidden in *The Barn*. That's what he was looking for the night he shot McArdle. I got him to talk by promising him some dope. Boy, what a yarn!

"He says Kildeen used to supply all the frails that lived in Mill Street. I asked him why he didn't breeze when Kildeen was jugged. He said he wanted to get that dope, and that if he got it he would have enough for the rest of his life. He swore that Kildeen wanted him to bump you off. Payment to be made in a nice lump of dope. He tried to get you one night, from the roof across from your hotel."

"So Kildeen was in on the dope racket too," said MacBride. "Well, that means he goes into Federal hands."

"Yeah. I got in touch with the Federal agents and they're up at *The Barn* now. Morio's goose is cooked. That reporter from the New York paper recognized him. His real name's Moriano. He's wanted in Pittsburgh for busting a girl's head—a year ago.

"When I had nothing to give him he went cuckoo. We had to put him in a strait-jacket. They tell me that Kildeen, out at the jail, is all hot and bothered."

"He's got cause to be," ground out MacBride. Then he sighed. "Well, maybe this'll scare hell out of the bohunks."

It did. Every man that had participated in the raid was given thirty days hard labor. The Federal man, after a two days' search, found Kildeen's fortune in coke in a hidden wall safe. They took him into custody. Pittsburgh police officials came into Millboro with extradition papers for Morio on a charge of murder with positive proof.

From his hospital bed MacBride, for two weeks, directed his men. Tulley was appointed Police Commissioner and carried out the captain's ideas of law enforcement. The streets of Millboro had never been more orderly.

On MacBride's first day out of bed, the new chairman of the Civic Committee said, "Captain, I know you must be weak, but we'd like to throw a banquet before you leave, in your honor. Tulley tells me that Lieutenant Banner and the other men are staying on for another month, to polish up the rookies, but that you're returning to Richmond City a few days hence. Do you think you could stand a banquet?"

"I could, but as a matter of fact I'm leaving tomorrow. I've got some Christmas shopping to do. Remember I've got a wife and a daughter. But throw it for my boys. They're good guys and they'll get a kick out of it."

A crowd saw him off at the station next day. He looked pale and a bit drawn, but his step was firm, his head erect, and he carried himself with a military snap.

A photographer waylaid him as he was stepping into the train.

"What, again?" clipped MacBride.

"Only a minute, Captain."

Kennedy, standing to one side with his bag in his hand, said, "Smile pretty, old tomato."

"You go to hell, Kennedy."

"Pretty!" Kennedy made faces.

MacBride had to grin.

The camera clicked.

"O.K." said the photographer.

MacBride, climbing on board, said, "Come on, Kennedy, you damn fool, and I'll play you some stud on the way up."

"Coming, old tomato!"

Alley Rat

A fight for a political job; gangster backing; a hold-up, murder, alley rats and— Captain Steve MacBride.

Chapter I

BUD MALONEY stood by the front windows of his roadhouse. He kept puffing nervously at a rag of a cigar. It was raining—cold winter rain—and the driveway was sheeted with thin ice. A floodlight streamed down from the top of the veranda, but beyond the radius of its glow was darkness, black and complete and final. Maloney wore a tux. His face was frankly hard, and now his lips were a tight, bitter slash above his cleft jaw.

Business was at a standstill. No wonder! There was a crowd there. But food was untouched. Men and women waited impatiently. One woman was crying in a handkerchief. The chairs were not arranged orderly at the tables. Some men sat with their backs to the tables, and a few stood, leaning against the edges of tables, smoking, waiting.

There was a platform against one wall, beneath a purple and gold canopy, and the orchestra pieces there were deserted. The musicians hung around. In the center of the dance-floor was a mass of broken glass. Directly above it was the skeleton of a chandelier. Waiters stood like images.

At the lower end of the dining- and dancing-room, directly in front of a door that led out to a parking space behind lay a man. He lay face downward. One arm was stretched out before him. The other was somehow cramped beneath his stomach. There was a slight twist to his body. A Borsalino lay a foot from his head; and about two feet from his outstretched right hand, lay an automatic pistol.

From time to time somebody or other cast a sidelong glance towards this motionless figure.

"Oh, when *will* they come?" cried an agitated woman.

"Keep your shirt on, kid," said the man with her.

His voice carried, and somebody laughed out loud. Another woman elevated her nose. "Common trash, Esme," in a whisper.

"Quite."

Maloney jangled loose change in his pocket. Luigi, his head-waiter—fat, sleek, soft, imperturbable—said, "The roads are slippery, Bud."

"Yeah. But I wish to hell they'd hurry. Think of it, Lu! Two thousand bucks cold cash!"

Luigi, whose pay would go on just the same, rolled a fat dark eye. "It's hell, Bud."

Two beams of light suddenly slashed through the drenched darkness, and icy raindrops sparkled. A motor roared.

Maloney said, "That's them!" and jumped for the door.

Feet thumped on the veranda. Maloney had the door open.

"Hello, Bud," said MacBride.

The captain rolled in out of the rain, his rubber coat crackling and gleaming darkly, a felt hat yanked down over one ear. Rain was on his face. He wiped it off carelessly and tongued a cigar from one side of his mouth to the other.

"Where's the stiff, Bud?" he clipped.

Moriarity and Cohen pushed in, shaking the rain from their overcoats like a couple of wet cats. Kennedy, casual, lazy, drifted in last. He wore no overcoat, merely a badly-pressed blue suit, with the coat collar turned up, and a wrinkled blue cap whose peak was out of true. He had his hands in his pockets and he did not seem to mind the rain or the cold. A damp cigarette butt, gone out, hung from one corner of his mouth.

Cohen rubbed his hands together gingerly. "How about a drink, Bud?"

"Sure."

MacBride, opening his black rubber coat, looked down the length of the dance-floor and said, "Cold, eh, Bud—dead cold?"

"Yeah. He got it smack in the heart, I guess. Drink, Cap?"

"Yeah."

The group moved over to the counter in front of the cloak-room. Luigi disappeared for a moment and then came back with a bottle and glasses.

"Help yourselves, boys," said Maloney.

MacBride poured out a stiff drink, swirled the liquor in the glass and flung it down neat. He rasped his throat and leaned against the wall.

"Now what happened, Bud?"

"Well, first, I was standing over there alongside the cash desk. Mamie, my cashier, was sitting behind it. Get this, now, Cap—no car drove up. The door there opened. Just before it opened a guy who was sitting by the front windows got up and went into the toilet, which is down here—see the door?—next to this hat room.

"Well, then the door opened. Two guys came in, shaking off the water and opening their coats. Before I knew it I was looking at two masks. They poked guns at Mamie and me and made her cough up. One guy pulled a black silk bag from his pocket and it opened up big. In there went my dough—two thousand berries.

"Mamie and me were shoved on into the dance-room, and the one guy covered Luigi and told everybody to put up their hands. Then they went down the tables, keeping me and Luigi ahead of them, and raking in jack and jewels from my guests.

"When they reached the end, they made me and Luigi turn around and told us to get back to the middle of the floor. We did that. Then this guy who'd been sitting by the window and who went into the toilet just before these guys showed up—he suddenly jumped out, and fired. The bullet sailed past my head and caught one of them guys square. That guy's gun went off and busted my big chandelier. The other guy with him grabbed the bag as the guy fell and lit out through the back door.

"All I remember is this other guy, the one showed up sudden like that—this other guy run past me like hell and sailed out the back door, too. We figured he was after the guy, and a lot of us ran to the door, too. But we couldn't see no one. We waited. We didn't hear any shots. That guy ain't showed up. Either he got shot and we didn't hear it, or he kept on running and maybe is still chasing that other guy. I dunno."

"H'm," muttered MacBride. "Well, let's look at the stiff."

He strode out of the lobby and into the dining-room. His windy blue eyes searched every face as he swung across the dance-floor. He stopped by the dead man, reached down and heaved him over.

"Garrity," he said.

"Hot diggity!" said Kennedy, kneeling.

MacBride caught hold of Garrity's gun and stood up, holding it in his palm, weighing it. He shot a look at Kennedy.

"Tex Garrity," he said. "Head of those South Side hoodlums."

"Late head," corrected Kennedy.

MacBride flattened his lips. "Cripes, this means hell, Kennedy! Garrity was no small tomatoes.

"That West Side gang have been trying to horn in on the South Side for months, and it seems as if they've hauled off and took out a nice slice."

MacBride turned to Maloney. "This guy who killed this bum here—what did he look like?"

"Small, dressed plain in a dark suit, and yellow hair. Not a guy you'd look twice at."

"And the other guy, the one got away."

"Tall, thin, and he wore a nice black overcoat and a derby. He talked fast and tough. He went about his business like he knew what he was doing."

"And the other guy ain't come back yet?"

"Nope."

MacBride jerked his thumb. "Ike, you and Mory go out and look around in the bushes."

Moriarity and Cohen went out. MacBride stood meditating, his eyes on the dead gangster. There had been rumblings lately of an impending gang feud. Local city elections were in the making, and the wards were naturally troublesome, and blood ran close to the surface. The West and South Sides merged to form the Fourth Ward, and Tony Maratelli, contractor and road-builder, was out to cop the

Aldermanic chair from Mike Mulvaney, ex-saloonman and present incumbent of that chair. Wherefore the Micks sang *East Side, West Side,* and the wops tried to drown them with *O Solo Mio,* and there was a hot time in the old town! And getting hotter!

As witness Tex Garrity, wild-cat chief—late—of the South Side mob, who with the audacity of his kind, had thrown a big party a week ago and sworn to high heaven and deep hell that Mike Mulvaney would continue as alderman.

Kennedy was drifting among the tables, getting an earful of how much so-and-so had lost. He was placid, sleepily genial, in the face of staggering figures.

MacBride went out to the lobby and called up the morgue. He came back into the dining-room, trailing cigar smoke, his open rubber coat flapping against his legs.

"Say, Cap," said Kennedy, "they got a haul. I figure that in cold cash and jewelry, twenty thousand was taken. Let's take into consideration the exaggeration complex, and cut it in two. That makes ten thousand, and Bud Maloney's two makes twelve. I've got a description here of the jewelry."

MacBride then went among the guests, taking down names and addresses and articles stolen. He nipped long-winded speeches on the part of outraged women nicely in the bud, having about him a blunt manner of formality that automatically revolted against extraneous detail; particularly the draft of women who, never hoping to recover their Teclas, bounced the monetary loss a couple of hundred percent.

Moriarity and Cohen came in, booted with mud, and Moriarity said, "Can't find a soul, Cap. But we found fresh ruts in the mud alongside the road, about a hundred yards up, where the car probably parked. Ike put his flash on the ruts. New tires, because we managed to make out the word Regal in the mud. Them Regal tires have the letters in the tread."

"That's using your eyes, boys," said MacBride.

Cohen said, "I wonder what the hell happened to the bird chased that other guy out."

"Maybe," shrugged Moriarity, "the other guy nailed him and when his pals seen it they dragged the poor guy in the car and dumped him out somewhere else, taking no chances on wounding him, but making a finish job of it in the car."

"Anyhow," put in Kennedy, "this gets the ball rolling. Garrity was bumped off, and there's a chance that the guy who did it was hooked up with the West Side racket. These two gangs have been itching for an excuse to play Fourth of July, and the South Side bunch will have a damned good excuse now."

MacBride broke in— "There's the morgue bus. We'll see this stiff off and then breeze. Ike, you and Mory better catch some sleep, because you're not going to get much from now on. I prophecy a lively bit of hell in this burg, and I'm going to camp at Headquarters myself. Bud, that liquor of yours is jake."

"Help yourself, Cap."

"Don't take it all," said Kennedy.

MacBride grinned. "Hell, if I left you alone with this bottle, Kennedy, you'd get plastered to the eyebrows and your sheet would never get this story."

Kennedy, with mock seriousness, said, "Captain, the gentlemen of the press—"

"Can that crap," chuckled MacBride, "and hold out your glass."

Kennedy sighed. "Good old tomato!"

Chapter II

MacBRIDE breezed into Headquarters, water trailing from his rubber coat. Sergeant Otto Bettdecken laid down a copy of *How to Make Money in Your Spare Time,* and sat back with a half-eaten hamburger in one hand and a half-drunk bottle of home-brew down on the floor by his left heel. Bettdecken was one of those voluminous men for whom Grand Rapids should build special furniture.

"You eating again, Otto?" jibed MacBride.

"Yeah. I get hungry around this time, Cap."

"Wipe the beer off your chin, Otto, and for crying out loud, be careful how you truck that stuff in here. I mind how a couple of months ago a Mayor's committee of inspection blew in, while you were out in the wash-room. I had to sit behind that desk like a damn fool till they went. I knew it was loaded. And it was—fifteen bottles of brew."

"I'll be careful, Cap—honest."

"Well, anyhow. Garrity was the guy bumped off at *The Blue Goose.*

Things are a bit muddled yet, but you'd better get in touch with all the precincts—especially those on the West and South Sides—and tell them to keep their eyes peeled. I'm going out on a private call. I'll be back in an hour."

Moriarity and Cohen came in, and MacBride said to them, "You can warm your pants, boys, or curl up somewhere."

"Thanks," said Cohen. "We just picked up some hamburgers, and if"—he grinned—"if Otto doesn't come across with a couple of bottles of brew we'll tell papa Commissioner."

"Blackmail!" said Bettdecken, and two-hundred-odd pounds wobbled with laughter.

Out into the wind and the rain went MacBride. Officer Joe Pigalli was at the wheel of the police touring car. MacBride hopped in beside him and said, "Shoot, Joe."

The black car plunged down the black, sleet-ridden canyon. The pavements gleamed beneath a corner arc-light. The rear end of the car slewed. Pigalli fought the wheel, shaking his head.

"Lousy night, Cap!"

"Yeah, Joe. Take it easy."

A side draft hurled frozen rain against MacBride's face. He spat sleet from his lips. A wet, dead cigar was in his fingers. He threw it away. They cruised through dark forgotten streets. They crossed a square where a few lights shone, then bored into another narrow street. Yellow lights, few and far between, stared through the wet darkness. The street bent to the right. A smeared electric sign stuck out from a brick-faced building:

ANGELO'S

"Pull up, Joe."

The car rolled to a stop, its tail slewing against the curb.

"Wait here, Joe."

"O.K., Cap."

A man moved in the doorway beneath the electric sign. The red end of a cigarette butt described an arc from his lips down to his side.

"How yuh, Cap?"

"Jake."

MacBride passed into a hallway. A girl stood by a cloak-room. A short, blunt-built man with a hair-brush mustache and a cast in one eye, sat beside her. This man got up, looked, grinned with a lot of gold teeth—but watchfully, not happily.

"Ah, Cap, how are you, Cap?"

"Hello, Angey."

"Watcha call rotten night, huh?"

"Yeah."

"Have de cigar, Cap."

MacBride took it, bit off the end. Angelo hastened to strike a match. MacBride leaned to get his light, then straightened, inhaled deeply, and shot smoke through his nostrils. Spread-legged, he roamed his eyes over the cabaret. A bawdy place, bivouac of loose women, truck drivers, longshoremen, and a sprinkling of clerks from mid-town sowing their oats. A pale-faced man slammed a piano hotly, and a crowd was on the small dance-floor. The sort of dancing where two stand on a spot and move everything but their feet.

"Get hot, boy!" someone yelled at the piano-player.

"Red hot, baby!" shouted a muscle-dancing girl—a chemical blonde, dizzily tight.

Angelo was uneasy. "Whassa matter, Cap?"

"Oh, nothing, Angey. Who's upstairs?"

"Ah—" He put his shoulders up alongside his ears. "Some boys, Cap."

"H'm." MacBride turned and climbed a staircase.

He walked into a large room containing six tables. A waiter was leaning in the doorway, picking his teeth. He tried to appear nonchalant; whistled and said, with forced cheerfulness, "Hello, Captain."

MacBride nodded, took his cigar from his mouth, put a quick shot into a cuspidor, and replaced the cigar in one corner of his mouth.

At one of the tables sat four men, and you wouldn't have picked any one of them as a model American. Two were big, heavy-jawed, roughly dressed. Another was small, with a beak of a nose and no chin worth mention. He looked like a rat, and he was. The fourth was well-dressed; dark, snappy suit, soft white collar, polka-dot tie. His hair was black as onyx, full of smooth, lustrous waves. He was good-looking in a dark, Italian way—about thirty. He had eyes that were as large and attractive as a girl's, and his skin was smoothly white, ruddy-cheeked. You're being introduced to Nick Sciacca, boss of the West Side mob.

Laughing-eyed Sciacca.... "Well, well, MacBride!"

Bunt Paoli, the rat-faced shrimp, shuffled a pack of cards. Rivigo took a drink and made a noise in his throat. Agosta, the other bruiser, licked a loose leaf of his cheroot back into place.

MacBride drifted over to the table, his rubber coat swishing. He took his cigar from his mouth.

"Garrity got bumped off tonight, Nick," he said.

Sciacca sat back. "That's interesting. I knew that Mick would get lead in his pants some day."

MacBride smiled—a tight smile, barren of mirth. "You know a lot, don't you, Nick?"

"A little bit, Cap."

"Modest guy!" chortled MacBride.

Sciacca's dark eyes sparkled, his teeth shone in a white grin. "Why the hell get worked up over a pup like Garrity?"

"I'm not worked up, Nick. But I will be if any guys start to crack wise with a gun. I suppose you've been having a hell of a time while I was down cleaning up Millboro. Well, get this—you, Nick, and the rest of you dagos—I'm back here in Richmond City, attached to headquarters. These elections are coming on, but that's no excuse for you guys to get loose with a gun. I mean it, Nick. Garrity was bumped off in a funny way. I don't know who did it, but I've got my hunches. Garrity was a louse—all right. You're a louse, too, Nick—a damn alley rat. If you gangs would exterminate each other, that would be all right. But you always go off the handle and bump off a cop or any other guy that gets in your way."

Sciacca said, "What the hell did you come down here for, to blow off steam or make a pinch? I don't know what the cripes you're talking about. You're all wet, and not from the rain either. Tie that boloney outside."

"You heard me, Nick. That killing was a queer one, and I don't know who was behind it. But I've got a sneaking suspicion, and I'm going to work on it. And this is what I came here to tell you: stay in the West Side, in your own backyard, and keep out of these election campaigns. The first sniff I get of you guys monkeying around, I'll flop on your parade."

Sciacca laughed. "Holy cripes, Cap, you give me a great horse-laugh."

"If you think I'm a lot of hot air, Nick, try knocking a ball out of bounds."

"Ah, lay off us!" rasped Bunt Paoli, smacking down the deck of cards. "Here we ain't bothering a soul, just sitting around and staying out of the rain, and you gotta come down here foaming at the mouth like a mad dog. Where the hell do you rate your nerve, big boy?"

"All right, all right," said MacBride, stabbing a forefinger at the group. "Wisecrack all you want. But I'm detailed to keep this city clean during the campaign, and I'm going to bust into any rat that slops up. Good-night!"

He pivoted and strode out.

"Don't get your feet wet!" called Sciacca.

But MacBride was on his way down the stairs. He tramped out into the rain, climbed into the police car, and banged the door.

"Shoot, Joe."

Chapter III

SOMETHING was doing at Headquarters....

MacBride, tramping into the central room, cursing the weather, saw several cops standing around, wet rubber capes thrown back. Sergeant Otto Bettdecken was hunched over the telephone, looking very much disturbed, and from an open door down the hallway, came the strident discord of voices pitched in anger.

"What the hell?" asked MacBride.

One of the cops nodded down the hall. "Jimmy Bone thinks he picked up something."

MacBride got out of his rubber coat as he strode down the hall. The door to his office was open, and from it issued the medley of voices. He brought up in the doorway, tipped back his soaked fedora, and shifted his cigar.

Kennedy was sitting on the desk, his legs jack-knifed, heels hooked on the edge and hands clasped about knees. He looked at MacBride and chuckled loosely, lazily.

"Hello, old tomato."

There were Moriarity and Cohen, shooting fast questions at a little fat guy who sat squirming in a chair and tearing his hat out of shape with nervous, dirty fingers. His face was shaped like a moon, only not so attractive. It was red and blotchy, crowned with a mop of tangled hair the color of terra cotta. He had wide pop-eyes, and he looked scared and did a lot of stammering. There was a tracery of blood on his left cheek.

MacBride clipped, "Who the hell's been socking this guy?"

"Ah, nobody's been socking him, Cap," shot back Moriarity. "The bum's crabbing all over the place."

Jimmy Bone, a motorcycle patrolman, young and serious, said, "I picked him up on Farmingville Turnpike, Cap. He crashed a car along the road just as I drifted by, and I pulled up. First thing I knew he was running away. What I wanted to know was, why should a guy run away and leave his car, even if he did skid off the road and smash a windshield? That's how his mug got cut up. I nailed him and frisked him for a gun, and I got one—a Colt's thirty-eight. I put bracelets on him and chucked him in my side-car and brought him here."

MacBride hung up his rubber coat. "What's his name?"

"Schneider, he says."

"What kind of a car?"

"Packard sedan."

"Take the number?"

"Yeah. She has Pennsy pads—00212. On the front left door is a place where there were initials, the kind I guess you cement on. Well, they were gone, but I could still make out the place where they were, due, I guess to the color of the rest of the car fading. She's not a new boat. The initials were *J.A.C.*"

"Anybody check up the pads?"

"I asked Sergeant Bett—"

Just then Sergeant Bettdecken loomed in the doorway. "Here we have something, I don't know what. That Pennsy number belongs to a flivver, not a Packard. Them pads were lifted from the flivver in a public garage last week, but the flivver wasn't taken. Now look here. There was a Packard swiped from in front of a guy's house named Dr. Train, about two weeks ago. The car wasn't his, but belonged to a guy named James A. Caldwell, of Jersey, who was on his way from New York to Montreal with his wife, and stopped at the doctor's to have something taken out of his wife's eye. His pads were Jersey, of course, number 4040X. This guy didn't get to Montreal, but went back to Morristown."

MacBride jammed his arms akimbo and looked at Schneider. "Stolen car, eh?"

Schneider crouched in his chair and held up one hand, as if he feared being hit. Cohen was aching to hit him.

MacBride turned to Bone. "You leave the car out there?"

"Yeah, Cap. Locked it and took the key."

MacBride reached for his coat. "Come on and show me the way."

They went out and MacBride climbed into the side-car and pulled the rubber wind-breaker up around his neck. Bone forked the seat, cranked up, and they shot down the street. The wind and the icy rain slashed at them, and ice formed on their faces. Farmingville Turnpike was a bleak, desolate stretch. Bone slowed down, peered keenly, then edged in towards the side of the road and pulled up.

The sedan was well off the road, nose down into a ditch, with slush up to its front hub caps and the limb of a tree sticking through the aperture where the windshield had been. MacBride got out of the side-car and said:

"Jimmy, swing your spotlight down on these wheels."

Bone wheeled his motorcycle around and then snapped on the big spotlight. MacBride shook his head.

"Now on the other wheel, the off side here."

The beam of light swept across the back of the car and stopped on the rear right wheel. MacBride bent down and almost put his nose against the tire.

"Boy!" he exclaimed, and stood up.

Bone said, "What?"

"This boat was parked near *The Blue Goose* tonight or I'm a wet blanket! Same tread as we found in the mud near the stick-up at the roadhouse—Regal tread. Give me the key, Jimmy. I'll drive this bus back and you carry on with your patrol. I'll see your name gets in the paper for this haul."

"Thanks, Cap. You know I'm trying hard for plainclothes. Getting married soon, and I'll need the pay."

MacBride grinned, the spotlight gleaming on his wet, chiseled face. "That's the stuff, Jimmy. Nothing like a wife. I've had one for over twenty years, and she's kept me young."

"Twenty years! Say, I didn't know you were that old!"

"Whadda you mean—*old!* Forty-two come a week from Saturday, and I feel like twenty-one. All right, boy—hop your iron horse and go places."

Young Jimmy Bone straddled his iron horse, roared the motor, smiled, waved, and streaked off into the darkness.

MacBride climbed into the car, started it, backed out, swung around and drove back to Headquarters. He parked the car at the curb and took the broad cement steps three at a time, at the risk of slipping on the ice and breaking his neck. He sailed into the central room like a blast of wind, but the wind was promptly taken out of his sails.

Kennedy was leaning against a pillar, and a droll, insinuating smile dragged at his lips and twinkled in his eyes.

"Well?" clipped MacBride.

"Schneider is flown."

"Yeah?"

"Yeah."

MacBride looked at Sergeant Bettdecken, who was just lowering a bottle of home-brew out of sight.

"Wipe your chin off, Otto!"

"Uh—ah—um—yeah, Lew Stein, of Stein, Riley & Bower, come in here with a writ. So we had to release Schneider temporary, it being the law."

MacBride snapped, "Who the hell let Schneider get in touch with his lawyers?"

Kennedy was laughing lightly. "Nobody, old tomato. But I guess Schneider's friends figured he was caught, and they got in touch with Stein, and Stein got in touch with Judge Hunkle—and there you are!"

"Damn these legal back-flips!" swore MacBride. "Why, Kennedy, that guy was driving a car with a rear right Regal tire. And it was a Regal tread mark we found out near *The Blue Goose!*"

"Thus and so, thus and so," sighed Kennedy.

"Where's Moriarity and Cohen?"

Kennedy said, "Were they sore? Hot diggity damn, they were! So they sneak out the side entrance, intending to follow Schneider. Well, that was ten minutes ago. They haven't popped up yet. They must be still gumshoeing along. If you've got a bottle of good Scotch in your desk, I might consider joining you in a drink."

"Oh, you might, might you!"

"Indeed and how!"

"Come on, you grafter!"

MacBride slammed into his office, yanked open a drawer in his desk, and hauled out a bottle of Dewar's.

Kennedy said, after the first drink, "Cap, take it from me, this thing is going a damned sight farther than you might think. It wasn't just an ordinary killing. It wasn't a chance killing. As far as I can see, everything was planned, timed, and went off like clockwork.

"Hasn't it seemed strange to you that the guy who was sitting alone by the window, got up and went into the toilet just before these other guys came in?"

"Yup. Kind of, Kennedy."

"It's funny, too, that he should come out again just as these two guys have cleaned up. He kills Garrity. The other guy grabs Garrity's bag and beats it, and that's the last of them. Now who was the guy that killed Garrity? Why didn't he come back? Was he killed by the other guy and his mob, or was he?— You get me, Cap?"

MacBride set down his glass. "Kennedy, I get you—and more. Garrity was framed! So help me living cripes, he was framed! From what little bit we can gather—rumor and the like—Garrity was the strong man who held the South Side hoodlums together. He was a friend of Mike Mulvaney's, and Mulvaney was depending heavily on him for a lot of votes. The catch is—why was he framed? If he was, then I've been shooting my mouth off to Nick Sciacca like a jackass, and Nick has every right to razz me till the cows come home!"

"The thing now is, Cap—who will boss the South Side hoodlums?"

"Ten to one, the guy who framed Garrity."

"Who's that?"

"Hell, Kennedy, I'm no genius! Schneider will have to appear before the District Attorney. Meantime, he'll be nicely coached by his lawyer and by the guys he runs with. That's the hell of it. But—I'm going to get my hands on Schneider again before he goes to trial. The trial will be for stealing a car. Those tire marks—hell, the testimony can be shot full of holes. The marks are washed away by this time, and that shyster lawyer will convince the jury that Moriarity was seeing things."

When Cohen came in, he looked down at the mouth. "Mory went home to bed, Cap. We tailed Stein and Schneider. But what the hell. Schneider goes down to the Moose Hotel and takes a room there. Then Stein breezes."

"Was Schneider living there before, or did he just register tonight?"

"Just registered. That guy may be yellow, but he ain't dumb."

Kennedy said, "You mean Stein ain't dumb."

"Go home, Ike," said MacBride, "and hit the hay. We've got a lot to do. Somebody's going to get hurt before he's much older."

Chapter IV

GARRITY got a swell funeral. He lay in state, in The Shamrock Funeral Parlors, and the crowd there was a big one. Of course, most of them had never known Garrity, but curiosity drew them. Some people make a habit of going to anybody's funeral, and Garrity had tacked up a notorious name in the neighborhood, and a lot of women get sentimental over the death of a colorful gangster.

Fat, slovenly women came, carrying babes in their arms. Girls came. They filed up to the coffin, muttered prayers, sobbed, filed away. The room was filled with flowers, and Clancey, the funeral director, wore a black frock coat, a winged collar, and the expression of a saint.

A Cadillac limousine drew up, and Mike Mulvaney, District Alderman, deposited a wad of chewing-tobacco in the gutter, assumed an impressive air, and plowed through the crowd. He stood beside the coffin, looking very grave, very sad, and his beefy lips moved in silent prayer. He sighed, turned around, bowed his head and strode into the large ante-room, where a lot of roughnecks sat around filling the place with tobacco smoke.

"Honest," said Mulvaney, "I never thought Tex would get mixed up in a thing like that. I'm sorry. He was a nice guy, a good guy. And he was so young. Well, that is life, like Father O'Rourke would say. All I can remember is Tex's smiling face. He was such a nice guy. Ah, me—ah, me!"

A bull-necked, broken-nosed man, wiped a tear from his eye. A black-haired woman in black, slim and red-eyed from recent crying, but now sullenly mournful, sat on a table and puffed on a cigarette. Dolly Kane. Tex Garrity's woman.

"I feel sorry for you, Dolly," said Alderman Mike Mulvaney.

"Forget it," said Dolly. She scowled.

A cross-eyed, slack-jawed misfit sniffed, cleared his throat and spat.

A tall, lean, quiet-faced man, who was leaning against the wall, hardly moved his lips but his words crackled: "You slob, you spit on my shoe! Wipe it off!"

"Didn't mean it, Spot." But he wiped off the shoe with his handkerchief.

A big man, in a black shirt, came weaving through the crowd, mingled with the group around the table, and jerked his thumb over his shoulder.

"Couple o' dicks."

There was a slight movement among the group. Dolly Kane took a quick puff on her butt, and it bobbed in one corner of her mouth as she said. "Cripes, do them guys have to come around?"

"Take it easy, kid," said the tall, lean, quiet-faced man.

An old woman, in the room with the coffin, suddenly started to wail. She raised her hands upward, rocked back and forth.

Dolly clipped, "What the hell's the matter with her?"

The slack-jawed misfit said, "Ah, that's Ma Finnegan. She ain't ever got over the time her kid Johnny was burned in the chair for bumping off Inspector Scholz, two year ago."

Dolly scowled. "Think we'd hired professional bawlers! Hell's bells, that dame howls like a sick cat! It ain't her funeral."

The tall, lean, quiet-faced man poked her gently. "Tone down, Dolly."

"Why, dammit?"

"Use your head, if you got one!" His voice was low, a barbed whisper.

Suddenly MacBride appeared, a clean-clipped figure of a man, dressed in a conservative blue suit and a neat, conservative gray hat. His hands were lounging in his pockets, and a fresh cigar was clamped between his teeth. He seemed to ignore everybody, and yet he saw everybody.

Alderman Mulvaney burrowed toward him. "Why, how do you do, Cap?"

"Hello, Mulvaney." MacBride went on cruising his eyes over the crowded rooms.

Mulvaney sighed. "Ah, me—ah, me! Death—death! It is sad, Captain."

"Yeah," absently.

"Uh—you want to view the body, Cap?"

"I didn't come here to look at dead ones, Mulvaney. I'm interested in the live babies."

"That's disrespectful to the dead, Captain!"

MacBride slid a derisive eye over him. "Be your age, Mulvaney. I don't have to act up to hold my job. And I don't see any reason why I should bawl over the death of a guy that once tried to wing me.

Death doesn't make me sob, Mulvaney. A dead rat is just the same to me as a live one—only less dangerous. Your stock in trade is acting up. You've got a position. I've got a job."

Mulvaney reddened. "If you feel that way, why'd you come down here? Can't you let people mourn in peace?"

"Let 'em mourn. What are you mourning—the loss of a good vote-getter?"

"Don't get sarcastic, MacBride!"

"Dry up, Mulvaney. I didn't start this conversation."

"Well, then don't hint out that Garrity was more to me than an acquaintance, or by God, I'll have you arrested for defamation of character."

MacBride sighed, wearily. He jerked his chin. "On your way, Mulvaney. I said I didn't start this gab."

Mulvaney straightened down his coat in flustered indignation. "Just watch how you talk; that's all. Remember, I'm Alderman here, and if I want to, I can make your job uncomfortable."

"Hello, Kennedy," said MacBride, turning and ignoring the Alderman.

"Hello, Cap. I'm down with the staff photographer to get a shot of the coffin going out."

Mulvaney heard and elbowed in. "Say Kennedy, they can have a picture of me, too. And look here, write up a story. They call me the Neighborhood Daddy, and that's what I am. No guy ever said I was snooty, and I always bend to lend a guy a hand. It's too bad about Tex, him holding up that roadhouse, but I knew him before he went bad, and I'm here to pay my respects to the—the sacred dead, no matter what he did. That's the kind of a guy I am, and that's why I'm going to be re-elected."

"All right, Mike," smiled Kennedy. "I'll remember that. The photographer's out front."

"Okey. Suppose I get the bereaved sweetheart of Tex's and sort of have us stand together."

"Sure," smiled Kennedy, head on one shoulder, eyes droll.

So Mulvaney went over and grabbed Dolly, and they went out through the front doorway. Dolly was taking out her powder compact, but Mulvaney shook his head. Then he put his arm around her shoulder in a very fatherly manner, assumed a tender, fatherly mien; and Dolly held a handkerchief to one cheek, and the camera clicked.

"Rich!" chuckled MacBride.

"Great campaign stuff, old tomato," drawled Kennedy. Then he elbowed MacBride's ribs. "There's Bud Maloney. What's he doing here?"

"I've been waiting for him," said MacBride, and signaled Maloney, who had just stepped out of a sport roadster. He came towards MacBride, looking around warily.

MacBride muttered, "There's a mob inside, Bud. Just walk in and shoot your eye around. If you see any guy resembles the guys got away, point him out."

"You know, when Garrity and the other guy came in, they had masks on, Cap."

"I know. But even so, something may be familiar."

Maloney went into the crowded anteroom. His eyes snapped over the crowd. He shrugged. He wasn't very hopeful. "There's a lot of guys here about the one's same build, Cap. One there—and there—and there's another one leaning against the wall by that table. He's just looking away."

"Hang around the door, Bud," said MacBride, and drifted over towards the table.

Half a dozen men—including the slack-jawed misfit—were sitting around, and the tall, lean, quiet-faced man stood against the wall, idly picking apart a dead cigarette.

"Hello, Cap," ventured the slack-jawed man.

"Hello, Chinky. What are you doing these days?"

Chinky shrugged. "Washin' dishes at a lunch-wagon."

"H'm." He jangled loose change in his pocket and caught the eye of the quiet-faced man. "Don't remember you."

"Why should you?"

"Nice shot." MacBride grinned and snapped the ash from his cigar. "I'm interested in new faces. Working here?"

"No. Visiting friends."

"These guys around the table?"

"No."

"Who?"

"Listen, what ever your name is. My name's Corcoran, and I'm Mike Mulvaney's new publicity man. Is there anything else you want to know?"

"Quick on the back-chat, aren't you?"

"That's my business."

MacBride replaced his cigar in the left corner of his mouth. "My error," he said, and pivoting, strolled away.

Mixing with the crowd, he finally reached the door and stepped outside into another crowd that was trying to get in. A short, shabbily dressed man, with a couple of days' growth of stubble, leaned against the building. MacBride presently stood beside him, and looking around over the crowd, muttered:

"Go inside, Charley. There's a tall, good-looking bird standing beside the table. He's got on a dark gray suit. You can't miss him. Take a good look at him, then hang around and follow him and see where he goes."

"Right, Cap."

MacBride moved away, and saw Maloney standing by his roadster. "Mind if I go, Cap?"

"Go to it, Bud."

"I thought there'd be nothing here."

"Not much, Bud."

Maloney drove off, and then Kennedy came out. "Any luck?"

MacBride shrugged. "It all depends, Kennedy."

Charley, a police rookie, wormed his way in through the doorway.

Ma Finnegan was wailing again.

Dolly said, "I wish somebody'd chuck that yap out!"

Chapter V

WINTER sun streamed in through the window of MacBride's office at Headquarters. Blue smoke coiled upward from his cigar. His feet were hooked on the desk. Kennedy sat on the desk, one foot dangling, the other on the desk, hands clasped around the knee.

"Mulvaney is in a tight pinch all right," said Kennedy. "Tony Maratelli will rate a lot of votes, no kidding. He's not as bad as he might be. Of course, if he gets in office, it will mean that his contracting company will get the job of building that new state road across the marshes. That's what he's after. He's a prosperous dago with lots of jack, and he spends like a sport. He'll get all the dago votes and a lot of others, and the position of his party gives him a good chance to fight for the reduction of gasoline tax. Mulvaney can't do that, because his boss is mixed up with the oil syndicate, and if they raise the tax, you'll see a fight for lower gas rates to equalize the tax jump. Believe it or not, Mulvaney's at his wits' end to gain popularity."

MacBride creaked in his chair. "And if he thinks he can drag in a gang to fight for him under cover, he's mistaken. Now I don't know what his game is, and I don't know where he picked up this guy Corcoran. They may be on the square, but until I prove it, they're crooked to me."

"This broad, Dolly Kane," drawled Kennedy. "She didn't seem worked up over Garrity's death at all. I saw her go off to the funeral with this guy you call Corcoran."

MacBride rasped, "She's a tart, Kennedy! A brazen-faced, hard-boiled little wench. She'll have another man before the sod on Garrity's grave has settled." He sat up. "Well, I've got Charley Myers, a cop that's just been made, dressed up like a bum and doing a bit of tailing. He comes from the sticks and he's not known in the city."

"Schneider's due to appear in court day after tomorrow, isn't he?"

"Yeah. And the District Attorney says I can have him for a couple of hours beforehand."

"Here's hoping, Cap."

"If he doesn't talk, it won't be my fault. Moriarity has a nice new piece of hose."

Kennedy slid off the desk, "See you again, Cap."

"S' long, Kennedy."

Kennedy went out. MacBride stood up, stretched, and went over to stand by the window. He stared abstractedly into space. It was a rough, brutal racket. Crude, brutal men held office, and in order to attain their ends, they lied, bribed, coerced and sometimes killed. The truth tasted bitter in the captain's mouth. Mulvaney protected speak-easies, had money in some of them, got men jobs and thereby bound them to his side. He pulled strings to make laws easier for factories, to erase marks against condemned buildings. His salary was only incidental to his graft, and he was not of a mind to lose the job that netted him that graft.

There was a knock on the door. MacBride turned and said, "Come in."

Charley Myers came in. "I followed the funeral, Cap, and then I followed this guy you told me to. He went to a nice apartment house—28 Mallory Street—with this here girl. I stood across the street, in a cigar store, thinking they might come out. But they didn't. But I saw the guy at a window on the fourth floor, fifth window from the left-hand side of the building. He was in his shirt-sleeves, and he had a glass in his hand. He was laughing at something. Then I saw the girl. She came over and looked out, and she was laughing too. He said something, and then she patted his cheek, and they disappeared."

"Good work, Charley. The damned trollop! I don't care a damn about Garrity dying, but she certainly must be a lousy bum to carry on with this Corcoran. All right, Charley. I want you to hang around there some more, and see if either of these two comes out or goes in with somebody else."

Charley grinned. "Sure will, Cap. Thanks for the job."

"Don't mention it."

Charley went out, whistling. This was better than pounding a beat in the sticks!

MacBride spent the remainder of the afternoon getting reports up to date. At six he grabbed his hat and coat and was on the way out when the telephone rang. He pitched hat and coat into a chair and caught up the instrument.

"Cap?"

"Yup."

"This is Charley. Say, can you meet me at Chester Square—northeast corner, in front of the cigar store? Maybe I've got a lead."

"Okey, Charley. Be right over."

He hung up, slapped on his hat and got into his coat as he walked out. He caught a taxi a block from Headquarters and hopped in. Early winter darkness had settled. The air was crisply-cold, invigorating. Stars were shining over the city.

It was a ten minute ride to Chester Square. MacBride got out, looked up one of the dark streets that rolled into the square, saw a smeared electric sign:

ANGELO'S

Charley Myers came out of the cigar store and drifted up beside MacBride.

"The broad came out of that apartment house alone and walked a couple of blocks and then got into a taxi. I hopped another one and tailed her. She came down here and the taxi went up Blinker Street. I saw it stop so I stopped mine right here. She got out and went in where you see that sign *Angelo's*. She hasn't come out yet."

"Good work, Charley." MacBride stood, hands in overcoat pockets, breath spuming out into the frosty air. "You can hang around here. I won't be long."

"Say, hadn't I better sort of slide in behind you?"

MacBride chuckled and clapped him on the back. "Don't worry, Charley. No danger there. Just hang around till I come out."

He turned and strode up Blinker Street. His footsteps re-echoed sharply. He swung into the doorway beneath the sign, and the man there started, then said, huskily, "Oh—hello, Cap."

MacBride nodded and went on in. The cabaret was almost deserted. The hat-check girl sat on a chair reading a newspaper. She looked up and smiled. MacBride nodded. He stood looking around quizzically.

A door in the rear of the lower hall opened and Angelo came out, humming merrily. But he stopped short when he saw MacBride, and perhaps he gulped. Then he came forward, forcing a grin.

"Ah, Cap! Sure glad to see you, yeah. Shake the hand."

They shook and MacBride said, "Glad you're glad to see me, Angey."

"Have de cigar."

"Sure. Thanks."

Angelo hastened to strike a match, and MacBride leaned over to get a light. He raised his eyes and looked right into Angelo's. His words came out with a cloud of smoke:

"Who's upstairs, Angey?"

"Not a soul, Cap."

MacBride stood back, took his cigar out of his mouth, looked at it, then looked at Angelo.

"Mind if I take a look?"

Angelo spread his hands. "I tella you, Cap—Jeeze, nobody he's uppa stairs."

"I'll look anyhow, Angey."

He shifted, gripped his cigar between strong teeth, and went up the stairs like a youngster. He stopped in the doorway of the large room wherein he had had his brittle chat with Nick Sciacca. The room was empty.

"Hell!" he muttered under his breath.

He backed out, stood at the head of the stairs, took one downward step, then paused. He looked around, back down the darker reaches of the upper hall. He had heard a woman laugh. He caught sight of Angelo standing at the bottom of the staircase. Angelo was looking up at him, motionless, his face a blank.

MacBride turned and drifted quietly down the corridor. A door marked the end of it. He listened. There were voices behind the door. Occasionally a woman's. He opened his overcoat, took his gun from a holster beneath his arm and shoved it into his overcoat pocket. Then he buttoned his coat. He heard a metallic clank.

He put his ear against the door, listening. The voices had stopped. His left hand moved and settled upon the knob. He turned it slowly. Then he shoved open the door and stood there. The door banged back against the wall.

The room was empty. There was no disorder. A single electric light, white-shaded, hung from the ceiling. There was a table with chairs around it.

MacBride stepped in. His eyes snapped about the room, alighted on a door. He jumped towards it, grabbed the knob, turned it, wrenched open the door. Darkness. But the light from the room showed him a narrow stairway that descended abruptly to regions below. He felt his way downward. He reached a landing, and his outstretched hand came in contact with a wall. He probed around. The staircase took a left turn. He followed it.

He bumped against a door below; opened it. He stepped into a small room, furnished with a table and a few chairs. Behind it, was another room. At the other end, was a chintz curtain over another door. He pushed it aside and looked into the main cabaret.

At the farther end stood Angelo, looking towards him—as if he had expected to see MacBride appear there. Angelo did not move. A cigar was motionless in his mouth.

A shot banged—muffled. MacBride galvanized and ran across the cabaret.

"Damn you, Angey!"

Angelo gulped and paled.

"Where the hell was that shot, Angey?"

Angelo looked pained. He was speechless, petrified.

The doorman rushed into the room, blurting, "Holy God!" And

then he saw MacBride and stiffened.

MacBride rushed past him, hauling out his gun. He ran into the street, into the cold night. He looked up and down. He saw a figure crawling on the sidewalk, twenty yards away. He ran towards it.

"Cap! Cap!"

"Good Lord, Charley!"

Charley sighed and lay back against a house wall. MacBride fell down beside him.

"Boy, boy!"

"I hung around—across the street, Cap. I saw the broad and two men come out of that alley. I thought—maybe—you'd got hurt. I ran towards them, pulling my gun. But one of the guys shot right through his coat pocket and— Oh, it hurts like hell, Cap!"

"Where, boy—where?"

"I dunno. Chest, I guess. They ran off, towards the square."

MacBride, kneeling, blew his whistle. Then he lifted Myers in his arms and carried him into Angelo's. His face was gray like granite and hard like granite. He put Myers down in a chair. He glared at Angelo.

"You—call an ambulance!"

Angelo reeled off to the telephone. MacBride turned and ran to the door. He blew his whistle again. He saw a running figure down the street, saw the flash of buttons and shield beneath a lone street lamp. He jumped out to the street and waved his hands.

A patrolman puffed up, swinging his nightstick. "That you, Cap?"

"Yeah, Shanzenbach. Charley Myers, a rookie, has been plugged. Come in here. Who's that coming?"

"Prob'ly O'Leary."

Patrolman O'Leary came running from the opposite direction.

"What's up, Cap?"

"Trouble."

MacBride turned and went back to Myers. Myers was pasty white, weary, broken. MacBride opened his shirt. It was bloody. Meyers' chest was bloody.

"God Almighty, Cap, I can't—hardly—uh—breathe."

"Try hard, Charley."

Angelo said, "I phone for de ambulance."

MacBride spun on him, leaped, caught Angelo by the throat. "You lousy greaseball, who was upstairs besides that frail?"

Angelo lost color again. His eyes popped, and his mouth writhed.

"Jeeze, Cap, you busta ma throat!"

"What I intend to do, dago, if you don't come across—and fast! You warned those guys by tapping a pipe."

His eyes were small jets of blue fire, his lips curled over long, hard teeth. He swung Angelo back and forth like a wet sack and slammed him violently into a chair. Chair and Angelo crashed to the floor.

"Get up, Angey—get up and talk!" panted MacBride.

"Jeeze, Cap, so help me, Cap, I ain't got no hand in dis!"

"Lay off that crap! I want to know who was up there. Listen to me, you pie-faced pup!" He bent down and held his rock-bound fist under Angelo's nose. "You spring it, see! I'll spread you all over this dump and send you up for twenty years if you don't talk!"

Sweat was running down Angelo's face. He gasped, groaned. "Nick... Bunt.... Holy Mother, Cap, they'll killa me—they'll killa me! But, honest. I ain't gotta no hand in dis. I can'ta help if them guys—"

"Pipe down! Close your dump and don't let me see it open! You find a hole and crawl into it. I don't want you, dago."

A bell clanged. Shanzenbach ran to the door. "Ambulance, Cap," he called back.

MacBride turned to O'Leary. "Let's carry Charley out."

They carried him out as a white-coated doctor leaped to the sidewalk.

"One of my men hurt bad, Doc. Burn the road for the hospital You go with them, Shanzey."

"Okey, Cap."

"You, O'Leary, hang around here and see no guys come back. Pick up anybody gets nasty."

The ambulance boomed off. MacBride strode toward Chester Square, winged a taxi and gave an address. Fifteen minutes later he alighted before the apartment house in Mallory Street. In the lobby there was a glassed-in cubbyhole in which sat a girl at a switchboard.

"Which is Miss Kane's apartment?"

"I'll ring Miss Kane."

"No you won't. I'm MacBride, Police Headquarters." He flashed his shield.

"Oh. Well, it's 430."

"Thanks."

MacBride got into the elevator, gave the room number.

"Miss Kane's out, sir."

"She is? All right, back to the ground floor and get the guy who has a pass key."

The manager appeared in the lobby, quite disturbed. A few words from MacBride, and they ascended the elevator. The manager opened the door marked 430 and MacBride rolled in, stopped, looked around.

"How long has she been here?"

"About three weeks."

"I want you to report to me as soon as she comes back."

He prowled around the living-room, into the bedroom. He came back into the living-room, noticed a large gray pasteboard box lying open on the divan. He picked up the cover.

SWANN & COMPANY

FURRIERS

55 Broadway Avenue

He jotted down the address. Then: "All right, Mr. Aronson. Don't forget what I told you."

"I won't, Captain. I'm awfully sorry—"

"Not your fault. Good-night."

Ten minutes later MacBride got out in front of the imposing establishment of Swann & Company. Since it was Saturday night, the store was still open, and MacBride strode in and asked for the man in charge. To this man he said, as he flashed his shield:

"Recently you delivered furs of some kind to Miss Kane, at 28 Mallory Street. I want to know what kind of a payment was made on it."

"Just a minute, Captain."

The man went off into an office and came out a moment later. He said, "Our records show that payment was made by check. The amount was a thousand dollars, and the check was signed by Nicholas Sciacca. Lady's fur coat."

"Thank you very much."

In the street, MacBride walked. The run of events had turned a complete somersault. He had reasoned that Dolly was taking on with Corcoran, Alderman Mulvaney's man. And here Sciacca, the head of the dago hoodlums, had bought Dolly a new fur coat. And Garrity had been Sciacca's deadliest enemy!

Chapter VI

KENNEDY lounged in a chair, one leg slung over the side, the other hooked to the edge of the desk. The peak of his cap had gone astray and was jutting out over one ear. He looked tired—but then he always looked tired.

"So you think Garrity was really framed, Cap?"

"Think!" MacBride stopped pacing the room and bent his eyes on Kennedy. "What the hell do you think? Garrity just under the sod! This brat going to her flat with Corcoran, and the two of them laughing by the window. Then a fur coat from Nick Sciacca! Then she goes to Angelo's, to see Nick. And they skin out. Why? Because they knew that if I saw them together, I'd suspect something dirty. And I do!"

"Get the woman, Cap—get the woman."

MacBride stabbed a finger towards Kennedy. "Listen, Kennedy. I'm going to get that frail. And Sciacca. If she yaps and tries to pull a sob story, I'll fan her. I've got all Headquarters looking for them—"

The telephone rang. MacBride picked it up. He said, "MacBride talking," and listened. His voice lowered, became tight. He kept nodding, saying, "Yeah, Shanzey.... Yeah, I see.... Yeah.... Well, s' long." And then he hung up and held the instrument gripped tightly in his hands.

"Poor Charley."

"Dead?"

MacBride mumbled something inarticulate and put down the telephone. His cheeks puffed as he blew out a long held breath. He dropped into his chair, planted his chin on his knuckles, stared into space—bitterly.

Then he suddenly got up, took his hat and coat, put them on and went out.

TONY MARATELLI, aspirant for the Aldermanic chair, got up from an overstuffed chair and beamed. He was a short man, built like a barrel, with rosy cheeks, thick black hair, and small, merry eyes. He was in carpet slippers, lavender shirt, purple arm-garters; his suspenders hung down, and he smoked a corn-cob pipe.

"Hello, Cap. Glad to see you, but what's the matter? Say, you look mad. How about a glass of Chianti?"

"Sit down, Tony."

"All right if I stand?"

"Sure. Listen. I want Nick."

"Nick Sciacca?"

"You said it."

Maratelli took a puff on his pipe, laughed. "Hell, you come to the wrong man, Cap."

"Listen. A cop was shot by the alley next to Angelo's, and Nick did it. I want him."

Maratelli's thick thumb scraped across his unshaven chin. He looked serious. "That's too bad, Cap. I'm sorry to hear—"

"Never mind that. Where's Nick?"

"I don't know. I s'pose you figure Nick and me are close friends, hey? Nothin' like it, Cap. Nick and me broke off a month ago. Look, I'm a business man first, then a politician second. I might be a lousy politician, but I'm a good business man, and I got plenty money, and I can buy votes if I need 'em. I ain't takin' no chances with a guy like Nick. He was a nice guy, and we had many a drink together. There wasn't no fight, Cap. I just told Nick that I was runnin' my own campaign, and because I own a big business, I couldn't afford to get mixed up with him. I want this Alderman's job, Cap, and you know why. Big business. I'll get all the road pavin', and things like that. I figure I can win easy. Mulvaney ain't got a chance. I'm sitting pretty, and I'm doin' it without strong-arm help from any gang."

"Tony, I'm serious. You always were a pretty square wop—"

"I'm tellin' the truth, Cap. If you don't believe me, maybe you will if you get Nick. My wops parade a lot and maybe there's some street fights, but I ain't startin' them, and there's no guys paid by me to start 'em."

"All right, Tony, I'll take your word for it." MacBride bit his lip. "But remember, if you're trying to gyp me, you'll get hell."

"I'll take hell, Cap, if I'm tryin' to gyp you."

MacBride went out, a little disgruntled, but glad in a way that Maratelli was playing straight.

He walked back to Police Headquarters. It was a good, cold night for walking. Nothing had turned out as he had anticipated. At one time certain that Corcoran and Dolly were in league, that lead was knocked into a cocked hat when he discovered that she was with Sciacca—and that Sciacca had bought her a coat. Now where did Corcoran come in? And why had Garrity been framed—and by whom?

Striding into Headquarters, he ran into Moriarity and Cohen. Both looked as though they had been through a deal of excitement.

Cohen said, "Well, Cap, now what do you think happened?"

"Shoot, Ike."

"Schneider was found in Haggerty Alley—with the back of his head shot off!"

MacBride stiffened.

"Yeah," said Cohen. "A woman in one of the houses heard a scream. She looked out of the window just in time to see a guy pitched from a machine. The machine kept going. Had no lights. She came down, saw Schneider dead, and ran for the nearest cop. Schneider's at the morgue now."

"So Schneider was taken for a ride," said MacBride. "Those guys were afraid to let him undergo another quiz."

"What Mory and me said."

"No word of Sciacca and the frail?"

"Nope."

MacBride strode into his office, uncorked the bottle of Dewar's, poured himself a drink and flung it down straight. He rasped his throat. He stood spread-legged, his hands thrust into his overcoat pockets, his eyes glued meditatively on the floor.

He pivoted abruptly. Moriarity and Cohen were regarding him. He gave them one look and then strode out, very purposefully.

Kennedy was idly chatting with Sergeant Bettdecken.

"Where away, old tomato?"

MacBride did not answer, did not look around. Jaw set, he banged out, looking very much like a man possessed suddenly of an astounding idea.

He walked rapidly away from Headquarters, and his heels struck the pavement with a hard, determined rhythm. He turned right at the next corner. He kept on, swinging from street to street, his breath trailing behind him. He was like a machine driving on and on with a certain grim intensity that it seemed nothing could deter from its chosen course.

Presently he reached a residential street. Old elms lined the way, and the houses were large—stucco for the most part, or brick—with spacious lawns and wide piazzas. He slowed down, peering keenly. He passed a flivver parked at the curb. It was empty. He went on.

Farther on, there was a black limousine parked. MacBride suddenly dodged behind a tree. A man was walking down from one of the piazzas. There was no mistaking the large, shambling bulk of Mike Mulvaney. He got into the limousine—into the front. He evidently had dispensed with his chauffeur—at least temporarily. MacBride heard the motor start. He ran along from tree to tree. He bent over and darted to the rear of the car as it was starting. He leaped on to the trunk-rack, held fast.

Looking back, he saw lights appear on the flivver he had passed—saw the flivver start away from the curb. He cursed. One hand slid into his pocket. The limousine gathered speed and the rear tires hummed beneath. The flivver made no attempt to catch up. It merely followed, not close enough for its headlights to reveal MacBride perched on the trunk-rack of the limousine.

But he kept his eyes on that flivver. It followed turn for turn. It occurred to him that he was in a precarious situation. If that was one of Mulvaney's bodyguards, the fellow might decide to shoot at any moment, and MacBride would have no comeback, since the other could say that he thought MacBride was a crook out after his boss.

It was a wild ride, for Mulvaney apparently was in a hurry. After a while they entered a narrow, deserted street, where the hum of the motor echoed clearly. Then the limousine slowed down, swung into the curb and stopped. MacBride dropped off and crouched behind the car. Looking back, he saw that the flivver had stopped. Then he saw it turn around, go back and disappear around the next corner. Now what the devil did that signify?

The door of the limousine had slammed. Peering through the windows, MacBride saw Mulvaney climb a short flight of three stone steps. He saw him press a bell-button. Faintly he heard a bell ring—one short and two long. A moment later the door opened and Mulvaney disappeared. The door clicked shut.

MacBride stepped from behind the car and stood on the sidewalk. He put his fists on his hips and ran his eyes up over the dark face of the three-story building. On the third floor he espied a thin sliver of light that seemed to escape through a crack in a dark shade. He scratched his jaw. He looked at the door and put his hand into his pocket, and it closed over the butt of his gun.

He climbed the three stone steps and rang the bell—one short and two long. He pulled down the brim of his hat and turned up his coat collar. He heard the lock click. The door opened. He shoved in, but a man blocked him.

"Now wait a minute, buddy—"

MacBride's arm rose and chopped shortly. His gun-barrel hit the man's head and the man sank without a murmur. MacBride stepped over him and probed his way through the darkness. He found a staircase and ascended it warily, careful of his footfalls. He reached a hallway, felt along it, found another staircase and proceeded. At the top, he paused.

One lighted transom shone in the darkness, partly open, and he heard voices. He put out his hand, touched the wall, and then tiptoed towards the lighted transom.

"…and you shouldn't have done it, Nick! My God, what did you think? You—"

"Ah, lay off, Mike. There was that guy coming at me, and I just cut loose from force of habit. I ain't caught, don't worry. And if I do get caught, you got to stand by me."

"Of course, of course! God!"

There was a moment of silence. Then Mulvaney— "Didn't that bell ring?"

"Yeah."

"Well, I don't see anybody coming in."

"I'll take a look," said another voice.

MacBride was square in front of the door when it opened. His gun was leveled.

"Only me, gang," he said.

Chapter VII

A SHORT, yellow-haired man fell back with a gasp.

MacBride stepped in. "Don't, Nick!" he snapped. "All you birds—hands high. Hello, Mulvaney."

Every man was frozen to his chair. Mulvaney turned white. Nick Sciacca's eyes blazed. Bunt Paoli was there. Dolly Kane was sitting on a cot, her new fur coat flung open. Corcoran sat beside Mulvaney.

"I don't get this at all," said MacBride. "Here's Nick, boss of the wop hoodlums, sitting with Mike Mulvaney and his publicity agent. And there's Dolly Kane, bereaved sweetheart of Tex Garrity, flashing a coat given to her by Nick Sciacca. Ain't this sweet!"

"How the hell did you get in?" rasped Sciacca.

"Through the door, same as Mike. I took a ride on the rear end of his car. I heard him ring the bell—one short and two long. I knocked the lookout for a loop—and here I am. Now what have you guys got to say for yourselves?"

Mulvaney swelled. "You've got your nerve, MacBride, busting into a house!"

"And you've got your nerve, Mulvaney, sitting with this bunch of rats. You—Nick, and you, Paoli—and yes, you, Dolly—I want you birds, the whole damned three of you, for the killing of my rookie Charley Myers."

"You're a damned liar!" cried Dolly.

"Am I? Don't kid yourself, sister. The three of you were sitting in that room upstairs in Angey's, and he flashed you that I was in the dump. Another thing comes up: Schneider was taken for a ride and had the back of his nut caved in. And the stick-up at *The Blue Goose*—and the killing—*and framing*—of Garrity!"

"Who framed Garrity!" snarled the woman.

"You, I imagine, among others."

Dolly cursed and threw her cigarette at MacBride. It bounced back off his overcoat. He stepped on it.

Mike Mulvaney was perspiring, though the room was not particularly warm. His lower lip hung down, wet and gleaming. His eyes bulged and stared dully. He was very much like a man in a trance.

Corcoran's face was deadly gray, his lips tight, his eyes shuttered, his nostrils quivering. Sciacca was half-smiling, and the ghost of a laugh was in his eyes; but the expression was fixed, glassy, adamantine, satanic and watchful. Bunt Paoli scowled, but he looked scared behind the scowl.

"The gang of you," said MacBride, "will come to Police Headquarters."

"MacBride," breathed Mulvaney, hoarsely, shaking his head, "you can't take me in. God, think of my position—my family, three kids! My wife'd die, MacBride, if I got mixed up in anything like this. You've got to give me a break."

"Are you asking for quarter?"

"Call it what you want. But don't you see, MacBride, you can't do this. I'll be ruined for life. My wife—my kids! Think of my position!"

"You should have thought of that, Mulvaney, before you got into this mess. You've always tried to high-hat me, and I see no reason why I should treat you any differently than these other bums. You made your bed, and now you're going to lie in it. I'm not Santa Claus, Mulvaney."

"Listen, MacBride. I'll come across with as much jack as you wan—"

"Cut that! I might weaken!" He grinned—a tight, ironic little grin. "Pick up that telephone, Mulvaney, and ask the operator for Police Headquarters."

Every man in the room stirred, and Paoli growled. Mulvaney opened and closed his fingers, and a sigh sucked in his throat. He shook his head—slowly, doggedly.

"No, MacBride. We've got to settle this right here. You can't take me in. You've got to name a price."

MacBride felt his scalp tighten. He was not unaware of the danger of his position. Each of these men was keyed up, cornered, deadly. They hung, as it were, on a hair-trigger. Mulvaney had everything at stake—his job, his reputation, his future life. All these lay in the hollow of MacBride's hand.

And MacBride shook his head. "No, Mulvaney. You're going in. You can't do otherwise. Why? Because Sciacca and Paoli and the woman were in on the killing of Myers. And Corcoran—well, Corcoran, how about that *Blue Goose* stick-up? And this yellow-haired guy—I'll bet Maloney will identify him as the guy who shot Garrity and then disappeared with the other bird. Mulvaney, reach for that telephone."

Mulvaney shook his head.

Then Dolly snapped, "It seems to me that all you guys are being buffaloed by one lousy cop. There's five of you here, and all of you are heeled. He can't shoot five guys. He couldn't even shoot more than one. What the hell's the matter with your nerve?"

MacBride laughed shortly. "Nerve! For crying out loud, I never saw an alley rat yet that had enough nerve to face a cop on the square!"

"Oh, you didn't?" asked Dolly.

"No. And the best thing you ever did was to help frame Garrity, who was nuts over you."

"Yeah?"

"Yeah."

She fell back on the cot, laughing. And then suddenly her face set and a gun went off in her coat pocket. The bullet put a hole in Mac-Bride's hat but did not knock it off. Sciacca streaked for his gun and so did Corcoran.

MacBride's eyes blazed. "Nick!"

Bang!

It was MacBride's gun. Nick was nailed to his chair, a look of horror on his face.

Bang!

Again MacBride's gun, and Paoli leaped up screaming and fell across Corcoran, who cursed.

"For God's sake, finish him!" roared Mulvaney. "We got to finish him!"

The woman jumped up and pulled her gun from her pocket. "I'll finish the big bum!"

MacBride had his gun on Corcoran and could not switch. Out of the corner of his eye he saw the woman, blazing with fury. But he fired at Corcoran, and Corcoran reeled backward and crashed a window with his head.

Then a gun boomed directly behind MacBride. He stiffened wondering if he were hit. But he saw the woman blanch, look dumbfounded. She dropped her gun, reached out a hand, then suddenly buckled at the knees and lay in a heap.

Kennedy stood in the doorway, cap over one ear, dead butt drooping from one corner of his mouth, smoke coiling from his gun muzzle.

The yellow-haired man sat back in his chair; face white, mouth open, muscles paralyzed. Mulvaney stood with his hands clenched, his head thrust forward, his shoulders hunched. His eyes popped with terror. Strange sounds creaked and groaned in his throat. Blindly he rushed for the door.

MacBride took one step, clubbed his gun and brought it down upon Mulvaney's head. Mulvaney, carried by the impetus of his lunge, collided with the wall, then slid to the floor and rolled over.

Gun-smoke, caught by the draft, whisked out through the broken window. Sciacca sat on the chair, chin on chest, arms hanging. Corcoran lay twisted beneath the broken window. Paoli lay face-down beneath the table. Dolly was curled up in her new fur coat.

MacBride put hand-cuffs on the yellow-haired man. The yellow-haired man stared transfixed at the table.

MacBride turned around and looked at Kennedy. Kennedy was looking at the woman, his head on one shoulder, a vague spectre of a smile on his lazy lips.

Smoke kept sliding through the broken window in swift streamers.

"Thanks, Kennedy," muttered MacBride.

"'S all right, Cap." He moved slowly and knelt down beside the woman. He bent her head back. He released it, and it fell forward again.

"Dead, Kennedy?"

"Yeah. Y' know, old tomato, I did her a good turn. She was in bad, so deep that not even the tabloids would give her a hand. And besides—it was either her or you and"—he shrugged—"I'm not sentimental about sex."

"H'm," mused MacBride.

He bent down and looked at Sciacca. He remembered that first shot of his. He had got Sciacca right through the heart. Paoli was dead. So was Corcoran.

MacBride suddenly turned. "I left a guy down the hall—"

"Yeah," nodded Kennedy. "He's still there, tied to a radiator."

"How'd you get here, Kennedy?"

Kennedy said, "Followed you. Tailed you to Mulvaney's place, and saw you hop on the back of his car. So I swiped a flivver that was standing nearby. Bet the guy's reported it. You'll have to smooth it for me, Cap."

MacBride grinned. "Yeah, I guess I'll have to."

Mulvaney stirred, rubbed his head, opened his eyes. He stared around dazedly, and then he fixed his gaze on MacBride. He shrank back against the wall. He moistened his lips.

"God, MacBride!..."

"What's the matter, Mulvaney?"

"Oh, God!"

MacBride picked up the telephone, and looking at Mulvaney, said into the mouthpiece, "Police Headquarters."

Mulvaney raised a hand. "Please, MacBride! Help me! Don't—don't! I didn't mean— I—I—"

"Hello. That you, Otto?... MacBride. Listen, send the wagon around to Number 40 Race Street.... Yeah. And call the morgue, Otto. Some guys played Fourth of July here. They got hurt."

He hung up.

Mulvaney held his face in his hands. He was sobbing.

The yellow-haired man spat. "Jeeze, what a guy!"

Chapter VIII

THE office of MacBride.... Moriarity stood with his back to the warm radiator. Cohen leaned against the wall. Kennedy had reversed a chair. He straddled it, heels hooked in the rungs, arms on the back of the chair, shoulders hunched and chin resting on interlaced fingers. Cap askew and one lazy eye squinted against the rising smoke of a cigarette.

MacBride sat at his desk, well back in his swivel chair, a drawer pulled out and one foot braced against it.

Mulvaney sat in a chair against the wall, broken and fear-ridden. Beside him sat the yellow-haired man.

"So Garrity was framed," said MacBride.

"It was that woman," muttered Mulvaney. "Damn her. She was nuts over Nick, and she was tired of Garrity. Corcoran came up from New York, and he and Garrity didn't like each other. I tell you, Mac-Bride, I was against it from the beginning, but these guys—these guys—"

"Aw, lay off that!" broke in the yellow-haired man. "You started it."

"What do you know, Smitty?" asked MacBride.

"I know that this yap is trying to steer clear of all the blame. I been identified by that guy Maloney, and I'm cooked. But this yap was in the know all along, and don't you let him kid you he wasn't. It was like this. Dolly was sick o' Garrity. Sure. She had him up to the neck, and she was gone cuckoo over Nick. Garrity was gettin' a swelled head, and Mulvaney didn't like it. He was gettin' scared o' Garrity and Garrity knew it and he was takin' advantage of it.

"Me and Spot Corcoran were down in New York, havin' hard times. We get a letter from Mulvaney. At least Corcoran does. Spot had lots of ambition, and we come on here and meet Mulvaney. Him and Corcoran was old friends, and Mulvaney tells us about Garrity. He says he wants a new right-hand man, and Corcoran's the guy for the job.

"It's like this. We meet Garrity, and Mulvaney tells him we're two guys who know our onions. Garrity asks us a lot of questions. He don't take to us, because he sees right off the bat that Spot looks like a wise guy and a good one. So him and Spot don't get on. Well, that's all right. It's the way it was supposed to be.

"Spot tells Mulvaney that Garrity or him has got to lead the mob, and Mulvaney says, well, he got Spot up here to lead it. By this time Spot knows Dolly pretty good, but he ain't fallin' for a broad. He sees she's sick o' Garrity, and he gets under her skin nice, and finds she's nuts on Nick, and she says she wished Garrity would get his.

"So Spot comes right out and tells Garrity that him and the gang is dead on their feet. So does Dolly, and that gets Garrity sore. Then Spot tells Garrity that he could teach him a lot of things. Garrity asks what, for instance. And Spot starts braggin' about the joints he stuck up in his time. So he kids Garrity into stickin' up the *Blue Goose,* and says he'll go with him.

"Of course, you know that Nick broke off with Tony Maratelli. Spot talks it over with Mulvaney and says, there's a gang we can use. You see, Spot had ambitions. It was his idea to put the two gangs together, then get rid of Nick and run the whole show. He got in good with Nick, and he had plenty of Mulvaney's money to hand over.

"Dolly works on Garrity into holdin' up the roadhouse, sayin' that it was makin' her sick when she had to hear about her man bein' afraid to do a job like that. So he falls for her line, and he falls for Spot's.

"I'm sent out there that night to sit around. We planned it nice, and Mulvaney here was with Spot and me when we planned it. He okeyed it. That's how Garrity was framed, and don't you let this guy tell you different.

"I got Schneider to drive the car. I wired him in New York and he come here. He wasn't so hot, but we didn't want a guy was knowed around here. That cop caught Schneider when he was tryin' to ditch the car after he'd took us home. We got him out through that writ, but he was all busted up and afraid to face trial, and Sciacca and Spot took him for a ride. They took him for a ride because Mulvaney was scared you guys would make Schneider talk—"

"You fool!" cried Mulvaney.

"Lay off, brother!" snarled Smitty. "I'm cooked, but I'll be damned if you're goin' to get off."

"He won't get off," said MacBride. "You see, Mulvaney, you're a rotten politician. You didn't have the guts to lose the graft you'd been reaping in for years. You're cooked, man!"

"Oh, God!"

"You should have thought of God when you planned all this dirty double-crossing. Brain? You haven't got one, Mulvaney. Because you played with alley rats, and I know, from over twenty years a cop, that a rat turns on his closest friend when he's cornered. Look at Smitty. A short time ago you two guys were working together. Now you hate each other."

"Think—think of my family!"

"I am. And in all truthfulness I can say that I'm mighty sorry for them. I'm sorry for your wife and your kids. But the law is the law, and you crossed it; you took a chance on ruining your family, and you did. You were money mad, and you were crazy for the standing which your position gave you. You couldn't lose like a man. Even now you're taking it like the yellow alley rat you turned out to be. Ike, lock these two guys up for the night."

Mulvaney sagged out, handcuffed to Smitty. Mulvaney choked and whimpered and groaned. Smitty cursed.

"You big bum, you!"

He had never hoped to say that to an Alderman.

MacBride pulled out some glasses and the bottle of Dewar's.

"Help yourself, boys."

They gathered around and glass chinked against glass.

MacBride filled his last and held it up. He eyed the amber liquid thoughtfully, his blue eyes keened, two vertical lines on his lean, corded cheeks.

"A toast to the old tomato," said Kennedy. "A toast to one hard-boiled captain, who gets loud-mouthed as hell sometimes, who makes a lot of blunders, but who always evens the score with a whale of a scoop. I allude to Captain Stephen J. MacBride. A fine, upstanding bulwark of the law, honorable and honest, who, I'm told, still kisses his wife like a newlywed and calls her baby mine—"

"Did you say toast or roast?" asked MacBride.

And he grinned into his drink.

Publication History

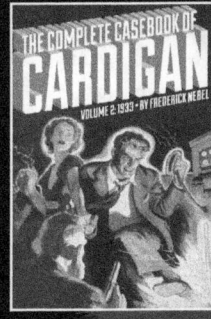

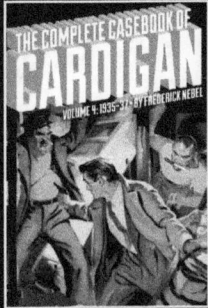

THE COMPLETE CASES OF MacBRIDE & KENNEDY

IN FOUR VOLUMES

BY FREDERICK NEBEL

Crimes of Richmond City

CAPTAIN STEVE MacBRIDE was a tall square-shouldered man of forty more or less hard-bitten.

Dog Eat Dog

WHEN CAPTAIN MacBRIDE was suddenly transferred from the Second Precinct to the Fifth, an undercurrent of whispered speculations trickled through the Department, buzzed in newspaper circles, and traveled along the underworld grapevine.

It was a significant move, for MacBride, besides being the youngest captain in the Department—he was barely forty—was known throughout Richmond City as a holy terror against the criminal element. He was a lank, rangy man, with a square jaw and windy blue eyes. He was brusque, talked straight from the shoulder, and was hard-

INTRODUCTION BY DAVID LEWIS

Coming This Fall From Altus Press

The Law Laughs Last

TOUGH precinct was the Second of Richmond City, lying in the backyard of the theatrical district and on the frontier of the railroad yards.

A hard-boiled precinct, touching the fringe of crookdom's elite on the north—the con men, the night-club barons; and on the south, the dim-lit, crooked alleys traversed by the bum, the lush-worker and poolroom gangster. On the north were the playhouses, the white way, high-toned apartments, opulent hotels, high hats, evening gowns. On the south, tenements, warehouses, cobblestones, squalor, and the railroad yards. The toughest precinct in all Richmond City.

Law Without Law

KENNEDY chuckled. "So you're back in the Second, Mac."

"See me here, don't you?"

"Ay, verily!"

The old station-house, blown up during the last election, had been rebuilt, and the office in which Captain Stephen MacBride sat and Kennedy, the insatiable news-hound, stood, smelled of new paint and plaster. Something of the old atmosphere was lost—that atmosphere which it had taken long years to create: dust, age-colored walls decorated with news clippings, "wanted" bulletins, likenesses of known criminals.

Two days ago MacBride had been

New Guns For Old

POLICE Captain Steve MacBride was on leave. He had it coming to him. As one of the main factors in the scouring of Richmond City's corrupt municipal government, he was due some little respite from the shield and the gun. With the passing of a self-seeking Mayor